Titles by Arthur James

Hants (2014)
Retro New England

Jason and the Kodikats (2013)
Children

The Adams Sisters

A Novel

By

Arthur James

Blackstone Books
New York, NY

ISBN - 13 :9780990448822

ISBN - 10 : 0990448827

THE ADAMS SISTERS

Copyright © 2015 by Arthur James

All rights reserved. Except for the use in any review, the reproduction or utilization of this work in whole or in part in any form by any electronic, mechanical or other means, now known or hereafter invented, including xerography, photocopying and recording, or in any information storage or retrieval system, is forbidden without the written permission of the publisher.

This book is a work of fiction. Names, characters, places and incidents either are products of the author's imagination or are used fictitiously. Any resemblance to actual events or locales or persons, living or dead, is entirely coincidental.

Publisher Blackstone Books LLC
New York, NY

info@blackstone-books.com

About The Author

Arthur James is a finance professional who lives in the Pacific North West. He completed a MBA in Seattle and holds a CPA. A Literature Professor friend told him that several short stories showed a flair for characterization and he continued to write. The first two novels were subject to more than a dozen revisions.

The children's novel, Jason and the Kodikats, which was set in Alaska was the first to be published. It was followed by a retro New England story called, Hants. Now it's The Adams Sisters romance, which is to be published.

Art married at 21 and took a yearlong honey moon in Australia. His former wife passed on several years ago in Santa Barbara, California. The couple had no children. The honeymoon set a pattern of traveling, whenever possible. Most of North America has been visited. Mexico and Costa Rica were long weekend jaunts. In Europe, Britain, Holland, Belgium, Luxembourg, France, Portugal, Spain and Italy have been explored. More recently, South East Asia was added to the itinerary.

Arthur went for full immersion in French and now counts it as a second language. Among older writers, he has a preference for Victor Hugo and in the best seller category, Danielle Steel and Nicholas Sparks.

Mr. James was raised a Roman Catholic and attended a number of Catholic schools. He skis, walks and likes the water. Volunteer work embraces giving time to both local and national political parties and sitting on the Boards of Arts Non-profits.

His writing technique is evolving and he has started to leave time referenced to the calendar behind. Projects on the drawing board include an 80-page plot draft for a religious thriller set in Boston and sporadic research for an international intrigue.

1 - The State Department

Samantha Adams had left Baltimore early that morning, after a quick shower and breakfast. At 29, she was in her prime. She liked the work she was doing as an Intern, at the Watch in the State Department, even if it meant being frequently on the road and obliged to stay away overnight on Department business.

She steered her metallic gold Lexus into the merge lane as the traffic approached the junction of Interstate 95 coming down from the north and turned into the Capital Beltway, which circles the District of Columbia. She always liked the feeling of coming back into her hometown and reached out to turn on the Citizens Band scanner. The first channel to come in over the speaker was the trucker's favorite. It was usually the best spot to pick up all the inside scoop on traffic snarls.

Almost instantly, a husky male voice crackled in over the airwaves. "Red Dusty jockeying Geronimo coming in from B-town. Chicken coop on the down ramp at first southbound exit on the B-Way just past Interstate 95."

She read every one of the trucker's words, checked the speed and eased her right foot back off the gas. In less than 3 minutes she saw a big red cherry on top of the long white cruiser, pulled off to the side, on the approach to the freeway.

"Yippee!" She laughed. "You're not getting this girl." The young woman turned down the scanner and picked up the cell phone from its cradle, which was mounted dash. It was programmed for easy dialing while driving. She pressed # 9, and then CALL and put the phone back into its receptacle. Dialing was audible from the speaker installed somewhere out of sight.

"Good Morning, the Watch, Roscoe Walters speaking, may I help you, please?"

"Sam here Roscoe, I'm calling to let you know I'll be there within the hour.

"Where are you?"

"I'm out on the Belt around the College Park exit."

"Are you taking the Parkway in?"

"I could, but it's always slow trying to get over from Anacostia at this time of the morning. In addition, I passed an overhead sign a few miles back, which said the southbound Parkway is under construction."

"Which means?" the man at the other end asked.

"I think I'll do a loop on the B-Way until I'm around Alexandria and then I'll come up the Jefferson Davis and over the Roosevelt Bridge."

"That way in is probably as good as any. I hate fighting the cross-town gridlock myself."

"I hope it's a good choice."

"Did you get us anything in Baltimore?"

"Yes Sir, Mr. Walters. I shot 36 frames with my digital over a six-hour period yesterday in and around the docks. They were downloaded to my notebook at the hotel last night. I attached the twelve most significant frames to an e-mail for you, before breakfast this morning. They should be in your mailbox now."

"Hold on a minute, until I switch programs."

"I'll bring them up on my notebook again too, while you are doing that, so we can discuss them.

"Good girl, I knew you were right for the Watch as soon as I saw your curriculum. Ok, I've got your pics up. Oh wow! Who do we have here? Who's this Oriental fella? He looks familiar."

"Sorry, no names or sound, just photos. That Oriental man was on a freighter named the Imperial Queen. I checked the registry last night. It's Liberian. He leaned over the rail for about an hour. The swarthy one with the scar over his left eye stopped by around 11 a.m. and talked to him from the dock. About 11:30 a.m., the man with the sunglasses arrived and went half way up the ramp. They talked for a couple of minutes and then the sailor on the rail threw him something quite small, just before disappearing inside the ship. I followed the man with the sunglasses.

"Back up a bit. Where were you when you took these shots?"

"They were all taken in South Baltimore. The Imperial Queen was tied up not far from a sugar company, along the inner harbor docks in Fells Point."

"Ok, then you followed sunglasses."

"That's right. He got into a late model delivery van. I have a plate number here somewhere. I followed him back out to East Fort, to a small plaza near the center of Fells Point village. He picked up something to eat and then went to a phone booth and made several calls.

When the phoning was done, he drove down through Fells Point, turned left at the end of the village and took an overpass. On the other side of the overpass, the van immediately entered the Port Covington container terminal. The first stop was a vacant parking lot about a quarter of a mile along East McComas St, near where there was a lot of lumber stacked behind fences. Mr. Sunglasses walked up to a large blue Port of Baltimore crane, just past the lumber.

It didn't look as if the crane was working, but someone appeared a-way-up on a platform, beside the door for the operator's cabin. The man on the crane waved, and then climbed down to the ground. They talked for about 10 minutes.

I couldn't get anywhere near them, without being spotted. Even the few pictures I took with the telephoto were not worth sending to you. When they finished talking, the man with sunglasses went back to his vehicle and drove right to the end of McComas to where it passes under a raised section of I95. There are some storage sheds and small wharves in a fenced off area, near the turn.

Those four men on your screen, who are wearing orange coveralls, came out of one of the sheds and approached the van on foot. They all shook hands and then Mr. Sunglasses and the man in a peaked cap hugged each other. A door opened on the side of the shed and a black four-wheel drive cruiser came out. Sunglasses jumped in and he and the driver sped off.

I couldn't get back to my car without being seen, so I had to wait, until the men in coveralls drove sunglass's van into the shed and shut the door behind them. By the time I got back on McComas, there was no sign of the black cruiser, so I went back to the Imperial Queen."

"Was there a name on the shed, where they put the van?"

"Yes! I have it."

"Put it in your report. I'll have somebody do a follow-up."

"Ok! After about two hours of waiting at the Imperial Queen, I was surprised on my perch by that man in the suit. He asked me if I was looking for something. I told him I was a freelance writer getting some pictures of the docks for an article. He said that he was Baltimore Police and that I shouldn't hang around the docks any longer than I needed.

About 20 minutes later the same oriental man as before came out to the rail of the freighter again. The Baltimore Blue stepped from behind a dumpster and called the seaman to come down onto the dock. It looked like he showed him his badge, when he arrived.

The Oriental man pulled a cell phone out of his pocket and made a call. A new, black SUV with tinted windows pulled up and stopped. The Oriental man opened the passenger door, took out a briefcase, gave it to the Baltimore plain clothes man and then he went back up the ramp.

I decided to keep up the surveillance, until the sun went down, but there wasn't any more activity."

"Great work Samantha. I'll send these photos to cataloging right away to see if we have any matches on file. I don't like the idea that the policeman stopped you. Sam, I don't want you to go around Baltimore anymore until I authorize it."

"Sure Roscoe, anything you say."

"Come and see me when you get in. I have something new, which came in yesterday. We'll call it your bonus for these pics and the long day on the docks. Gotta go now. See you later."

"See you later boss," she said pressing the end call button on the cell phone and then switched off the notebook. I wonder what's in the new assignment she thought, slipping a silver CD into the player.

The golden capsule cruised past the Exits for Washington Parkway while its driver kept beat to the music with the palm of her hand, on the steering wheel. Suddenly a cell phone's buzz broke her thoughts and she turned down the music.

The Adams Sisters

"Hello, Samantha Adams speaking," she said with a professional tone.

"Samantha, where are you child?"

"Mom, what are you doing calling me?"

"I wanted to know where you were. I was worried. You didn't call last night."

"I stayed on the job until near dark and then checked into a motel. Some pictures had to be downloaded from the camera into the notebook and then cropped to size and converted to thumbnails before I emailed them to Mr. Walters. I ate an apple, took a shower to wash Baltimore's Docks off me and fell asleep. Sorry Mom, I just forgot to call you. "

"Well, I asked you, where are you?"

"I'm out on the Beltway, headed for the office."

"I thought that Masters in International Relations was going to get you a good job."

"This is a good job, Mom?"

"It seems more like a traveling sales position to me. You're always out on that road."

"That's how it works, when you're an Intern. Believe me Mom, it's great. I'm getting a new assignment, when I get into the office."

"Ok Honey, you're the one that's living in your shoes, but personally I'd prefer something that requires less running about."

"Marsha, your years are catching up with you."

"Supper is at six dear. Will I tell Mrs. Yamato to set a place for you?"

"Yes, I'll be there at six. I must go Mum. Traffic is getting heavy. I'm just crossing the Potomac River now. The No. 1 one is coming up fast on the right. I don't want to miss it.

"Talk to you later."

"There I'm in Virginia now, bye Mom."

"Bye Samantha!"

The No. 1 became the Jefferson Davis Parkway, as it cut through Alexandria. Looking off towards the east, Samantha saw a steady stream of planes landing at Ronald Regan Airport, out on the Potomac flood plane, which is a short distance south of Arlington, and directly across from the mouth of the Anacostia River. In the distance, the spire of the Washington Monument was rising high above the city. Samantha glanced briefly towards the west, as the Lexus sped passed the Pentagon.

The command center for America's worldwide military forces was built during World War II. The building remains the headquarters of the Department of Defense. It has five sides, which are 921 feet each on the outer walls and 360 feet each on the inner courtyard yard. There are 17.5 miles of corridors connecting its 92 acres of offices. Even today its working population is around twenty thousand people.

When Samantha looked to her left again, rows of white crosses in the Arlington National Cemetery had replaced the Pentagon and then they too were gone as car and driver began to negotiate the approach to the bridge. A low monumental structure known as the Arlington Memorial Bridge connects the National Cemetery on the Virginia side of the Potomac with the Lincoln Memorial on the Washington side. Two heroic, gilded Italian statues anchor the Washington end of the bridge. One is called The Arts of War and appropriately its nearby twin, The Arts of Peace. Before she had time to think of it, the Lincoln Memorial was in front of her. Now it was only a two block drive up 23rd Street NW to the State Department.

The State Department is located in Foggy Bottom, halfway between the Lincoln Memorial and George Washington University and a little east of the Watergate Complex and the Kennedy Center. It's a long, low eight story federal building, which occupies a full city block.

In a way, the Department of State is part of two worlds. On one side, it's an extension of the President. On the other, it's part of the Administration. Like the White House, it's called upon to frequent, mix and mingle with foreign dignitaries. Unlike the Administration, one of its main concerns is culture, art, and history.

The main entrance hall of the Department of State is a handsome space with thirteen-foot high ceilings and a Tabriz rug on a mahogany floor. A huge chandelier hangs over the center of the room. Doorways leading away from the hall are arched. Pieces of period furniture are located along the walls.

The main diplomatic reception rooms are located on the top floor of the building. When visitors leave the eighth-floor elevator, they come into an area known as the Edward Vason Jones Memorial Hall. It too has a thirteen foot ceiling and its paneling is modeled after that of the drawing room at Marimon, an early 18th-century house in King George County, Virginia.

The suite of rooms, which make up the diplomatic reception rooms are: the Thomas Jefferson State Reception

The Adams Sisters

Room, the John Quincy Adams State Drawing Room, the Benjamin Franklin State Dining Room, the Walter Thurston Gentlemen's Lounge and the Martha Washington's Ladies Lounge. The rooms and lounges are furnished with over one hundred and fifty 18th-century tables, sideboards, chairs, sets of drawers and paintings.

Among the many paintings is Fitz Hugh Lane's, View of Boston Harbor. Within the open center of the picture, Lane frames the distant but distinctive dome of Bullfinch's statehouse, a feature of many Boston Harbor paintings.

The State Department building is not only a center for diplomatic receptions; it's also the home of the Ralph J. Bunche Library. The Library is the oldest federal government library. It was founded by the first Secretary of State, Thomas Jefferson, in 1789.

The Library has a large and important collection of unclassified and published information sources on foreign relations. Foreign relations is defined broadly to include books about foreign countries, world history especially since the American Revolution, international organizations, like the United Nations and the Organization of American States.

Samantha pulled up to the entrance of the underground parking. Immediately, two security guards came towards her car. While one verified her department identification tag, the other moved around the Lexus with a mirror on wheels, checking the underside of the vehicle.

Security had seen her many times, but the new regulations required them to process each new arrival, no matter who it appeared to be. When the yellow barrier arm folded up, she drove forward over the metal floor, which would spring up suddenly, forming a three foot high solid steel wall, should a vehicle try to go through without stopping. Her parking spot was at the far end of the second level of the underground bunker.

Once she was in the staff entrance lobby, Samantha lay her notebook computer and purse on the scanner belt and walked through the metal detector gate. After she had retrieved her possessions from the far end of the belt, she walked over to the high counter and swiped her ID card through the reader. A guard behind a glass window verified that her face was the same as that, which came up on his monitor, before buzzing her through.

The Operations Center or the "Watch" is part of the Executive Secretariat. It's open around the clock to alert and brief Department officials on overseas news and events and to coordinate the Department's response to emergency situations. The Watch also provides selected communications support to Department officials.

Roscoe Walters was a project manager at the Watch. He had been with the Department of State 16 years. At the beginning of his career, he had been attached to The Organization of American States Office. From there he had gone to the UN Delegation. For the past five years he had been attached to the Executive Secretariat, at first in General Briefing and now in Special Projects.

As Manager of Special Projects, he had a considerable amount of autonomy. He and his people did a lot of investigation and research; however, they had no police powers. Special Projects was assigned a substantial part of the budget allocation for the Watch. All Walters asked of his people was that they keep good records on their expenditures. A receipt was a start. Whether the expenditure was appropriate or not was another matter.

Samantha Adams was on a one-year internship at the Watch. Roscoe Walters liked what he saw in Samantha. She had a Masters in Political Science from Penn State, in International Relations, but she wasn't your typical college type. She did the grunt work like a regular civil servant and he took note of it. She would never know, but one of the photos taken in Baltimore the day before had already been matched and was on its way to the Secretary with a short briefing. That made him and the Watch look good.

Roscoe Walters saw a thick-set man in a wrinkled suit standing in front of the glass wall of his office. He got up from behind his desk and went to greet the visitor,

"Hi, come on in. You must be Special Agent Arnold Steinberg from the African Intelligence Division?"

"That's me."

"I didn't know if you got my voice mail. Have a seat," Walters invited, motioning towards a chair.

"Thanks," the Special Agent said as he sat down. "Mind if I ask you a question?"

"Sure, go right ahead. What would you like to know?"

"How did you find me?"

"How, well to make a long story short, I was running a general search query in the Department's database, at my level of access, which is quite high. My question concerned Nigeria, during the past month with several sub-criteria like

The Adams Sisters

USA, Washington, and the US Government. There was a lot of data. I came across a day report that you filed, after a White House general diplomatic reception."

"Which one?"

"The reception where a Nigerian named Colonel Jocommo was present."

"Oh yes, I remember that night, go ahead."

"You said that the SS Agent on duty for that event had been annoyed, because the Colonel had breached security and talked personally with the President, without a formal introduction."

"That's correct, that's what I said in my report."

"Do you remember how this supposedly accidental meeting was managed?"

"Sure, their embassy received the usual invitation and RSVP'd that the Ambassador, a Dr. Ojibwa would attend with the visiting Colonel Jocommo. The Dr. arrived in their embassy car with two military in uniform and another African, who was dressed in their traditional costume.

I noticed the gentleman in the tribal robes moving around the floor. He seemed quite assured of himself. I guess the SS simply figured that he was a previous visitor and didn't put a tag on him.

When the President stepped out of his circle to refresh his glass from a passing waiter, Jocommo did the same and there was a short interaction between them. It was enough. When the SS Captain on duty that evening asked the President with whom he had been talking, he was right on. He even knew what gift he would be receiving from the Colonel at their official meeting the following day."

"Poor man, they'll probably have a Secret Service waiter follow him around after that evening."

"Probably!"

"Are you a bit of a specialist on Nigeria Mr. Steinberg?"

"A bit."

"Like what?"

"Well, of course, they had that Biafra genocide a number of years ago."

"I remember that."

"Then there's their relationship with England. They're still closely engaged with the English. England's Prince Charles has been there at least once during the past year.

The Army took over during the 80's and there was a coup among them in '92. A new constitution was adopted in 1999, and a peaceful transition to civilian government was completed. They have oil, but the people are poor. They also have the largest population on the African Continent. However, Mr. Walters, you didn't invite me here for general information."

"No! Actually I am more interested in scams originating in Nigeria, especially international scams and ones involving Americans."

"Then you read my profile?"

"Yes!"

"Mr. Walters, I have followed a dozen scams out of Nigeria over the past five years and at least two dozen Americans have been stung by them during that time period. It's like investigating shadows. Nobody will say a word until they are sure that they've been had. You know the silence of greed.

The scam artists are a very international group of people. They live or study in just about every country on the planet, including Russia and they're no dumbbells. They try all kinds of ways to get a cut of that oil action. Some of them aren't too ethical either."

"Would this possibly look like one of their scams?" Walters asked, taking a letter out of its envelope and passing it to him?

"Yes Sir, this is a prime example, right down to the cross on the T's. If you don't mind my asking, where did you get it?"

"By accident, the addressee had moved."

"That's typical. I've cataloged several like this. The first time I thought the recipient might be in with them; however, later I learned they send out hundreds of these letters and address them to people they find listed in business directories."

"Thank you, Mr. Steinberg. You just stopped me from trying to find the person to whom this was sent."

"You were going to investigate this letter?"

"It falls within the scope of the State Department. The Watch has a very general mandate. I'd like to investigate many items, which come my way, but I must keep an eye on expenditures. Every one of my Special Projects, which doesn't bear timely, useful information according to an established grid, gets me a bad mark in the big black book. I am often a tad over budget. If I go too far over, someone else will have my job. I don't suppose I could ask you not to mention this visit in your daily report."

"Sorry, but it's like me seeing Jocommo. Everything goes in the daily report, or someone else will have my job."

The Adams Sisters

"Then it looks as if I have started another Special Project. I better do my paperwork, so that my daily report matches yours."

"You are going to investigate that letter?" Steinberg asked.

"I don't know yet, but I am intrigued. That's a lot of money this Dr. Ossaga is offering."

"All I can say is good luck. Those letters have earned me several reprimands for unauthorized expenditures too."

"Thanks for the warning, Mr. Steinberg. I know you're quite busy so I won't hold you up any longer. Thanks for stopping by."

"No problem, Mr. Walters and like I said, best of luck."

Special Agent Steinberg hadn't gone long when Roscoe noticed a slender, well-dressed young woman in a navy blue jewel-neck jacket and flared skirt, waiting for his signal to enter. He smiled and she came in.

"Hey Sam!"

"Hey Boss!"

"Sit down, please."

When she was seated, he passed her an envelope. "Tell me what you notice about this."

"It has been opened."

"Besides that?"

"The stamp is from Nigeria."

"Keep going."

"There's no return address."

"That's better. So what would you do with it, if you found it in your letter box?"

"Probably throw it in the garbage, if I didn't know the person to whom it was addressed."

"Not even curious."

"Nope! When I was studying, I moved almost every other year. Lots of people don't do a proper change of address. I received many pieces of mail that were not for me. If there wasn't a return address on the envelope, to which I could draw an arrow, then it went in the garbage."

"Really?"

"Really!"

"That's about the same as the fella said who turned this in. I wanted to see, if it was a normal reaction."

"So why did he turn it in, if he threw it in the garbage?"

"He said he was waiting on the phone for 5 minutes listening to background music. The envelope in his waste basket caught his eye and he decided to see if there was a return address inside while he was waiting for the other party to answer the telephone."

"That sounds legit to me."

"Are you sure? This one could get expensive and I would rather stop now than make a mistake."

"Then it's a project?"

"It could be. You don't think some jerk just found an envelope in a trash can, wrote up a letter to stuff into it and then turned them both into the Department for a laugh, do you?"

"That is entirely possible Sir, but the first part of what you said sounded normal to me."

"Ok, let's suppose you're waiting on a phone, you're bored and you see this envelope that you threw out, because there was no return address to which you could draw a return arrow. What would you do next?"

"I might wonder if there was a return address inside and reach down and pick it up." She stopped and smiled. "That came out automatically, Mr. Walters. I forgot for a minute. The other man said he did the same."

"That's ok Samantha, open it."

**

June 15th, 20xx
Lagos, Nigeria
Fax: 234-90-405427

TO: *The President*
Caravel Holding Corporation
1643 – F Street
Baltimore, MD
123569

Dear Sir,

The Chamber of Commerce in Lagos recommended your name to me. The Chancellor of the Chamber said that you have a reputation for being an astute businessman and always open to a profitable opportunity.

I have a proposition for you, and I hope that you will be interested.

Nigeria is a very troubled country. There are many factions. Quite a few highly respectable people are on blacklists and cannot do business in the ordinary manner. My colleagues and I are among these poor unfortunates. However,

The Adams Sisters

we think that we have devised a way to get around this unfortunate situation, with your assistance.

If you would let us transfer US$ 15,000,000 to your bank account in the United States, then there is a way out for us. After the money is in your country, we will advise you as to what items we would like to purchase for shipment back to Nigeria. Your commission for your services would be 10%.

If you would be interested, please contact us at the above fax number and supply us with your bank account number and routing information for the transfer of the funds.
Sincerely,
Dr. Lawrence Ossaga

**

She looked up at her superior without a word.

"So what do you think?" he inquired casually.

"I think I would throw it back in the waste basket."

"Why?"

"Mr. Walters, nobody just sends 15 million dollars into the US, to a total stranger. Besidest, where would these Nigerians get that kind of money?"

"So you think it's a scam?"

"Of course it's some kind of a scam."

"Do you know that hundreds of Americans have been taken in by letters like this over the past 10 years? There could be many more who haven't officially complained."

"They must have more money than brains, Sir."

"It's called greed, Samantha. They have a little and they want more."

"Barnum Bailey said it a different way," she commented.

"Yes, I agree, they're suckers too, but they are also Americans and they pay us. We have to try to do the best job we can, in spite of them."

"What job is that Mr. Walters?"

"Samantha, how old are you?"

"Twenty-nine, Sir," she replied without hesitation.

"I know you're not married. Do you have anyone serious in your life?"

"I have a few friends from when I was growing up here in Washington, who I see from time to time; however, I'm not really looking. Once I thought I had a long term relationship on the go when I was in New York, but it went sour. That's partly why I asked for a transfer back here."

"And you have been with the Department how long."

"Five years in New York and three months here with the Watch in Washington."

"Then you could be career material."

"I hope so. I really do hope so."

"Let me tell you something Samantha. This letter may be an opportunity for you to bring yourself to the attention of the folks, who will decide if you'll stay on at the Watch, after your internship. It's not a big project. There's nothing strategic to it. This type of thing is a nuisance that everybody wish would stop, but nobody seems to be able to sink their teeth into it.

Before you arrived, I had a visit from a Special Agent, who's in African Intelligence. He's been following Nigerian financial scams on and off for 5 years. He said it was like tracking spooks. You never hear anything, until someone gets stung and by then the bad guys have all disappeared."

"I see, but why me?"

"You're new around here. I need to keep a lid on this. We aren't the Secret Service or the FBI. The service we provide is research and advice; however, sometimes to deliver the product, we must go beyond the library walls."

"To places like the Baltimore Docks?" she added.

"You follow me. You've been here three months and I like what I see. You act on your instincts. I made a note in your file the other day to the effect that you were similar to a quarterback moving through your assignments. I always get something, like that picture this morning in my email, and I am able to make a touchdown for the Watch. "

"Thank you."

"Maybe it's your style. There aren't many other interns wheeling around in a Lexus equipped with a CB Scanner."

"You know about the scanner?"

"You forgot to turn it off in the parkade one day. Our electronic security picked it up on a routine sweep. They went into your car and turned it off."

"They went in my car, but how?"

"That's what I said, but they replied that it might have been a remote bomb that even you didn't know about."

"Thanks for telling me and I do sort of think of myself as a little bit of a road warrior."

"If you want this one, Samantha, it's yours. You'll be Project Captain and I'll be your only assistant. "

"My assistant, what happened to my Manager?"

"Oh, I'll still be Manager, but I just don't have time for the nitty-gritty of the project. There are a dozen others on the go just now. However, I would really like to take a look into this letter. If we could make even a small breach into these Nigerian Scams, it might help me get out of here."

"Where do you want to go?"

"I'd like to go to the Department of State's Executive Office. This is my 16th year in service. The Executive Office would be a nice way to round things off." The short, tanned and athletic civil servant replied.

"I see."

"Are you in?"

"Yes, Mr. Walters, Sir, I'm in."

"Great!" he exclaimed reaching across the desk to shake her hand.

"Where does my assistant suggest I start?" she asked.

"How about doing your due diligence on Nigerian Scams."

"Got you," she said standing up. "I was just on my way."

She went to the door and started to open it.

"One more thing Samantha."

"Sir?"

"This one is just between you and me. Don't let anyone here at the Watch know what you're working on."

"Any special reason?"

"I'm over budget and there is no budget for this type of investigation."

"I understand, mum's the word," she said closing the door behind her.

****

2 - The Adams Family

"Hey, Preppy!"
"Hey yea!"
"Do yea Preppy?"
"Yea...I do."
"Then do me a favor: three Honey Brown Ales, two Caesars, four Vodka Shooters with whipped cream heads and a glass of Sauvignon Blanc."
"Coming right up, Lady."

Saturday night at the The Wave was a hot spot with some of the older college crowd and young professionals, who frequent the nightlife in Washington and Georgetown. The club was located between New Hampshire Avenue NW and 19th Street NW, at number 21 Dupont Circle. It occupied the ground floor and second level of a building, upon which a pending development permit had been registered.

Probably, Dupont Circle is Washington's liveliest neighborhood. Its street life and intellectual notoriety are fed by the abundance of bookstores, cafés, art galleries, and restaurants, which are all within easy walking distance of each other. Once, the area was known as Washington's Newport. Today, except for the Massachusetts Avenue corridor called

The Adams Sisters

Embassy Row, it's a neighborhood of brownstone townhouses and redbrick turrets.

The attractive young black waitress watched Preppy prepare her order. His hands moved fast. Two more waitresses, both blonde, arrived at the service station. They began giving the young barman coy smiles, trying to catch his attention. The server, who had been waiting when they arrived, finished scooping the loose change up off her tray and put it in the little Navajo clay dish that was suction cupped onto the tray's flat surface. The rugged looking young man arrived with her beer order.

She smiled at him like the two blondes had done and queried, "You're new here, aren't you?"

"Been here since Tuesday this week, but I'm only replacement help. I've been mixing and pouring at the owner's place over in Adams-Morgan. Guess one of their boys here broke his ankle playing ball."

"That was Tommy."

"They asked me, if I would see them through to the first weekend in September, after Labor Day."

"Are you going to?"

"Sure, why not, as long as you girls don't over work me too much."

Then he was gone. She watched him flip a bottle of vodka high into the air, catch it behind his back and then pour an ounce into each of four shooter glasses. When the clear liquid was topped with a creamy brown layer of liqueur and a dab of whipped cream, he hustled back to where she was waiting.

"What about yourself?" he asked. "This is the first time I've seen you."

"I'm part time. I come in when they call me, if I'm not busy."

"Let's see, I still owe you 2 Caesars and a Sauvignon."

"Yes, you do!"

"Be back in a sec."

Five feet down the bar, the other two waitresses, were getting restless. "Com'on Tod, you said you'd be nice tonight." He only smiled back and kept right on working.

"There, you are," he declared, placing the rest of her order on the tray.

"Thanks, Tod."

"That's not fair."

"What's not fair?"

"I don't know your name and you already have mine."

She smiled again, flicked her shoulder length black hair backwards, slipped her hand in under the tray and said in a low voice, "It's Christina, but call me Christa." Then she turned, and roller-bladed across the polished concrete floor, disappearing into a maze of crowded tables, which were located under a mezzanine that was held aloft by an upright, eight-foot high structural steel I-beam.

A few hours later, she hung up the roller blades inside her locker in the waitresses change room and gave the combination lock dial a good spin, to mix up the numbers. It had been a busy night, and she had earned $75.in tips.

A few more of the waitresses came through the door as she was leaving. "Nite Christa, see yea next time."

"Yea!" she replied, but knew that there wouldn't be many more next times as 4th year of medicine at Georgetown U was proving to be much busier than 3rd year had been. The final year of medicine had forty-eight weeks of clerkship duties, many of which fell on Friday and Saturday evening.

It had cooled off outside. Thank God, she thought. The Wave had been like a steam bath all night long.

Her new, metallic powder blue BMW roadster was parked near the back of the staff level of the parkade attached to the building, which housed the Wave. When she was close enough, she aimed the alarm deactivator that was on her key chain and pressed the white button. Up ahead, a sharp audible beep sounded. Once comfortably seated and with the motor running, she pulled a small lever on the dash and the hood folded back into a compartment behind the back seat.

There were still quite a few cars on this level. The small blue vehicle made its way through them towards the exit and into the lane, which opened onto New Hampshire Avenue NW. An old black Audi rag top waited at the sidewalk for a break in the flow of traffic. There was a blond in the passenger seat and a blond squeezed into the rear compartment seat.

The Audi's right-hand turn signal was blinking. The driver glanced quickly to the left then turned right towards the Circle. At that moment, Christina saw it was Tod the barman, who was driving. She gave a little burst of gas and followed fast, coming up beside the sports car in the swirl of automobiles, which were weaving their way around the park and fountain that are located in the center of Dupont Circle.

The three young people in the Audi looked over at her. Tod smiled, and the two waitresses waved. She saw his lips moving, saying "Good Night", but couldn't hear the words over

The Adams Sisters

the roar of the traffic. The small black car tuned right, at the coffee shop, into the north bound access-street for Connecticut Avenue NW, which passes underneath Dupont Circle.

"Have fun Preppy," she called back, then moved into the curb lane herself and turned into P Street NW.

She followed it over the bridge that crossed Rock Creek Parkway and drove along until 30th Street NW. The BMW sped along, then turned left onto R Street NW and continued west along it for two blocks, before slowing and turning into the red brick paved driveway of her family's house.

There were three other cars parked in the insets along the curved driveway. That meant her sister was home tonight. She let herself in and went immediately to her room up on the second floor of the west wing.

It was almost noon, when the young woman awoke the following day. She pulled on a white terry towel robe, went into the adjoining bathroom to splash a little water on her eyes and then made her way down the wide fanning double staircase. A woman stopped her vacuuming and greeted her cheerfully,

"Morning Miss Christina!"

"Morning Mrs. Yamato. This is Saturday. Don't you ever take a break?"

The woman in a black dress wearing a white apron replied, "Friday is my ballroom dancing night, so I left early yesterday and didn't get a chance to finish my to-do list. Today I'm only here until after lunch." Then the maid turned her attention back to the rug.

When she arrived in the kitchen, Christina found her mother writing checks at the kitchen table. At fifty-five, Marsha Adams was still an attractive woman, even in a house coat. She had high cheek bones and distinct features. During the winter, she attended a fitness club three times a week and jogged five miles between sessions during the spring and fall. To beat Washington's summer heat, she pedaled a stationary bike inside her air conditioned home.

"Morning Mom!" she greeted on her way to the fridge.

"Morning, it's almost noon. You were out late last night. I turned the TV off at one and you still weren't in."

"I worked. They called during the afternoon. One of the girls was sick. It was Mrs. Yamato who gave me a message. I thought she would have told you."

"Yesterday afternoon she left early. It was her ballroom dancing night, and her dancing partner had invited her out for dinner, before they went to the studio. I didn't have a chance to talk to her. This morning I had to get a start on these bills before they shut the phone off on us."

"Next time I'll leave you a note, Mom."

"You know, Christa, sometimes I wonder about you."

"Wonder what Mom?" she said, sinking her teeth into a slice of watermelon.

"I don't like the idea of you being over at that bar serving all those people."

"It's great fun, Mom. They're all young. There's never any rowdiness. Last night I made $75 in tips. Most of them are college kids or they're doing some kind of postgraduate work. There are a few professionals like lawyers. It isn't a regular job. I've only been called three times, since Easter. My courses haven't been affected. I have one of the best grade point averages in my promotion, and I scored in the top ten percent on the first part of USMEL."

"Don't any of the team ever ask you where the car came from that you are driving?"

"Lots of them have nice cars. Last night there was a new barman. I saw him drive off in an Audi. Maybe his dad is a senator."

"You and I both know that an Audi isn't a BMW."

"Not quite, but almost, anyway I always park it at the very back of the staff level."

"I hope you didn't tell Sebastian you still haven't got past that college crowd?"

"He doesn't have a clue. Right after one of the times the Wave called to see if I could work, he phoned to ask me if I wanted to go out with some of his friends. I told him part of a clinical, which I must do, was being held at the DC General that evening."

"Ok girl, I was young once too. It's just that your father has worked so hard to get this family up above the lot of common black folks. He doesn't quite understand why his daughter wants to do waitressing."

"There are lots of black kids at the Wave, Mom. One night I even saw Theodore Walton the third there with that Baptist Minister's daughter."

"Really?"

"Honest to God," she replied, crossing her heart. "Anyway, I probably won't be accepting many more shifts. I'm getting too busy again. If Dad says anything, tell him I said working part time at the Wave over the last three years has helped me keep my head clear, so I could get those A's he loves so much."

The Adams Sisters

"I can't chit chat with you now Christa. Your father will skin me if I don't get these checks out, and then I have to do something with this hair of mine, before this evening, but I do have one last question. Have you heard anything from the school yet?"

"I already made my elective and clinical selections for the next block. They were supposed to e-mail me my class and clinical rotation schedules."

"When does the next block start?"

"First week in October."

"That's in about six weeks."

"I know, I should go and check my e-mail now to see if there is anything in it. Also, there are a couple of chapters I must read if I'm going to go with you and Dad tonight."

"Watermelon isn't enough to start the day on."

"I'm trying to stay skinny."

"Come back down for lunch. It will be in about half an hour."

"Is Sis around today? I saw her car in the driveway, when I arrived this morning."

"Yes, she's having lunch with us."

"Ok! See you in half an hour." Then she was gone back upstairs.

Christina's room opened onto the back yard. There were a few trees and some bamboo, which had grown up, but she had a clear view of the playing court that her dad had put in, when she and her sister were still in grade school. His girls weren't interested in piano or ballet classes, so he gave them half a tennis court and half a basketball court. Through the open window, she heard the pop, pop, pop of a tennis ball being whacked and pushed back the curtain to see who was playing. It was her father, all in white, smacking a ball against the cinder block wall, which formed one end of the court.

She went over to her desk and shook the wireless mouse to animate the 17" LCD screen. The connection to the Internet was always open. Her computer had a wireless link to a DSL router that was located downstairs. She clicked on the email icon, and two messages downloaded to the screen. A short, 'You have new mail!' tune sounded from the speakers under the desk.

The first message was the confirmation and the schedules from Georgetown University that she had been expecting. She clicked to print it out. The title on the second message said, ' DC Meets.' It looked like junk mail, but she opened it anyway.

There was the usual warning after the header to effect that this message was not in contravention to the federal communications legislation and unless you replied; there would be no following up. The message read:

**

Welcome to DC's newest hot spot for people wanting to meet new friends!

Now you can register your profile, free of charge, at DC Meets. The following categories are available: Women Seeking Men, Men Seeking Women, Women Seeking Women, Men Seeking Men and Pen Pals. Your anonymity is guaranteed in two ways. First you chose your own nickname for your profile. Second, you receive your own personal e-mail address at DC Meets. All messages to or from it have the originating e-mail address stripped away. The only way for someone who reads your profile to contact you outside of DC Meets is if you give them your regular e-mail address or telephone number.

You have probably seen many Personals and Matching sites while surfing the Internet. What makes us different? Registration is free, and you must give us a valid driver's license number. In addition, we will only register Zip Codes, which are located inside the Capital Beltway.

To register and get your free user name and password, go to http://www.dcmeets.com.

**

Why not have a look she thought? There were still 20 minutes before lunch. The Web address was highlighted, so she clicked on it, activating the browser. The site quickly came up on her screen. Several seconds later a graphic loaded, that showed the Washington Monument with a heart on the pinnacle. DC Meets was inscribed into the Monument in embossed letters. A small door at the base of the Monument flashed Enter. She clicked again to enter.

The next screen was a menu of choices: About DC Meets, Members Login, Registration, Policy & Rules, Disclaimer, and Webmaster. She had been into many of these sites before but had never registered. Another day, a message from DC Meets might not have provoked a response from her and would have only been deleted without even being read. However, today it hit a positive chord. Recently she had overheard several waitresses at the Wave talking about people they met on-line.

By the time, she had finished filling in the 4 registration screens with her interests, likes and dislikes, personal habits

The Adams Sisters

and hobbies, a call for lunch sounded from downstairs. She clicked on the Submit Profile button and waited for the confirmation of registration to come up on the monitor.

Congratulations on successfully registering with DC Meets. Your user name is Night Shadow. Your Password is 2467cv. Please write these down and keep them in a safe place. She jotted them on a Post-it Note and stuck it to her old wooden student, desk, under the mouse pad.

Christina's parents and sister were already sitting in the dining room. Mrs. Yamato, their small, intense Japanese American maid, was pouring her dad a glass of ice tea.

"Hey, Sis, what was keeping you?" her older sister asked.

"Hi Samantha, I was checking to see if all my elective course selections were confirmed."

"And?"

"Got every time spot I asked for."

"Great!"

"So what's up with you, anything new at work?" Christina asked.

"Not much, I was in Baltimore Thursday."

"Mom said so. What were you doing?"

"Taking pictures down by the docks."

"Were they good guys or bad guys?"

"There aren't any good or a bad guy as far as the State Department is concerned. Our mission is simple to collect pertinent, timely and useful information. At least that's what I'm told, by my boss, Mr. Roscoe."

"Is this Mr. Roscoe a sweetie?"

"Christa!" Her mother interjected. "You're talking about our government."

"Afraid not, Sis. He's fiftyish with a receding hair line, but he does work out, and he's in not bad shape.'

Charles Adams lowered the Sports Illustrated, which he had been reading, at the head of the table and looked out over the top of his half frame reading glasses at his daughters. He was a tall slim man with pleasant features. His tight knit frizzy hair was turning a salt and pepper grey. No matter how much he ate, he never seemed to gain much weight.

"Civil servants don't have to be sweeties," their father scolded softly. "We pay them and they make sure our work gets done."

The sisters looked at each other with big eyes and giggled. Mrs. Yamato chuckled and began to take off her apron. "Ok folks, I'm history. See you all on Monday." The

Adams waved bye to her back, as she went out through the swinging door to the kitchen.

"To change the topic," Christina said. "What did you do last night sis?"

"I went for drinks with an old crowd that I've known since high school."

"Meet anybody in particular?"

"You might say that."

"Who?"

"Do you remember Ronnie Williams?"

"Oh yes, he was the one who came to pick you up at the front door with a basketball in his hands."

Charles put down his magazine. "I remember him too. What's that little black mutt doing with himself now?"

"He's Manager of Fleet Sales at Potomac Motors."

"That's not bad, fleet sales can get you big bucks if you work at it."

"He is not suffering."

"No, Fleet Sales isn't bad," Marsha Adams added. "Don't forget, when I met you Charles, you were just a hair dresser."

"I know Honey, and if a black mutt like me could get up in this world, anybody can."

"So are you going to see him again?" Christina asked.

"Actually he's going through a divorce and it seems a little sticky. I did give him my cell number though. You know, for coffee or lunch sometime."

"There now," her mother added with a tone of satisfaction. "That's what you need, a little escorting to help you forget that nut from the Yonkers."

Samantha's face dropped back flat. "We'll see Mom," she remarked. After that, an uncomfortable silence settled over the table, and the four of them started to eat the BLT sandwiches and potato salad that Mrs. Yamato had left on serve-yourself-platters, in the center of the table.

Samantha had come back to Washington hurting. She slept in her old room and ate with them, when she was around, but she hadn't really come back into the little family. Marsha, Charles, and Christina let her be and didn't try to include her in anything.

Charles Adams ran a very successful general insurance brokerage on the north east side of Washington. When the girls had been very young, they lived in Washington. However, once a down payment was saved, he had moved the family into the diaper town suburb of Georgetown.

The Adams Sisters

The senior Adams had not always been in insurance. Barber was the trade that the Marines gave him. Two days after being honorably discharged, he found a job in Baltimore; However, Charles didn't want to make barbering a career, as it was evident from the civilian wages he was earning that it would be a long time before he could even think about the things he so wanted in life. By chance, he learned that hairdressers earned twice as much more in fees and tips than barbers did for the same number of hours worked.

Once he was back on his feet; the former Marine had applied for and received a veteran's student loan. It had been more than enough for him to stop barbering and take the one year Certified Professional Plus hair styling program offered at the Baltimore Institute of Professional Hair Design.

The course hadn't been a snap. It started with learning the difference between dozens of different pairs of scissors, combs, brushes and electric clipper attachments. Then there were the rollers and heat treatments. He had a lot of trouble matching hair coloring with a person's natural pH acidity factor. The students were even taught how to build crowns from fine copper wire, cover them with hair and then merge them with a woman's own hair to make the high styles, which awe everyone.

Once certified, Charles moved back onto the edge of the old Trinidad neighborhood, where he had grown up, in North East Washington. At first he took a couple of ordinary jobs in beauty parlors, where the hairdressers changed every other week. However, after a while word got out with the old crowd that he had known, while growing up, and it wasn't long, before he established a regular clientele.

Charles was able to buy his way into one of the better salons on the periphery of the North East Capitol Hill district of Stanton Park, by showing the manager his customer list. It included the number of times each woman had been to see him in the past year, what she had done to her hair and its dollar value. The manager said that if he kept even a quarter of his old clientele, there would be a chair for him. Over half of the list followed him to the new location.

It was quite a classy shop. There were 15 cutters, 6 washers, and a beautician. The beautician's name was Marsha. Now she sat at his right hand side eyeing their two grown daughters.

He first learned about selling insurance when Marsha took him home to meet her parents. Her dad had sold insurance most of his life to people in and around the Capitol. Over Sunday night supper, her father made jokes about having to go to his policyholder's houses on their payday to collect premiums, so their policies wouldn't lapse, and his commissions get reversed. It was Marsha's dad who steered him towards the home study program for the Life Underwriters's License.

Selling insurance began as a part time activity. He passed out his business card to every one of his customers at the beauty parlor. Many of them talked to their husbands, and he ended up selling them insurance at their home, after his day of cutting hair. When Charles left the salon to take up his new calling on a full time basis, Marsha left too. They were married, when he was twenty-seven and she twenty-five.

Within five years of starting to sell insurance, the former hairdresser made it into the Million Dollar Club, which is based on one year's gross sales. At that point, the company he had been writing for, offered him a branch manager's job. He accepted and learned much, much more about the insurance business and how much money one could really earn.

As a branch manager, he could still sell, but in addition to commission on his sales, he received a percentage of the commission written by all agents at his branch. If they left, their policies went into a house account, which he also controlled. It was when he became a branch manager that the family moved to Georgetown.

Several years ago; the opportunity came along to buy out a general broker, who wanted to retire. Charles put a second mortgage on the family home in Georgetown, left the branch manager's job and went out on his own. The brokerage was a success.

When he took over the book, the firm was carrying life, fire and casualty lines from 12 different companies. Now fifteen years later he had 30 companies on the roster and had added products such as loan insurance, receivables insurance, export insurance, key man insurance and a hand full of miscellaneous products like Savings Bonds, T Bills, annuities and even mutual funds. Ninety agents placed orders through his brokerage. This week he had a meeting with a company from Zurich, which wanted him to add their travel insurance package to the firm's menu.

The girls were getting up from the table when their mother said, "Don't forget about the Club tonight, if you have nothing on."

The Adams Sisters

Samantha looked at her father, squinted her eyebrows and asked, "What Club?"

Before he could reply, Christina inquired, "Are you doing anything this afternoon, Sis?"

"Nothing definite," her sister replied, "Why?"

"How about a game of tennis and I'll tell you all about the Club."

"All right."

"If you're busy this evening," their mother continued. "There's always next time."

"It's ok Mom," Christina said, coming around the table to kiss her mother on the cheek. "She'll tell you for sure later, but for now, it looks as if it's a maybe. Anyway, I'm going. Are you still leaving at 7:30 p.m.?"

"We'll be meeting up with the Johnston's in the Club at seven thirty, but your father and I will be leaving here at 7 p.m. sharp. Sebastian, Gene, and Penelope will be with them. Gloria said that Sebastian was asking after you, when he called home this week.

"That's because I beat him at tennis the last time he was here, but he is kind of nice anyway."

"And he has all that money dear."

"Money s-money mom, I haven't even graduated yet.

Her mother chuckled and replied, "No, but you do like earning $75 in tips."

"Who's Sebastian?" Samantha asked.

"I'll be ready at 7 sharp Mom.

Come on Sam. I'll fill you in on the way to the park. After that, you can decide for yourself if you want to come with us."

"Have a good game girls," Charles Adams called after them as they went through the swinging door into the kitchen. Then he winked at his wife, picked up the Sports Illustrated he had been reading and headed for the den.

"Gotta go Hon, the Red Skins game is starting on TV. It'll be over in plenty of time for me to get fixed up for this evening."

"Okay, Dear, I have a few things to attend to. I'll come in and watch the game with you, when they are done."

"See you later then," and he was gone.

The Adams house was located on the north side of R Street NW, between Wisconsin Avenue and 32nd Street NW. It was a two storey, solid red brick building with a hip roof. About 10 years ago, Charles Adams had a contractor put a full height dormer in the roof on both the front and back and built one large room on the third level, which had a view across the street to the south and out over Georgetown looking north. All the windows were double hung and fitted with black wooden shutters that really functioned.

There was virtually no front lawn, as it had been converted into a curved driveway and brick paved courtyard for parking. However, there was an island of green, inside the semi-circle formed by the two foot high red brick retaining wall, which followed the inside of the driveway. An ornamental cast iron lamp post was set in the grass, between the sidewalk and the curb, in front of the house.

An old, low stone wall, which ran from the sidewalk to the house, divided their property from a neighbor to the west. The back of their property dropped 15 feet to the level of a blind lane.

When the house was being built, a solid concrete double garage was also built underground, at the lane level. There was a staircase inside the garage leading up into the house and an outside concrete stairway, beside the garage, leading up to the back yard. At the bottom of this outside steps a heavy wooden gate opened out onto the lane. It was always kept locked. The half tennis court and half basketball court were built on the concrete roof of the garage.

Samantha had recently moved back to Washington from Manhattan, after applying for and being successful on the Intern exam at the State Department's Watch division. Her mother suggested that she put her Manhattan apartment furnishings in a mini-storage and take up her old room, on the second floor of the family's home. Her daughter had accepted on a temporary basis.

The first couple of months in the new job at the Watch had been hectic. There were a lot of study sessions and overtime. That meant missing meals, being away frequently overnight and several weekends. She really hadn't made contact with much of what was going on in the family.

That evening's dinner invitation at the Club was the first time the family had even offered to include her in anything. The fact of the matter was, Samantha had been through an engagement, which went sour in Manhattan. Her parents and sister wanted to give her time to get by it.

Christina and Samantha walked east along R Street's red brick sidewalk in shorts, sleeveless tops, and runners. They were carrying tennis racquets and a tube of balls in their hands. The older sister's hair was pulled back tight in a twist,

The Adams Sisters

while the other's was a shoulder length tangle of wisps held in place by a wide, polka dot band.

Each house along the block was unique. Two were white and made of wood. A number of them were built of red, orange or yellow bricks. One of them had a wide veranda the full length of the building and the house on the corner of 32nd Street NW had a red brick turret recessed into the junction of two outer walls. Dumbarton House was located on the far corner, at the other end of the crosswalk. The historic site was surrounded by a high red brick wall into which was set a white granite slab. It bore an inscription by Mildred Bliss concerning the place of gardens in the humanist way of life.

Dumbarton house was built in 1798 on the heights above Georgetown, on a 705 acre estate owned by a Scotsman. Today it served as the headquarters of the National Society of the Colonial Dames of America. Next after Dumbarton was Montrose Park, which ran back from R Street about a quarter of a mile to where it meets Dumbarton Oaks Park and Rock Creek Park.

Rock Creek Park is one of the most beautiful urban parks in the United States and one of Washington's hidden treasures. This 2,800 acres of wilderness follow Rock Creek through the city for six miles, from where the creek mouth meets the Potomac River near the Kennedy Center to the border of the District of Columbia with Maryland. It's a gorge with ravines and pockets of heavily wooded forest. In Mount Pleasant, it cuts through the National Zoo. Pierce Mill is about the halfway mark up through the park. Corn and flower were ground there in the 18th century. The area north of the Mill is known as the Nature Center. In addition to the wild deer, this section enclosed a golf course and an Equestrian Center, where there are pony rides and the opportunity to take riding lessons or board a personal horse.

Across the street from Montrose Park is a plain, old brick building called the Jackson Arts Center? Once it had been the Jackson School. Both Samantha and Christina had gone there for their primary grades. The old pipe monkey bars that they climbed on were still standing at the back of the building, in a play yard that is enclosed with high red brick walls. At the entrance to Montrose Park, there' was a small sun dial on a pedestal. It had always been the unofficial clock for neighborhood children playing in the park, as long as anyone can remember.

Signs indicating the rules and hours of closure were in English and Spanish. There are a number of picnic tables scattered under the trees. The sisters followed a well dressed woman who was walking a poodle. She stopped to take a plastic bag from a roller on a post, into which were to go any dog droppings.

The girls turned onto a path, which branched off from the main walkway. It led down a gentle grade to series of clay tennis courts. No one was playing.

"So Christa, what club are you and mom talking about."

"Dad's got a club now, Sam. It started out as a place to take business acquaintances and then he took a family membership. You should have him put your name on the register."

"What club did he join?"

"The Cabot Golf, Hunt and Equestrian Club"

"Where is it?"

"West of Bethesda, on the River Road, but inside the Beltway."

"That was kind of a ritzy area, if I remember correctly."

"It still is," her younger sister laughed.

"Is it a white people's club?" Sam asked casually.

"Nice serve," Christina complemented her. "There are lots of white people, but there are also quite a few black people too."

"How many is quite a few?"

"Lots, you'll see if you come for dinner with us. The Johnston's are black. We're meeting them."

"How many times have you been there for dinner?"

"I'd say that we've eaten there a couple of times a year, since Dad joined, but the real attraction for me is the horses. I go there riding, whenever I can squeeze it in between all the courses, labs and clinical sessions in medicine."

"I suppose Charles has taken up golf now, too?"

"No. He plays tennis and swims once in a while."

"And Mom?"

"She just goes for meals and plays tennis with Dad sometimes. I told her she should try the lawn bowling. She said she would, if I bowled with her."

"Did you?"

"No, it's mostly old black and white ladies who lawn bowl together. I'd feel out of place."

"Maybe I'll offer to bowl with her."

The Adams Sisters 31

"That would be appropriate. I'm sure she'd like it. When she was in the regular indoor bowling league, in Washington, she never missed a night."

"Who are these Johnston's that you're meeting and who is Sebastian?"

"Mom and Mrs. Johnston met first. Now we're all quite friendly. Mr. Johnston owns some apartment buildings. They live in Chevy Chase. Sebastian is one of their sons. He lives in Philadelphia.

He's sort of a business type. You know red suspenders and pin striped suits. He's President of a small venture capital company. I think there is some connection with the Philadelphia Exchange too.

We were introduced last spring. He had tickets to the Philadelphia Symphony and jokingly asked me if I wanted to go. I had just written two really tough exams and wanted a change, so once Dad offered to pay for the hotel, I took Sebastian up on his offer.

Sebastian came home to Chevy Chase about every second weekend during the summer. We've played tennis a couple of times, and I've started to meet some of his friends. He's a pretty cool guy. Mom has already started her eligible bachelor thing."

"What do you think?"

"I don't know. You know me. I'm just school, books, tennis and horses, until I graduate. Outside of that, I've a part-time summer job lifeguarding at the pool, which is about 8 hours a week, and I'm an on-call waitress at a bar called the Wave, over on Dupont Circle. There hasn't been too much time for dating, during four years of honors Biology and now three years of Medicine.

"How old is Sebastian?" Samantha asked, returning her sister's volley.

"Thirty-one."

"If I was in the looking mood, he might make a better match for me, I mean as far as age goes."

"But you're not in the looking mood?"

"Definitely not," the older sister hollered as she ran forward to a return a serve that was dropping short. "Last night with the old gang was the first time I've laughed since it happened."

Now they were standing together at the net. "Want to talk about it?" the younger Adams asked.

"Maybe, my guess is you're still a virgin?"

Christina felt her cheeks grow warm, before replying, "Yes."

"There's nothing wrong with that Sis. I was too, until this last fellow, and I dated quite a few boys."

"That's what makes it so bad I suppose, but if you don't want to talk about it."

"No, it's okay. I'm getting better. He was a black boy I met when I was doing my Masters in Philadelphia. At school, it was only a casual acquaintance. Then I bumped into him again in New York, after I went there to work for the Department. He grew up in the Yonkers and Manhattan was his playground. At first, he was only showing me around. Then we started going out.

One thing lead to another and we were talking about if we were married. We were in upstate New York for a weekend of sightseeing, and he said that since we were almost engaged anyway and would be getting married, when it would be convenient, why not get a room together. I went along with the suggestion.

We kept dating, but a ring never materialized and a wedding date was never set. I drifted into sleeping with him on a regular basis. One day I said to myself it all had to stop. I phoned him and told him that I had bought a ring and I wanted him to give it to me. I said I wanted him to meet Dad.

A couple of days later he showed up at lunch with a real classy, lady. He introduced us and then said he had changed the locks on his apartment and had taken an unlisted telephone number. They both stood up to leave, without even ordering and she purred at me, 'Tough luck girl, I got him now".
"That's the last I ever saw of him."

If you tell Marsha that I bought my own engagement ring, I say you're lying, and I'll never talk to you again in my life. Besides him and me, you're the only other person who knows."

"I've forgotten it already Sam, I promise."

"Then I guess you and I will be dining at the Cabot Golf, Hunt and Equestrian Club tonight, Miss Christa Adams.

"Excellent, we'll tell Marsha and Charles, when we finish this match."

As they were crossing the intersection at 32nd Street NW, on the way back to the house Christina laughed, "Guess who bought a house down that way?" with her arm pointing in the direction of S Street NW.

"The Queen of England?" Samantha joked.

"Try the punk rocker Lady Rose, and rumor has it she paid 2 million."

****

3 - The Johnston's

The Cabot Club was located deep in the Northwest sector of the District of Columbia, more properly in Montgomery County, Maryland. It was an area of rolling hills, streams, lakes, estates, country clubs and a substantial population of those who would be known as the upper middle class, if America had classes. The Club was easily accessed from the whole of the District, either via the Capital Beltway or one of several main arteries such as Wisconsin Avenue, Massachusetts Avenue or Macarthur Boulevard, which radiate out from the hub of Washington.

Charles Adam's black Mercedes moved slowly out into R Street NW. and turned east towards Wisconsin Ave., where he made a left. After a block, he turned right onto Reservoir Road and traveled along it, until the merge with Macarthur Blvd., just past Georgetown University. Macarthur Blvd. followed the Potomac River in a northwesterly direction, and it wasn't long before thick, lush green trees surrounded the roadway on both sides. Christina pulled out a medical text book and began to read.

Samantha settled back into the soft velvet upholstery and gazed through the automobile's window. It was almost as if time had been turned back. She forgot about the State

The Adams Sisters

Department and Manhattan. Up front, a steady flow of words passed between Charles and Marsha. Their easy conversation was like a lullaby to her ears. She was back in her little family. It felt so secure. Neither girl noticed when they turned up Wilson Lane and then onto the River Road NW.

The Club was located on a long rectangular property comprised of four hundred acres of fields, rolling hills and tree lots, which sloped down gently from River Road NW. Booze Creek flowed through the center of the property. The Club House, Lodge, swimming pool, tennis courts, lawn bowling, Pro Shop, rifle range and stables were set well back from the road and far from prying eyes. Even the golf course was concealed behind a five hundred foot wide band of mixed trees, growing all along the border with the public road.

The Mercedes turned off the River Road NW and passed through two high stone pillars to which were fastened heavy iron gates that were wide open. The paved, winding road, which lead up to the compound was lined with cedars, hedges, and overgrown honeysuckle bushes. Several times there was a break in the thick, close wall of vegetation and Samantha saw golfers out on the fairways to the left. Some walked and pulled a cart, others sped along in electric carts.

Half way from the stone pillars at the entrance onto this private property and the cluster of buildings that formed the central compound, the Adams family, arrived at the first of two forks along the drive. Off to the right, a four-foot by four-foot brown wooden panel hung in a frame on two pieces of chain. Heavy block lettering spelled out the word, RANGE.

Samantha turned to her sister and asked, "What's up that way?"

"Shooting!"

"What kind of shooting?"

"In the summer time it's mostly skeet. You know small clay disks."

"I saw skeet shooting, when I took a cruise around the Caribbean," Samantha informed her.

"Did you try?"

"No, I like shooting, but I'm not a duck hunter type. Shooting at targets is of more interest to me. What else do they have at the Range besides skeet?"

"There's a 10 bay, outside rifle range, which ends in a concrete bunker filled with sand. Also, there's a long low building where they shoot at paper targets with pistols. I've never been in, but Dad said there's a button you push and your target comes up to you automatically, along a track, so that you can see how close your bullet came to the center of the target or put up a fresh one."

"That might interest me."

"Reservations for everything are made at the Club House or over the phone. You should have Dad put your name on the register."

"Could he do that?"

"Sure, you're family," her younger sister replied and then called to her father. "Dad, don't forget to add Samantha's name to the register, while we're here today.

"Good idea, Christa," he replied. "I'll register your sister first thing."

By then they had arrived at the second fork in the road leading up to the Club House. The spur went off towards the right again. A similar wooden panel swung lightly in the breeze and on it was written the word, STABLES.

"I don't have to ask what's in that direction," Samantha laughed.

"It's really great," Christina exclaimed. "I go there as often as my course work permits. There is an exercise track and an area set aside with gates and jumps. The club owns about 20 horses.

There are three trails on the property. One is totally in the trees. On the other two, there are open stretches, where it's possible to get up a good gallop. There's even one spot, where you can gallop downhill."

"Sounds exciting, but I'm not really a horse lady, Sis."

The Lodge, Club House and other buildings around the compound came into view. They were all made of stone; about five feet up from the ground and then white stucco took over, until the roofs, which were covered with orange clay tiles. It looked very Spanish. The parking lot was surrounded by honeysuckle hedges. At first glance, it was difficult to see, if there were many guests.

The four wings of the Lodge formed a narrow X, which pivoted about the main entrance, reception desk, lounging area and large open fireplace over which hung a huge copper hood. The front wing, on the south side of the building, housed the kitchen and a small dining room on the ground level, which only served breakfast. The indoor swimming pool was located in the back wing along with a sauna and exercise room. The rest of the Lodge was filled with guest rooms, which were quite heavily used by the members now that there was a zero

The Adams Sisters

tolerance policy for driving over the alcohol limit. The Lodge and the Club House were connected by a wide brick and glass passageway that looked something like a green house.

The main floor of the Club House, where a large dining room was located, opened out into the garden, which contained a wide stairway leading up to the second floor deck and the inside lounge. Both the garden and the upper deck offered a view towards the Pro Shop, which was located about 500 feet from the Club House in a low stone and stucco building. The first tee of the golf course was visible to outside diners. At the back of the Club House were located a billiards room, several racquetball courts and a sports bar. Upstairs, there were meeting rooms and a small ballroom adjacent to the lounge.

The eight tennis courts and lawn bowling were found on the west side of the lodge. Another one storey building similar in style to the Pro Shop contained both ladies and men's locker rooms and showers. The stables were situated north east of the buildings, behind a grove of trees. The compound area, composed mostly of the Club House, Pro Shop, and Lodge, was off limits to horses

The club had over 3,000 full memberships and another 1,000 social memberships. Initial full membership was $27,000, and annual dues for both types were $1,800. Activities such as golf, horseback riding, and shooting had a fee attached to them and were restricted to full members. The social membership gave access to dining, the bars and ballroom as well as the sports facilities, on the west side of the Lodge.

Charles Adams steered along the winding route to the parking lot. Covered walkways ran along both sides of the parking lot to the Club House and Pro Shop. The walls of the walkways were made of sheets of Plexiglas, which stopped one foot from the ground and about six inches below the flat overhanging roof, so that the wind could circulate properly. Samantha followed her mother and sister across the open parking lot towards the main entrance to the Club House This evening she was wearing a peony pink cap sleeve shirt, pleated front cream color pants, and thong sandals.

"Where are we supposed to meet them, dear?" the elder Adams called from behind.

"Gloria said that we should meet them for a drink on the upstairs deck around seven. Our dinner table is reserved for seven thirty."

"Lead away then, I'll bring up the rear."

Marsha entered the Club House and took the inside stairs to the second floor. She crossed through the back of the Lounge and walked directly to the open French doors leading out onto the deck. As soon as they stepped through the opening, Mrs. Adams saw a hand waving from a table near the outside railing. It was Gloria. The women's eyes met, and they smiled simultaneously.

Charles wife turned and looked back at him. "They're just over here dear," she said and started to make her way through the tables.

Christina was second to arrive at the Johnston's table.

"Hey yea, Sebastian."

"Hey, Christa, what's happening?"

"We're arriving!"

"Glad you could make it."

"When the Adams say they'll come, they do."

"I know that, I was only ribbing you. Come sit beside me, I've been saving you a place."

Don't mind if I do. You're looking mighty spiffy tonight, Sebast.

"Well, thank you, Ms. Adams."

"Mama there's a place for you, right in beside Mrs. Johnston," the younger Adams daughter said.

"All right Christa. I see it."

"Hi Gloria."

"Hi Marsha."

Samantha and her father seated themselves in two unoccupied chairs beside Mr. Johnston

"How are you folks doing this evening?" the waitress asked.

"We're fine!" Charles replied to the waitress.

"Would you like to order anything or are you moving straight on to the dining room?"

"I'll take a whiskey," the elder Adams answered. "Make that a double whiskey, please Miss."

Marsha looked at him, and he winked back. "Better make it a single, please Miss."

Sebastian took the lead. "Christa, who's the lovely lady the Adams have brought with them this evening?"

"Sebastian Johnston, this is my sister Samantha.

"I think I known your sister from some place. Did you ever live in Philadelphia, Samantha?"

"I went to school there, at U Penn."

The Adams Sisters

"Was it grad school?"

"Yes, it was my Masters."

"That's it then, I remember your face from the Grad Lounge or some Grad function."

"I went to the Grad Lounge sometimes with my friends ," Samantha replied. "What did you study?"

"Wharton, MBA."

"Oh, you're one of those biz guys."

"Yea," he smiled lowering his gaze, which had been fixed on her face. "What was your Masters in?"

"International Relations."

"What are you children talking about there?" Mrs. Adams interrupted.

"Nothing Mama," Christina replied. "I'm introducing Sam to Sebastian."

"'Now it's my turn," Sebastian continued, "this is my brother Gene, his wife Penelope, and that's my paternal grandfather Norbert. Everybody, this is Christa Adam's sister, Samantha."

"Pleased to meet you all," Penelope exclaimed. Gene gave a little wave, and the granddad nodded to both of the sisters.

"So Sebastian," Christa said. "What's up? I mean like what have you been doing since the last time we talked? "

"I've been so busy, believe you me."

"I believe you."

"I started setting up the financing for two companies on the Philly exchange this week. I'm trying to get them through to a Red Herring."

"A what?" Charles asked, looking into his whiskey glass.

"A Red Herring, Mr. Adams. That's a preliminary prospectus for a public offering."

"Could have fooled me son," Sebastian's father Harold added. "I thought it was something to eat."

The elder Johnston, Harold's father, Norbert interrupted his son, "I didn't know they served red herring at this Club, Sebastian. Maybe that's what I'll order tonight."

"Sorry, Dad and you too grandfather, a Red Herring is not fish. It's a financing document," Sebastian laughed.

Gloria came to her son's rescue. "A Red Herring is biz-kids talk. You two should know that by now."

"Oh, excuse me!" the elder Johnston exclaimed, holding his hand over his mouth

The women all laughed.

"So what do you do, Samantha?" Gloria Johnston asked.

"I'm with the State Department here in Washington. Actually, I've just come back to town in the last three months. Before that, I was with State in Manhattan for 5 years."

"I simply adore Manhattan," Gloria exclaimed. "I can't imagine anyone leaving Manhattan for Washington."

"I may go back," Samantha replied with a touch of longing in her voice, "but for now there's opportunity and advancement in Washington."

"Then you are not married?"

"No!"

Mrs. Johnston smiled at her and added, "Good luck and welcome back to our town."

"Thank you."

Samantha turned her attention towards Gene's wife, who was clad in a natural sateen shirt dress. "What do you do Penelope?"

"Gene and I have two boys. One is seven, and the other is eight. Besides taking care of them, I take care of Gene. He works in Dad's business," she said gesturing towards the elderly gentleman, who had thought that a Red Herring was a fish. "They're in property management and rentals.

In addition to taking care of all my boys, I work part time at an art gallery in the Bethesda village, Monday, Wednesday and Friday afternoons."

"What type of paintings does your gallery carry?"

"Our inventory is mixed. Currently, there's a little African-American, some Native-American, some Latino and about forty percent main stream."

"Are you from Washington?" Christina's sister continued.

"No. I'm from Phoenix. My family is also involved property management. That's how I met Gene. We were at a National Property Managers' convention here in Washington. I'm a RPM, a Registered Property Manager. So is Gene."

"I've never been to Phoenix," Samantha informed her.

"You shouldn't miss it. Phoenix is a hidden pearl in a very arid land. If you're visiting Phoenix, you're nine-tenths the way to the Canyon."

"The Canyon?"

"The Grand Canyon, it's only about 6 hours' drive north."

"Thanks, I'll remember that."

Christina's mineral water and Samantha's Cinzano arrived.

"I bought a painting, well a reproduction from Penelope yesterday," Sebastian injected.

The Adams Sisters 41

"A painting, you mean a reproduction," Grandfather Johnston mimicked. "What are you going to do with it?"

"Hang it in my office in Philadelphia, Grandddad."

"What's sort of a painting ..... dancing girls?"

"No, it's called, "Cabin in the Cotton."

"Cabin in the cotton, what's that all about?"

"It's just a painting Granddad. I was helping Penelope with her commission quota. There's a cabin and a woman in a red bandana and red polka dot skirt standing with a man in a white shirt. The cotton fields in the background look like the sea. A big white sea."

"Are there any mermaids in that big white sea?" the old man jested.

"Sorry, Granddad."

"You are a good boy Sebastian. I'm glad that you went to that Red Herring school in Philadelphia. If you had of liked collecting rent for us, your brother Gene wouldn't have that job today. If he weren't out collecting your Dad's and my rent, there wouldn't be any Penelope in DC, to sell you cotton on canvas."

"I like art too," Charles interrupted them. "I even bought a painting of the sea, but I never think of the water when I look at it."

Old man Johnston looked at him deeply and repeated, "The sea, Mr. Adams?"

"Yes Sir, Mr. Johnston the sea. It's called The Little Captain."

"Are there any mermaids in it?" the elderly Johnston jested again.

"No."

"Then why did you buy it?"

"It reminded me of hair."

"Hair?" the old man exclaimed.

"Yes hair, women's hair. The waves curl into themselves like women's hair just after it comes fresh out of a roller. There's beauty in women's hair, Mr. Johnston; it's like the sea. It simply takes a certain type of eye to see it."

Marsha cleared her throat loudly, and Charles got the hint. No talking about his hair dresser days tonight.

The elderly man continued, "No mermaid, but at least your sea has women's hair in it."

"Maybe I'll come by and see your Little Captain someday."

"Any time you wish, Norbert. Our door is always open.

"I've seen the original of Cabin in the Cotton," Christina said to Sebastian.

"Where was that?"

"At the Smithsonian, last spring," she replied.

"Do you remember who the painter was?" he cajoled.

"Sure. Pippin, Horace Pippin, he was black."

"That's right Christa."

"He was one of the black American boys who went to fight in the war in Europe," she added.

"Do tell," Sebastian joked, trying to hide the fact that he knew very little about Pippin.

"A German sniper shot him in the arm," the young woman continued. "When the wound healed, he decided to take up painting."

"That's the Hun for you," the elder Johnston said. "If Pippin had of come to collect rent for me, no sniper would have got at him."

Samantha noticed a bewildered look on her sister's face and realized that she didn't know what to say to Norbert, whom she suspected was trying to bam-booze them.

"I'm no connoisseur of art," Samantha said, "but I like sea paintings too."

The old black man looked at her. He knew instinctively that that it would not be appropriate to talk of mermaids. She had that no fooling around look about her.

"Which seas do you like, Miss Adams?" Norbert Johnston pressed her.

"The sea in the North West."

"You mean our Pacific North West?"

"Yes!"

"I've never been there," Norbert replied cautiously.

"I have," she assured him.

"Which artist are you referring to?"

"Callahan, Kenneth Callahan," the elder Adams sibling replied.

"Which work?"

"Shore Scene"

"What's in it?"

'There are skeletons of fish swimming in the ocean and gulls walking on the sand."

"I like that Miss Adams."

"Well, thank you Mr. Johnston."

The waitress came by again and announced, "Any time you folks are ready, your table is waiting in the dining room."

"Thank you, Miss," Marsha said. "We'll finish our drinks first. Then I'll give you a little wave."

The Adams Sisters

Gloria looked over at her son Sebastian and Christina. She wondered if they were taking to each other. She hoped so. The Adams' weren't as rich as she would have liked, not like Penelope's folks, but Christina was a good clean girl, and she would be graduating from medicine in the spring. It would be nice to have a Dr. in the family.

Marsha looked over at her daughter Christina. She wondered if they were taking to each other. She hoped so. Charles and she had worked too hard to get her through to the right kind of people. In the mother's mind, it was the only reason for belonging to this club.

She wanted Christina to marry into good society. She and Charles had got up in the world, but it had been such a struggle. Secretly she was of the opinion that it was just as easy for a woman to fall in love with a rich man as it was for her to fall in love with a poor one. If ever the love for him wore thin, a woman could always amuse herself spending a rich man's money.

At first she had thought that her daughter would meet someone at medical school, but so many of the boys there seemed to be on student loans. There was no way to tell if they came from money. Marsha was just as glad that Christina's bookishness discouraged them. However, here at the Club, it was a completely different world. It was well, let's say a more controlled environment. There weren't any student loan boys getting through to this outside deck.

Charles wife remembered the first time she had seen Gloria Johnston sitting in the lounge waiting for Gene and Sebastian to shower, after a game of tennis. At that moment, she was only another black woman at the Club, and they had only smiled at each other. Then, when the boys came up, she thought instantly that either one of them might do. However, Gene turned out to be married. That just left Sebastian. It had taken some doing, but she had managed to engineer a meeting between the older Johnston boy and her daughter, without his mother or Christina suspecting a thing.

Now Sebastian had been to the Adam's home for dinner several times. She had watched the two young people play tennis together, against the cinder block wall in their back yard, from behind the curtain of the upstairs bedroom window. Christina had even accepted his invitation to go to Philadelphia one weekend to hear the symphony, after Charles offered to reserve a room for her at the Gallery Hotel, which is in the center of the cultural district. To the best of her knowledge, at

27, her daughter was still a little girl. She and Charles had worked so hard to keep it like that.

Norbert Johnston slipped his arm in around Samantha's elbow, when the two families began moving towards the gently sloping outside stairs, which led down into the garden and on into the dining room. "Why don't you come and sit beside me for supper Samantha? You can tell me more about that painting of fish skeletons swimming in the ocean, and I'll tell you a little bit about the Johnston's."

"That's very gracious of you, Mr. Johnston."

"Call me Norbert, Samantha."

"Okay Norbert."

The waitress seated them at a long table near the window. Just two or three isolated couples were eating at the outside tables on the patio, but the air conditioned dining room was three quarters full for the Saturday evening second seating. They had a view of the Pro Shop and could see a line of hand pulled golf carts near an open double door on the side of the building. A boy with rags sticking out of his back pockets was busy cleaning the heads of the clubs and irons before he wheeled the carts inside.

Samantha ordered wine. Christina didn't drink. The plates and glasses came and went. Their conversation flowed back and forth.

"So what do you do at the State Department, Samantha?"

"I'm an Intern, Norbert."

"I thought you said that you had been with them for five years."

"I have."

"And you're still an Intern."

"I was with the Department for almost five years in Manhattan and now I'm with the Watch in Washington. It's a special unit; you might say it's a nerve center. Candidates for the Watch must have at least 5 years' experience in State before they will even consider you and then, if you're accepted, you start as an Intern."

"I see."

"Are you from Washington, Norbert?" Samantha pressed.

"Yes I was born here, but originally our family came from the Eastern shore of Virginia, not far from Eastville. Later they moved into Eastville. I've been told that they have the oldest continuous court records in the United States in that town."

"What did your family do in Eastville?"

"They ran a general store."

The Adams Sisters

"And before that?" she plied.

"They were farmers, tobacco."

"Did they have their own farm or were they sharecroppers?"

"No, they had their own place," Norbert said with pride. "My great, great, great grandfather whose name was Antonio came to Virginia in service, around 1621. He served as a servant and after a set period of being indentured, he was given his freedom. He married a freed woman named Mary, who had also served as an indentured servant. When they were married, they took the family name Johnston. Antonio and Mary ended up owning a 900 acre farm on Virginia's Eastern Shore and grew tobacco. Their descendants never became slaves. Over successive generations, the farm was split up. My line sold their section and opened up a general store in Eastville."

"Penelope mentioned that you were also in the brokerage business but that Sebastian had moved all that to Philadelphia."

"Not really brokerage in the sense of the word that is understood today. We were into futures, cotton and tobacco futures," he said with a serious tone in his voice. "It was a sideline that started in the general store in Eastville.

At first my family took a few tobacco futures from local farmers, in exchange for goods. The futures were resold to wealthier people for a small profit. Later they started buying both tobacco and cotton futures from farmers for cash, which they had borrowed from the bank, using their store inventory as collateral. The futures always resold easily, and the loans were paid back quickly. There was always enough of a margin in those transactions to make it worthwhile for the Johnston's.

Even though I never lived in Eastville, my father had worked in the store, before moving to Washington, and he taught me all about buying and selling tobacco and cotton futures," Norbert explained. "My son Harold wasn't interested and neither was my grandson Gene. They like buildings. Our little company owns and manages quite a few of them, both residential and commercial. Sebastian was the only one, who showed any interest in futures, so I taught him all I knew. He doesn't trade tobacco or cotton futures anymore. These days the money is in gold futures. It seems there's a thriving gold exchange in Philly."

"That's very interesting Norbert. I'll have to talk to you again sometime. I've always wanted to know more about the stock market, but have been keeping my savings in mutuals."

"Oh, mutuals are okay too. I own a bit of them myself, but not as much as I in the past. They lost quite a bit of value in the 90's, so I sold part of what I was holding.

Why don't I give you my card? I usually lunch out two or three times a week. It's always nice to have an attractive, young escort, to bring the envy out in the tables around you."

"I'd like that," she said, accepting the card. "Do I call you?"

"Yes, call me anytime and say that you're free for lunch. I know that you Administration people are always on the run. My agenda is not heavily booked anymore. I mostly go in and sign a few checks. My son and grandson take care of everything."

"It's a deal then," Samantha said, shaking the elderly gentleman's hand. "We'll make them envious over lunch."

It was 10 p.m. before both families left the Club. As he was leaving, Gene told Charles that he would call him during the week about getting insurance on a new building of theirs.

Sebastian pushed Christina's chair back in under the table for her and enquired, "Any plans for Labor Day weekend?"

"I'm not sure. Dad was saying something about Atlantic City or Virginia Beach," she replied.

"I don't know if I'll be coming to Chevy Chase. It's the last long weekend, before Thanksgiving; however, I'll call you. If we're both in town, how about playing tennis?"

"Sure, as long as you don't mind, if it turns out like the last time."

"Somebody has to win," he laughed.

"You're right," she blushed and smiled, before adding, "Maybe I'll let you win next time."

****

The Adams Sisters

4 – Fishermen's Wharf

The morning following supper at her father's Club, Samantha, arrived for work at the State Department refreshed, and felt very positive about herself and her job. There wasn't much at the Watch or the Main libraries concerning scams originating in Nigeria. Most of the information available, in hard copy, read like the CIA Fact Book – population statistics, economic and agriculture statistics and a summary of the country's history. She decided to try the Internet. The State Department's postings, to the Internet, were more informative than anything she found on the library shelves.

The Departments postings were divided into travel and business warnings. She found a copy of the general travel warning, which had been renewed many times, on Africa.Net.

**

WARNING

"The Department of State warns U.S. citizens of the dangers of travel to Nigeria. Violent crime, practiced by persons in police and military uniforms, as well as by ordinary criminals, is an acute problem. Harassment and shake-downs of foreigners and Nigerians alike frequently occur throughout the country.

A visa is required. Promises of entry into Nigeria without a visa are an indication of a fraudulent scheme. Proof of a valid entry visa is required to be able to leave. Business scams involving foreigners are widespread.

Nigerian scams usually involve offers to transfer money, lucrative sales or contracts with large commissions. Scam artists pose as officers or ministers of the Nigerian government. Correspondence is usually written on seemingly genuine ministerial stationery, replete with official stamps and seals.

In addition, Advance Fee Fraud (AFF) schemes abound. After enticing you with offers of lucrative contracts or cash transfers, you will be required to provide up-front or advance fees for various taxes, attorney fees, transaction fees or bribes. These schemes are known as "4-1-9" fraud after the section of the Nigerian penal code, which addresses fraud schemes. Americans apprehended on Nigerian soil, who are involved in an AFF, will be subject to local law.

Passports are a hot commodity. Their loss or theft should be reported to the U.S. embassy or consulate immediately. In addition to violence, thief, and fraud, contagious disease is prevalent. Evidence of yellow fever and cholera vaccinations are required.

The Department's Web site, at http://travel.state.gov, was much more explicit in a posting titled, 'Tips for Business Travelers to Nigeria'.

"Money Transfer: The operator claims to have a large sum of money, usually millions of dollars, which needs to be transferred to a "safe" bank account abroad. The Central Bank of Nigeria is often, though by no means always, mentioned. You, as a safe bank account owner, are promised a percentage of the huge sum, just for use of your account. You may be asked to provide a blank check, signed invoices, letterhead and bank account information, or to send money for transfer taxes. Some businesses have found their account looted by the persons to whom they sent account information."

**

Samantha looked down at the photocopy of the letter that Roscoe had given her. It fit perfectly with several of the points mentioned in the 'Warning' and the 'Tips for Business Travelers'.

She wondered how Americans could be so foolish as to believe letters like the one she was holding. There was so much information available on the Internet that citizens could access. She also wondered how the scam artists could be still

The Adams Sisters

sending out this junk, when there were so many public warnings.

The following day, she had a chance to talk with her Section Chief, Mr. Walters.

"How are things going, Samantha? I know I've been giving you a lot to do lately, but we are short staffed at present with the tail end of annual vacations."

"Oh, I'm managing Roscoe."

"Have you had a chance to do anything with that letter I showed you, the one from Nigeria?"

"As a matter of fact, I did do a bit of research. State turned out to be the best source of information. Here are a few print outs I pulled off our Web site."

He quickly scanned the sections, which she had highlighted in yellow.

"This is excellent! I wasn't aware that the Department had gone into this issue in such detail. With so many projects on the go, one can't keep up on everything we're doing."

"So where does this put us?" his Intern queried when he had finished reading.

"It means the research you've done is legit now."

"How's that?"

"I couldn't justify the resources needed to send you off freelancing on a stray letter. However, since the Department is this concerned about the issue, it's fair game for us at the Watch too."

"What do you want me to do?"

"I'll have to see if I can find a few bucks somewhere. Check with me tomorrow. There are a number projects, which haven't been bearing much fruit lately. I might decide to trim them back and reallocate some of the funds to Nigerian scams."

"Ok!"

The following day she went into her superior's office a little before noon. He was smiling. "How's my assistant on the Nigerian Project today?" she joked.

"He's doing fine."

"Did he find me some budget credits?"

"There's enough to get started."

"What did my assistant have in mind for a start?"

"I talked with four agents and an information officer, after you gave me those Internet postings. We, the Administration, have quite a lot of general information. However, the ability of the U.S. to extradite Americans from unlawful business deals in Nigeria is extremely limited. Since the mid-1990's, quite a number U.S. citizen "victims" of scams have been arrested by police and held for varying lengths of time in Nigerian prisons. The police don't always let the U.S. embassy know.

These people are reluctant to come forward and complain to us, when they get back home, as they fear further prosecution here. We do hear about them and the deals through unofficial sources."

"So, we're either in at the beginning or hear about the end, but we never see the sting in operation," the young woman summarized.

"That's right."

"I would like you to set up shell business and then fax this Ossaga from it. We have already had the embassy check out his fax number. It's unlisted. The Nigerian telephone system is very underdeveloped, and the government has told us that they simply don't have the resources to investigate the several thousand inquiries that they receive about these letters every year. There's no way that our equipment can trace his fax number back to an address. Even if we could, we might only find a call forwarding machine.

These people have killed in the past, so they should be considered dangerous. We are not the FBI, the CIA or the Pentagon. You are never to expose yourself to any situation where there would the slightest possibility of having to call on one of those agencies for help."

"I understand."

"You will have to be a very responsible young lady and keep yourself focused at all times. This is real life, not the movies."

"I understand Sir."

"As I said, this project will remain between you and me. We don't want the boys, here at the Watch, to come sniffing around."

"Yes Sir."

"Now that we understand each other Sam, where do you think you'll start? What can I do to be of assistance to you?"

"I think I should learn something about business shells. I'll feel my dad out first. He's in insurance and might have some ideas. My sister is also friends with someone who's involved with brokerage. He might be helpful."

"Good, I'll accept that for a start, but remember, this is confidential, and you're never to make any connection with the Department, while you're talking to them."

The Adams Sisters 51

"There won't be any accidents."

"Then you're on your own, but keep in touch. As your assistant, I should know as much about project as you do, at all times."

"Right you are and one more thing, thank you very much, Mr. Walters," she said, extending her hand out across the desk towards him. He took it and shook it lightly.

Roscoe watched her leave his office. He was feeling very pleased with himself. He was happy that his Intern was responding so well. For him, this was make-believe work, but it was an excellent way to get an Intern through the first few months at the Watch.

That evening after dinner, Samantha, went into the living room where her father was reading the Washington Post. "You busy Dad?"

"No," he said, setting the paper down on the couch beside him. "What's on your mind? You look serious. You're not coming to tell me that you are moving out, are you?"

"No," she laughed. "You'll have plenty of advance warnings. I might start to take a look around for a one bedroom apartment this fall, but I probably won't get through to it until after Christmas."

"You're welcome to stay with us, as long as you want. This is a big empty house for your mother and me, when you girls aren't around. Anyway, what's on your mind?"

"I want to ask you about business?"

"Go ahead, shoot."

"If I wanted to set up a business, how would I go about doing it?"

"Do you want to start up a business? I thought there were some rules against civil servants carrying on a business."

"There may be, I'll worry about them if and when."

"What kind of business would you like to go into?"

"I don't know, import/export, maybe African crafts.

"You've never showed much interest in your African heritage. You've always been the high-tech, Miss America type, why now?"

"I'm only using crafts as an example. Maybe I'll import oil from Nigeria."

"That's better."

"Ok, if I wanted to import oil from Nigeria, how would I go about doing it?"

"First, you'd be wise to have a business."

"Ok, let's start with me setting up my company. How would I do that?"

"Samantha, there are basically three types of companies. The smallest is the sole proprietorship. There are about 3 million of them in the US. We Americans use them to do everything from painting houses to launching new products. In addition to proprietorships, there are private limited companies and public limited companies."

"What's the difference?"

"Cost, liability, structure, you name it.

If you want to set up a proprietorship, you'll have to think up a name for it, do a search to make sure that nobody else is using that name and then register it. The search and name registration will run you about $100, but then you'll be legally able to contract in the name of Sam's African Imports.

A proprietorship is an extension of you. You finance it, and you are personally responsible for all debts. If anybody sues Sam's African Imports, they're really suing you."

"That sounds a little risky to me."

"It can be. That all depends on what you are doing."

"Why would anybody bother getting into a trap like that?"

"Because Sam's African Imports can write off legitimate business expenses and Samantha Adams can't"

"I see. What about the others?"

"Once you get your name registered, you could incorporate it. Incorporation would separate Sam's African Imports Ltd. from you personally. You could still own 100% of it, as long as you hold all the shares. You could also sell shares to other people to get money to pay for your oil inventory or you could pay them for their services with shares. Your incorporated company has to file its own tax return separate from you. If the company gets sued, creditors can't come after you personally except under special circumstances, like a personal guarantee.

If your private corporation does really well, you might try to get it listed on a stock exchange and then it would be a public corporation."

"Why would I want to make Sam's African Imports Ltd. a public company?" his daughter continued.

"Sometimes it is easier to raise money on an exchange than to get it from a bank and people are more willing to hold shares in a public company, because there is a better market for publicly traded shares, when they want to get their money out."

The Adams Sisters

"That's great Dad, thanks; I won't hold you from your newspaper any longer," she said starting to get up.

"No problem, Sam," he replied, unfolding the Washington Post again, "any time."

Several weeks later, while rummaging through her purse, Samantha came across a business card that Norbert Johnston had given her at the Cabot Club, the evening they all had dinner together.

She clicked open the Organizer on her computer. There was nothing scheduled between 11:30 a.m. and 2 p.m. today. Why not she thought? There couldn't be any danger in having lunch with a man who was in his seventies.

The mouse pointer went to the side of the Organizer, and she started to click out his telephone number, on a digital keypad, which had appeared on the LCD screen. A woman's voice answered from the small speaker placed on the back of her desk.

"Capital Property Management, may I help you please," she said with a professional manner.

A microphone attached to the monitor picked up Samantha's voice. "May I speak with Mr. Norbert Johnston, please?"

"One moment, please."

"Norbert Johnston speaking."

"Mr. Johnston, this is Samantha Adams, remember me?"

"Samantha! Why yes, dinner at my son's Club, I was wondering if and when you would call."

"I won't chit-chat, in case you're busy, but I was thinking of you and thought I'd see if you were available for lunch today."

"What time?" he exclaimed with boyish excitement.

"Say twelveish," she replied.

"Great, where?"

"Where do you usually go, when you want to impress the boys with a new lady friend?"

"Where are you now, Samantha?"

"I'm at my office, corner of 23rd Street NW and C Street NW, and a little south of Washington Circle."

"That's not far from me. Our headquarters is in Mount Pleasant. I could pick you up or meet you almost anywhere. Do you like seafood?"

"I was raised on it. My Dad bought bushel baskets of Chesapeake Bay crabs, down at the Maine Avenue, Fishermen's Market. We boiled them on the BBQ in the back yard and then gorged ourselves on a picnic table."

"That's an idea," he reflected. "There are several great restaurants next to the market. We'd have a choice of buffet or ordering off the menu. Would you like me to pick up or meet you there?"

"That's a super idea, Norbert. I haven't been around the Fishermen's Wharf since coming back to Washington. I think I'd prefer to take my car. Do you carry a cell phone?"

"Yes, I have one," the seventy year old replied.

"Good, I'll park and wait for your call. When you arrive, give me a buzz at 202-466-4454. I'll walk over to your car."

He chuckled into the phone, "Twenty years just fell away, and I haven't even left my chair."

"That's why you asked me to call you for lunch, Norbert," she said with a smirk.

The elderly man laughed, repeated her cell number and said he would see her soon.

Washington owes its existence to its river front location on the Potomac, where it meets the Anacostia River. In the olden days, the Seventh Street wharf on, Washington Channel, was one of the busiest ocean-going ports in America. Today it is the site of the Washington Marina.

The Maine Avenue, Fish Market, is located directly on the river, beneath a mammoth highway overpass. It's a conglomeration of permanent, open-air stalls where the bounty of the Chesapeake Bay and the Atlantic Ocean is spread out on shelves covered with crushed ice or on racks, which are surrounded by clouds of hot steam.

The stalls are frequented by locals in search of seafood, by civil servants on their lunch break from the nearby L'Enfant Plaza federal office buildings and tourists. However, the closest most out-of-towners get to the Wharf are the massive, modern waterfront restaurants, along Washington Channel, south of the Nation's Yacht Club.

As soon as Norbert hung up from speaking with Samantha Adams, he put his phone on voice mail, grabbed his straw hat and headed out of the office with only a quick, "see you later, I'm gone for lunch," to the receptionist who stared after him.

Mount Pleasant is mostly a residential area, partially surrounded on the West by the National Zoo and on the North by a branch of the Rock Creek Park. Once absentee landlords had let the buildings get run down, but the neighborhood was on the way back up. The Johnston's had relocated the head office of their, Capital Property Management firm to a renovated building on Newton Street, which they owned.

The Adams Sisters

Norbert had reserved the penthouse in the building for his personal residence, even before the renovations started. He liked living in the midst of urban life. Both his office window and the living room window of his condominium looked out on Mt. Pleasant Village, which is a cluster of small stores, a bar, a hairdresser, a barber, an accountant and a real estate agent. Cars park on both sides of the median in the middle of the Village. Norbert was proud of the large green and white sign secured to a post on the median, which read, DRUG FREE NEIGHBOURHOOD. He headed a committee that had convinced the City to install this sign.

Norbert had a high powered telescope set up on a tripod, behind a light silk curtain, in his living room, and a comfortable, easy chair strategically placed so that he could watch the neighborhood for hours and never be seen. If he even suspected that he saw drugs in the street, on the roofs or even in the apartments into which he looked, he would notify the Police immediately. It was thanks to the efforts of residents like him that the neighborhood was on its way back up.

A yellow Porsche emerged from the parking garage in the basement of the building, with Norbert at the wheel. He stopped to check both ways for traffic on Newton Street. A roll down steel door closed silently behind him. On the sidewalk, a group of young boys in a circle yelled and hollered in Spanish, as they kicked a small bean bag between them. He drove slowly to the corner, turned the vehicle into 16th Street NW and began to cruise south, towards the distant Washington Monument.

Samantha too had left her office almost immediately, when she hung up from talking with the elderly Johnston. After clearing the parkade, she drove to Independence Avenue and followed it east as far as the Maine Avenue turn off. While stopped at a red light, she flipped down the visor and freshened her lipstick in the tiny square mirror. She found a non-metered parking spot for the gold Lexus along Maine and then set off on foot to meet her lunch date. As she passed by the Market, the sweet, pungent smell of steamed jumbo shrimp became almost overwhelming.

The young woman had only reached the walkway leading up to the entrance of the flagship, of a family of the mid-Atlantic fine seafood restaurants, when her cell phone buzzed. She flipped it open and answered, "Hello!"

"Hello Samantha?"

"Yes, this is Samantha."

"This is Norbert."

"Hi Norbert, where are you?"

"I see a sign that says Nation's Yacht Club. Where are you?"

"I think I see you Norbert," she giggled. "Wave so I can be sure. Yes, it's you. Here see me. I'm waving at you now."

"Ok, I see you too. I'll be right over."

Samantha was surprised to see the elderly Johnston's office attire, which consisted of a black and white striped seersucker suit, a grey and silver silk tie and black loafers. She looped her arm into his at the elbow and steered him through the restaurant's double glass wooden doors, past a huge ship's wheel and on towards the Hostess station. A tall black woman in an expensive paisley dress greeted them.

"Good afternoon folks! Is this the first time you've visited our house."

Samantha nodded and replied, "Yes!"

"You may order from the menu or you may help yourselves from our 75 item, all-you-can-eat buffet. The upstairs," she indicated a wide mahogany staircase with red carpeted stairs, "is reserved for menu only service. Downstairs service, which includes the patio, is for both menu and buffet service."

"We would prefer the patio, Miss," Norbert told her.

"And we're going to try the buffet," Samantha added.

The hostess signaled to a waiter, who came immediately.

"These guests are going to sample our buffet today, Richard."

"Please follow me folks," the youth, in black trousers, white shirt, black vest and a black bow tie invited. "Are we sitting inside or on the patio?"

"The patio," Norbert replied.

He showed them to a large square table outside, which looked directly onto the Nation's Yacht Club. "Could I get you anything from the bar?"

"Not for me," Samantha replied. "Ice tea will be fine."

"I'll have the same," Norbert added.

"Would you like a jug of ice tea?"

"Yes, a jug would be perfect," they replied together.

"Fine! Just go over, get in line and help yourselves. You may go back to the buffet as many times as you wish."

They each took a very large dinner plate from a dishes caddy and began to move through the day's hot features, which were arranged in stainless steel steam trays. The choice

The Adams Sisters

included: baked fish, breaded spiced shrimp, steamed clams, steamed crayfish, seafood jambalaya, seafood Newburg, steamed mussels, scallops, assorted smoked salmon, and crab legs. This was followed by a heat lamp section that included: skewers of blackened salmon or tuna, fried shrimp, deep fried clams, fried fish fillets, huge mussels, sea oysters, pickled cockles and miniature crab cake.

Since they had come for the self-service seafood, they didn't go to the salad bar or the soup and chowder bar. I'm not taking rolls either," Samantha told Norbert. "There's still dessert, if I have any room after this, but I already think that my eyes are bigger than my tummy."

"You can always come back for dessert."

She smiled at him and headed towards their table. The waiter had left a 2 quart jug of ice tea with cubes, as well as a roll of paper towel and a silver bucket into which they could place shells, shrimp bodies, skewers and bones.

"I am glad you called," he said. "It was turning out to be another boring day. How long have you been away from Washington?"

"Eight years in all."

"That's quite a spell."

"After I finished a BA in American History at Georgetown, I found a job at the library in Philadelphia, through student services. When I was an undergrad, I'd never even thought of doing a Masters. The idea started to grow in my mind while I was working at the library. I ended up registering at Penn State, in Franklin College and spread the courses and Master's thesis in US International Relations out over two and a half years.

When the grad work was done, I wrote the Civil Service and State Department exams. The Department offered me a spot in Manhattan. In addition to our delegation to the UN, there were at least one hundred supporting staff, who occupied the whole floor of a downtown New York office tower. During the first year, I was with the Administrative Affairs Section."

"What did they do?"

"Lots – human resource services like expense budgets, security, communications, and conference operations, but to name a few. Then I spent two years with the Resources Management Section, which monitors the administration of the United States, UN budget. It's the unit that deals with the State Department's Secretariat on all management issues relevant to American interests, in a strong and effective United Nations."

"That sounds like an official reply, which was etched into your brain."

"Are you insinuating indoctrination?" she laughed and then continued. "After Resource Management, I moved along to the Press and Public Affairs Section. That was the part I liked the best. I actually got to go into the UN quite frequently."

"What did you do there?"

"We were responsible for explaining to the media and public our country's participation and policy concerning the United Nations. Sometimes I prepared news releases and other times; I was a spokesperson to both domestic and foreign accredited journalists. I also organized briefings to civic groups. Occasionally, I went into colleges and universities and spoke to students myself."

"So that was 5 years in New York."

"Right and eight years away from my home town in all," she summarized.

"I know the government moves its team around quite often, but maybe you'll get to stay here in Washington and get back in touch with your roots."

"I hope so. I've already been out with some old high school buddies, and it was lots of fun."

Over dinner, they talked about the stock market in general and a few mutuals in particular. Samantha waited patiently and then steered him towards the topic, which had prompted this lunch meeting.

"Tell me, Norbert, if you were going to start up an import/export business, would you go for a proprietorship or a limited company?"

"I would probably begin with a proprietorship and if it survived, turn it into a limited company. Why do you ask?"

"I am just curious about the business process. My studies haven't really equipped me very well to understand the business side of life."

"Business is like every other discipline, formal schooling is nice to have, but it will only take you so far. Eventually, anyone who is serious must roll up their shirt sleeves and plunge in"

"If you wanted to start up a business, what would you do?"

"I'll be honest with you Sam, I'd probably buy one. There are so many excellent businesses for sale. First I'd take look in the classified section of any newspaper. If I didn't find what I wanted, I'd run an advertisement describing exactly what I was looking for."

The Adams Sisters

"Really!" She sounded amazed. "I always thought business was such an exclusive domain, beyond the reach of ordinary people."

"You've been watching too much television, my dear. Business is ordinary people coming together to earn their living. But you have a job, so I don't think that you'll be hanging out your shingle anytime soon."

"No," she joked. "I don't think that I'll become a DBA."

"A what?"

"Doing Business As," she replied, a bit unsure of herself.

"Oh," he laughed. "I thought DBA was some new kind of Biz-degree from that Red Herring crowd."

When she got back to the office, Samantha phoned a paper in Baltimore to find out how much it would cost to run an advertisement in the Saturday edition. The ad she faxed them along with her Department credit card number and expiry date read as follows.

'BUSINESS WANTED: Seeking established proprietorship, which is not operating. Willing to pay up to $500 for your registration, stationery, and records. Reply in confidence to Box 4576, this paper.'

****

5 - Georgetown

Georgetown was a thriving colonial tobacco port on the Potomac River that was formed by Scottish tobacco merchants, in 1751. The town was part of Maryland, before integration into the new capital. During the Civil War, local sympathies were mostly southern.

The beginning of the C&O Canal was actually Rock Creek, the dividing line between the capital and its suburb. Several hundred yards upstream from the Potomac River, the canal branched off to the west and flowed through Georgetown, parallel to M Street NW. The Canal is now part of the National Park Service. Sometimes, strollers along its banks can watch Park Officers take the "Georgetown" barge through the locks.

Since 1787, African Americans have been parishioners at Holy Trinity Catholic Church, on 36th Street NW, between O and N Streets NW. For more than a century, it was the only place in Georgetown where they could worship.

Sebastian phoned on the Thursday, before Labor Day weekend, to take a rain check on his tennis game with Christina. One of his clients had invited him out on his yacht for the three days. He said they were going to work out the final phase of a five million dollar financing deal while trolling for tuna.

The Adams Sisters 61

On Friday afternoon, before the long weekend, the Wave called and asked Christina if she could work both the Saturday and Sunday evenings. She accepted Saturday but told them it would be her last time. She was getting busy with a clerkship and was required to do some evenings at the hospital. Charles and Marsha Adams went to Atlantic City alone.

There were a few lulls at the Wave, before 10 p.m. on Saturday night. Once Christina and Tod got past his warm up jokes, they chatted easily together.

"Did they schedule you for Sunday evening too?" Tod asked her, while she stood at the waitress station.

"They offered, but I said that I couldn't make it."

"How come? With the long weekend, there should be a good holiday crowd."

"Actually this is my last night, Tod. I told management I couldn't accept any more shifts."

"Why's that?"

"I'm in school."

"What school?"

"I'm in my fourth year of Medicine at Georgetown U and it started in July. Besides the courses, there are the clericals. My schedule is too heavy. This is my last year, and I don't want to take any chances."

"Is that a fact?" he jested.

"Yes, really, that's what I'm all about Preppy."

Carefully he began to stack clean glasses into a deep cooler, between him and the bar top while continuing to talk to her. She noticed the perfect part that ran through the center of his straw blond hair.

"This is my last weekend too," he informed her without looking up. "I'm working tomorrow in the evening, but I told the owner I can't take anymore after that."

It was her turn to pose the questions. "How come?"

"I'm in my fourth and final year too, and it started in May."

"Fourth year of what?"

"A Doctor of Veterinary Science program at the Virginia-Maryland Regional College of Veterinary Medicine."

"I've never heard of that school," she continued eyeing him with skepticism. "Where's it located?"

"There are three campuses, two in Virginia and one in Maryland. My first three years were completed at Leesburg and Blacksburg in Virginia. I elected to do a 12 month Fourth Year clerkships at the Avrum Gudelsky Veterinary Center, on the University of Maryland campus, in College Park."

"Why there?"

"There're a few reasons. My family lives in Silver Spring. It's only a zip along the Beltway to the UM Campus. Also, they have a very good Equine Studies Program. The state house in Annapolis has funded the program generously over the past few years."

"So Preppy is going to be a Doctor?" she snipped

"Not an MD, but yes, don't I look the type?

"Nope, I figured you'd go surfing in California for the winter."

"That would be nice, but duty calls."

"So what have you been doing, since the last time I saw you here?" she asked, with the skepticism gone from her voice.

"This week I've been taking seminars on bioterrorism at the US Department of Agriculture in downtown Washington."

"What kind of terrorism?" she exclaimed.

"It was part of appreciation week for the role veterinary medicine plays in protecting the Nation from bioterrorism. One seminar was on the West Nile virus. There were a number of presentations concerning the implications of bioterrorism and biosecurity, on the poultry production facilities situated on Maryland's Eastern Shore."

Just then, a group of six young people came through the door and sat down in Christina's section. She straightened up, took hold of her tray and declared, "Duty calls!"

He smiled and whispered, "Hasta Luego"

"Adios, Preppy," she replied and was gone.

Jesuit-run Georgetown University is the oldest Roman Catholic University in the US. Founded in 1789 as Georgetown College, the school's location in the nation's capital has helped build its reputation for excellence in several faculties. Many alumni are prominent in government. The school has four undergraduate schools that offer seven bachelor's degrees, as well as medicine and law. Its men's basketball team, The Hoyas, usually show well. The campus population is approximately 12,000.

The medical school came into being in May of 1851. A group of local doctors monopolized the clinical facilities of the Washington Infirmary. Four excluded practitioners decided to improve their livelihood by setting up a medical school and dispensary of their own. The president of Georgetown College granted their request that it be considered the Department of Medicine.

The Adams Sisters

The first woman applied to and was accepted by the medical school in 1898. There was dissention among the faculty. She had to take a special course in anatomy, in private, with the anatomy professor.

In 1903, a University Hospital was built on land donated by the College. The Sisters of Saint Francis came from Philadelphia and took full charge of it. The first patients were five local volunteers, who had been wounded at Guantanamo Bay in Cuba.

Today's School of Medicine is a large red brick building, set quite a way back from the Potomac River. It's part of the Medical Center. The Center's other components are the University Hospital, Dahlgren Medical Library, Lombardi Cancer Research Center and the School of Nursing. The highest point in the Medical Center is a white, domed gazebo, built on top of the square, wooden tower that sits on a low-pitch roof into which are built high narrow dormers.

The University is private, but the Medical Center is even more private. There are rules covering confidentiality, especially where patients are involved. There are rules covering contact with the media. No demonstrations are tolerated. Needless to say, the Medical Center is a smoke free environment.

Fourth year is divided into 4 quarters. It starts in July and ends with graduation, on Memorial Day weekend, at the end of May. It consists of forty-eight weeks of required clerkships, twenty weeks of electives and four weeks that may be used for a vacation or additional electives. There are two twelve-week blocks of clerkships and two twelve-week blocks of electives.

The first quarter was almost over, and Christina had twelve weeks of electives coming up, before the Christmas/New Year's break. All summer and during the month of September she had been doing a clerkship at DC General Hospital, in Washington. Recently she had decided that she would apply to do her Internship at DC General too. It was entirely possible that she wouldn't be accepted; however, the rumor was that applicants were given points for having done their clerkship there, provided there was nothing negative in their supervisors' reports.

On a cool morning during the first week in October, Christina walked westward along R Street NW to where it ended, at the intersection with 38th Street NW and then turned south towards Georgetown University. The South Cottage Club playing field was located at this intersection. She wore dark slacks with a crease in them, a beige cotton blouse and white jacket. It was the standard dress code for women at the Medical School. While she walked; she talked on a cell phone to her best friend, Jewel Simpson.

When the young medical student arrived at a wide, double unit of cement steps set into the slope, which rises from Reservoir St. to the Medical Dental Building; she stopped and looked up, before starting to climb the steps. Six tall white columns, which hold up the roof over the building's entrance, rose up from a ledge above the five brass double doors.

The main lobby of the Medical School was made of rich brown, polished wood. A wooden bench runs along the back wall. Above it was a painting of a woman in bed who was being treated to by a doctor. On the other side of the bed two interns, a young man and a young woman, looked on. Christina went to the School's Administrative office to hand in the Internship Request Form.

Once she had received a receipt for the Request Form from the Assistant, the young med student returned to the corridor and headed towards the back door of the building. She walked across the plaza towards the Pre-Clinical Sciences Building, which also accessed the Dahlgren Medical Library. Jewel Simpson would meet her there, in the Coffee Shop.

As she walked, Christina felt a piece of paper chaffing at her leg from inside the right pocket of her slacks. She put her hand in her pocket and pulled it out. It was the e-mail message she had printed off, before leaving her bedroom. Someone who called himself Yellow Cloud had replied to the profile that she had posted on DC Meets.

He said he liked her user name, which was Night Shadow and that he was a student and would like to know more about her. Christina didn't know if she would reply. What if there were some way that he could find out who she really was. She had never done anything like this before. She felt apprehensive, but also excited. Nobody but Jewel was going to find out about DC Meets.

Jewel and Christa had known each other seven years now. The friendship had started in the first year of Biology, when they were both frosh. Jewel had fallen in love during the first year of medicine, with a boy named Benjamin, who was in Dentistry. Now they were engaged. The two girls had stayed best buddies through it all.

"Hi Christa," a girl with a tight, blond ponytail said as she approached.

The Adams Sisters

"Hey, yourself Jewels!"

"Are we going to the library, straight away?" Christina's friend asked. "I just got back from my clinical and wouldn't mind a small break."

"Great, I don't really feel like cooping myself in there yet either. What time are you meeting Ben?"

"He's working at the Student Dental Clinic this afternoon, so the earliest that he will be free is 5 p.m. I told him I'd be waiting outside the clinic. We're having a quick supper and then we're both coming back to the library."

"Let's have coffee then," Christina continued. "I have something I want to show you."

"What?"

"You'll see."

When they were seated, Christina took the piece of paper from her pocket and spread it out in front of her friend. "Read this and tell me what you think?"

Jewel stopped reading almost immediately. "Who's Night Shadow?"

"Me!"

"I don't get it. Where did this thing come from?"

"Back during August, I received some junk e-mail from one of those online mix and match dating sites called, DC Meets. For a lark, I joined up. This is the first reply I've had."

"What did you put in your profile?" her friend asked. "This guy seems interested in you."

"Do you really think so?"

"Oh, definitely, you can tell by the way he lets you see himself and by the things he wants to know about you. Did you reply yet?"

"No!"

"Are you going to?"

"I don't know? This is a whole new experience for me. I've never done anything like this before. I thought I should take my profile down."

"You could talk with him online. You don't have to meet him."

"What would I say?"

"He's only a guy Christa, answer his questions and then ask him a few questions yourself."

"Do you think I should tell him I'm black?"

"You didn't post a picture? Usually, people post a picture with their profile on these Web sites."

"No, I didn't submit a picture."

"You're lucky to have received a reply, with no picture. Some girls set up four or five different pictures of themselves, but never get a reply. And the answer is no, I wouldn't mention anything about color, unless he asks. "

"Isn't that being dishonest?"

"Not really, as long as you don't lie, there is nothing dishonest in it. Besides, he might be asking two or three girls the same questions. This Yellow Cloud doesn't need to know if you're black or white, unless he asks."

As they walked to the Dahlgren library, they talked about the email.

"What did you put in your profile?" Jewel continued. "It must have been good to hook a guy without a photo."

"I can't remember it all, but I did talk quite a bit about horses and riding them."

"He must be a horse nut too. I saw the word horse in at least three of his questions."

"Let's forget Mr. Yellow Cloud for now," Christina said abruptly, as she was feeling awkward. "What did you finally settle on for your third quarter clinicals?"

"Internal medicine, obstetrics, and gynecology. How about you, Night Shadow?"

They both burst out laughing.

"Pediatrics and family medicine."

"You're going to end up being a baby doctor." Jewel kidded.

"Maybe of my own babies," the Adams girl replied. They smiled at each other and laughed again. Then Christina became serious. "I want to ask you something. You can tell me it's none of my business if you want."

"Go ahead; I can only say that it's none of your business."

"Are you and Ben still not doing it?"

"By it do you mean sex?"

"Yes!" She felt herself blushing.

"We haven't done a final yet, but we've come pretty close."

"Really, I always thought that Jewish guys were fast movers."

"When they're with a Jewish girl, they have to follow the rules. After graduation in May we're getting married and then Mrs. Benjamin Denton is going to do it, all night and all day, right through to the next day."

"Better watch out that you don't become pregnant." They both burst out laughing again.

The Adams Sisters

Next day Christina had to go in to DC General. It was raining. The air in the hospital was close. It seemed as if many people had stored up their problems all summer and then with the arrival of fall, had decided to come in for a tune up. At the end of the shift, she was beat.

Traffic was moving slowly with the rain. The trip back across town took an hour. Inside the BMW, the roar of the rain, pounding down on the fabric top, drowned out the music coming from the radio.

Back at home, Christina found the small red light on the side of the phone in her bedroom blinking. The signal meant that there was a message in her voice mailbox. She didn't feel like listening to her messages, but keyed in the numeric code anyway, while getting undressed. There was only one message.

It was Sebastian. He was in Washington and wanted to see her. There was a number to call. Nobody answered. The voice mail at the other end of the line came on. She started to talk after the beep.

"Hi Sebastian, this is Christa. I got your message. Yes, I'd like to see you too. I'm working at the hospital in the morning, but I'm finished at one p.m. Why don't you come by here after that? We could go for a walk if it isn't raining. There are lots of parks in this neighborhood.

I just came in from work, and I'm really exhausted. I'm going to catch up on some sleep, before my next shift. See you tomorrow."

The following afternoon when Christina arrived, Sebastian's black suburban with tinted windows was parked beside Marsha's silver Lincoln. She pulled into her usual spot, got out and went immediately into the house. She could hear her mother's voice. It was coming from the direction of the back deck, which jutted out from the French doors that were built into one wall of the dining room. As she approached, she could see Sebastian's head.

Her mother was the first to notice her and waved. Sebastian's head turned around just as her daughter was waving back. Christina greeted the young man with a light touch on his shoulder. His arm came up off his lap, and his fingers closed softly around her elbow. Mrs. Adams smiled approvingly.

"I'll be right back Sebast. I feel all sweaty from work. I need a shower."

"Go right ahead dear," her mother interjected. "Sebastian and I will finish our ice tea while you freshen up."

It didn't take long, before she was back a in white camisole tee shirt, seventeen inch coral pedal pushers, matching kidskin f ats and her hair pulled back with a brightly printed scarf.

"Are you ready Mr. Johnston?" she crooned.

"Yes I am, Ms. Adams," the young man chuckled, standing up.

"You two have a good walk," her mother called after them as they walked back through the dining room to go out by the front door. Both of them turned and waved at her.

"Where are we headed?" Sebastian asked when they turned left at the sidewalk and started to walk east along R Street NW.

"There's a Lovers' Lane between Dumbarton Oaks Park and Montrose Park. The earth road may be a bit washed away in spots by the rain, but it's a good walk and it goes all the way down to Rock Creek Park."

"Will I be all right in these leather shoes?"

"Oh, they'll be fine," she assured him. "So what brings you to Washington in the middle of the week?"

"I'm on my way back to Philly from St. Petersburg in Florida, where the firm was proposing small business loans to Russia entrepreneurs."

"Any takers?"

"Oh, there're all takers, if we offer them cash, but venture capital doesn't work like that. If a project is going to be a money maker, it has to do something that really needs to be done, and I must be convinced that it will do the job the way the users want it done. When I get back to Philadelphia, I must ask a few people some questions about software, to be sure the projects we're looking at are viable."

She looked up at him as they started down the old road. "You didn't stop into see me to talk about software."

"No, you're right; I want to talk to you about hardware."

"What kind of hardware?"

"A house, I would like to build one, and I'd like you to help me design it."

"I don't know anything about designing a house," she protested evasively then landed a light punch on his left bicep.

"But you are a woman, you see differently than I do. I would probably only stick rooms here and there or let some architect decide for me."

The Adams Sisters 69

"What's the matter with your Dad and Gene? They must have lots of building experience."

"I don't want then to have any part in it. I only want you to be involved."

"Why?"

"Because I like your style, look at that outfit you are wearing today."

She pressed him. "Sebastian, you're not answering my question."

"Well, someday I might ask you to live in it," he joked.

"That was better, but you're still avoiding my question. Most people have a long list of things to talk out before they start talking about building a house together. We haven't talked about any of them."

Sebastian burst out laughing and slapped his palm against his raised thigh. "Christa, you're a hard woman to bargain with, but I'm not exactly talking about anything. I'm simply extrapolating into the future."

"Why don't we extrapolate down this road and see what we can postulate?" she joked.

"Yes, let's do that," he replied, taking hold of her hand. "But you know Christa; I've made a lot of money. I've already made as much as my Dad, and I still have 35 years left to work."

"And building a house is a good investment," she postulated and continued. "Sebastian, you must know a lot of girls. I see them smile and give you a little wave, when we play tennis at Cabot. I'm sure that when you're ready to extrapolate somebody into a house with you, there will be lots of takers."

"I'm sure that's true, but they're not Christa Adams. There's only one like you that I have ever met, and it's you."

Christina blushed and laughed. "Did anybody ever tell you that you are an outrageous flatterer, Mr. Sebastian Johnston?"

"Will you think about it?"

"Helping you design a house?"

"Yes, design a house," he replied, smiling and lowering his eyes.

"Where's this house going to be built?"

"In Philly."

"Do you have a building lot picked out?"

"No."

"Sebastian, how can you design a house, when you don't even know where you're going to put it?"

"See what I mean, a woman sees things different. Guess I better find myself a building lot. Thanks, Christa."

"I'm very busy with 4th year and I have the second part of the USMLE coming up in March."

"The second part of what," he asked?

"The US Medical License Exam," she replied.

"You won't have to inconvenience yourself the slightest. I'll bring everything here to you."

"Ok, I'll think about, but let's talk about something less serious than building houses."

"Thanks," he said, leaning over to press his lips against her forehead. "I'll see if I can get a lot by Thanksgiving. Let's make a date for Thanksgiving right now. That will help me focus on finding a lot because I'll want to have something to tell you."

"Thanksgiving is six weeks away, Sebast. That's a long time to plan ahead. What if a client wants you to spend the weekend on his boat?"

"It won't happen, but you're right; it's a long way ahead to make plans. You might have something on with your family."

"Not might about it, I will have plans with them."

"Let's make it early in the day then."

"How early?"

"I'll reserve a court at the Club for 11 am. We can have a quick game, a light lunch, and I'll tell you where I'm at with the building lot."

"Ok, 11 am, it's a deal. Do you see why they call this place Lovers' Lane? Here it is mid-afternoon in the middle of the week, and we're talking about a date that's going to happen in six weeks."

"I know, this place has good vibes. How far down does this road go?

"We can walk down to Rock Creek. You could even take your shoes off and soak your feet in the water if you felt like it."

"I feel like it."

"Good, so do I," she exclaimed, pulling him forward by the hand.

They talked and played by the water for an hour before Christa suggested, "We should be getting back soon, Sebastian. We've been gone quite a while, and I still have about fifty pages to read, before turning in tonight."

"Are you going to work, at home?"

"I don't study very well at home. There are too many distractions. I'll probably go up to the library on campus."

The Adams Sisters

"Let's head back then," he agreed, finishing lacing up his shoes.

Sebastian didn't go back into the Adams house. She walked him to his suburban and waited until it had cleared the entrance to the driveway. On the way into the house, the young woman remembered the conversation she had with Samantha, in tennis court at Montrose Park. Now she understood better how her sister had slipped into that relationship in Manhattan.

Mrs. Adams was in the kitchen, when her daughter came in and she called out to her, "Is that you Christa?"

"It's me Mom."

"Come here for a minute, would you."

Her daughter went in.

"Did you and Sebastian have a nice walk?"

"Yes, it was fine. Guess what?"

"He asked you to marry him."

"Don't be silly, he wants me to help him design a house."

"What kind of a house."

"A house for himself in Philadelphia."

"If a woman helps a man create his house, she usually ends up living in it."

"You never know!"

"I knew you two were right for each other."

"Don't go jumping to conclusions, Mom."

"That's the way it always starts dear. I might have a few ideas on a house for you myself. I hear that he's made a lot of money."

"That's what he says too."

"You know, Christa, I'd like to see you and Sebastian married."

"I couldn't help but notice, Mom. Anyway, I'm going to put a few things in a plastic container for a snack and then I'm off to the library. I have a few chapters to read for tomorrow. Tell Mrs. Yamato that I won't be here for supper."

"Okay, you run along and do your studying. I'll tell her not to set a place for you. I'll tell her to leave a plate in the refrigerator."

That evening the young woman decided to go to Lauinger Library, which is located on the South East side of the Main campus and is used by the general student body. There would be less chance of meeting anybody she knew there.

Lauinger Library is located not far from the university's most infamous entrance – the stone staircase that was first used in Alfred Hitchcock's classic, 'Thirty-nine Steps'. More recently, they were the steps that the good Father Damien tumbled down to his death in, 'The Exorcist'.

When Christina arrived at the library, she left her books in a carrel, went to find a computer and logged into DC Meets. When her In Box came up on the screen, Yellow Cloud's message was still there. She clicked on the Reply button and Re: Greetings! Appeared in the Subject line.

**

To: yellowcloud@dcmeets.com
From: nightshadow@dcmeets.com
Subject: Re: Greetings!

Hi Yellow Cloud,

Thanks for your message. I want to say that this is the first time I have ever done this. I am not really sure why I'm replying to you. There are a few things you have to understand from the start.

I don't want you to know who I am. If you try to find out, I'll delete my profile at DC Meets. I don't want you to ask me any questions about where I live or what I do, as you might use my answers to find out who I am. If you are agreed to these conditions, then we can have an online conversation.

Hoping to hear from you soon.
Sincerely,
NS

**

When the message had cleared the screen, she logged out and went back to where she had left her books. It was 11 p.m. before she folded them up, and headed back home for the night.

****

The Adams Sisters

6 - Sam's Business

When Samantha Adams wasn't out on the road or in her office, she spent most of her working hours in the Bunche Library at the State Department doing research. After running multiple searches in the Department database and even designing a few special SQL queries, she had found more information on the Nigerian scams in the Library than was available on the Web site. There were even some classified case histories, which greatly broadened her scope.

This morning she was in her office, and the dialer window popped up on her computer screen and began to beep. She had a call. The view button was flashing to indicate that the caller had their conferencing camera turned on. She clicked on the icon to answer. Immediately the small camera on the top center of her monitor was activated and began to transmit to the other party.

The dialer returned to its place on the status bar, and a 4" x 4" video window opened on the screen. It was Roscoe Walters.

"Hi Samantha!"
"Hi Roscoe!"
"You're looking quite chipper this morning."
"I'm feeling quite chipper too."

"What's up?"

"Everything is going great," she replied.

"How great?"

"I'm not spending much money and I have us set up with what you might call a fast company."

"That's excellent. Now, tell me the rest."

"After talking with my Dad and a family business acquaintance concerning shell companies; I ran an ad in the Baltimore Sun, offering to buy an on paper set up for a business. The Baltimore Sun was chosen, because the Nigerian scam letter was addressed to Caravel Holdings, in Baltimore, There were six replies. I ended up taking a small business called Baltimore General Services.

It's a proprietorship, which has been operating for two years. The owner sold me the registration, stationery, and a rubber stamp seal for $500. With a valid registration in hand, I contacted one of those virtual offices sites on the Internet called Fifth Dimension Offices and opened up a business account in the name of Baltimore General Services.

It's a very good deal, Sir. They provided me with Baltimore phone and fax numbers. I have live voice and voice mailbox service. Everything will be relayed to my private cell phone here in Washington.

If the other party in Nigeria faxes, I get a beep and can download his fax immediately to my cell phone or notebook as e-mail. If I want to send him a fax, I just type up a message on my notebook and e-mail it to his fax number @fifthdimension.com. Their computer turns it around and faxes it to the number I give in Nigeria.

There's a distinctive beep on my cell phone, when a live call is coming in. If I'm available, I can have the call forwarded to me simply by answering. When I don't answer, it goes into a mailbox. Later I can either listen to it or download an e-mail of the call. If I want to call him, I call Fifth Dimension first and then key in his number. No matter how hard he tries, he won't be able to get past that Baltimore telephone number."

Walters had an amazed look on his face. "Do they really have offices like that out on the Net?"

"As a matter of fact, there are quite a few. Some of them are amazing, but they get more expensive. This is just a standard business package. Except for the newspaper ad, I've paid everything in cash. Nothing can be traced to the Department."

"Be sure to turn in your receipts."

The Adams Sisters

"I will. Last night I sent a fax to the number that was on the letter. I'm waiting to hear back now."

"What did you say in your fax?"

"I said the company to which he had sent his letter no longer occupied those premises and it had been forwarded to me bundled with some more return mail. Since there was no return address on the outside of the envelope, I had opened it and had found only a return fax number.

I told this Dr. Lawrence Ossaga that I had a small company and would be interested in his proposal if he would be willing to do business with me instead of Caravel Holdings."

"Have you got a copy of the letter there?"

"Yes."

"Let me see it, please."

She clicked down through the directories on her hard drive, found the letter file and put it into an email message to him. Almost instantly, she could see him reading it on the screen.

"Good girl. I'm glad you signed as Angelou Adams. This is a long shot, but you shouldn't take any chances. Another thing, in any contacts you have with him, always call him Dr. Ossaga. Those people are quite touchy about respect."

"I will Mr. Walters, Sir."

He smiled at her and laughed, "Okay, Ms. Adams, carry on and let me know when he makes contact. Bye."

She said, "Bye!" and his image disappeared from the video window on her screen.

In addition to the project work, there were many training exercises in the Watch internship, which had to be fit in when it was opportune. Interns were on the honor system as far as fulfilling the training exercises were concerned. However, there was a multiple-choice control on them after six and twelve months. One of the exercises involved familiarizing oneself with the Foreign Affairs section of the Library of Congress.

Intern Adams reached for the mouse and then clicked the search button on the status bar, at the bottom of her monitor. She typed in Phone Directory. Two choices came up, Public Directory, Government Directory. The second was clicked. A blank query box materialized. This time she typed in the words Library of Congress. In a second, a list of twenty-five departments was on her screen. She chose Information Services and the number began to be dialed.

It didn't take long. The attendant at Information Services said there was a general orientation tour starting in an hour. It was a perquisite for the tours of specific collections such as Foreign Affairs. There was just enough time, so she reserved a spot on the tour. Before locking down her keyboard, she bundled up several back issues of two of the Department periodicals, State Magazine and Dispatch Magazine, which she had borrowed from the Bunche Library and then quickly left for the parking garage.

The Library of Congress is housed in three buildings, located at the rear of the Capitol on Independence Avenue. The quickest way there, from the State Department, was to skirt around the Lincoln Memorial and pick up Independence on the south side of the Mall, which is a long rectangle of green lawns, stretching from the Lincoln Memorial in the west to the Capitol in the east. Once on Independence Avenue, the Washington Monument loomed ahead, in the direction that Samantha was headed.

The Monument or obelisk is the tallest masonry structure in the world. At its pinnacle, 555 feet 5 inches above the surrounding plaza, it is twice as high as the Capitol and ten times higher than any other building in Washington. It was built to honor America's Revolutionary War hero and first president.

At that time of the day, the pure white spire's long, hazy shadow didn't fall over the rectangular lake, known as the reflecting pool, which is between the Monument and the Lincoln Memorial. Samantha looked to her left briefly while passing the pool. For a split second, she was reminded of the film, Forest Gump.

Driving up Independence Avenue, she saw the white come of The Capitol first and then a few minutes later located the green dome of the Library of Congress, just off to the right. Between the Library and her were the Smithsonian Castle, the Air and Space Museum and the US Botanical Garden.

The Library of Congress is the American equivalent of the British Library or the Bibliothèque National in France. It occupies not only the historic Jefferson Building, but two other structures – the Art Deco Adams Building and the more modern Madison Building. From the outside, the Jefferson Building looks more like an Opera House in Paris than a Library. In the Great Hall, a huge stained-glass skylight illuminates the richly colored mosaics, which cover the vaults of the ceiling and expansive floors below.

There weren't many tourists around the Jefferson Building that day and Samantha went straight to the Visitors Theatre for a 12-minute orientation film on the Library. After the movie, she

The Adams Sisters

went to the Great Hall. A group of 25 people was just leaving with a library attendant. Some of them were equipped with earplugs, so that they could listen to a translated version of what the guide was saying.

Samantha's group was all Civil Servants, many of them Interns like herself. Their guide led them up a marble staircase to the Main Reading Room, a rotunda 100 feet in diameter under a dome 160 feet high. Computer terminals give access to the 75 million items on 350 miles of bookshelves. In addition to giving the visitors in the group a user's manual to keep, the guide took them through a stunning series of screens using a notebook and projector and then on a summary tour of where the various collections were physically located.

When the tour was finished, she went to the Information & Publications Office. There were a large number of books, magazines, manuals, guides and bulletins available. She picked up - a general guide to the Library, a map of the Special Collections, as well as information on the Digital Library and a How To brochure, which explained access to the Library of Congress Catalogue over the Internet, from her office or from home.

As she walked back to her car, the Intern looked over at the Capitol Building and thought to herself, I'll have to go through you too, when I get a minute. I wouldn't want any of the staff at the Watch to think I'm a hillbilly if Congress ever comes up as a subject of their conversation. She decided to spend the rest of the afternoon reading and absorbing the guides that she had picked up on the first part of the Library exercise.

On the way home that evening, Samantha stopped into a video rental shop near the corner of M and Wisconsin Streets in Georgetown village. The attendant was able to find her a copy of the Forest Grump video. As she stepped back out onto the sidewalk, the huge clock over the bank on the corner, indicated 4 p.m.

When she entered the Adams house, Mrs. Yamato came to greet her.

"Ms. Samantha, you're early."

"I have some reading to do, so I decided to bring it back here."

"There won't be any dinner served this evening. Your parents are out and aren't planning to be home, until later this evening."

"I'm not hungry anyway, Mrs. Yamato, I'm watching my weight."

"There are plenty of things in the fridge, just help yourself and put your dishes in the dishwasher. I'm leaving soon, but I'll turn it on, when I come in the morning. "

Samantha went upstairs and set the books, magazines and video on the bed. Her room was beside Christina's and looked out on the same back yard. She looked around and saw her notebook computer on an old desk.

"That's right," she thought out loud, "I was going to keep a diary of the Nigerian Scam assignment on my personal notebook too. I should do an update, before starting to read."

When the notebook's screen came up, she clicked on the icon for the Notes program. It filled the viewing area in a second. She went into Mobile and then logged into her office at State. It didn't take long to replicate the project files on State's server with those on the machine in front of her.

When the replication was done, she started to read. A little after five, she went downstairs to rustle up some cold cuts and salad. She was just starting to read again when the cell phone sounded in her purse. A short dial tone was followed by two longer tones. It dialed again. She scrambled for the purse and pulled out the cell. That was a signal from Fifth Dimension Offices that she was receiving a fax and could view it by e-mail if she wished.

The phone opened revealing a small lithium screen. She pushed on the download button and four lines of text began to scroll across the viewing area at a time.

**

To: Baltimore General Services@5th_dimension.com
From: operations@5th_dimension.com
Subject: Dr. Lawrence Ossaga

October 21st, 20xx
Lagos, Nigeria
Fax: 234-90-405427

Dear Ms. Angelou Adams,

I have received your letter in which you explain how you acquired my letter to Caravel Holdings. My colleagues and I checked and for some unknown reason; there no longer seems to be a telephone listing for Caravel Holdings.

Ms. Adams, Caravel Holdings, was recommended to us by the Chamber of Commerce in Lagos. You, however, are an

The Adams Sisters

unknown to us or to anybody in Lagos. Baltimore General Services isn't even in the current business directory.

In your letter, you are proposing to take the place of Caravel Holdings if we will accept your offer. I discussed the matter with my colleagues. They have agreed to consider your request. However, they would like to know more about you.

We would like you to fax us a copy of your birth certificate, your current driver's license, and your passport. When they receive these items, they will decide.
Yours very sincerely,
Dr. Lawrence Ossaga

**

When the message terminated, a few lines from Fifth Dimension Offices said that the text would be transferred to her mailbox from which it could be downloaded.

She turned off the screen and snapped the cell phone shut. A flood of thoughts swept through her head. For a moment, she felt afraid. Her hands were trembling noticeably, but she went to the notebook, logged into Fifth Dimension and collected the message. It took a second to print out and then she could see it all at a glance. I don't even have a passport, she though and I don't really want to fax a copy of my license and birth certificate to Africa. What if they come looking for me?

Through the open window came the sound of the back door, off the kitchen, being closed hard. She went to the curtain and saw Mrs. Yamato walking across the tennis court towards the cement staircase, which led down to the heavy wooden gate that opened onto the lane leading out to S Street NW.

A strange feeling came over her. She felt as if she was doing something wrong. She had only felt like this once before. It was when she had faked her engagement to her family and friends. Being involved in this scam almost made her feel as if she was a criminal. The literature from the Library of Congress no longer appealed to her.

Fortunately a portable TV with a built in VCR, which was hers from Manhattan, had not gone into storage. She closed the door to her bedroom, placed the DVD into the drawer and settled back to watch the movie. It was almost over, when she heard Christina come in. Samantha didn't really want to talk to her sister just then, so grabbed the headset and plugged it into the TV. Christina wouldn't hear any sound coming from her sister's room and would think she was sleeping.

In the other room, Christina was aware of nothing. She was so used to being alone in this house. She was tired and lay down on top of the bed. In a few minutes, she plunged into a deep sleep. Forty-five minutes later, she awoke with a start. On the way downstairs to find something to eat, the younger sister noticed that her older sister's bedroom door was open. She was sure it had been closed a while ago.

Christina came back upstairs with coffee and a slice of lasagna, which had been warmed up in the microwave. Then she logged on to DC Meets and checked her e-mail. In a few seconds, a pop-up-box appeared on the screen, which said, "You have new mail!"

There was only one message. She clicked to open it. The young woman felt her throat tighten. The communication was from Yellow Cloud.

**

To: nightshadow@dcmeets.com
From: yellowcloud@dcmeets.com
Subject: Greetings!

Hi Night Shadow,

Thank you for replying to my message. It's ok by me if you want to stay anonymous. I won't ask you any trick questions. I think it's prodigious that you are even willing to communicate with me.
Bye for now,
Yellow Cloud.

**

Christina was thrilled. She thought his reply would be suggestive. She printed out his message to show Jewel, the next time they were together. After it had printed, she folded the sheet of paper and slipped it into a textbook.

She clicked on the reply button and began to type.

**

To: yellowcloud@dcmeets.com
From: nightshadow@dcmeets.com
Subject: RE: Greetings!

Hi Yellow Cloud,

Thanks for reassuring me about my confidentiality. You seem quite sincere. I'll try to be the same with you.

I've really never had a friend, who was a boy.

There was one boy, whom I did get close to, but it was only at school. Sometimes we did our assignments or took

The Adams Sisters 81

coffee breaks together. It was fun. We laughed at everything. When he graduated, a company in California hired him, and he moved there. I wrote him twice.

That's all for now; I have to go and read some chapters for tomorrow.
Bye,
Night Shadow

**

She clicked on the SEND button, and it was gone.

All of a sudden, Christina felt panicky. She didn't know why she had written what she did to a stranger. She wished there was some way to bring the message back, but it was too late.

Just then, she heard someone coming in downstairs. She thought it might be Samantha and went to investigate. It was her parents taking off their coats.

"Hi Christa!"

"Hi Mom, where were you two?"

"Some old friends from our East Side days invited us to dinner, so I went to meet your Dad at his office. Did you eat something?"

"Uh ... some lasagna."

"Is Samantha here?"

"Her car was here when I arrived, and I think that her bedroom door was shut, but I dozed off fast. When I woke up her door was open. She may have gone out."

"Her car is still in the driveway. Is Jewel upstairs with you?"

"No, why?"

"I don't know. You have a strange look, like you were eager to get back upstairs to someone."

"No, there's nobody here, but I have to go back to my reading. I just came down to see if you were Samantha."

"Come back down and watch the news at 11 p.m. with us, if you're still awake. Maybe your sister will be in by then too," her father coaxed.

"Ok, Dad, see you later."

Samantha arrived early at the State Department building the following morning. She dialed Mr. Walters's direct line, but he hadn't arrived yet. She left a short message asking him to call her, when he got in. The call came at 8:20 a.m.

"Hi Sam, what's up?"

"May I come to see you Roscoe?"

"Sure come now, before I get busy."

When the Intern walked in, he sensed immediately that something had happened.

"Have a seat, Sam."

Before he could say anything more, she put the printout of the fax from Nigeria on his desk and sat down.

He read it twice and then looked at her. I see now what's making you nervous.

"I don't even have a passport, Sir," she blurted out anxiously.

"Haven't you ever traveled outside the US?" her superior said skeptically

"No, and I've heard that only about 7% of Americans have a passport."

"It's unusual for people who work in State not to have one. We're always among that 7% statistic. "

"I thought I'd see our country first, so I've never needed one."

"There's a lot more to see besides the USA on this planet," he reminded her.

"I'm like that," she defended herself. "I even have a Stars and Stripes bathing suit."

"What have you seen in our country?"

"Lots of things."

"Like what?"

"Niagara Falls, Yellowstone, Yosemite, Mount Rushmore, the Oregon Dunes, the Mount St Helen's volcano."

"You are absolutely right Samantha. Rushmore has been on my to-do-list for 20 years. In any case, I wouldn't let you fax a copy of your real passport to this Ossaga. Now, beside no passport, how do you feel about this letter?"

"Apprehensive. I keep thinking that maybe they will get through to me."

"I don't think anybody could get through that set up on the Internet that you described to me. Do you have any idea what it's like, where this Lawrence character faxed from?"

"A little, I read up on it."

"Their level of technology is like a cave man compared to yours. Their telephone system is so old that we can't use any of our equipment on a number to fit it with an address. Some girl wearing headphones may have plugged wires into a switchboard to get this fax sent to you. I don't really see how they do it. There are supposed to be about 5,000,000 phone numbers in the country, but there are only 2,000,000 in the

The Adams Sisters

phone books. Any American company that goes there relies totally on satellite phones."

"I didn't know that."

"If you want out of this project Sam, I'll give it to one of the boys."

"I didn't say I wanted out. I was only a little worried."

"We'll fix you up with a passport, driver's license, and birth certificate. They won't get you past the police or immigration, but they'll be good enough for these fellas. Are you still in?"

"Yes, sure."

He pushed for a line on the speakerphone and then dialed three numbers.

A jovial voice answered, "Documentation, Ron Oliver here. How may I help you?"

"Ron, this is Roscoe Walters at the Watch."

"Oh, hi Roscoe, what's up?"

"I need a passport, driver's license and birth certificate for one of my interns."

"No problem, send him on down. What's the name?"

"It's a young lady. Her name is Samantha Adams, but make up the docs for Angelou Adams."

"I do my best work, when the operative is a girl. Send her down."

Walters scribbled a room number on a post-it-note and handed it to Samantha.

"Thanks, Mr. Walters."

"Any time, and keep me up to speed about what's going on."

"I will."

"One last thing, you shouldn't take those fake papers out of the building, unless you really need them. The Administration knows we do things like that, but officially the practice is frowned on.

"I'll leave them in my desk."

He gave her an extended thumb up and suggested, "Sam, you should get yourself a US Passport. Eventually, you're going to need it for your job."

She extended her thumb in agreement, smiled and left.

****

7 - Philadelphia

For many, the Cradle of Liberty is a welcomed rest stop between the Big Apple and the Nation's Capital. In reality, the Tri-state area is much, much more. Philadelphians live in three worlds. First, there's the city. When they want to go into themselves, they retreat to the west, into the Pennsylvania hinterland. If they're feeling extrovert, they cross one of the city's three bridges into New Jersey. Camden is directly across the Delaware River from Philadelphia and from there; it's only a short drive to Atlantic City and the beaches south of it along the Delaware Cape.

Philadelphia is an old American City as well as a new American city. It's the city of the Independence Hall and the Liberty Bell. It has also been voted the best Restaurant City in America. There's a restaurant nearby for every taste! In addition, it's Africa's new black elite's favorite city.

African culture abounds. If your mood runs towards music, there's an African American Cultural Awareness Concert, at the Opera Company of Philadelphia, in February. In June, the African American Consumer Show is held at the Convention Center. Those who are really hip about their roots can be

The Adams Sisters

found schmoozing at the African American Extravaganza at Penn's Landing, on the Delaware River, in August.

The Philadelphia Stock Exchange is located on Market Street between 19th and 20th Streets, on the edge of the Museum District, which is about four streets due south of Logan Circle and five blocks east of University City. It was founded in 1790 as the first organized stock exchange in the United States. Today it's housed in an eight level; block long, landmark structure of horizontal ribbons of metallic gold interspersed with tinted plate glass windows. Sebastian Johnston's office is located not far from the Exchange.

Sebastian owns an old colonial house in Chestnut Hill, in Northwest Philadelphia. It's a neighborhood full of a classy section of shops and homes resembling a quaint English village. Chestnut Hill is sometimes called a little city in Philadelphia, because of it's convenience for those working in the city. From the downtown core, they have two choices - the Schuylkill Expressway or the East River Drive.

In spite of being so well equipped, Sebastian was rarely at home except to sleep. Since it was too far to drive, when he only wanted a meal; he preferred to eat at several of Philly's gentlemen's clubs. His favorite was M's., which features a full menu, from casual dining to multi course dinners, all day through late nights, with exceptional wine, champagne, cigars and a lavish complimentary buffet every weekday at 5:30 p.m.

Sebastian had invited his older brother Gene, his wife Penelope and their two sons over to Philadelphia for the weekend. The adults had gone out dancing Saturday evening. Sebastian had asked one of the girls from his gym to accompany him.

Now it was already Sunday. Penelope sat in the living room, listening to a birch wood fire crackle, as she skimmed through the Cosmopolitan magazine, which she had stuffed in her overnight bag. She could hear the brothers' voices coming in off the back deck, through the open sliding glass door in the kitchen.

Autumn was almost over. It was a cool November afternoon outside. The brothers were in Sebastian's hot tub.

"Sebast!" Gene exclaimed. "What was all that talk last night about you selling this house? This is a great place."

"I know it's fabulous, but I'm getting past it. I want to build something of my own."

"But you have everything here, not to mention just a hop, skip and a jump to your office."

"At first I thought about building here in Chestnut Hill."

"And?" His older brother queried him.

"Like wow, you would never believe the regulations governing these few blocks of old houses."

"I believe you. Don't forget I do real estate for a living. I've seen just about every type of zone, ordinance, and regulation that has been dreamed up. You didn't even have to tell me that this place was crisscrossed with, 'do this, don't do that, thou shalt not'. Look at these houses – heritage to the eyebrows. They're always the worst. Tell me what they told you at City Hall?"

"The short and sweet, currently, there is no new construction being permitted in Chestnut Hill. The planning department is only issuing renovation permits. There's even a heritage group in town, which buys up old dilapidated places and puts them into a historic trust, until someone wants to get a permit to do a Reno on one of them.

I thought I might be able to get around the regulations by tearing down this house and building a new house on the lot. One of the architects in the planning department looked out over the top of his half glasses and said, 'we don't issue permits to tear down homes like yours, Mr. Johnston'."

"No guff, you mean you can't even tear down your own house," Gene exploded.

"No, Sir."

"How long are we going to allow this encroachment on private property to continue in America?"

"You tell me Gene."

"So what are you planning to do?"

"I have to find a building lot, or a house that is permitted to be torn down."

"So we are back to finding a building lot again."

"Right."

"Why don't you forget about building and stay here? Living in this place says lots about you. It's almost like a designer signature."

"That may be, but I need to build a house."

"Need to, what are you talking about brother, nobody needs to build a house."

"I do."

"Why?"

The Adams Sisters 87

"It is part of my plan to hook that Adams girl, Christa. You remember her. She sat beside me at the Cabot Club that evening we had dinner with her family."

"What!" his older brother exclaimed.

"Gene, don't look so stunned, you're married."

"But she isn't your type Sebast."

"Exactly, I'm getting past my kind. Bachelor's babes have their place, but at a certain point in every man's life, they have to finish. I can't be running around in silk pajamas, with party girls in Manhattan or Miami, for the rest of my life.

Besides, when you get through to it, Philadelphia is a real straight, small town. I want someone who will fit in outside the bed, someone who's respectable. You know what I'm talking about, a homemaker. I need slippers, a fire, a dog and maybe even a kid or two, exactly like you and Penelope."

"Why don't you go for her sister Samantha? She'd make a better match for you."

"Christa and I have already started hatching a story. Samantha and I met the same time as you and she did. I don't know the slightest thing about her."

"She grew up in Washington. I could have one of my boys write you up a sheet on her."

"Gene, I said it's Christa."

"Okay, Brother, it's Christa. Mind if I ask one more question?"

"Shoot!"

"Does she know she's the one?"

"Sort of, but not exactly."

"Sort of," Gene laughed, splashing water at his younger brother. "You kill me. What if she doesn't want to be, Mrs. Sebastian Johnston?"

"She will want to."

"How do you know?"

"Because she's going to design the house I'm building, then supervise its construction and furnish and decorate it. It'll be hers. If she wants to live in it, she'll have to marry me."

"Mind if I tell you something little brother?"

"Go right ahead."

"You are one foxy Brother."

"Why thank you big brother. I take that as a compliment coming from you. Let me add that if I weren't a foxy Brother, I would never have made as much money as I have. "

"I'm envious green of that skill you have with the greenback."

"Granddad said he offered to show you, but you weren't interested."

"I was young and chasing Penelope, when he was offering," Gene explained. "Do you know how many times I flew to Phoenix, in the two years, before we got married?"

"No, but it must have been enough, she married you."

"I still think you'd be better off building a house with someone like Penelope."

"When we go inside, I'll ask her if she wants to build a house with me."

"Paws off Johnston," Gene exploded, splashing water at him again. "She's classified material and I am the only one with the password."

"Then it's Christa?"

"Ok then, it's her?"

"Now that we have that settled, I need your help."

"What kind of help?"

"I am running short of time. I told Christa I'd have a building lot by Thanksgiving. I thought I'd be able to pick up an old wreck here in Chestnut Hill and do a demo. Since the Planning Department killed that thought, I need an alternate site and fast."

"Where do I fit in?"

"Gene, you said it yourself, you do real estate, you've seen every regulation that they can dream up. I'm very busy at the office, until Christmas. Every time I venture near real estate, I feel like I am in kindergarten. Securities are my line. I need you to find me a building lot by Thanksgiving."

"Ouch!"

"I'll make it worth your while. I'll give you a beginner's course in trading gold options and start you off with 10% of the value of the lot you find, deposited into a private brokerage account."

"Well, if you put it like that, I might be able to come up with something. Have you any idea what the house is supposed to look like that you want to put up on this lot to be? It makes a big difference on the area in which I should look."

"I was hoping that Christa would be able to take care of that little detail, but she's too busy. There can't be too many distractions until she graduates and gets licensed in the spring. My secretary went through a pile of magazines and picked out the ten houses she liked best. I've chosen one of them for the basic style."

"Have you got the picture here?"

The Adams Sisters

"Inside, let's get dressed and I'll show you."

"Good idea, I've had enough hot tubing for one afternoon. All that booze I drank last night has been sucked straight out through my pores and into that whirlpool."

Penelope heard them coming in. She was sitting on the chesterfield, with her legs crossed, filing her nails when they appeared in the doorway, rubbing their heads with thick, white, terry-cloth towels. The young woman was wearing light grey tweed lounging slacks and a black merino-wool, hooded pullover.

"You boys have a good soak?"

"Super, you should have joined us."

"I already had my make up on. Next time tell me you're going tubing before I put it on."

"Right." Gene confirmed.

"Can I fix you anything, while you're getting dressed?"

"Sure," her husband said. "What were you thinking of?"

"How about Irish Coffee? I already went through your little brother's kitchen and liquor cabinet. He has all the ingredients."

"I'll take an Irish Coffee too," Sebastian said, winking at her.

When the Johnston brothers arrived back in the living room, three cut glass mugs were waiting on a tray on the coffee table, the fire had been refreshed and melodies from a Diana Ross CD were filling in the background.

"Guess what, Penelope," her husband exclaimed.

"I don't know Gene. You know I'm not a good guesser, tell me."

"Try Honey."

"Sebastian is going to run for President."

"Close, Honey, but not quite. Sebastian was dead serious last night when he said that he was going to build a house."

"Why that's wonderful news Gene."

"How's that?" her husband queried.

"I'll be able to sell him some more paintings," she smirked.

"Penelope," Sebastian protested. "You know I paid too much for the last painting I bought from you."

She laughed, "I'll give you a volume discount to do the whole of your new house."

"Have you ever thought of selling stock, Penelope?"

"I thought about it once, but there were too many numbers," she snickered. "I like art better. The gallery buys low, and I sell high, to folks like you, for a handsome commission."

"I'm going to report you to the Peoples' Court if you keep talking like that. They're rumored to be very partial towards creative people."

"Sebastian, I am the Peoples' Court. If you don't stop in at my gallery again soon; I'll find you guilty."

"Then what," he pressed her?

She gave him a naughty look and put her chin up high before replying, "Then Gene, and I and the boys won't be able to come over to Philly anymore on the weekend."

Gene interrupted their fun, "Forget about the Peoples' Court you two. Sebastian, show me that picture of the house."

Sebastian retrieved it from the buffet drawer and handed a folder to Gene, who was now sitting beside his wife. "This is a picture of the concept I am going to start with. An architect will produce a pencil sketch from this. Then I'm taking the sketch to my designer to have her make any modifications, which she thinks would be appropriate."

The house was three stories high and finished in beige stone. There were rooms containing bay windows on both ends of the ground floor. The room on the far right jutted out from the main house about eight feet. Its hip roof met the main roof at a perpendicular angle. The second floor had one wide dormer, which started over the front entrance. The third floor was built under the eaves and was lit by several narrow dormers built high into the steep 'A' frame roof.

All the windows had black shutters. The bay windows had black sheet metal roofs jutting out from above them. The front door was a single black slab, flanked by two narrow windows, which ran up to the transom. Trimmed green bushes were planted up close to the house, and there was a low hedge around the front entrance. No garage was visible. Several trees dotted the wide lawn.

"That's not bad for a start," Penelope said. "You could do a lot with a place like this. I prefer this style to those new concept homes with irregular levels and huge slabs of glass. Even if you don't want to now, you could always build a wing on this side of the house. "

"This definitely wouldn't fit in around Chestnut Hill Sebastian," his older brother said with authority. "It feels more like the burbs, almost country even. I see it in a little wooded grove, where the nouveau riche are building their hideaways."

"Then you approve?" Sebastian asked, without saying that it was quite similar to the Adams house, without the west wing.

The Adams Sisters

"Yes I approve," Gene replied. "Penelope, I am going to find Sebastian a lot, where he can build this."

"That's very generous of you, Gene."

Sebastian looked at his brother. He knew that Penelope was touchy about her husband putting money into the market because he had never taken the time to study it.

"In return, Penelope, I am going to give him a special private course on how to trade gold options."

"Granddad already tried that."

"Granddad's program was futures, cotton futures in particular. He would never say when to buy and when to sell in his course. I am going to tell Gene what to buy and when to resell it."

"It's getting late in the year Sebastian, are you going to wait until spring to start building?" she asked.

"The building starts in the spring."

Gene spoke up, "I promised Sebastian that I would locate the perfect setting for his castle before he comes home at Thanksgiving."

"I like it when families can work together like this," she said. "Sebastian, I'm going to have you give my brothers your course, when they're here next summer."

Sebastian wondered if she meant the options program, but thought it safer to clarify what she was referring to. "Course?" he queried.

"Your course, on how to co-operate and help each other in the family," she emphasized.

"Sure," Gene agreed, "we'll give them the family program won't we Sebastian."

"No doubt about it brother, they're on. I've already logged their reservation."

Penelope started to gather up the emptied cups. "If we are going to head back home early Gene, you two should start thinking about getting that Bar-B-Q fired up. I like my steak well done."

"Where are the boys Dear?" her husband asked shyly.

She called back over her shoulder to him, "They're upstairs in the den. Didn't you hear them when you were changing?"

Her husband followed her into the kitchen. "I didn't hear a peep. What are they doing?"

"Sebastian has a couple of dozen videos his den. When I looked in, they were watching Star Trek."

"I didn't hear any video while I was getting dressed."

"They must have figured out how to make the headphone's work, because the sound was on when I was up there."

"Maybe they found a girlie movie?"

"There aren't any. I checked every title, before I let them go into the den."

"Then it must be headsets."

If they don't show up on their own, at least five minutes before the meat is ready, I'll go up and tell them it's time to wash their hands."

He slipped his arms around her waist and enquired, "Everything all right, Honey?"

"Yea, I'm glad we came over. I like the boys to have more contact with their uncle. A visit like this lets them understand more of what he's about. They don't see this side of him when he drops by for a meal at our place or when we all meet up at Granddad's."

He snuggled his head against her neck. "What have you been doing all by your lonesome, while the boys and I have been out of sight?"

"I read my Cosmopolitan. Did Sebastian tell you who that girl was that he invited to come dancing with us last night?"

"Yup."

"Who was she?"

"He knows her from his gym. She's in his jogging platoon. There are about thirty of them in the group. They run eight miles every Saturday morning at 7 am."

"What does she do?"

"Some sort of an administration assistant in an office downtown."

"When is he going to stop running around with office girls and get a proper woman?"

"That's what this house building idea is all about."

"Are you really going to find him a lot?"

"It's nothing, Penelope. I'll call one of my contacts in Pennsylvania and have him take a look around. You saw the house. I have a general idea of what he needs. He won't even have to go very far from here. Montgomery County is full of little nouveau riche enclaves. He offered me ten percent of the value of the lot as a finder's fee, but I'm not going to take it. He's my kid brother."

"We have plenty of money dear," she said. "His little course on options will be payment in full. When you're confident enough to trade, I'll put ten thousand in a joint

The Adams Sisters

account, and you can try to make it grow for us. If you lose it, we won't talk about options anymore."

"It's a deal," he said, kissing her on the cheek. "I better go on out back and give him a hand with the Bar-B-Q."

"Ok, see you later," his wife purred.

The following morning Sebastian was up at 6 am, did an exercise routine, showered, dressed and was on his way down the Schuylkill Expressway, before seven o'clock. He was Chief Executive Officer and majority shareholder of Liberty Capital Corporation, a small private venture capital and investment banking firm, which he had started. He would have liked to keep one hundred percent of it, but in order to get good directors; he had been obliged to let thirty percent of it go. However, there was a shareholder's agreement, which stated that if any of the Directors wanted out, they had to sell their shares back to the corporation.

When Sebastian had finished at Wharton, he probably would have been required to go in and take a desk and phone at one of the brokerage houses in Philadelphia or Manhattan, if he hadn't had capital of his own. This stroke of good fortune was all thanks to his grandfather. When the young Johnston was still in high school, he had bought and sold his first cotton future. He had bought and sold them all through his undergraduate years and then later, while in grad school. It was while he was in the MBA program that he started to migrate towards options, especially gold options.

Although Sebastian had never worked in an investment-banking firm, there were lots of good people around who had. They only needed to be paid. At the firm's start up, the young man had taken most of the wealth he had accumulated from selling futures and options and exchanged it for shares in Liberty Capital. That money was used to hire quality people.

However, even experienced staff was not enough. The firm needed to make strategic alliances in the investment community. That's where the directorships came in. Liberty was affiliated with one of the local firms that had a seat on the Philadelphia Exchange. It also became a member of a group, which acted as an upper level downstream for the securities that each other issued. The third directorship had gone to one of the mid-range Philadelphia law firms that specialized in securities.

Liberty had its own in-house counsel, who had been a junior in the law firm, which held one of the ten- percent directorships. In addition, there was an in-house CPA, who was the CFO. Besides them, there were three people who had investment banking experience in operations. They handled all the documentation for Red Herrings, Prospectuses, IPO's and the like. There was an IT Manager, a professional executive assistant, four administration assistants and a receptionist. With Sebastian included; they were twelve in all. He had learned much and still was learning a great deal from all of them.

Liberty worked on a fee-for-service basis, and a commission on the money raised. It was a lot of work, long hours and many missed weekends, but the dividends he was receiving, in addition to his salary were, giving him a high six figure income. Sebastian didn't regret not going into real estate with his family.

When Gene had a minute on Monday morning, he contacted an associate in Philadelphia.

"Earl, this is Gene Johnston from Washington speaking."

"Hi there Gene, what's up?"

"I won't take up too much of your time, as I know we're all busy on Mondays, but I need a little bit of information."

"Sure if I have any, it's yours."

"A friend of mine wants to buy a building lot in the Montgomery County area, north-west of Philadelphia. According to the association directory, there are about seventy-five realtors operating in that quadrant."

"I know the directory has become so bloated over the past five years," Earl said on the other end of the line.

"That's why I called you. I need the choice narrowed down."

"What kind of a fella is your friend?"

"Sort of a cross between a Yuppie and an up and coming nouveau riche."

"That would be Daniel's Properties Ltd."

"Anybody in particular?"

"Let me see, what page is that on in the directory?"

"Page 268."

"Ok, I have it. Let's see. I know for a fact that Jenkins has left them. There, Willard Hawthorne that's your man, He's in their Norristown office."

"Great, much appreciated Earl. Call me anytime. I owe you one."

"Think nothing of it Gene. Give me a buzz back, if Willard can't help."

The Adams Sisters

It took a week for Willard Hawthorne to come up with three prospective sites. One was in Roseglen, another in Gladwyne and the third was the other side of Belmont Hills on the way into Welsh Valley. He e-mailed Gene pictures and addresses of all three. Gene immediate e-mailed them to his brother's office.

Sebastian didn't have any free time, until the weekend. After his run on Saturday, he set out to hunt down the addresses that Gene had sent.

Roseglen was nice, about the same distance from the city as Chestnut Hill, except that there was direct access to Interstate 76 or the Schuylkill Expressway so it would be faster going to and from the office. There were some very expensive homes in the area. He found the lot by locating it between two houses, which had street numbers on them. The price was right, but the street didn't say 'Yes' to him, so he moved on to Gladwyne. The lot there was not at all to his liking, but he liked the street. The rear of the lot sloped off quickly into a swampy gully, and it was a far drive to the freeway, so it would be like commuting into Chestnut Hill again.

Sebastian took out his map to see where he was in relation to Belmont Hills. The third address was on Conshohocken State Road, which he could pick up in Gladwyne and follow straight through. The lot was on a plateau, on the west side of Conshohocken State Road, about six properties before the intersection with Hagy's Ford Rd.

Once he passed Hollow Road; the asphalt began to climb. The houses were well spaced, and there were lots of trees and expansive front lawns. They were a bit like estates, only more modest.

At the top of a long upward grade, he spotted a space where there should be a house, but there wasn't. He started to count the houses from this spot. After the sixth one there was an intersection, and it was called Hagy's Ford Rd. Not bad, he thought turning around to drive back to the vacant lot. His black suburban turned into the overgrown driveway and stopped in front of a fallen branch.

On the other side of Conshohocken Road, opposite the lot, there was a deep ravine. On the north side, there was a three-story white stucco house with a double chimney running up one of the end walls. It was almost hidden by the trees that surrounded it. On the south side, a two story stone structure was set well back from the road, and it had a paved driveway.

Sebastian went to examine the remains of a concrete foundation in the center of the lot. It was scarred black. Obviously there had been a fire, probably many years ago.

He drove up to the intersection with Hagy's Ford Road, where there was a bus stop and turned left. The first on the left again was Tower Lane., and the young investment banker took it. He drove around the development, without making any snap opinion. Most of the houses were ranch style, about 15 years old. There was a Catholic Church and a sign out front of a large structure read, Welsh Valley Middle School.

Sebastian was feeling positive about this location and returned to Conshohocken Road. He drove back down the hill to Hollow Road, where he turned right and followed it until he arrived at Interstate 76. There was an entrance ramp to the freeway going south. The sign said 9 miles to Philadelphia. He entered the freeway's southbound ramp and in a minute was in a stream of cars headed towards Philadelphia.

Sebastian left the freeway at the next exit, drove under an overpass and came right back onto Interstate 76 headed north. In a few minutes, he was back at Exit where he entered and moved into the right hand lane. Soon he was on Hollow Road again. It was a lot quicker to Conshohocken Road, now that he knew where he was going. This just might do; he thought for a second time as he drove back onto the abandoned property.

The following week he got Willard Hawthorn's number from Gene. They bargained for fifteen or twenty minutes, before settling. Hawthorn agreed that he shouldn't be obliged to pay for the removal of the old foundation since he had specifically asked for a building lot. Sebastian told the realtor to give him a call when all the papers were ready. Once off the phone, he took his checkbook out of the desk drawer, and then had his secretary courier the deposit to Daniel's office in Norristown, to the attention of Willard Hawthorne.

****

The Adams Sisters

8 - Thanksgiving

Thanksgiving fell on Thursday the 28th of November. It would give a four-day weekend to many since they considered Friday to be an unofficial holiday. During the preceding week, everyone tried to get as much of an advance on what they were doing as possible. No one wanted to be too far behind, when they came back after the break.

The Adams sisters were both preoccupied with their electronic relationships. Christina had received an e-mail, from Sebastian. He was definitely coming on the weekend. Their lunch at the Club was on. He had found a building lot and had pictures of it as well as the surrounding houses. He also had an architect's sketch of a proposal for the house and would bring it all with him, to their lunch at noon on Thursday.

Samantha and Dr. Lawrence Ossaga had undeniably made contact. She hadn't heard a word from him for over two weeks, after sending the copies of her ID. Then Monday morning of Thanksgiving week, at about 5:30 a.m., she had been wakened from a sound sleep by the beeping of her cell phone, which was usually left on the night table.

Not fully conscious, at first Samantha didn't realize that the call was coming from Fifth Dimension Offices and that it was a voice transmission.

"Hello."

A heavy gruff voice said, "May I speak to Ms. Adams, please?"

Without thinking, she said, "This is Ms. Adams. Who is calling?"

The words were slow, "This is Dr. Lawrence Ossaga, Ms. Adams."

The young woman sat up in bed and brushed her hair back out of her face, "Where are you, Dr. Ossaga?"

"I am in Nigeria, in Lagos."

"I sent the information that you requested, but you didn't reply," she told him. "I wondered what had happened to you."

"I was out of the city with my business. When I returned, I found your fax. I gave the copies of your documents to my colleagues. They only contacted me today."

"What did they say?"

"They're interested in your proposal, to replace Caravel Holdings; however, they need more information."

"What type of information?"

"They would like a copy of a blank check from your company bank account."

What luck, she thought! The day after faxing a copy of her special department passport, Samantha had been in Baltimore for the Watch and had stopped by one of the local banks to open a commercial account. The checks should be arriving at the Post Office Box in Baltimore soon if they weren't already there.

"That will be no problem, Dr. Ossaga. I don't have my checkbook here with me, but I can fax a copy of a voided cheque to you shortly."

"Now I must speak seriously with you Ms. Angelou Adams."

"Go ahead Doctor."

"Have you told anybody about what you are doing with us here in Lagos?"

"No, nobody."

"Good, I can't stress to you enough that the success of our project depends on absolute secrecy. You must never, speak to anybody about it."

"I understand."

"In addition, you must only communicate with me personally on this subject. Often my work takes me out of the city for several days or a week. If you call and someone else answers, don't give them any information. If someone calls you

The Adams Sisters

from Nigeria with a message from me or wants to discuss the project, say that they have the wrong number, and you don't know what they are talking about."

"I understand. Do you mind, if I ask you a question?"

"Go ahead."

"Are you a medical doctor?"

"No, I am a Ph.D. and I work for the Nigerian government."

"I see."

"Remember absolute secrecy," he repeated. "No one must know."

The contact was beginning to fade and then return.

"I promise Dr. Ossaga, not a word." She was smiling.

"Thank you, Ms. Adams." The connection broke, and the line was filled with static. She tried to call him back, but a recording of an officious female voice came on the line. "I'm sorry, all circuits are busy. Please place your call again later."

The young Washington bureaucrat sat in her bed in completely amazed, repeating every word over many times. His voice was very heavy and African. There was a British accent in many of his words. She wondered what he looked like.

Quickly she began to focus. It would be at least four hours before the bank would be open, and she could call to verify whether the newly printed checks had been mailed. Her system was demanding coffee, so she pulled on a thick terry towel robe, stuffed the cell phone into her pocket and headed for the kitchen.

The caffeine cleared her head. If the checks were in the Post Office box, it would be better to head for Baltimore right away. However, this was too short a workweek to make an unnecessary trip. Then it occurred to her to try and call the Post Office. It was almost 6 a.m. There might be someone on duty.

It took several calls to locate the correct building. A night security guard answered the phone.

"There might be somebody in that area Miss, I'll try to transfer your call."

A sorting clerk answered. At first he said he wasn't authorized to give out any information on the contents of the public boxes. However, he did relent and when to verify. Yes, there was a package in her box. The main doors opened at 6 a.m.

Samantha went back upstairs and turned on her notebook. Quickly she brought up the Notes screen and sent a message off to Mr. Walters explaining what had happened and that she would be in later, as she was going straight to Baltimore from home.

In addition to the email from Sebastian, Christina was also receiving messages from Yellow Cloud. They were now into their sixth mutual exchange. She was intrigued by him.

It was his knowledge of horses and the things that he told her about them, which prompted her to ease up on the heavy conditions, which she had imposed, when they first started messaging. She told him that as long as they didn't mention specific places or people, she thought she was ready to discuss more than horses with him. On Tuesday evening after supper, she downloaded a fresh message from DC Meets.

**

From: yellowcloud@dcmeeets.com
To: nightshadow@dcmeets.com
Subject: Read my message before the attachment.
Attachment: yellow_word_association.doc

Hola Night Shadow,

It's really prodigious how we seem to be on the same wavelength. I find myself logging in almost every day now, to see if there's a new message from you.

In your last message, you suggested that Internet meetings might be a more pure form of interaction between men and women than physically meeting because as you explained, physical appearances, tone of voice and gestures can have such an influence on the recipient of these signals.

Maybe platonic would be a better word than pure, and I don't think that Internet meeting sites for men and women are all that new. Lonely hearts clubs first appeared in European newspapers in the 15th century.

Both Internet meeting sites and lonely hearts clubs are similar in that we can only know what the other person chooses to tell us about themselves. When two people are in physical contact with each other, it's harder to control the simultaneous exchange of information. I think that people involved in an email relationship tend to analyze the sender's words, more than they would oral speech because they're looking to see beyond the written words.

Would you like to play a word association game? Here are five words: white, test, animal, fun, talk. . Without thinking too hard, tell me what you associate with each one of them. After

The Adams Sisters

you send me your associations, open the attached file to see what I associate with these words.
I am going to have Thanksgiving dinner with my family. Besides my parents, my two younger brothers and two younger sisters will be here. I think family is important
Lol, YC

**

Christina had also been analyzing his words and what he said to try to gain an insight into him. One thing she picked up on was the way he used the word 'prodigious', in a manner similar to how other people used the word 'awesome'. When she asked him about it, he told her that he tried not to be swept up by every buzz word that was going around and yes – had replaced awesome in his speaking habits by prodigious. He didn't know of anybody else who used the word. She decided to reply to him, before starting her assignment for that evening.

**

From: nightshadow@dcmeeets.com
To: yellowcloud@dcmeets.com
Subject: RE: Read my message before the attachment.
Attachment: night_word_association.doc

Hola YC,
It's true what you said about how physical presence affects us. If you were here, I'd probably be wondering if my hair was ok or, if I was laughing or smiling too often or not enough. I'm sure I would be watching the expressions on your face to see, if I could tell what you were thinking, instead of listening to what you were saying.
Here's what I think of when I see your words: White = White House; Test = getting my driver's license; Boots = horses; Fun = laughing with my best friend at school; Talk = talk shows on TV.
I think e-mailing may or may not be platonic. It all depends on the two people who are in the e-mail relationship. If we have an emotional response, then it's because the other person has entered under our skin somehow. That's more than platonic. However, if communications remain nothing more than a conversation, I think that it would probably be platonic.
I am going to be busy on Thanksgiving myself. We're also having a family dinner. Besides my parents, I think that my older sister will show up and my aunt, my mother's sister has been invited. She's a widow and her children live too far to

come. Actually my sister has been living in New York during the past few years and didn't come home much herself, so I am hoping that she will eat with us.

Sometimes when I read your messages I find myself thinking, 'Hey I'm a little like that too.'

Now I'll give you five words: country, bar, mother, sick, hate. Don't look at my associations in the attached file, until you send me yours.

I must go now. Hasta Luego. ...NS

**

On Wednesday, Christina decided that she would go horseback riding, before meeting Sebastian for lunch and called to reserve a horse for nine o'clock the following day. That evening the alarm clock was set for 7 a.m. Thursday morning she was gone, before anyone was up, but left them a note on the kitchen table. The streets of Georgetown were deserted.

During all the years that Christina had taken lessons or had only gone horseback riding in the Equestrian Center, in Rock Creek Park, she always wore jeans and cowboy boots. The first time she visited the paddock area at Cabot; she thought it amusing to see everybody dressed as if they were competing in a horse show. Then she learned it was the Club dress code.

The young woman arrived at Cabot Club well before eight, parked the BMW and went to the change rooms, where she kept her riding clothes. Half an hour later she was walking along the path that went from the Club House to the stables. She wore high black boots, white spandex pants, and a black riding jacket that came down to her hips, a white turtle neck sweater and a steel helmet. Her hands were sheathed in grey kid gloves, and she carried a riding crop.

There was a light land fog that morning. It shimmered through the paddock, which lay beyond the stables. In the distance, she could see a horse chopping on the dewy grass. Several club members were milling around in front of the stables, waiting for the attendants to bring horses out from the barn or in from the paddock. Christina waited her turn.

At nine o'clock sharp her name was called, and she stepped forward to explain her preference in a saddle. Once mounted, the attendant adjusted the stirrups and the horse began to walk away from the wooden structure, when it felt a slight tug on the left bridle.

The Adams Sisters

Christina had the horse for an hour and a half. The stable attendant told her to let the animal warm up, before attempting any trotting or galloping. Horse and rider turned off into the trees and followed a well-worn track until it emerged in the field. It wasn't long before the beast under her began to canter. They both knew the trails and runs well. The horse voluntarily picked up speed and began to gallop, whenever the terrain would slope downward.

The way Christina worked the trails was intentional. At ten after ten, she turned the steed around, pressed her heels into its sides and gave a sharp whack with the crop. They were off into a straight fifteen-minute gallop, before reining in near the stables.

The attendant held the bridle, while she dismounted and then asked her if she would put the horse in stall number 10 to cool off, until he had the time to clean it up. Once she had closed the bottom half of the stall door behind the horse, Christina began to make her way back outside. As she passed by stall number 5, she stopped to look in, through the open top half door.

A chestnut brown horse was lying on its side, in the straw at the rear of the stall. A man in a long white lab coat was bent over it. She heard him talking softly to the animal as he rubbed at the front of its shoulder with a piece of cotton cloth. Then he held a syringe up in the air, got a bead of liquid on the tip of the needle and pressed it into the horse's shoulder, where he had been rubbing.

The horse snorted and shuffled its legs as if it was going to try to get up. The blond man in a white coat pressed his two hands against the horse's body and applied his own weight, all the while continuing to talk. The horse resisted once more; then flopped back down on its side. Before Christina could think, the medical attendant stood up and turned towards the open upper stall door. Their eyes met.

"Preppy!" she gasped. "What are you doing here?"

He replied with a question, "Christa, how did you get here?"

She recovered and answered, "My father's a member at this Club. I've been out riding."

By then he too was over his initial surprise, "This is part of my practical. I'm on call this weekend?"

"What practical?"

"Don't you remember? I told you, I'm studying to become a Vet. This horse is one of my patients."

He walked forward, lifted up the latch and said, "Would you like to come in?"

She stepped through the opening and he closed the lower door behind her.

"What's the matter with this horse?"

"She has a cold."

"A cold?"

"Yes, a cold, horses get colds exactly like we do."

"Can I go closer?" the young woman asked.

"Be my guest."

"I saw the syringe. What was in it?"

"I gave her an injection of a mild sedative mixed with a general antibiotic."

By then the young woman was down on her knees in the straw.

"Do you mind if I touch her?"

"Not at all."

Her hand reached out and smoothed the animal's head, "Is she going to go to sleep?"

"No, it wasn't that strong. I only gave her enough to keep her down, so she'll rest."

"This is fascinating."

"Yes, it is fascinating and soon it's going to be my full time job."

She looked at him and smiled, "I didn't know Vets made house calls, but I must say you have an excellent bedside manner."

He looked at her, and a broad grin spread across his teeth, "That's right; you're a Med. student."

"The student part is almost done for me also. Soon it's going to be my work. I graduate in the spring."

"Now I remember. You wanted to intern at DC General."

"Did I tell you that too?"

"Yes you did."

She stood back up. "I must have been feeling very good that night. Usually, I never talked to anyone around the Wave about what I did outside of work. I was only part time you know."

"Yes, I remember."

"Have you been back?" she inquired.

"No, I'm done too."

"How did you get here?"

"Came along the Beltway from Silver Spring and took Exit 39 at River Road."

The Adams Sisters 105

"Sorry about calling you Preppy," she apologized. "It slipped out. I was so surprised. I have to go now and get cleaned up. I'm meeting someone for lunch in the Club House."

"Come on then," he said, lifting up the latch. "I'll walk you to the door."

"Do you come here very often?" she asked.

"I usually get a call to come in on Saturday morning, and end up being here until noon. I don't get paid for this, but the Club does pay something to the School. I get the hours, and School gets the hay. Since I'm their regular, the Club did give me a social membership."

"I don't suppose a social membership includes riding the horses."

"No, but I can take any one of them out for a gallop, to check it over."

"Maybe we'll see each other riding someday."

"Maybe we will." They were at the door." Have a good lunch Christa. Nice seeing you again."

"Yes, nice seeing you too, Tod," then she was gone.

Sebastian was waiting for Christina, when she came into the dining room. She made her way towards him and accepted a kissed her on the cheek.

"I called your house," he told her, slipping off his dark brown suede jacket, which he placed on one of the spare chairs at their table. "Your mother told me you went for a ride."

"It was fabulous. I would go riding two or three times a week if I had the time."

"Let's eat first," he prompted, seeing the waiter approaching them. "I'll tell you about the lot and house after we have finished."

"Fine with me."

She ordered oyster chowder and a Kaiser smoked meat submarine; then the waiter went away. They did some catch-up and talked about her ride until the food arrived. While they were eating, she inquired, "Sebastian, do you mind if I ask you about your work?"

"Not at all. What would you like to know?"

"Is it your company or do you work for somebody else?"

"I'm the majority shareholder, 70% and I also draw a salary."

"Did you get the money to start it up from your family?"

"No, I earned every cent, buying and selling securities."

"How do you know what to buy and sell?" she asked.

"The market is like Anatomy, it has to be studied."

"I've heard investment banking is a very competitive business and lots of firms don't last long."

"Competitive isn't the word, Christa. It's savage. Even your own people will sell your investor list to the other side of the street."

"How did you ever manage to break in, if it's like that?"

"I started planning, while I was at Wharton. I made friends with every African student I could. In addition, I've become active on several committees in Philadelphia, which are involved with Africa or Africans. I'm also head of the African section of the U Penn Alumni.

There's an enormous amount of money flowing out of Africa. A lot is coming to America. For some reason or another, Africans like Philadelphia. I try to get acquainted with as many of them as I can. My firm even sends them birthday cards.

These new arrivals are picking up a growing percentage of the securities that Liberty Capital issues. As a matter of fact, this niche absorbs about 40% of our private placements. They're the cornerstone of Liberty's clientele. Nobody has succeeded in gaining their confidence as I have. All the information I have on them is kept on a memory stick, in a safe."

"I don't understand how those people can come here with money?" she remarked. "There seems to be such poverty in Africa."

"I never ask them where it comes from."

"Then it could be money from an illegal source?"

"It could be, but when you talk about Africa, you have to adjust your concept of what's legal and illegal. Sometimes illegal the only way to get things done."

"Give me an example."

"In some African countries, when the government changes, payments stop on all contracts made by the former administration. It doesn't matter whether money is due or not. Sometimes the people who didn't get paid must resort to strategies, which may appear to be illegal, to an outsider, if they want to get paid.

"It must be a terribly hard place to live in. I'm glad that I was born in America."

"Me too, Christa, me too."

When all the dishes had been cleared away, they ordered coffee and Sebastian pulled a file folder from the leather satchel at the side of his chair.

The Adams Sisters 107

"This is the house as it stands now," he said putting the pencil sketch down in front of her.

"That's not bad looking. You have good taste. Let me see where you're planning to build it. "

He lay four photos down over-top of the sketch. This is the lot, looking in from the road. There were two photos are the neighbors, on either side. This is a shot taken near the old foundations, looking out towards the road."

"The sketch of the house fits well with this property."

"Thanks, Christa, it was pricey, but I took it anyway."

"How much?" she asked.

"Two hundred and ninety thousand, but there are two acres."

"I don't have any idea of the value of real estate, but that' is a sizable amount of money to pay for an empty lot. How far is it from Philadelphia?"

"About fifteen minutes, if the traffic is light."

She stared at the sketch for several minutes. There was a certain something about it, which she couldn't immediately place. Finally, she picked up a pencil and pointed, "It wouldn't hurt to build a wing off in this direction, right about here."

She had taken the bait. Sebastian was glowing.

"I would never have thought of that Christa."

She continued, "Sooner or later you might want more space, even if it's only for guests."

"Excellent!"

"How much do you plan on spending?"

"I can go another $500,000 on top of the land and hopefully I'll be able to sell the house in Chestnut Hill, as soon as I move in here. The equity I have in that house will be enough to allow me to be creative with some new furniture and landscaping."

"You can do a lot of building with a half million dollars," she assured him

It was already two thirty, when they finished going over the sketch and photos from a number of points of view. Sebastian had to be at his father's house for five.

"There you have it, Christa. It's Thanksgiving, and I have my lot. Are you going to give me a hand?"

"That was our deal, wasn't it?" she replied looking him straight in the eyes.

"It was."

She looked at the whole thing again and spoke, "If I were to help, you wouldn't presume anything else, would you?"

"I don't quite catch you."

"What I am saying is that, if I were to take a personal interest in the designing and building of your house, there wouldn't be any presumption that we could cut any corners."

"What kind of corners?"

"In my mind, when a man and a woman live together in the same house, they should be married, regardless of who designed it."

"In my mind, it's the very same."

"Then it's a deal Sebastian, I'll give you a hand."

"Thank you, Christina," he said softly, picking up her right hand and kissing the back of it. "This is your copy. I'll put it all together in this folder for you. Now we should be gone. This is family dinner evening, all over town."

She picked up the folder and slid it into her wide shoulder bag. "Yes, it's getting on. I should be going back. I'll work on this project in my spare time, and there'll probably be a lot of questions, so I'll leave them in your e-mail for you. You can send me an answer, when you have a few spare moments."

"How do you feel?" he asked, reaching for his jacket.

"Excited, I'm not a designer; I'm not married, and I'm getting to design a house." As she was standing up, Christina leaned over to kiss him on the cheek, and then inquired, "What sort of a time-line are we on?"

"I'd like to start building in spring" he replied, taking her by the elbow. "Come on, I'll walk you to your car."

****

9 - The Blizzard

The Christmas festive season begins early in Washington. Lights start to appear around the beginning of December. The city stays lit up straight through to the Epiphany or the Festival of Kings, in January. The selecting and lighting of the National Christmas Tree are always significant events, no matter who happens to be the President.

There have been all sorts of trees. Some years live trees have been planted on the Ellipse between the White House and Constitution Avenue. Other years have seen trees planted in the flower bed, in front of the White House. In 1954, an arrangement of smaller decorated trees, representing the states, the District of Columbia and territories was set up as The Pathway of Peace.

It's always a matter of pride to an individual state, when they provide the National Christmas Tree. The tallest ever, cut tree came from Arizona, in 1965. It was over one hundred years old and stood ninety-nine feet tall. The U.S. Post Office has issued a commemorative stamp depicting the National Christmas Tree.

This year the honor was bestowed on Fraser's Christmas Trees of Spokane, in the state of Washington. On December

2nd, an eighteen and a half foot Noble had been presented to the First Lady. She chose to display it in the Blue Room of the White House throughout the season, to be viewed by millions.

Dr. Ossaga and his colleagues had received the Baltimore General Services voided check in late November. After another delay of a week, there started a series of calls and faxes between the Nigerians in Lagos and Samantha Adams to get the routing and SWISS numbers for the international funds transfer to her company's bank account. She sent them a copy of the company seal on December 19th.

On December 20th, the 3rd Quarter of the fourth year of Medicine ended at Georgetown University. The fourth Quarter began on December 21st. Christina was back in clerkships from the first day. She was also scheduled to work at DC General on Christmas Eve, Christmas Day, Boxing Day and New Year's Eve.

Between Christmas and New Year's, the State Department was on slack time. Many of the staff took a few days of their annual vacation, so they had a whole week off between the two holidays. Samantha was going to Orlando, in Florida for New Year's Eve and New Year's Day, with some of her old crowd, for the Citrus Bowl. They would be twelve in all. She was sharing a hotel room with a woman named Tiffany, whose husband was onboard an aircraft carrier, in the Mediterranean, for the next three months. The two women had played intramural volleyball on the same team three times at Georgetown U.

Christina saw Sebastian twice between December 26th and 30th. She gave him the modifications, which she had to suggest to the main structure of his house. In addition to the wing at the back, she added a greenhouse, a garage, and car port. In all, she made six significant contributions. He was pleased. In fact, he sent the rough sketch with her modifications to his architect, as soon as she gave them to him.

Apart from seeing Sebastian and working, Christina spent several hours e-mailing Yellow Cloud over the holidays. They had sent each other electronic Christmas cards. They even went up in a Chat group a number of times and carried on a simultaneous conversation on the screen. It was still only in joking; however, they were talking about what if they were to meet each other offline and if they did, where would it be.

Samantha and her friends flew to Orlando early in the morning of Tuesday, December 31st. They were in plenty of

The Adams Sisters

time to get to their hotel and then go out to find the seats, which they had reserved in bleachers on Rosalind Avenue, to watch the Citrus Bowl Parade. Downtown Orlando closed early for the extravaganza. The parade started at noon. There were 24 floats, 24 bands, many specialty units and the two marching bands from the competing teams.

After the parade Samantha and Tiffany went back to their hotel for a quick snack, a shower and a change of clothes. Around 8 pm they met the others in the hotel lobby; then boarded three taxicabs for the Atlantic Dance, which started at 9 p.m. at Disney's Boardwalk. Their $200 tickets included a stunning array of cuisine to select from, champagne all evening long, and dancing, until 2 a.m., in one of the world's largest ballrooms. At midnight, the nets on the ceiling opened to let thousands of black and white balloons float down on the dancers, who now moved from one stranger to the next, hugging, kissing and wishing them Happy New Year.

The Citrus Bowl game kicked off at 1 p.m. January 1st at the West Church Street Stadium, in front of 70,000 spectators. From where they were seated in the grandstand, Samantha could clearly see the lake through the open end zone. At 5 p.m., they all went to the Church Street Station, for the post-game party.

The following morning, the group of twelve drove over to St Petersburg, on the Gulf coast, in a rental van. They spend the day swimming in the shallow warm waters, for which that city's beach area is noted. When Samantha came out of the women's change rooms wearing her Stars and Stripes bathing suit, Ron Williams stopped short, smacked the palm of his hand into his forehead and exclaimed,

"Wow, Sam! How did I ever miss?"

"You just wouldn't take your mind off that basketball you were always toting around and so I found someone who liked to dance."

"Well, I assure you; my basketball days are definitely over, and I've learned how to dance."

"So, I saw last night."

"Maybe we'll make a comeback," he said, flashing a wide grin.

"Who knows, maybe we will," she replied, pulling the sunglasses down from on top of her hair, before heading off towards the blankets that were already being spread out on the sand. The swimming was great, as long as you watched out for the Portuguese man of war, which were drifting along with the help of the wind and current.

The day ended when they left the van at the Orlando airport and boarded a jet for the flight back to DC. It was raining as the plane's the tires touched the runway, at Ronald Regan National Airport. An airport shuttle bus took them to the car park. Tomorrow was a workday for most of the group, so the goodbyes were short.

"Sam, mind if I give you a call during the week?" Ron Williams hollered to her as she was slamming shut the trunk of her Lexus.

"Don't go and forget you said that," she hollered back.

"I won't and Happy New Year again."

"You too Ronnie, Happy New Year."

She took the George Washington Parkway North to the Francis Scott Key Bridge and came into Georgetown on M Street NW, before telephoning home to let them know that she was back and would be in soon. Driving up Wisconsin Avenue, the rain began to freeze at the edge of the windshield and the wipers kept sticking on the film of ice. The driveway to the Adams house was also coated with a layer of ice. Charles was standing at the front door as she approached the house. He took one of her bags.

"Thanks, dad."

"I think you just got back in time, Kido."

"How's that?"

"The 10 p.m. news said that Regan Airport getting icy in spots. They're sending salt trucks out, but warned that they may be forced to close several runways."

"I believe it. My wipers were freezing on the way home. We'll have to do something with that driveway of ours too. It's getting quite slippery."

"I'll take some salt out with me in the morning," he said, closing the door behind them then added," come on into the living room. We have a fire going. Your Mon is dying to hear about your weekend."

Samantha left her bag in the hall, followed her dad in and sat down beside her mother on an elegant natural white, classic style leather sofa. Marsha had recently redone her living room over in Natuzzi. Charles went back to the semi-circle stuffed arm chair, where he had been reading, and listened to his daughter tell of her New Year's in Orlando.

The following morning, traffic, was at a crawl. The driving lanes were wet and stained white with salt. The curbs and

The Adams Sisters

shoulders of the roads were full of slush. At the slightest upward grade, car tires would begin to spin. The radio said that the snow would melt off during the day and it did. However, more rain and freezing rain was forecast for that evening.

In spite of the weather, the State Department was starting to come to life again, after the holidays. The first item on Samantha's to do list was to log into Fifth Dimension, to see if there were any messages. One fax, which had been converted into e-mail, was waiting to be downloaded. It came quickly across her screen. She printed it out immediately and began to read.

**

December 31, 20xx
Dr. Lawrence Ossaga
Lagos, Nigeria
Fax 234-90-405427

Dear Ms. Angelou Adams,

I am pleased to tell you my colleagues are satisfied that you can be of assistance to us with your company, Baltimore General Services. Now it's time to divulge more of our project to you.

Nigeria was under military rule for many years. After the transition to civilian government was thorough, there were growing signs of insurrection in some areas, parts of the civil service had stopped functioning and exports of oil were dropping. In order to secure the value of our currency on international markets, the government suspended payment of all internal and some external debts for an undetermined time, even though funds existed, in the Nigerian Central Bank, to cover most of them.

The country is approaching its first real general election, since the transition to civil government. In light of this, the government has decreed that an attempt should be made to pay some of the more important debts, which the government has outstanding. The President has asked the Debt Reconciliation Committee, to review the veracity of all claims. I am a member of this Committee.

There are 13 people; myself included, who sit on the Committee. We review each claim for payment and identify the funds, which were originally made available through the national Treasury, to the Central Bank. Two things have occurred within this committee.

First, there seems to be far too many debts being repaid to people who are currently allied with the government. Most of them are Ibo. Far too few payments are being made to people of other ethnics and especially far too few to Moslems. Second, blocks of funds have been located in the Central Bank, which are no longer identifiable. Possibly, the owners of those debts have died or left the country.

Certain interests, who are not Ibo, approached me to see if I could do something to speed up the review and payment of their debts. The Debt Reconciliation Committee ceases to exist, once the upcoming democratic elections are held. These gentlemen are my colleagues. Given the current circumstances, which exist within the Committee, it's not likely that my colleagues' claims will be reviewed and paid, before the Committee is dissolved.

There exists a bias in favor of settling foreign claims within the time that we have left. The Committee is especially interested in settling any outstanding claims with American companies as the US is our largest customer for oil exports.

My colleagues have proposed to transfer their outstanding debts to your company, Baltimore General Services. There are two groups, and they are willing to make the transfer to you under two invoices. In one group, there are four sub-contractors to be paid. In the other group, there are five. The total of the two invoices is 15 million US$.

My job is to obtain the necessary Committee approvals for payment and choose one of the unidentified amounts in the Central Bank as belonging to your company. In return for my services, I will receive 20%. Your function will be to supply us with a bank account outside of Nigeria to which we can transfer 15 million US$. Following that, you will purchase the goods, which my colleagues select and have them shipped to Nigeria. In return for its services, your business will receive half of what I will be paid.

Time is of the essence. The elections could be announced any day, and I would lose all access to files and the Central Bank. Before we move along to the next step of the process, we must know that you fully understand everything I'm saying.

Please confirm reception of this fax and ask for any clarifications you require.

You are our partner now. I cannot stress to you how important it is that you maintain absolute confidentiality and secrecy about this project. If word were ever to get out and come back to Nigeria, we would all lose our lives.
Yours Faithfully,
Dr. Lawrence Ossaga

The Adams Sisters

**

Samantha couldn't believe her eyes. His letter was exactly the same as the warnings on the Department's Web site. She had to see Mr. Walters. Without bothering to phone him, she left her desk and walked quickly along the corridors, until she arrived in the sector where his office was located. He was going through the doorway as she rounded the corner. The Intern followed him in and sat down unnoticed while he took off his coat and hat. Turning around, he burst out laughing,

"Samantha, how did you get there? I didn't see you, Happy New Year!"

"Happy New Year, Mr. Walters. I hope I am not too soon."

"You're the first one here, so you're at the top of the list. It's on a first come, first served basis today."

"Good! I've something to show you. I think it's what you've been waiting for."

"Let's see."

She passed him the print out. He scanned it first and then went back to reread and absorb the details.

"This is absolutely incredible," he exclaimed. "Do these people think you're an imbecile?"

"I agree, all of this is mentioned in the warning that the State Department has on the Net."

"Simply incredible, they're even going to use the Central Bank. We're through to them this time, Sam. I'm going to keep this copy for my record if you don't mind."

"No, I have a file on my machine."

"Have you thought about what clarifications you're going to ask this schemer Ossaga to give you?"

"Not yet."

"Make them sound good, these guys have probably heard every angle there is."

"I know, that's why I'm going to call and speak with him directly. I haven't called him yet. It's always been he who has called me."

"Good idea, it will appear to be a more genuine reaction on your part. I'll leave it to your discretion. There's just one thing, before you run off."

"What's that?"

"Not a word to anyone in this Department. We'd have them tapping our phones. They'd probably try to have it taken up and let the Secret Service handle it."

"Mum's the word, Dr. Ossaga," she replied, with a laugh. "Mum's the word."

"Yes I know, you're getting it from both ends," her boss agreed. "Now, I've got to find a way to write all this up, so that it doesn't look like what it is."

"What is it?"

"It's an incredible swindle of basically honest people. It shouldn't be long now before they ask you for some money. After that, they'll want you to fly to Nigeria."

"Probably!"

"Well' I'm telling you right now, you'll never set foot in that country. I don't care what you have to tell them, but there is absolutely no way you're going there."

"I understand you, Sir," she said, standing up. "I'd be afraid to go there anyway."

"So would I Samantha," he added scanning the print-out she had given him another time. "Give me a call if anything comes up."

"I will, see you later, Sir."

Lagos was eight hours ahead of Washington. During the day, the Watch Intern tried fifteen times to dial Nigeria. It was a time consuming process. First she called Fifth Dimension Offices and keyed in a code after a computer answered. When she was informed that her call had now been forwarded to Baltimore, thus masking its origin, she would dial Dr. Ossaga's phone number. After many beeps and bongs, a recorded female voice with a heavy African accent would cut into explain that all circuits were busy.

It was 5 o'clock. She was weary. She decided to go home, to have supper and to stay up, until midnight trying to get through to Lagos.

The temperature had begun to fall as most Washingtonians headed home at the end of the day. In many areas, hail was being driven down on the city by a strong sou'easter wind. It was a good night to be home and to stay home.

On Tuesday, January 7th, a few computer weather forecasting models indicated the possibility of a major East Coast storm soon. On Wednesday, weather models produced at the European Center for Medium-Range Weather Forecasts showed a strong storm headed towards the US East Coast.

On the 8th, television stations issued winter storm watches for the mid-Atlantic. Some called for more than a foot of snow. That night the temperature fell below freezing along the eastern seaboard. The day's rain became a frozen nightmare.

The Adams Sisters

At those temperatures, salt was ineffective. Special supplies of chemicals, which worked regardless of how low the temperature fell, had to be spread on the Capital Beltway and DC's streets. Each mile of open lane required tons of the preparation. Applicator trucks moved slowly everywhere. In the morning, traffic was a long continuous snarl. In spite of being late, most people made it in to work.

At 3 p.m., on January 9th, Greensboro, N.C. measured 10 inches of new snow, tying the record for that date. Snow began falling at Regan National Airport around 9 p.m. During the night, huge currents of wind pushed humid air in from the Atlantic Ocean. When the water-laden air hit the cold front centered over the Mid-Atlantic, the humidity condensed into snow. By morning, the barometer had dropped 20 bars and the Capital was engulfed a driving blizzard. A foot of tiny, hard ice pellets had fallen, and winds as strong as 75 knots per hour were being clocked.

Schools and agencies of the federal government started announcing closures for the day at 5 a.m. By noon, the weather bomb had dropped 20 inches of heavy snow on Washington. The wind pushed it up into high drifts in many places. Visibility was down to less than a hundred yards on the Beltway. Many tractor-trailers were sighted on their side in a ditch. Exit ramps were blocked. Out on Interstate 95, stalled freezer trucks began to run out of the fuel that kept the coolers going.

In the city, there was no place to park. Along the main arteries, people abandoned their cars several feet from the curbs. The vehicles were surrounded by banks of snow, as high as their roofs, as soon as a plough went by. Lynchburg Va., Washington, Philadelphia, Baltimore, New York City and parts of the Boston area came to a standstill.

The police ordered everybody to stay off the streets, who did not have absolutely necessary business to take care of. In those cases where it was necessary to go outside, the radio said to walk. Cars, which became stuck, had to stay where they stopped. There were no tow trucks available for private vehicles.

DC General Hospital issued an urgent request to the city and surrounding area on Friday afternoon. Ambulances were stalled and delayed everywhere. They were not equipped to get through the snow that was found off the main streets. Any resident having a four-wheeled drive vehicle, preferably with a winch attached to the front bumper, was asked to report to the hospital's Emergency. The request was repeated multiple times during the weekend.

Early Saturday morning, a second storm came barreling down out of the Great Lakes, crossed Pennsylvania and met the weakening Atlantic storm head on. By 6 a.m., it had dropped another seventeen inches of snow on the Capital. Weathermen nicknamed it, White Wand.

DC General Hospital is located on the East Side of downtown Washington, nineteen blocks beyond the Capital Building. Within walking distance of the hospital gate, is the Stadium Armory Metro Station, which is on the Blue Line. Christina was scheduled to work, in the Emergency, both Saturday and Sunday.

On Saturday morning, there was not a chance in the world that any of the Adams family cars would make it out to the street. Snow had drifted up as high as the front door latch. The low hedges in front of the house were covered. It was impossible to tell where the driveway ended and the street began.

The closest Metro station to the Adam's house is Dupont Circle. The closest Metro Station to Georgetown commercial district is at Foggy Bottom, across Rock Creek, in Washington just south of Washington Circle.

Christina put on a pair of loose nylon jogging pants over cotton twill khakis, a yellow nylon ski jacket over a woolen turtle neck sweater, a woolen stocking hat belonging to Charles, mitts, heavy lace up boots and set off to climb out over the snow to R Street NW. The snow plow hadn't been down their street in two days, and there were no vehicle tracks.

She deliberated about which way she should go. If she went down the back way and crossed over Rock Creek to Dupont Circle, there was a very good chance that she would have to break a trail all the way. If she went out to the corner of R and Wisconsin, she could probably follow a tire track down Wisconsin and then go over to the Foggy Bottom Metro Station. She began to move slowly, lifting her knees high and then setting them down again, over and over. It took an hour to reach the Foggy Bottom Station.

Many people were lined up inside the Station, waiting for the next train. The Blue Line starts in Virginia, south of Alexandria near the Beltway. It follows the Potomac up past the Pentagon and crosses into Washington along the north side of the Watergate Complex. Eventually, the train did come, and it filled to standing room only. After many stops and starts

The Adams Sisters 119

and waits, as the Metro wound its way through the heart of Washington, Christina did get across the frozen city and clambered off at the Stadium Armory Station.

The Hospital is a conglomerate of three multi storey red brick buildings, connected together by wings and tunnels. It's set well back from street, in a huge field, which overlooks the Anacostia River. The complex contains the Health Care Campus, a Sexually Transmitted Disease Clinic, a Detox Clinic, a Women's Services Clinic as well as a TB and Chest Clinic. The DC Jail is located south east of it along the river. There are two intriguing structures towards the North. One is the JFK Stadium. It's a massive concrete oval, which dominates the skyline. The top of the walls look like a flying saucer or a roller coaster track. Across the street is the Armory, which is the home of the DC National Guard.

Outside the Hospital, a crew of men in orange overalls worked continuously, pushing the snow back. Two were on small snow blowers keeping the sidewalk open. A tractor, equipped with a blade & heavy link chains on the rear wheels, went back and forth over the asphalt approach from 19th Street SE to the loading dock, where the electronic sliding glass doors were located. Some men worked with hand shovels scooping up what the blowers and tractors couldn't get. A lone figure carried a shovel full of salt in one hand and used a flat wooden stick to spread the salt, where the ambulances and four-wheel drive trucks were pulling up to unload.

There were more private vehicles and drivers than there were ambulances. These volunteers' vehicles were identified by a triangle of neon-orange plastic attached to the outside aerial. Their drivers wore white armbands. They were bringing in accident victims, people who had frost bite, others with heart attacks from shoveling the heavy snow, and of course, there were pregnant mothers, who were starting into labor as well as gunshot wounds, and old people who couldn't breathe. Anybody who didn't absolutely need to be hospitalized was being sent home, as soon as they were treated.

It was 9:30 a.m., three hours after leaving home, when Christina signed in to start her supposed to be 8 o'clock shift. They were all glad to see that she had arrived. She took off the outerwear, put on her uniform, and then reported for duty in the Emergency Department. There were people everywhere; some were in the waiting benches, but many were just slumped down on the floor with their backs up against the wall. The corridors leading away from the Department were lined on both sides with wheeled stretcher beds.

The med student worked steadily until 4 p.m., when she was told to take a short break. She was sitting in a small staff lounge, just off the Emergency when Dr. Edwards, the Chief Duty Doctor came in and called everyone to attention.

"You've probably all heard by now that we are in the second storm, which has moved down from the North-West. The police are being forced to close more roads to all, but essential travel. I know it took some of you hours to get in today. We all congratulate you on your courage and persistence.

The Hospital is making overnight space available to anyone, who is scheduled to work tomorrow. We will also provide space for anyone who will volunteer to work tomorrow. Please give your names to the duty nurse. We'll notify you later where you will sleep."

Christina gave her name to the nurse, as she walked back to the Emergency. When she arrived, there was a black SUV pulled right up to the sliding glass doors. The driver and one of the snow crew were unloading someone from the back floor of the truck onto a wheeled stretcher. She went to see, if she could help them.

"What is the nature of this patient's problem?" she asked when she reached them.

The man wearing a stone colored canvas coat with the volunteer arm band replied without looking up, "She's in labor. I think she's lost blood."

Christina went around to the side of the bed to help them get the woman on to it. As she slipped her arms in under the laboring woman's back, the volunteer driver looked at her.

"Tod!" she said emphatically, controlling her surprise.

From the moment Tod Evans had decided to respond to DC General's public request for volunteer ambulance assistance during the storm, he knew there was a possibility he would run into Christina Adams and had mentally prepared himself for the moment.

"Good afternoon, Dr. Adams."

"Where did the truck come from?" she asked, recovering her composure. "As I recall, you drive an old sports car."

"I do, an old Audi. This SUV belongs to my Dad."

"Don't tell," she joked, "you volunteered because you wanted to see me in action."

"Do you want the truth?" he joked back

The Adams Sisters 121

Yes."

"I was logged onto the UM chat site Friday evening and one of the other guys said he had borrowed his dad's Jeep and helped out here all day. I decided to do the same thing."

They had the sick woman on the gurney and started to wheel her inside.

"It was very considerate of you, to give up your day to help the hospital like this," she said with a more friendly tone.

"I don't mind helping out," he affirmed. "There are a lot of people in need and the system is being pushed to its maximum."

"Do you know how long it took me to get here this morning?" she asked.

"How long?"

"Three hours!"

"Wow!"

Dr. Edwards came over to them.

"Miss Adams, would you prepare the admittance chart for this woman, please."

"Certainly, Doctor."

"Mr. Evans can we get you anything, coffee, a sandwich. This must be you're fourth or fifth load?"

"It's the fifth Doctor. Yes, I could use a coffee and a sandwich."

"Miss Adams, when you're finished with the chart, would you get Mr. Evans a coffee and a sandwich, please?"

"Yes Doctor."

While Tod was eating, Dr. Edwards came up again. "It's almost four thirty, are you going to be able to handle another run this afternoon."

"There's a lot of snow falling Doctor, but I'll go out once more."

"I really appreciate it Tod" the medical man assured him. "The police have called in another accident and I don't have an ambulance to send out."

"Is it serious?"

"They said it was a head on. One person is dead, and two are seriously injured. Here's the location the officer gave me."

Tod looked at the writing on the notepad, "I know where that is," he said tearing off a sheet of paper.

"I'm going to send a Medic with you."

"Whatever you think is best, Doctor."

"Be sure to gas up at our pumps, before leaving."

"I will."

"Am I mistaken, or did I see you talking with Miss. Adams."

"We were talking. She and I both had summer jobs at the same place a while back."

"Good. Do you mind if I send her along with you."

"Not at all Doctor."

"While you're gassing up, I'll tell her to put some warm clothes on."

Christina was waiting at the loading dock, when Tod pulled up in his father's four wheel drive, after topping up the gas tank. She opened the back passenger door and placed her medical bag, as well as a cardboard box containing plasma and plastic tubes, on the seat. When she climbed into the front seat, he asked, "Do you have everything?"

"I hope so."

"Where do you live that it took you three hours to get here this morning?"

"I live with my parents, on R Street NW, not far from the Georgetown University campus. I walked all the way over to the Foggy Bottom Station this morning to get the Metro."

"That's a long walk in this weather. You should be about ready to quit soon."

"I'm sleeping over at the Hospital tonight, so I'm going to work, until I get tired."

"I see."

"What does your father do that he has this big vehicle?" she inquired.

"He's a Public Accountant with a small practice in Silver Spring."

"Did Dr. Edwards tell you what we are going after?"

"Two people in an accident and a third is dead," he replied. "I hope there won't be three dead, by the time we arrive back at the Hospital."

The back wheels of the vehicle began to slide sideways. "Not too fast," she warned. "We don't want to join the list of casualties."

"Yes Mam," Tod joked, saluting with his right hand.

"By the way, I like your coat," she said.

"It's a Fergie."

"What do they call that one?"

"An original field coat."

"Nice name too!"

The radio was on, and the weather report broke in every five minutes. Philadelphia was in the same shape as

The Adams Sisters

Washington. She wondered what Sebastian was doing. She hoped he had the good sense to stay in.

It took almost an hour to get to the accident. Night had fallen. A police cruiser was stuck in the snow up to its floor boards, beside the two cars that were still locked in a head on collision. The officers were standing outside waiting for them. Tod didn't dare drive too close to the edge of the road. The soft snow might hide a sharp drop off onto the ditch. The policemen came to meet them, when he stopped.

"Boy, are we glad to see you two."

"Where are the victims?" Christa asked.

"We have them in our cruiser, with the heat running, but the gas gage is reading empty. We tied off their wounded limbs with our belts."

"Are they conscious?" she asked.

"No, Doctor."

"How difficult is it going to be to move them?"

"There are bone fragments piercing their skin in various places."

"Tod, give them the stretcher and then turn around so your rear door is facing the wreck. I'm going to go over to the cruiser with the officers."

A woman was laid out on the back seat, and a man was in the front. They both appeared to be dead, but she could still get a pulse.

"Were they in the same car?"

"No, the woman was with the dead man. The man in the front was driving by himself."

"We'll have to move them one at a time. Ease the stretcher in under the woman first," she instructed them.

It took about five minutes to move each victim. When Tod and the officers went back for the man, she stayed behind and set up the intravenous for the unconscious woman. Once the rear hatch was secure, the officers locked their cruiser and climbed into the front seat with Tod. Christina stayed in the back with her patients. She gave them an injection of a stimulant to help keep their motor functions going and hoped she didn't lose them.

It took longer to drive back to the hospital than it had taken to go out to the accident. There were more cars off the road now. People were waving at them from the ditch, but Tod didn't stop. They arrived at the Emergency Department at 7 p.m. Several attendants rushed out with wheeled stretchers.. When the victims had been transferred, Christina went up to the driver's door and Tod lowered the window

"That's some bedside manner you have," he said.

"Thanks, Tod, I really didn't know I had that in me."

"I've got to head home now."

"Maybe I'll see you again sometime," she said, with genuine warmth in her voice.

"You never know. Maybe we'll bump into each other at the Cabot Club, in the spring."

"I'll keep an eye open for you," she promised. "You should get going now. The weather is only going to get worse."

"Don't work too hard tomorrow," he cautioned her.

"I'll try not to. You drive carefully on the way home."

"I will," he said putting the SUV into gear. "Nite!"

"Nite Tod," she replied as the vehicle began to move away.

****

10 - The Evans Family

Founded in mid-1840, Silver Spring is the largest and oldest business district in Montgomery County, Maryland. It experienced significant growth in the late 1920's and early 1930's when several new industrial and commercial enterprises clustered along Georgia Avenue and the B&O rail line. The subsequent development of new retail and service outlets, supported by a system of public parking lots, helped Silver Spring become a thriving commercial center serving both the Montgomery County suburbs and the middle and upper income areas of northwest Washington, D. C.

This period of prosperity was short-lived. New regional shopping centers attracted shoppers away from Silver Spring. When the big chains eventually left, other retailers closed their businesses. Vacant storefronts popped up throughout the central business district. Even the opening of the Metro station in 1978 was not enough to change what the municipality had become.

Today Silver Spring is near the end of the North-South Metro Red Line, which starts north-west of Washington in the southern Montgomery municipality of Bethesda, runs into downtown Washington near the Capitol Building and then heads back towards the North. Silver Spring is the first stop in

Maryland. The mural on the side wall of the station shows penguins going through the turnstiles, boarding the metro cars and then sitting down to read their newspaper or a pocket book on their ride into downtown Washington. This mural says it all.

The office of John Evans & Associates, Certified Public Accountants, is located on Colesville, not far from the Silver Spring Metro Station. When the sign was painted, associates had been envisioned. Once there had actually been an associate. He stayed one tax season. Since then, the associates, who were genuinely needed during tax season, tended to be accounting students, who were working on their CPA.

It was a one-man practice, which generated sufficient revenue to pay the office rent, the mortgage on the family home and feed, clothe and educate his wife and five children. There was always a little left over for extras. Last year some of the extra had gone to purchase a new four wheel drive SUV, which replaced the family's Volvo station wagon.

In his early career, John had been working for a large regional firm of 26 accountants, in Baltimore. It was a salary job. He was sure he could do better on his own. He met wife Jenny through a referral from one of his small business clients. She had recently returned from California and opened a small flower shop. All she really needed was a hand to set up her bookkeeping. When he didn't present an invoice, she had invited him to go with her and some friends one Sunday, to visit Assateague Island State Park. Even though John Evans had been brought up in Maryland, just outside of Baltimore, he had never been to Assateague Island and so accepted the invitation.

The long barrier island, which is located off the coast of Maryland and Virginia, is built by sand that persistent waves have raised from the ocean's gently sloping floor. Occasional storms drive waves and sands so forcefully that the beach and shoreline change dramatically, from year to year. Summer mostly means the lure of beaches and mild surf, where shorebirds trace the lapping waves back down the beach. Behind the dunes, one finds the island's forests and bayside marshes. Wild ponies wander between the marshes and the surf.

The outing with Jenny was such a contrast to the life that the young accountant was living. His non-paying client turned out to be a genuine and sincere person. On the way back to Baltimore, he asked her if he could call her socially. It wasn't

The Adams Sisters

long before she was supporting and even urging him to leave the large regional accounting firm he was working for and strike out on his own. She had family around Silver Spring, and they moved there, after getting married.

Tod was their first born. He was fair-haired from birth, just like his mother. A year later he was followed by Ester and then eleven months later by Gwyn. The couple stopped there with making a family, because the practice wasn't generating the revenue, which they had imagined it would.

Eventually, the young accountant had been able to diversify his practice away from doing year- end financial statements for small, usually owner-operated businesses and corporate and personal income tax returns. When the revenue stream evened out several years later, with the addition of business plans, bookkeeping services and computer installations, the couple toyed with the idea of maybe trying to have another boy. They were twice blessed with twins whom they named Morgan and Miles.

When the twins were born, the Evans house began to be pinched for space. At first the den had been converted into a nursery; however, it was only a temporary solution. They decided to take a chance. There was a new development in Woodside Park, which was located north of the V shaped intersection between Georgia Avenue and Colesville Road.

After many discussions and running dozens of 'What-if' scenarios, an offer led to a down payment on a two storey red brick colonial style house, located on the eleven hundred block of Noyes Drive. It had long narrow windows facing the street and double chimneys on both ends. From the front, the house was deceiving small, but the structure did go quite far into the back yard.

Noyes Drive was lined with oaks, and there were no curbs. Lush green lawns ran straight out to the pavement. There was and still is a visible absence of fences in the neighborhood. When they bought a house, there were only three cement steps coming up to the front door. Over the years, the couple changed everything, starting with the front entrance.

John's first project was building a low red brick retaining wall. It was about ten feet out from the front of the house and ten feet in from each corner. The three steps up to the front door were replaced with three steps built into the wall Lamp posts were added on both side of the opening. The still youthful Evans shoveled earth into the enclosure, until the ground was raised up six inches below the front door sill. A concrete sidewalk and square pad were poured in front of the entrance and a roof supported by double columns soon appeared above the square concrete pad. Grass covered the space between the sidewalk and a thick 15 inch yew hedge that was planted along the inside edge of the low brick retaining wall.

Tod's adolescent need for privacy resolved itself when the basement was finished, adding a bedroom, laundry room and office to the dwelling. It turned out to be a stroke of luck for him. Whenever the house was bubbling over with family chatter, he could always withdraw into the cave as he called his room in the basement and get his schoolwork done. There was never a problem, if one of his buddies wanted to sleep over. A fold up camp cot, already made up with bedding, was stored in the laundry room. Later, when he started to go to dances and date, he would come in by a back basement door, and nobody was ever sure at what time he arrived.

The eldest Evans had been popular at school. There always seemed to be a girl who was interested in him or one that he wanted to get to know. As far as he could remember, his first crush occurred in grade three, and he felt sad for weeks, when the girl moved away.

Besides girls, sports had always been important to him. Baseball was his game, and his youth had been a never ending series of Pee Wee, Little League and Babe Ruth ball tournaments. He liked pitching and managed to pitch a lot. If minor league baseball had been more developed in the DC area, he might have gone further and become a pro-ball pitcher.

Tod's first summer job came between the sixth and seventh grades. Actually, it got underway in February of the sixth grade. Since he was the eldest, he had to help his Dad in the office, during tax season. John Evans would prepare the individual returns and paper clip the attachments to it. His son's job was to make two copies of the return and two copies of the attachments.

One copy was for the office records, and one copy was for the client. The original went to the IRS. The top right hand corner of the first page of the client's copy received a red stamp saying, CLIENT'S COPY. He would put the office copy in a folder, print the client's name on the tab if it was the first time return and then file it alphabetically. The following summer he manned the phones for six weeks, while his father was out circulating and leaving a business card where ever there might be potential.

Later there had been many summer jobs. Once he had helped on a residential housing project, another time it was in a hamburger and soft ice cream place. After his first year of science at the University of Maryland, the Student Placement office offered him a summer stevedore position on the docks in Baltimore. The job had involved a lot of driving; Silver Spring to Port Fells and back every day, but the pay was super. Several other summers he'd worked in DC bars.

The previous summer had been his second season to work as a barman for a small outfit called Coastal Entertainment. They had five good clubs. The shifts were long and always involved weekend work, but the tips were more than the regular pay he earned. Eight years of university would end, come graduation in the spring. He was one of the few in his crowd, who hadn't mortgaged his future with a hefty student loan.

No one in the Evans family quite remembers when Tod's interest in animals and especially sick animals began. His mother told him that she remembered him fixing birds' wings after they flew into the windows of their home. He couldn't recall doing that. What he did remember though was the time their dog Patches died.

When he was thirteen, one of the neighbor's children contracted a light case of jaundice. The Evans dog Patches became very ill not long afterwards. The veterinarian said it was hepatitis and prescribed an antibiotic. The dog slept in the laundry room, beside Tod's bedroom, in the basement. Together the boy and the family pet had fought the illness for weeks, but the animal kept getting weaker. One day when he and Ester came home from school there was a pool of urine on the floor, where the dog lay. The parents and their children buried Patches at the back of the family garden.

The young man's real interest in animals matured while studying science at university. In biology and zoology, dogs and cats were used as subjects in the dissecting labs. One day Tod came home and told his family that he was thinking about applying to Veterinary School after he finished the BSc. His parents said if that was what he wanted, then that was what he should do.

Being one year younger, Ester was always one year behind her brother at school. She was quiet, but everybody knew her because she was Tod's sister. Secretly some of the girls even envied her, because she was frequently asked out by one or other of her brother's friends. Ester studied Math at the College Park campus of the University of Maryland and drove back and forth with Tod, whenever it was convenient. The rest of the time she took the Metro to Fort Totten station and transferred there to the Green Line, which runs through MU.

Shortly after her brother announced that he was going to be a Vet, Ester told the family that for over a year she had been planning to transfer to UM Law School after Math, if she was accepted. In addition, she informed them that if accepted, she planned to enter the Navy Judge Advocate General's Corps Student Program, which permits law students to commission in the inactive Naval Reserve, while attending classes. Upon graduation, the successful completion of a bar examination and the Navy officer training course, she would serve on active duty for four years, beginning as a lieutenant.

Gwyn had been the baby of the family until the twins were born. Her indecision and flightiness were blamed on this early spoiling. She changed her academic stream three times, before graduating from high school and spent every spare moment and cent she could get on art and painting. She didn't want to go to college and instead enrolled in a private institute in Washington, where she studied textiles. During the summer between the two year certificate program, Gwyn had been hired by a small fashion house in Manhattan, and she knew exactly where she was going, as soon as she had a diploma in hand.

The twins were like night and day. Morgan was athletic. He took all the ribbons every track and field day and had already run in two public entry marathons. He wanted to go into the Navy and had told everybody that he would be attending the Naval Academy at Annapolis, from grade nine on. Miles was a nerd. He spent more time in front of a computer screen than he did sleeping. While in junior high, he had written a program for a computer game contest, which a local software firm bought for twenty-five thousand dollars. He told everybody that he was going to MIT, just as soon as accepted.

The first real problem appeared in Tod's life during the spring of the fourth year of science. He was dating a tall, hot brunette named Angie. They had been seeing each other since Christmas of the third year. Her dad was General Manager of a pharmaceutical complex near Raleigh, in North Carolina. Angie

The Adams Sisters

wanted him to come back home with her to Raleigh after graduation. Her father was offering him a first class position in one of his firm's laboratories and Angie's mother was offering to put him up in a small apartment the family had over the tool shed in the back yard, until he and her daughter worked out their plans. Tod didn't know whether he was ready for marriage yet, but if push came to shove, he had a feeling that he wouldn't resist too hard.

Tod sent a transfer application to the Virginia & Maryland School of Veterinarian Medicine during the summer, between third and fourth year. The Veterinary Faculty only accepted thirty people a year from Maryland. He didn't think he would make it, so he went along with Angie's plans for him, and never told her about the application to do specialist studies. Then the Veterinarian Faculty's conditional letter of acceptance came at the end of March. All he had to do was pass the final term with the same marks he had been receiving all along.

Tod didn't go to Raleigh. When he showed Angie the conditional letter of acceptance and said that he was going to take the place he had been offered, she grabbed the letter and tore it into pieces. She asked him if he thought she was going to sit around and twiddle her thumbs waiting on him, for another four years. An argument started between them, which had no resolution. She was his first serious girlfriend and it hurt. After that, relationships were a summertime fling, which never went past Labor Day.

When he left DC General, after saying good night to Christina, Tod would have liked to take Central Avenue east to the Beltway and then up to the Silver Spring Exit. It was one of his usual runs. However, the radio was on, and he could hear what the DJ's were saying about driving conditions, out on the Beltway. White Wand was not letting anybody through. Better to stay on the main city streets as much as possible, he thought to himself, just in case the SUV did get stuck. From the Hospital, the young man went up 19th Street to Independence Avenue and drove east towards the Washington Monument. At 7th Street, he turned right and headed north. Eventually, 7th Street would become Georgia Avenue NW and it would take him directly to Silver Spring. As he drove, he thought about the day and the injured people he had seen.

He felt a little strange about interacting with Christina Adams the way he had during the afternoon. Working in a bar was a job, but it was also a fun time. He had never seen what even one of the dozens of waitresses, who yelled and hollered at him for service in the bar did, after the summer was over, and not one of them had ever seen beyond the blond with the muscles, who poured their drinks. Giving a horse an injection or volunteering to help accident victims was real time. Today was the second time he had seen Christina and the second time she had seen that he wasn't really Preppy at all. Even if she was going to be a doctor he had to admit, she was good looking and definitely had a great build. He wondered if they would bump into each other again.

At 11 p.m. he turned off the ignition at the Evan's house on Noyes Drive. It looked as if all the family had gone to bed. The house was a lot quieter now than it had been when they were all there. His parents were very pleased to have him staying with them while he finished the last year of the Veterinarian program.

Ester had been accepted in Law and had transferred to the Baltimore campus of the UM. This year she was doing her Maryland Bar and in the spring would be entering the US Navy as a lieutenant. Gwyn had gone back to Manhattan with her diploma. She soon tired of fashion houses and was now working in the planning department of a large garment manufacturer. She matched textiles to styles of clothing and had recently scored big with a project to use micro fibers in designer uniforms for nurses. Morgan and Miles were both gone too. Morgan was an upper-class midshipman at the US Naval Academy in Annapolis, and they hoped soon to be a commissioned officer. Miles was at Caltech in Pasadena. He had received a scholarship from a Silicon Valley company.

Before he went downstairs to his room, the young man poured a cup of coffee from a half full carafe that was sitting on the base of the coffee machine. Then he put it into the microwave oven to warm up. He pulled out a ham from the refrigerator, carved off three thick slices, opened the plastic container of potato salad and put three big scoops beside the meat. There was fruitcake on the back of the counter. It was wrapped in plastic, but there were several generous pieces individually wrapped. He added two of the wrapped pieces to the plate, grabbed the coffee cup and turned out the kitchen light.

His bedroom was warm in the winter, as the furnace was located in a small room on the other side of one of the walls. With a broadband connection, his computer was always on. First he clicked on the Internet Radio icon on the desktop and selected an alternate music station. Then he logged into his

The Adams Sisters

Internet account at the University of Maryland to check his e-mail. There was a message from one of the other students in the veterinarian program. There was one from his sister Ester inviting him to come over to Baltimore to see her new apartment and to meet her new boyfriend, who worked for JAG. There were a couple of pieces of junk email. One was advertising a multi-level marketing scheme that would earn you $15,000 a month. There was another advertising to put your photograph on a T-shirt. He deleted them both.

Next he logged into the University of Maryland, Chat site. There were seventy-five people online. He started to watch the lines scrolling fast down the screen. It looked like a marathon, and they all talked of nothing, but the storm. He watched for a chance to join their conversation. It was like trying to cut into traffic. Finally, he spotted a question, which was going unanswered. It had been posted by someone using the code name Crazy House. He'd seen that handle before and quickly typed a reply ' No Crazy; it's closed. I just come in from out there.' He hit the Enter key and saw his comment appear on the screen beside his handle, which was Doczoo.

Doczoo: *'No Crazy, it's closed. I've just come in from out there.'*

Almost instantly, another line followed his.

@lost: *'Welcome aboard, Doczoo. What were you doing out that way?'*

Quickly he typed his reply,

Doczoo: *'Driving volunteer for DC General.'*

@lost: *'With your buggy?'*

Doczoo: *'No my Dad's.'*

@lost: *'Any dead ones?'*

Doczoo: *'Yea, one on my last run.'*

Crazy House: *'Do tell Doczoo, tell us all.'*

He sat there and talked to them until he couldn't hold his head up any longer.

Doczoo: *'It's 1 a.m. guys, I gotta crash. See you next time.'*

@lost: *'Nite Doc, thanks for the news.'*

Crazy House: *'Bye, bye Doc. I'm crashing soon too.'*

He put the computer into sleep mode and went to bed.

****

11 - Doctor Ossaga

On Saturday morning January 25th, Samantha was buried deep, under a down filled comforter. Her mind fought against sleep while it tried to make contact with the day. Slowly she began to awake. Her right hand clawed at the blankets covering her head, to clear a breathing hole. The limb was numb with sleep. She rubbed it fast on her naked thigh, until pins and needles confirmed that her circulation was returning.

Cautiously she opened one eye and then the other. A small red light blinked steadily on the cell phone that was beside the alarm clock on the bedside table, indicating that she had a waiting email message. There was still too much sleep in her puffy eyes to focus on the one square inch cell phone screen, let alone read an email message. However, it would probably be legible on the notebook. The question - was she inquisitive enough to get up.

It was another five minutes, before curiosity impelled her to flip back the blankets, slip on a white terry towel robe and go over to her old wooden desk. As soon as she logged into the email account at Fifth Dimension, Dr. Ossaga's latest message filled the LCD screen.

**

The Adams Sisters

To: baltimoregeneralservices@5thdimension.com
From: operations@5thdimension.com
Subject: Fax from Lagos

January 25, 20xx.
Lagos, Nigeria
Fax: 234-90-405427

Angelou Adams
Baltimore General Services

Re: About Me

Dear Ms. Adams,
Now that you have become our partner, it's time I tell you more about myself and the project.

My father was Chief of a tribe of 700,000 people. The majority of us were from the same ethnic group. About 15% of the tribe belonged to a minority group. In addition, the tribesmen were equally split between Christianity and Islam. My father was progressive. The minority was well treated, and several of them sat on the Advisors Council. Our Chief was a hereditary function. I was supposed to succeed my father.

When I was 18, being Chief didn't interest me at all. I made it very plain to everybody concerned that I didn't want to take the function. There were objections, from the the most conservative elements of the tribe. Eventually, my father accepted my decision. In fact, he even counseled me.

Speaking as the Chief, he said that if he should suddenly die, it would be very difficult for me to resist the tribe. They might even take me prisoner and force me to be their Chief. He suggested I find a legitimate excuse for leaving the village.

He told me when I was gone, he would make his Advisors Council, an elected group. Then, he would help set up a municipal type government. He said, "A structure will be in place and ready to start to assume more importance, when I pass on."

Not long after this conversation, I told my mother I was thinking of joining the British Navy on a two-year contract. She didn't like the idea, however many young men in Nigeria were serving in the British Forces. After my father had said he thought that 2 years in the Navy would be a good preparation for the next Chief of his people, the matter was settled.

I served out my contract with the Navy but didn't renew it. I was honorably discharged in London. While I was still in the

Navy, I had applied for and was accepted at a university in England. My father resigned as Chief and the process of forming a municipal government got under way. Eventually, he was elected the first Mayor. When he died, a new mayor was elected. During all that time, I remained in England and finished a Ph.D.

After I returned to Nigeria, I stayed away from my village and went to live in Lagos, which has been the real center of the country for many years, in spite of the fact that Abidjan is the Capital. In Lagos, I joined the administration. The military regime appointed me to the Debt Reconciliation Committee, because of who my father had been and the President kept me on as part of his transition strategy. However, I have been advised my term will expire when the next general elections are held.

I have done a great deal for my Nigeria as a civil servant. Now I dream of doing something for my father's people. When the Debt Reconciliation Committee is dissolved, I will have no work responsibilities, I'll be able to devote my time to the project, which I've been thinking about for a long time.

The reason why I originally became involved with the contractors, who are transferring their claims to Baltimore General Services, was that the money I will receive for my part in the affair will be sufficient for me to turn one of my dreams into reality. If anything went wrong in our partnership with you, my idea would die. I might even die too if my involvement were ever found out. I must stress the need for absolute secrecy to you again.

My country and the world in general are full of thieves and opportunists. Fifteen million dollars is very attractive to many people. You must not say anything to anybody about what you are doing. Please promise me Miss Angelou, in your next fax to me or over the phone, if we succeed in making contact.
Best Regards,
Dr. Lawrence Ossaga

**

Samantha yawned. She was getting tired of this insistence of his concerning secrecy. What did he take her for anyway? She knew he was a thief and so did he. She clicked open the Notes program on her notebook, found Mr. Walters's name in the address directory and then started to compose a brief message to him.

**

To: Roscoe.Walters@statedept.gov.us

The Adams Sisters

From: Samantha.Adams@statedept.gov.us
Subject: Ossaga

Dear Roscoe,
I've had another message from that old thief, Ossaga. Now he's claiming to be a defrocked Nigerian tribal Chief. He also says he has a Ph.D. from an English University. I've already assured him a number of times that I've observed absolute secrecy with regards to everything he has told me, but he's asking me to put it in writing or better still, telephone him and reassure him verbally.
I know it's the weekend, but before I try to contact him, I thought I'd message you to see if you have any special instructions. If you happen to be checking your e-mail messages, give me a shout.
Bye for now,
Samantha

**

Once the message was sent, she went to take a shower and to pick up a cup of coffee in the kitchen. When Samantha arrived back in her room, she began to get dressed in between sips of coffee. She had just finished pulling the bed spread up over her pillows when a three-note tune sounded in the room. She looked over at the computer. The center of the LCD screen contained the familiar message window saying, "You've got mail!" A few clicks on the roller ball mouse brought the new email message into view.

**

To: Samantha.Adams@statedept.gov.us
From: Roscoe.Walters@statedept.gov.us
Subject: RE: Ossaga

Hi Sam,
I've been pounding away on the keyboard at home, paying my bills and catching up on personal correspondence. Lucky for you the remote access to the Department was still open. I was updating my agenda book for the week, when your e-mail message came through.
If Ossaga is still insisting on absolute secrecy, he must be getting ready to give us something more substantial. This has been a long one way street with you supplying all the information.

I know it's the weekend and there's an eight or nine hour time difference, but if possible, I believe it would be a good idea to contact him verbally. You have a very pleasant voice on the phone. That might reassure him.

Ah, there's my wife calling to see if I'm finished paying our bills. We're having three couples over this evening for supper and two tables of bridge. I'm off to the store to help her with the groceries.
Talk to you soon,
Roscoe

**

Bridge, hum, she thought. He really does have a dark side. I could see him playing Poker, Black Jack or even Roulette, but Bridge. Then she looked at the clock and did a mental calculation. It should be about supper time in Nigeria. Maybe I'll try calling Mr. Larry Ossaga.

She composed the number and switched it to the speaker phone on the desk beside her. There was a lot of static and them a horn that sounded at 10-second intervals. After waiting for two minutes, she moved to hang up the call just as someone said, "Hello," on the other end of the line. It sounded like a young girl.

"May I speak to Dr. Ossaga?"

She heard the girl calling out, "uncle, telephone, a lady."

A minute later a deep African voice, which she now recognized, said, "Hello!"

"Dr. Ossaga, this is Angelou Adams calling from the United States."

"Good evening, Miss Adams. I am glad you called. This means you got my fax?"

"Yes, it was waiting on my machine this morning. That's a very interesting story you told me about yourself."

"It's not a story, Miss Adams. It's all true, every word."

"I'm sure it is. I believe you and that is why I am calling you. I want to assure you that you have absolutely nothing to worry about. I haven't mentioned our communications to another living soul. Your secret is absolutely safe with me."

"That's very encouraging, Miss Adams. It's what I was hoping to hear you say.

"By the way, are you an uncle?" she asked.

"No, not really, but that's what the girl next door calls me. She comes over to clean my house on Saturday and today she offered to stay longer and prepare supper. I've invited her to stay and eat with me."

The Adams Sisters

"That was very nice of you."

"Nice, Miss Adams!" he exclaimed. "She asked me if she gets paid too during the time she's eating with me."

"Oh, I see. What did you tell her?"

"Only if she washes all the pots and dishes after the meal."

"I see! Do you play Bridge Dr. Ossaga?"

"I played a lot in England, but very infrequently here in Lagos. Not many Nigerians know the game. Why do you ask?"

"Oh, no reason, only curiosity, do you mind if I ask you a personal question?"

"What question?"

"About your age."

"No, go ahead."

"How old you are?" she inquired hesitantly.

"I'm thirty-three," he replied. "Now then, we should be ready to discuss the next step in the plan."

"Which step is that?"

"The invoices."

"The invoices, I don't understand Doctor. I thought you were going to transfer money to my bank account. What do we need invoices for."

"As I told you in a previous fax Miss Adams, a number of creditors are going to transfer their claims to your business, Baltimore General Services. The invoices are what is behind the transfer of the 15 million $US to you."

"I see."

"Do you really?"

"I think so."

"I have the invoices and a cover letter already to fax to you. I'll just finish my evening meal and then take care of it."

"That sounds better. I'll wait for your fax."

"Don't sit beside your machine Miss Adams. It could take hours of redialing to get an international line."

"Okay, I'll get your next fax, when I get it. So I guess this is bye for now."

"Bye for now, Miss Adams."

The line dissolved into a heavy static.

Samantha went back to her day. The weather was warming up. Outside the thwack, thwack, thwack of a tennis ball hitting first the brick wall built at the back of the Adams mini-court and then the mesh of a racket, sounded over and over. She drew back the curtains. It was her father.

He wasn't dressed for tennis. His bare feet were shoved into a pair of worn running shoes, and he was wearing khaki shorts and an ordinary white T-shirt that wasn't tucked in. She followed his arm, back and forth. His whole body went into each return. Samantha cranked the window open and called out,

"Hey, Dad, do you want a game?"

He looked up. His eyes were searching the windows. She waved.

He waved back and replied, "sure, come on down."

"I'll wear my scrubs."

"These are my scrubs too."

After an hour, Charles had to excuse himself as he had an appointment to have his car checked up. His daughter went back inside, had a second shower; and then dialed into her secret office on the Net. There was a fax waiting. As usual, she downloaded it as e-mail. There were 4 pages. The first was a letter from Ossaga; the second was a letter addressed to the Nigerian Debt Reconciliation Committee. In addition, there were two sample invoices addressed to the NNPC. She printed them off and then sat down to read his letter.

**

To: baltimoregeneralservices@5thdimension.com
From: operations@5thdimension.com
Subject: Fax from Lagos

January 25th, 20xx
Lagos, Nigeria
Fax: 234-90-405427
Tel: 234-90-044572

Angelou Adams
Baltimore General Services

Re: Invoices

Dear Ms. Angelou Adams,

In addition to my letter, you will find two sample invoices and a sample letter to the Director of the Nigerian Debt Reconciliation Committee. A letter to the Director and the two invoices should be reproduced on your letter head paper and company invoice stock. Be sure to copy the contract numbers and the dates on the invoices exactly as I have indicated.

At our personal expense, my associates and I have registered your company, as a foreign supplier in Nigeria. Both invoices are dated correctly. This means that your business was legally operating in Nigeria for two years before you

The Adams Sisters

invoiced the Nigerian National Petroleum Company, for work completed.

We have transferred the work done by 9 Nigerian nationals for the NNPC into two contracts. The first contract is WAR-36p-63c-71. It covers pipeline installation and well casing installation, for which our people were never paid. The second contract is HAR-17p-6l-72. It covers pumping stations, and repairs to generators and a lighthouse, also for which our people were never paid.

The long form of these two contracts, which deal with all the work and material specifications have been placed in the files at the NNPC. Baltimore General Services is the name of the company that appears in all the documentation as the company to which these two contracts were granted. We have also placed all the required subcontract forms in the files that show you subcontracted the work out to nine local firms owned by Nigerians. All the field reports, as well as NNPC job inspection reports, have been placed in the files, as back up material. There is also proof that Baltimore General Services paid all local contractors for the work performed. The only thing that remains now is for your company to get paid since the two contracts have been duly completed.

When you have reproduced the letter to the Director and the two invoices on your business stationery, please fax them back to me. I'll see that copies of the two invoices are placed in the files at the NNPC.

I will also make sure that your letter and two invoices are properly stamped as officially received by the Debt Reconciliation Committee and that they go into the Director's In-Basket. Once you fax them to me, you must never communicate with anyone about this affair besides me. I may be watched or there's always the possibility we have a traitor among our group. After I get your letter and invoices through to the Committee, my so called associates may think they have little more need of me. It would be easy for them to try to cut me out and start dealing with you directly.

You must work very quickly at this Ms. Adams. We have already wasted much precious time. Please complete the letter and two invoices and fax them back to me as soon as possible.

The success of this project depends upon absolute secrecy. Thank you for calling me to reassure me that all is well.

Best Regards,
Dr. Lawrence Ossaga.

**

Samantha was taken aback by what she had read. This was supposed to be a simple transfer of money to her bank account. Now it was fake registrations, fake contracts, and fake invoices. She didn't like it According to all the documentation that she had read at the Watch, the people running these scams would ask her to send money at some point to cover costs. Ossaga hadn't asked for a dime yet.

He really is a slick thief she thought. He's trying to make me believe that he has paid to register my company and paid to have documents placed in the NNPC files that will help transfer 15 million dollars to my bank account. No wonder so many Americans have been taken in by these schemes. These people con you into thinking that they are your friends. Next she turned her attention to the two sample invoices.

**

(Company Logo Here)
(Company Name Here)

INVOICE No. 5689:   *December 31, xxxx*

The Nigerian National Petroleum Corporation
Contract Administration Division
100 Commonwealth Plaza
Abuja, Nigeria

CONTRACT No.
WAR-36p-63c-71

1. Excavation, preparation and back fill of the trench along assigned pipeline route between Port Harcourt and Warri. ($400,000 US$)
2. Supply of 15" steel, fiberglass wrapped pipe according to specifications. (2,000,000 US$)
3. Welding together pipe sections. (1,300,000 US$)
4. Laying of welded pipe in specially prepared trenches. (900,000 US$)
5. Supply of 10" steel pipe to be used as oil well liner. (1,400,000 US$)
6. Installation of the liner in prescribed wells around Warri, Sapele and Eku in southern Nigeria. (2,000,000 US$)
Total   **(8,000,000 US$)**

The second invoice read as follows.

(Company Logo Here)
(Company Name Here)

INVOICE No. 5793   *December 31, xxxx*

The Nigerian National Petroleum Corporation
Contract Administration Division
100 Commonwealth Plaza
Abuja, Nigeria

CONTRACT No.
HAR-17p-6l-72

1. Construction of 5 pumping stations on pipeline between Warri and Port Harcourt. (2,800,000 US$)
2. Repairs to 5 diesel electrical generators along the pipeline. (700,000 US$)
3. Construction of pipeline and tanker connections along oil loading wharfs at Port Harcourt. (1,500,000 US$)
4. Construction of the lighthouse at the entrance to wharfs where oil is loaded at Port Harcourt. (2,000,000 US$)
Total   (7,000,000 US$)

Then there was the cover letter.

(Company Logo Here)
(Company Name Here)
January 26th, 20xx

Dr. Abdul Bakar
Director of the Nigerian National
Debt Reconciliation Committee
25 Floor, First Africa Tower
8 Liberian Way
Lagos, Nigeria

Dear Dr. Abdul Bakar,
I understand your Committee is responsible for assuring payment of past contract work done by foreign companies in Nigeria, on behalf of the government or its corporations.

In March xxxx, Baltimore General Services bid on and then negotiated the modalities of two contracts that were being tendered by the Nigerian National Petroleum Corporation. The *contracts were **WAR-36p-63c-71** and **HAR-17p-6l-72**. A stipulation of the contracts was that no payment would be made until evidence of satisfactory completion of the specified work was submitted.*

All work specified in the two contracts was completed on schedule and according to specifications. At each stage, the appropriate inspectors came from the NNPC and examined the materials, the field reports, and the completed work. Copies of all official inspections were submitted with progress reports to the NNPC in Abuja, throughout the life of both contracts.

In spite of the above-mentioned facts, my company has not yet received payment for the materials and work performed. Our contract price included progressive interest payments that would be due up to the end of xxxx.

The non-payment of these two contracts has caused great financial hardship to Baltimore General Services and has impaired its ability to obtain credit or financing. The company has been in good faith.

I am including copies of two invoices, which were duly sent to the NNPC in Abuja at the end of xxxx. My company would greatly appreciate any consideration that your Committee would give this matter.
Sincerely,
A. Adams, President

**

Samantha was feeling impatient. There was too much fiddle, fiddle in this. She had been so sure that she was going to crack some sort of an international swindle, but all it ever came down to was faxes and more faxes to Nigeria. She didn't need to bother Mr. Walters again. She would just send these invoices back to that silly African this very weekend. No wonder he didn't have a wife. What woman would let her husband run around in such a make believe world? Can you imagine living with someone who thought they were on a Committee that had access to excess funds in the country's central bank?

It was Monday morning and Samantha was just getting ready to go off to the office when her cell phone signaled that she was receiving something at her cyber office. It would be late afternoon in Lagos. Ossaga would probably have had time to go over the letter and invoices she had sent him. She grabbed her shoulder bag, cell phone and lap top then headed down the wide stair case wondering, if she had made some

The Adams Sisters

mistake on those documents that he was now going to point out to her.

Samantha stopped at the traffic light on M Street before it crosses the bridge over Rock Creek and becomes Pennsylvania Avenue, on the Washington side. The ordinary American spends an average of six months waiting at traffic lights, during their lifetime. She decided to make use of the time and pushed the buttons on her cell phone to activate the e-mail function. Only three lines of text were visible at a time, but she was able to scroll through the entire message, before the light turned green.

**

To: baltimoregeneralservices@5thdimension.com
From: operations@5thdimension.com
Subject: Fax from Lagos

January 27th, 20xx
Lagos, Nigeria
Fax: 234-90-405427
Tel: 234-90-044572

Angelou Adams
Baltimore General Services

Re: Release Certificate

Dear Ms. Angelou Adams

I received your letter and invoices and showed them to my associates yesterday. They took copies and are going to have them put in the files at the NNPC today. I made sure your letter and invoices received the Reconciliation Committee's official stamp showing the date of reception. Now there remains but one thing for us to obtain. It's called a Release Certificate.

A Release Certificate is issued by the NNPC in Abuja. It states that all documents concerning your claim are on file and that they have been examined in relation to the contract and have been found to support your claim for payment.

This certificate must be applied for and signed in front of two witnesses from the NNPC at their offices in the Capital, by a duly authorized officer of the company, which is applying. My associates and I can't apply for this certificate for you. You must come to Nigeria and do that yourself.

As I have said before, we must act quickly. The Committee's mandate will not go beyond the call for elections. I urge you not to delay in this matter. Please look into making travel arrangements today. I'll take care of your

accommodation and ground travel once you are in Nigeria. Please contact me as soon as possible to let me know when you will be coming here.
Best Regards,
Dr. Lawrence Ossaga

**

The light changed green and Samantha's metallic gold Lexus moved ahead in the traffic. Finally, she thought, Ossaga has shown his hand. He wanted her to go to Nigeria to sign some papers and he would take care of her accommodation. She wondered how many Americans had gone beyond this point. If they had gone to Nigeria, they would probably have been robbed or held for ransom. What a racket, she thought, wait till Roscoe sees this.

Half an hour later the last four messages from Ossaga were laid out on Walters's desk.

"The answer is No, Miss. Angelou Adams," he said with a wide smile breaking across his face.

"I know it's No, Sir," she said, laughing along with him.

"The government of the United States does not send State Department Interns to Africa, even if it means cracking the scam of the century."

"I wouldn't want to go any way Mr. Walters. You said it yourself one day; some of the people who have gone to Nigeria have never come back."

"Good, then we understand each other perfectly."

"What are we going to do then Mr. Walters?"

"We, this is your project Samantha. What are you going to do?"

"I'll string him along."

"You'll string him along? He's the one stringing you along."

"I know that Sir. I was thinking about it yesterday. If he were living in the US, he'd probably be in a psychiatric hospital for having delusions of grandeur."

"Or schizophrenia," her boss added. "If we lose control of this, the Department will have us committed to a psychiatric hospital. Don't forget, Intern Adams, this can never leave that guy's fax machine."

"It won't."

"What are you going to tell him?"

"I'll tell him I can't go. I'll say I have business commitments, other companies, a second job, a sick mother who I take care of."

The Adams Sisters

"What if he says that you won't get 50% of his 3 million dollars, if you don't come and sign for the Release Certificate?"

"I don't know."

"Why don't you tell him that you will contact a lawyer in Logos, who can represent you with the NNCP? Say you will give the lawyer a limited power of Attorney for only this project."

Samantha smiled at him, "Thanks, Roscoe, I knew you'd get me by it. I won't take up any more of your time now, Sir," she said, gathering up her things.

"Any time Sam."

"Bye."

"Bye"

Samantha went back to her office to think. All 27 faxes she had received from Ossaga were like a funnel, leading through to this. She knew now how it had happened to those other people. Even though her head said no, she felt as if she might be losing something. Their greed must have got the best of them.

She drafted a reply to him that she would finalize and fax later in the day.

**

January 27th, 20xx
Baltimore General Services
P.O. Box 9355
900 E. Fayette St.
Baltimore, MD 21233

Dear Dr. Ossaga,

You and I live in very different worlds, but we do have something in common. We both have a heavily scheduled agenda. You work for the Nigerian federal government and I am trying to run two companies.

My position with Baltimore General Services is very demanding. In addition to it, I have a consulting business and have recently started working on a contract for the US federal government. There's never enough time.

Dr. Ossaga, I am very sorry, but it is really impossible for me to come to Lagos. In the beginning, this was supposed to be a simple transfer of money to my bank account, which I would turn around and send back to you in the form of goods and equipment. You and your associates were able to register my company there. Isn't there some way that you could sign for this Release Certificate?
A. Adams.

**

The following day Ossaga's reply arrived.

To: baltimoregeneralservices@5thdimension.com
From: operations@5thdimension.com
Subject: Fax from Lagos

> *January 28th, 20xx*
> *Lagos, Nigeria*
> *Fax: 234-90-405427*
> *Tel: 234-90-044572*

Angelou Adams
Baltimore General Services

Re: Release Certificate

Dear Ms. Angelou Adams

I received your fax of yesterday and showed it to my associates during the night. You are our partner, and you are causing us a great amount of distress.

We accepted you as a partner in this project, at your express request. We have incurred substantial expense to register your company and have the files rebuilt at the NNCP. We have expended a lot of energy, and we have exposed ourselves to a significant risk on your behalf. All partners must do their fair share.

I urge you to stop this delaying and let us know when you will arrive in Lagos. Please reply without delay.

Best Regards,
Dr. Lawrence Ossaga

**

Samantha and Ossaga sent faxes back and forth for the rest of the week. She stopped being the polite American businesswoman, who wanted 50% of 20% of 15 million. On Friday night, he called.

"Ms. Angelou Adams, please."

"This is she."

"Ms. Adams, this is Dr. Lawrence Ossaga."

"I recognize your voice, Dr. Ossaga."

"Ms. Adams, you must stop this nonsense. You're causing my associates and me a great deal of anxiety. We are ready to act. All that is required is the Release Certificate for the Committee."

The Adams Sisters

"I realize that Dr. Ossaga, but I can't get away. If you had told me in the beginning that I would be required to go to Nigeria, I never would have entered into your project."

"But you are a partner, Ms. Adams."

"I am not a partner. I am only a business person who is going to let you use my bank account and who will then act as your representative for the purchase and export of whatever you want from the USA, provided that it's not guns."

"You have wasted so much of our precious time, Ms. Adams. The elections will be called any day now. You are a hard woman. You're going to deprive poor Nigerian villagers of the water that my pumps would have given them. Look into your heart Ms. Adams. Can you really do a thing like that? You're a black person yourself. Every time there's a drought many people die. You will be condemning more of them to death."

"Dr. Ossaga, it's very unfair of you to say that."

"Then come to Nigeria."

"I have a proposal for you."

"What's your proposal?"

"I will get a lawyer in Lagos and will issue a limited Power of Attorney to him. He can go to the NNCP and sign for the Release Certificate on behalf of Baltimore General Services."

"A lawyer to represent your company!"

"Yes a lawyer. If you're serious, you shouldn't have any objections to that."

"Objections?"

"Yes, do you object to me contacting the Nigerian Bar to have them recommend a lawyer to me?"

"The Bar!"

"Yes, the Nigerian Bar."

"No, Ms. Adams, I don't have any objections to a lawyer."

"Then it is settled."

"Ms. Adams, I must make some inquiries here for you. There are many lawyers, but there are also many sides. Our plan must not be exposed to a lawyer, who has a history of hostility to our side. He could get suspicious and start investigating. We are sure that we have covered everything, but if a lawyer from the wrong side were to discover one little item that we missed, it could become very dangerous for us."

"Ok, then, you'll have to find us the right lawyer."

"Yes Ms. Adams. I will find you a lawyer. We have found a way around this problem. I will fax you his name and how to contact him on Monday. Just one word of caution, you must never reveal my name to him."

"I won't."

"Promise me."

"I promise."

"Then good bye for now, Ms. Adams."

"Good bye Dr. Ossaga."

As promised, his fax came on Monday. He had found someone named, Ibrim Offuya. Samantha had his fax number, telephone number, and address. It was time to update Roscoe Walters. Two days later, the conferencing signal beeped on her screen, while she was working. It was Walters. She opened the connection immediately and his head appeared in a small window on the monitor.

"Hi Samantha!"

"Hi Mr. Walters!"

"I had our people in Nigeria check out this Ibrim Offuya. There's somebody of that name registered with the Bar, but he doesn't have the same address as Ossaga gave you. Also, the fax and telephone numbers he sends are both unlisted. Would you like to see a picture of the office address that Ossaga sent for this lawyer fellow?"

"Sure."

"I'll just pop it up in a second window on your screen."

"Wow, what's that?"

"It's called a public address. They're quite common in Africa. You buy a box in one of these walls. There's a steel door on the end of these double sided walls. Several times a week the post office goes there to put any mail received for this address in from the back. Would you like to see 2456 Palm Court?"

"Huh!"

He popped up a picture of a six inch by six inch steel door with heavy hinges set into a cement wall. It was secured with a very thick combination lock. The numbers 2456 were etched into the steel.

"Do you see now why I said Ossaga is not coming out of that fax machine?"

"I see."

"Bye for now, Sam."

"Bye Sir."

****

12 - Assateague

Warm, mid-February winds, continued to blow up from the Gulf of Mexico and bathe the mid-Atlantic region in a reprieve from winter. Any vestiges of snow or ice in DC simply vanished. The ground dried up, and early buds began sprouting on the tree branches. The State Department Intern felt her blood flow strangely. She had a desire for change, to be on the go. It was Mrs. Yamato who put her finger on what she was feeling.

"I think you have spring fever, Miss Samantha."

"But it's not spring yet, Mrs. Yamato."

"I know, that's what I told my daughter too."

"What did she reply?"

"She said it was spring inside her head."

"And"

"And, she wants to find an apartment of her own."

Just hearing the words, apartment of her own was like a shot of soothing medication to Samantha's system. She looked about the kitchen. Everything was so massive, so finished. It was the same in the living room and the dining room. This was her mother's domain. She didn't want to be this old yet. She wanted her old life, in her Manhattan apartment, to come back.

"What did you tell her?"

"I said if that was what she wanted; then she should start window shopping, and I would help her decorate when she found a place."

"Just like that?"

"I was young once too Samantha. I know my daughter must find a husband. It's always easier to coax one of those goofy young men into the trap, if you don't have to keep on making excuses about an old stick of a mother with a cast iron hair-doo, who keeps showing up with yet another tray of scrumptious Japanese tea and snacks."

"Mrs. Yamato, would you do me a favor?"

"What favor, Miss Samantha?"

"Would you tell that story, exactly as you told it to me, too my mother?"

"Are you looking for a husband too, Miss Samantha?"

"I don't know yet, but I think I might have spring fever."

It was as if a huge weight had been lifted from her. She took her tea and Japanese snacks and went upstairs. Christina's bedroom door was open, and she could see her sister reading at her desk. Her hair was wrapped in a white towel. The older sister strolled in through the open door.

"Working here this morning, Sis?"

"Yes!"

"What are you reading?"

"Pediatrics. I'm into Step 2 of the USMLE."

"What's that mean again?"

"United States Medical Licensing Examination."

"What's in it?"

"Clinical." Samantha frowned at her. "Step 2 assesses whether you can apply medical knowledge, skills, and understanding of clinical science essential for the provision of patient care under supervision and includes emphasis on health promotion and disease prevention. I need to pass step two or I can't graduate."

"I'm glad I didn't have to do that one, the GRE was bad enough. So, when does all this testing finish. Since you entered Georgetown, your whole life seems to have nothing but a continuous examination."

"I'm getting there. I'm in the February, March, April test mode. It's computerized. I'm doing it at the Philadelphia PTS."

"The what?"

"The Philadelphia Prometric Test Center. It's on the U Pen Campus."

The Adams Sisters

"Are you writing at the U Pen Center, so you can see Sebastian?"

"No, I'm only lucky. Jewel had to accept to do hers in Chicago. Other people I know are doing theirs in Houston, or they wouldn't have scores in time for graduation."

"Want a bite?"

"Is that one of Mrs. Yamato's snacks?"

"Yes."

"No, thanks. I'm watching my weight. If you eat too many of those things, you'll end up losing control."

"Mrs. Yamato told me that her daughter was looking for an apartment."

"I know. She told me last week too. Can you really blame her daughter though? How can she keep a decent dress size with her mother shoving all those sweet things into her, every time she comes home?"

"I might look for a place too. I haven't decided yet, if I will, but her telling me about her daughter reminded me of how much I miss my own space."

"I'm the same way," her younger sister confessed. "Once I'm finished interning at DC General, I'd like to find an apartment."

"By then you may have become Mrs. Sebastian Johnston and even have your own house."

"We'll see," Christina rebuffed with a smile.

"Are you going to the Library to study this afternoon?"

"Ordinarily I would be; however, I'm meeting Sebastian at the Club for lunch, so I reserved a horse for 2 p.m."

Samantha stood up from the bed, where she had been sitting and declared, "I won't waste your time with small talk. Have fun this afternoon Sis," As she left, she passed the Japanese pastry under Christina's nose tempting her one last time.

The Samantha sat in the stuffed arm chair, which was beside the window and looked about her. This was a little girl's room, and she wasn't one anymore. I should go out and pick up a rental paper she thought. Then she noticed one of Ossaga's faxes on the table beside her. It was the latest, the one, which gave her information about a lawyer, Ibrim Offuya. She decided to call the Nigerian legal man. Much to her surprise, the call, went straight through. A high pitched, almost effeminate voice answered.

"Hello!"

"May I speak to Ibrim Offuya, please?"

"Speaking, what can I do for you?"

"Mr. Offuya, my name, is Angelou Adams. I'm calling you from the United States?"

"The United States?"

"Yes that's what I said, the United States."

"Have I won something?"

"I don't understand, won something."

"Yes, you know those American TV shows that call up a stranger and tell them that they won something."

Samantha laughed out loud, "I wish I could oblige you Mr. Offuya, but I'm calling you in your professional capacity as a lawyer. I'm a business person in the US, and I need someone to represent me in Nigeria."

"I see. How did you get my number? It's not listed."

"The Nigerian Bar gave it to me."

"They don't have it. At least I've not given it to them."

"Well, it was them who gave it to me, your fax number also."

"I'll have to call them. I don't like my numbers being given out. In any case, how may I help you?"

"I need to give a limited Power of Attorney to someone in Nigeria to represent my business. Would you be interested?"

"That all depends. What does your company do?"

"Several years ago we built a pipeline and overhauled an oil pumping station in your country."

"I see, and what are you doing now?"

"We are trying to collect on two contracts?"

"I see. Are you a Miss, a Mrs. or a Ms. Adams?"

"I prefer Ms. Adams."

"Well Ms. Adams, with no intention to cast aspersions on yours or your company's integrity, I believe that you are aware or should be aware that there are probably one hundred rackets operating out of Nigeria, all with slight variations, but all with the intent to either swindle vast sums of money from the Republic of Nigeria or unsuspecting foreigners. Do you know what I am talking about Ms. Adams?"

"I have heard about the scams Mr. Offuya and I have read the US State Department warnings, but I assure you Baltimore General Services is not part of any swindle."

"Are you familiar with the Nigerian penal code?"

"I'm sorry Sir, but I'm not."

"Section 4-1-9 deals with Advance Fee Fraud and its very comprehensive. Since I live in Nigeria, I would be arrested and charged under the Law, if ever I became even remotely involved in a fraud coming within jurisdiction of Section 4-1-9."

Mr. Offuya, I assure you, I'm not calling about an Advance Fee Fraud."

"So you say, Ms. Adams and you might truly believe that you are part of nothing beyond a simple business transaction, but the reality behind what you have been told could be completely false. Representing foreign companies in collection matters with the government of Nigeria or its affiliates such as the Nigerian National Petroleum Corporation can be a very risky activity for Nigerian nationals if anything goes wrong. It could mean summary execution by secret morality squads or years in prison from which there is very little chance of ever exiting. Personally I prefer not to take the risk."

"That's exactly why I have asked the Nigerian Bar to refer me to someone like you and I assure you that you would be well rewarded for your services, should you take on my business."

"And what is your business, Ms. Adams?"

"Baltimore General Services has two invoices with the NNPC, which date from xxxx. All the field reports, all the inspection reports and every other requirement for payment have been submitted. I have been in touch with the NNPC and told all that remains for a recommendation to the Debt Reconciliation Committee is a Release Certificate from the NNPC.

At the present time, it is totally impossible for me to go to Nigeria and handle this affair. In addition to Baltimore General Services, I am a consultant and am currently working on a very demanding contract with a US government department. I would like to give a lawyer in Nigeria a limited Power of Attorney to do nothing, but sign the Release Certificate on behalf of Baltimore General Services."

"As the Americans say, Ms. Adams, you seem to have your ducks in order, at least from your point of view, but lots could still go wrong. There have been many incidents reported in Nigerian newspapers of other international companies who showed up in Nigeria to sign the release documents for the NNPC only to learn that the file had been lost and even worse, field reports and inspection reports had been forged. Some of their representatives were arrested."

"I assure you that nobody will be getting arrested in this matter."

Arthur James

"I'll tell you what, Ms. Adams; you fax me a copy of your invoices and any documentation that you have received from the NNPC or Debt Reconciliation Committee. When I have reviewed them, and if they seem in order, I will fax you instructions to transfer $1,000 to me via Western Union. You will then phone me and give me the secret code so that I can have the pick-up made. Your $1,000 will cover my review of your documents and one visit by me to the NNPC to verify the veracity of your claim and that all the documentation is in your file and appears to be legitimate. If everything seems in order, then we will discuss the terms and the cost of the Power of Attorney. Does that sound fair enough to you?"

"I wouldn't have it any other way, Mr. Offuya."

"Well, I'll say good day to you, Ms. was it Angelou?"

"Yes!"

"Ms. Angelou Adams, and one last request, please don't give my telephone or fax number to anyone else."

"Certainly Sir, you may count on me."

Christina closed the medical text book and set it aside. She decided to check her email at University, before getting ready to go to Cabot to meet Sebastian for lunch. There was only a short note from Jewel saying that she had received her message and wouldn't look for her in the Library on Saturday. While she was at it, she decided to check her In Box at DC Meets. There was a message from Yellow Cloud. Since they had both taken Spanish as their foreign language in high school, lately they'd been sending each other messages in the language.

**

To: nightshadow@dcmeets.com
From: yellowcloud@dcmeets.com
Subject: Café

Hola Night Shadow,
¿Cómo estás? ¿Te gustaria ir a tomar un café?
(How are you? Would you like to meet for coffee?)
Si no, no hay drama!
(If not, no drama!)
Buenas noches,
Yellow Cloud

**

Christina replied briefly,

*

To: yellowcloud@dcmeets.com

The Adams Sisters

From: nightshadow@dcmeets.com
Subject: Re: Café

Quizas
(Maybe)

Hasta Luego
Night Shadow

*

She logged out of DC Meets and went to get dressed.

Sebastian was waiting in a deep soft leather sofa, on the far side of the cold fireplace at the Club's front entrance. He called out and waved as she came through the door.

"Christa!"

"Hi Sebast!"

She sat down beside him.

"How's things?" he inquired.

"Oh, I'm simply swimming in it. I was reading Pediatrics all morning. The second step of the USMLE is about the only thing I see anymore. However, I did manage to make some adjustments to the sketch of the house you gave me. I've penciled them in on a photocopy. I'll spread it all out here on the table if you like?"

"Yea that would be excellent!"

They went through the modifications she thought would be appropriate for the next twenty minutes. Each change was discussed in detail. Sebastian wanted the why's and where for's. When it was finished, he suggested that they go inside for lunch. She gathered all the sheets of paper together, put them back in a plain file folder, attached the clip and handed it to him.

During the meal, they discussed medical school, the upcoming exam, her internship and their families. Once the coffee was served, Sebastian looked at her seriously and touched the tips of the fingers on her right hand.

"You know Christa, that's a lot of busy, busy, busy that's coming up in your life."

"I know!" she acknowledged.

"There still isn't going to be much time for you and me for almost another year."

"I've been thinking about that too. It really isn't fair to you to be alone in Philadelphia."

"I'm not exactly alone."

158 Arthur James

"I know you have friends, Sebastian. You couldn't go to U Pen and work in that city all this time and not meet people. I sort of expected that you had a social life, but I really don't want to know about it. You're a very attractive man. I'm sure the ladies don't let you by without a smile. But from my side, you knew how it was from the day your mother and my mother introduced us.

I'm just friends with anybody, until I get this medicine thing signed sealed and delivered. It's hard to get a place to intern. Some people have been notified that they'll have to do a time share intern arrangement, between several smaller centers in Maryland and Virginia."

"I'm going to be honest with you, Christa. When we were introduced, I was on the rebound from a Florida party girl. I had even told my mother I really wanted to meet a nice family type of girl and settle down. Everything I've said to you or done with you, since we met has been legit. Even this house is legit."

"I've never had any doubts you weren't straight forward with me, Sebastian.

"You know I had an architectural illustrator prepare the preliminary sketches of the house for me."

"I could tell it wasn't you who had made these sketches, Sebastian. They're professional."

"It was somebody I knew from U Pen."

"A she somebody?"

"Yes!"

"And?"

"And I had an accident. We had to meet several times to work up the sketches and then she started phoning. All we did was talk about the house. She wanted to see the lot where it was going to be built, so I offered to take her up to Welsh Valley on a Sunday afternoon, about six weeks ago. Since then we've had three or four diners together. We were small talking last week over drinks, when she said she would like to live in a house like that. I don't remember what I said, but we started talking as if she maybe would."

"Have you slept with her Sebastian?" Christina demanded angrily.

"No!"

"Well, I think you need to do some thinking about you and me and you and this illustrator. I'm sorry, but I can't be a part of it. If I get emotional about this, I could very likely miss the MLE. I've put so much into it for all these years. I think I would have a depression and maybe die, if I don't make it through them."

The Adams Sisters

"I understand you perfectly, Christa. I went down the same road with GMAT. You'll see; it's nothing."

"Sebastian, I reserved a horse for 2 o'clock. I think I better go and get changed into my riding clothes."

She stood up and picked up a small black leather backpack purse from the chair beside her.

"You don't have to walk me out Sebastian." She turned and left without even telling him she would be doing the USMLE at the Philadelphia Prometric Test Center.

It was 1:50 p.m. when she exited the women's change room and walked across the sandy soil towards the barn to tell the stable attendant she had arrived. When she entered the barn door, it took a minute or two for her eyes to adjust from the bright sunlight outside. When she could see clearly, it was too late. The tall, muscular blond male in a white lab coat had seen her and began to approach. She was feeling reclusive, because of the conversation with Sebastian, but put on a wide smile and greeted him.

"Hi Tod, I didn't expect to see you again so soon."

"Neither did I. It's simply prodigious!"

"What did you just say?" she asked impatiently.

"I said neither did I, but the Club called last night. They have two sick mares."

"No, I meant what did you say after neither did I?" she repeated.

"Oh, it's simply prodigious."

"That's it, prodigious. I've never heard anybody use that word before."

"Neither have I. It's something I invented to break the habit of saying awesome."

"It's you! This can't be."

"It's me what?" he asked good-humoredly.

Christina was so astonished and frustrated all at the same time that the words, Yellow Cloud, slipped out. Now it was his turn to absorb the reality of what had just happened. The smile disappeared from his face.

"You...Night Shadow?"

"Oh, this too much," she burst out angrily. "I can't take any more of this today, first Sebastian and now you. How did you track me down?"

"I didn't track you down."

The stable attendant came up to them leading her horse, which was already saddled.

"Miss Adams, your horse is ready."

She looked at him and then at Tod. She could feel her throat beginning to tighten and tears coming in at the corners of her eyes.

"I'm sorry, but I won't be going out riding today. I have to go."

She turned and ran back towards the women's changing room. It didn't take long to get out of her riding attire. Soon she was out on the River Road and then on the Macarthur Blvd. NW. When she arrived home, she had regained herself control and walked upstairs as if nothing had happened. She went straight to her computer and logged into DC Meets. It took but a few short clicks to delete her profile and then close her account.

On Monday, Samantha didn't say a word to Mr. Walters about the telephone conversation she had over the weekend with the lawyer, Ibrim Offuya. On Tuesday, she received a fax, which had been converted into email by Fifth Dimension Offices.

**

To: baltimoregeneralservices@5thdimension.com
From: operations@5thdimension.com
Subject: Fax from Abuja

February 11th, 20xx
2456 Palm Court
Abuja, Nigeria

Dear Ms. Angelou Adams,

I received your faxes and examined everything very carefully. Fifteen million dollars is a very large sum of money to be owed. I am surprised that you haven't gone bankrupt.

Be that as it may, your affair interests me, and I am willing to go one step further and examine the Baltimore General Services file at the Nigerian National Petroleum Corporation office here in Abuja.

I am a much respected lawyer here in the Federal Capital. I don't really want it to get out that my name is involved in this affair, no matter how legitimate it may be – and if I may add, that particular point has not yet been established.

My articling student's name is Banjo Olawole. I would like you to make two $500 transfers to Banjo, on two different days, from two different Western Union locations in Baltimore. When they have been completed, please phone me personally and give me the secret words for each transfer.

If that is satisfactory to you, I await your call.
With much sincerity,

The Adams Sisters

Ibrim Offuya
Barrister & Solicitor
 # 98256

**

Roscoe Walters was in meetings, in downtown Washington, all day Wednesday. Samantha stopped by her bank at noon and withdrew $1,000. She called Mrs. Yamato during the afternoon and said that she would have supper with a friend. As soon as she left work, she joined the stream of cars headed east on Independence Avenue and then turned onto Pennsylvania Avenue. Before long she was driving north along the Anacostia Parkway, headed for the Beltway and then on to Baltimore, where she would transfer $500 to Banjo Olawole, at a Western Union counter, using the secret words: *Liberty Bell*.

When Christina came in on Wednesday night, Mrs. Yamato told her a man had called. There was no message. He would call back later. She was finishing the last of her evening meal when the phone rang. Mrs. Yamato had already gone home. Charles Adams went to answer the call.

"Christa, it's for you."

She excused herself from the table and went and took the receiver from her father.

"Hello!"

"Christa, it's me Tod. Please don't hang up. I must talk to you."

"One moment, please. I'm going to take this on another phone."

Charles was already walking back to the dining room.

"Daddy."

"Yes?"

"I'm going to take this up in my room. Would you please hang up, when you hear me answer on the other phone?"

"No problem, but make it quick. I just thought of something I want to say to your mother and I don't want to forget it."

"I'll be quick."

She picked up the phone in her room and said, "Hello," then heard the downstairs phone click.

"Tod, how did you get this number?"

"That day during the blizzard at the hospital you told me that you lived with your parents on R Street near Georgetown U. There's only one Adams on R Street NW."

"Why are you calling me?"

"You said maybe to my last email asking you if you wanted to have a cup of coffee and I couldn't get back to you because your profile is gone."

"I deleted my profile."

"Why?"

"Tod, you know who I am. I'm so embarrassed about saying all those things to you in the email."

"There was nothing wrong in what we said and what about me? You know me, and I told you all those things too."

"You didn't call me up to ask me to go for coffee did you?"

"No."

"Then why did you call?"

"You said maybe and I didn't want to lose it."

"Even after you know who I am?"

"Yes, even after I know who you are."

"How did you pick me out of the thousands of girls, who are registered at DC Meets?"

"I ran searches by keywords on the profiles that didn't include a picture. There were about ten of you who had horses in your interests. I printed out the ten and analyzed each one then gave them a number from one to ten. Yours was number one, so I contacted you first."

"Have you contacted the others?"

"No, you replied and I was too busy to be having conversations with more than one girl online. I'd like to talk to you face to face Christa – away from the Internet, away from the Wave, away from Cabot Golf, Hunt, and Equestrian Club."

"And where would that be? You can't come around here."

"Have you ever heard of Assateague Island?"

"Yes, it's one of the barrier islands off the Maryland coast."

"There's a state park there. The park is inhabited by several dozen bands of wild ponies."

"I've seen pictures of them," she informed him.

"On Sunday I'm going to Assateague to collect data on the ponies for a course assignment. I'd like to take you there to show you the ponies.

"Tod I can't just go running off to some state park on Sunday. I don't even know your last name. What about studying?"

"My last name is Evans. You could study in the car on the way there. It's about a two hour drive."

"But you would talk to me."

"No, I wouldn't."

"Then I would talk to you."

The Adams Sisters

"Does that mean you'll come, Christa?"

"I don't know, Tod. Maybe we should leave it in the email."

"You were thinking about coming out of the email, in the last message that you sent to me."

"Tod, I sent that message to someone named Yellow Cloud, but everything has changed."

"Nothing has changed Christa. You're still you, and I'm still me."

"What time are you leaving?"

"I thought I'd get underway about 6 a.m."

"That's so early."

"I could make it later."

"No keep it at 6."

"Does that mean you are coming?"

"Where am I going to meet you? You can't come to the house."

"Name a spot."

"There's a park down the street called Montrose Park. I'll wait for you on a swing."

"I won't be late."

"I have to go Tod. I'll see you Sunday."

"Okay, I'll see you Sunday. Don't forget to bring your camera, the ponies are gorgeous, and Christa."

"Yes."

"Thank you."

"Now I really have to go Tod, bye."

"Bye."

Thursday evening Samantha went back to Baltimore. She transferred another $500 to Banjo Olawole, at the Western Union counter, in a drugstore using the secret words: *Ben Franklin*. On Friday, she called Ibrim Offuya to give him the two sets of secret words. Near 4 p.m. Roscoe Walters face appeared in a pop up window on her computer screen.

"Hi Sir, how were your meetings?"

"There was a lot happening, but I came out alive. How was your week? Hear anything more from those gold diggers in Africa?"

"As a matter of fact I did," she answered and then quickly updated him.

"I wish you hadn't gone and spent a $1,000 like that."

"You weren't around, Sir," she explained, defending herself. "I won't submit a receipt for the thousand dollars if you'd rather I didn't."

"No, it's ok this time, but don't send any more money, before I authorize it."

"I won't Mr. Walters."

"I have a few more people on my list, whom I haven't seen all week, and I want to drop in on then via this screen, before they leave. You have a good weekend Samantha."

"You too Mr. Walters," she replied and his face disappeared from her screen.

At ten to six Sunday morning, Christina left a note on the kitchen counter saying she had gone to the University early to get a good day of studying in. After doing so, she closed the back door behind her, crossed the yard, walked down the cement stairs and unlatched the heavy door, which opened into the dead end lane behind the house. It was cool. She was carrying a shoulder bag in which she had put two lunches, a pair of gloves and her digital camera. She went around the block and came up in front of Dumbarton House. There were already two people in Montrose Park.

Tod showed up at 6:05 a.m. He parked the car and walked towards the swings. She was wearing hiking shoes, khakis and an open lightweight, quilted rose vest on top of a light blue fleece pullover. He took the empty swing beside her and said, "Hi." She was smiling. He knew the day was going to go down well.

"Did you have breakfast?" She shook her head no. "Neither did I. Let's grab some donuts and coffee to go. Know a good spot nearby?"

"There's a place down on M Street in Georgetown village. They open at 6 a.m. on Sunday."

"Good we'll stop there. You ready?"

"Yup." They lifted themselves off the swing seats and went to his car. "You sure this car will go that far?" she joked. He didn't reply.

A half an hour later they sipped hot coffee and nibbled donuts as the Audi sped along P Street. Not long after passing through Dupont Circle, they turned onto Rhode Island Avenue. It leads into Maryland, where they switched to the Annapolis Road, which headed due east.

"Weren't you going to do some reading?" he inquired.

"I didn't bring a book."

He looked over at her smiling, "Then we're talking?"

She turned up the end of her nose and replied, "That's what today is all about, isn't it?"

The Adams Sisters

"Okay, to get us warmed up, we must make one stop along the way."

"Must?" she joked

"My mother prepared a care package for my brother, who is at the US Naval Academy in Annapolis. She wants me to drop it off."

"I didn't know you had a brother at Annapolis. Tell me about him." From that point on, until they turned off Route 50 to go down into the City of Annapolis, Tod told her about his family.

After becoming the capital of Maryland in 1695, Annapolis also became the first peacetime capital of the United States. Today there are two Annapolis's, the old inner harbor downtown, which has been designated a National Historic Landmark and the rest, which is like anywhere in contemporary America. As travelers arrive from the freeway, the first hub is the traffic circle formed by the streets skirting the circumference of the State House. The other hub is the harbor, which has made the town world-renowned as America's Sailing Capital.

Main Street in Annapolis is full of pubs. West Street is home to a strange collection of clubs, art galleries, and restaurants. The United States Naval Academy is located at the end of College Street. The Academy is a 338 acre campus known as the Yard. Like all midshipmen, Morgan Evans lived in Bancroft Hall, which he and everyone else called; Mother B. Jimmy Carter is among the Academy's alumni.

Tod found a place to park on King George Street. From there, they proceeded on foot to the Academy's Gates. They were stopped by a brisk, lean guard in full uniform, who was carrying a heavy rifle. Both visitors showed picture ID and the military man let them pass on in, after scanning the box Tod was carrying, with a portable metal detector. It was only a little after seven, but Morgan was waiting for them outside. He was clad completely in white, with a flat peaked disk cap propped on his head.

"Hey Morgan," his older brother hailed. The young man snapped up straight and saluted. "At Ease!" Tod said with a low awkward voice. The young, soon to be 2nd lieutenant smiled and relaxed.

"What did you bring me, Tod?" his brother prompted. "It sure is a big box."

"Mom said it was a care package for you and that I wasn't to open it, so your guess is as good as mine."

Christina stood off to the side watching them. This was the first of the new Tod that she was seeing, outside the computer. She found it curious the way the two boys jostled with each other."

"Morgan, I'd like to introduce you to someone."

"Sure," the younger brother said looking at Christina.

"This is a friend of mine, Christa Adams."

"Pleased to meet you, Christa."

Christina felt shy. She didn't know what she should say, "Hi Morgan, your brother and I are going on a field trip to Assateague, to observe some of the pony bands and collect data."

"Oh, cool, I wish I was going with you," the uniformed young man said, stepping towards her, with his cap under one arm and an outstretched hand.

She shook hands with him then stepped back a pace, before adding, "Why don't you come with us?"

"I'd love to, but we're on parade this afternoon. Have you ever been to Assateague before?

"No!" she replied, squinting into the rising sun. "Why?"

"You have to be careful of what Tod tells you."

"Morgan, she doesn't have to know," Tod interjected.

Christa flashed a devilish glance at the older brother then exhorted, "Yes I do, Morgan. Tell me."

"The last time I went to the island with him, he had me collect a bag full of this strange looking sea weed that he wanted to analyze at home, because he thought the wild ponies might be eating it. When we took it home, my mom had to tell him that it was dried pony manure, which had been exposed to saltwater and the sun." He started laughing, and Tod gave him a light punch in the shoulder.

Just then two other students, who were dressed the same as Morgan, came out of Mother B. "Hey, Morg, what'cha got in the box. You know the rules, one for all and all for one."

"That doesn't apply to boxes from home."

"Sure it does, just think, if we were stranded on a desert island there wouldn't be any yours and ours."

"Sorry guys, but the Academy isn't a desert island."

Tod interrupted them, "Anyway, Morgan, I can't stay too long. We still have a long drive."

"You two go ahead. I have a small question of protocol to settle here. Nice meeting you, Christa. Have yourselves an excellent day."

"We will," they said and headed back to the car.

The Adams Sisters

The Audi stayed on Route 50, which went all the way to Ocean City. During this leg of the trip, Christina opened up somewhat and told him a little about her sister and parents. About two miles before Ocean City, they turned off on to a secondary road and followed it for ten minutes, until they arrived at the Assateague Island Visitors Center, which was closed for the season. The old Audi continued on over the small humped bridge to the island.

The name Assateague comes from a Native American word meaning, 'marshy place across'. The 37 mile long island is split in two by a fence at the Maryland-Virginia state line. Legend has it that a Spanish galleon loaded with horses was shipwrecked along the beach in the 1600's. The ponies of Assateague have been made famous in the novel called, 'Misty of Chincoteague.'

Tod had obtained an Off Road Vehicle Permit to drive the Over Sand Vehicle Route along 13 miles of beach area, because he was equipped with a set of boots for the rear wheels of the car, which made them similar to a pair of tractor wheels. Once Tod wrapped the tracks around the rear wheels, and secured them well, they drove along the Over Sand Route to the half way mark and then he parked behind some dunes. Christina got out and stretched. He unloaded a backpack from the trunk and looped it over his shoulders.

"How much work do you have to do here today?" she asked.

"It shouldn't take me more than three hours."

"Good! I'm going to go exploring for a while and take some pictures. Who knows, maybe I'll see a wild pony. If you're not done, when I get back, I'll give you a hand."

"Oh, you'll see a pony, it's guaranteed. That's why I parked at this spot."

"Are you hungry? she asked.

"A little."

"Wanna have a sandwich, before I go. I packed two lunches."

"Love one," he replied. "How about coffee, I have a thermos."

"Love one," she mimicked playfully.

After their snack Christina set off walking southward along the dry sand. Busy little sandpipers ran up and down the beach. It was a warm day, and the wind was in her face. Beach grass grew out of every dune. The sand was littered here and there with little bits of the sea. There were lots of snail and mussel shells as well as blue crab claws.

Something caught her eye being flipped over and over in the surf. She approached the water. It was a horseshoe crab shell. She remembered learning in primary school that the horseshoe crab crawled along the ocean floors, when the dinosaurs inhabited the earth.

The young woman had walked for half an hour before there was any sign of ponies. Then as if by magic, she spotted fresh tracks in the wet sand. She unstrapped her camera and followed the trail, which led away from the water into the dunes. Coming over the ridge of a dune, she saw four dark brown ponies grazing on beach grass. One had a white mane and two had white from their knees down to their hoofs. They hadn't heard her approach in the soft sand, and because she was downwind of them, they hadn't picked up her scent.

Quietly she slipped her digital camera out of its case and took several shots. Suddenly all the ponies' heads reared up in one motion, and four pairs of black eyes stared directly at her. It was over in several seconds. They startled, turned about and disappeared over the top of another dune. She started to follow their tracks. They led back down towards the wet sand. This time she was careful.

She went back into the dunes and walked in the direction that the ponies had gone. When she spotted them out in the surf, she lay down in the sand and used the zoom on her camera. Soon she had half a dozen shots of four wild ponies splashing about in the surf. That's called being paid she thought, getting up and continuing on.

After five minutes, she heard the whining of a pony, somewhere in the dunes and began to take her steps very cautiously. The animal's call became much clearer. She was sure it was over the next ridge of sand, so dropped down on her hands and knees and crawled forward. Her eyes just came over the top of the dune, and she froze still. Not fifteen feet in front of her a mare stood facing into the breeze with a foal lying in the sand at her hind legs. It was obvious that the mare had given birth, but a short time ago. A membrane sack was still attached to the mother and foal. Christina took as many pictures of the two as she could from her laying down position in the sand.

The young medical student didn't want to disturb the new mother and her child, so she crawled backwards down the face of the dune and didn't stand up before she had wiggled

The Adams Sisters

completely over the top of another ridge of sand and down into a hollow, which had formed on the other side.

When Christina stood up, shook the sand out of her clothing and then looked at her watch. She had been gone an hour and decided to go and find the Over Sand Route, which she would follow back to Tod's car. Along the way, there were several patches of marsh on the east side of the Route. At one point, a tall blue heron walked up out of the water and looked at her very wisely, before returning to its hunt for food.

Tod was three quarters finished his to do list, when she arrived back at the car. She helped him with the last of his chores and then the two of them gathered up his equipment. When all his gear and samples were stowed away in the trunk of the Audi, they sat on a log and finished off the sandwiches and coffee.

"So, did you find any ponies?" he inquired.

"Oh, yes!"

"Any in the waves?"

"Yup."

"What else?"

She felt a little strange but told him anyway, "I found a mare giving birth in a dune."

"That is a rare sight. I've never seen it in the wild, only in the barn."

"I have at least half a dozen digital pictures of them. When I download them to my computer, I'll send you a few by email."

"I'll give you my email address at home."

"Thanks."

In spite of several bursts of conversation, they were both quieter during the drive back to Washington than they had been that morning. As they entered Georgetown, Tod asked her where she would like to be let off.

"You can take me to my house."

When he stopped the car in the curved red brick driveway, she turned towards him and began to speak slowly.

"I had a great day Tod and I thank you very much for inviting me. You're a nice boy outside of the computer, and I don't regret my maybe. I really learned a lot about you today, and I have it all squirreled away in my mind.

Now I must be serious with you. I don't really have the time or mental resources to think a lot about today because I must put all of me into graduating and getting by the second step of the Medical Licensing Examination. I want you to give me your telephone number, and when I've cleared all the hurdles, I'll give you a call. Maybe we can go out for coffee. If you try to call me, before I'm ready that will spoil everything. I might even get frustrated with you and say something I would regret."

"I understand perfectly," he said while writing his phone number and email address on a note pad that he had taken from behind the sun visor. "I also must get through the end of Forth Year."

She opened the car door, then reached out and touched the top of his hand with two of her fingers. "Bye Tod, good luck with the end of your program."

He watched the thick red door close behind her, before putting the car in gear and driving off.

****

13 - Oxford Circus

"Is it relevant Samantha?" Roscoe Waters asked, seeing the young woman standing in the doorway of his office.

"Yes Mr. Walters."

"Ok, sit down. I don't mean to be brief with you. It's Al-Qaida. They're giving all of us the willies, with the classified information they're releasing on their Web site. The President is wondering if they have moles in the State Department."

"I'm sure it's only talk, Sir."

He looked at her, took a deep breath and said, "You made me feel better already. What's on your mind?"

"I've heard back from the lawyer, Ibrim Offuya. According to the Nigerian Bar fee schedule, the maximum he can charge is one tenth of one percent for summary acts of procedure or representation, when the value of contract in question is more than five hundred thousand."

Roscoe laughed, "Why can't terrorists be about money too? So, in other words, this little Nigerian lawyer wants $15,000 from Uncle Sam to prepare you a Power of Attorney with Dr. Lawrence Slick."

"Your calculation is the same as mine, Sir."

"Even if it went no further that means they would have earned $16,000 for taking the effort to send a couple dozen faxes and make a few phone calls. That's probably about twenty-five or thirty times what an ordinary person in Nigeria earns in a year. If they're doing the same thing with four or five American business people a year, they're living like kings."

"I was thinking the same thing, Mr. Walters."

The Watch Director asked, "Do you know that any amount of money transferred through Western Union, which is over $10,000 must be reported to the government?"

"I wasn't aware of that," she replied despondently.

"They'd be onto you and me in a minute and that's if I could even find the money."

"I hadn't considered the possibility that they'd be on to us, Sir, but I had my doubts about you authorizing that amount of money for a Power of Attorney."

"You're right, I can't authorize this expenditure; still, it has been good Sam. We've learned quite a bit more about these Nigerian advance fee frauds, by seeing this one from the inside. Now we'll release the file and everything you have into the general archive system.

"Archive, Sir?" she repeated with astonishment.

"This is peanuts, Samantha, and it's not what we're really paid to do. It was a good little assignment. You learned a lot, and nobody knows what you've seen, but me. Your Internship is almost over. I've told all the staff here at the Watch that I'm inviting you to sit down at the table with the rest of the family. There won't be any more Manhattan."

"This is incredible, Sir – Mr. Walters – Roscoe," she exclaimed. "I can't believe I made it. Now I can really start to look for an apartment."

"Yes you can," he agreed, "and there's more. Since you'll soon be feasting with the rest of us, you may as well get used to the main course."

She laughed and asked, "What's on the menu?"

"For the present, it's terrorism."

"Oh, I love terrorists, Roscoe," she told him enthusiastically. "I'll take them for breakfast, lunch, and supper."

Her boss was smiling. He liked it when an Intern came into the Watch to be part of the permanent staff. They were always so eager. "Go and see Mrs. Robinson in Command. Tell her, I said she should issue you our Basic Manual on Terrorism. You can take it home, but don't lose it or someone might say you're a mole."

"Should I kiss you now or when the Internship is officially finished."

The Adams Sisters

"Wait till it's done – when I tell everybody you're officially one of us."

She stood up, shook his hand and went off to see Mrs. Robinson. That evening, while she was reading the Manual, Dr. Lawrence Ossaga telephoned. He wanted to know how things were going with the lawyer. She told him that he had agreed to accept if she paid him $15,000.

"Well, you're going to of course?"

"I put the matter to my Board of Directors today. I'm sorry, Doctor, but they won't authorize the spending of any company funds for this Power of Attorney. Some of them have advanced money to the business. They said this has gone far enough. They said it sounded like another Nigerian financial scam."

"Then I'm lost."

"I'm very sorry to hear that Lawrence, but we all must accept the restraints of reality. I live with a Board of Directors, and I can only imagine what you live with."

"That means my Father's people are going to continue dying."

"How's that Doctor?"

"If there won't be any pumps; then there won't be any good water. My father's people will continue to drink the water from the surface ponds that surround our villages. The water becomes brackish at the height of the dry season and several times a year the ponds become incubators for parasites. If the people ingest these organisms, microscopic bugs will cut their insides to pieces."

"Dr. Ossaga, this is the second occasion that you have mentioned pumps. To what are you referring?"

"With my share of the money, I was going to have artesian wells drilled and equipped with pumps in or close to each of the villages that my father once presided over. That would give each village a clean, reliable source of water, year round."

"Isn't that a problem for the state? What do they do with all the money they get from selling that oil?"

"The government won't buy water pumps with the oil money. I'm sorry to say, but not much oil revenue trickles down to the people. Most of it goes to pay for luxuries for those who are in power."

"Wouldn't you like to spend your share of the $15 million on luxuries too?"

"Ms. Adams, I have studied many things, but there is nothing in what I studied that will put clean, reliable water in the mouths of my people. You Americans have a saying, "Money talks, and cash is King!" The saying is as applicable in Nigeria as it is in the US."

"You should have gone into business and used the money you would have made to help your people."

"Sometimes I think I should have taken the Chieftain from my father."

"But then your father's villages would never have reached democracy."

"Angelou, democracy is only a word. Nobody can give democracy. It must be chosen, and the necessary sacrifices made to put the structures in place, so it will work. Democracy is a very fragile commodity, in a very furious world."

"I know" she replied. "The French too have a proverb, which sums it up well."

"What is their proverb?"

"Man is a wolf for man!"

"They understand much."

"Are you a wolf, Dr. Ossaga?"

"I am not a wolf, Ms. Adams and that's why I can't help my people."

"You shouldn't say things like that Lawrence."

"It's true. Do you know why I phoned you?"

"To see if Ibrim would accept to do a Power of Attorney, so that you would be issued the Release Certificate."

"There was that, but there was another reason."

"What other reason?"

"I was going to tell you that several hours ago the President of Nigeria announced that general elections are to be held during the first week of April."

"That wasn't much of a warning."

"It was enough for us. One member of the Debt Reconciliation Committee tendered his resignation. Others are thinking of resigning too."

"Are you thinking of resigning too?"

"I was going to stay long enough to get Baltimore General's invoices authorized and the money transferred."

"Do you think they will authorize the invoices?"

"Yes."

"Listen to me Larry. Don't resign yet. I'm going to use my own personal money. We must hang up now. I'm going to try to contact Mr. Offuya. We might still be able to get the Release Certificate signed in time."

The Adams Sisters

"Thank you, Ms. Adams. You don't realize it, but you may save the lives of dozens of people a year, for a very long time to come."

"Goodbye Doctor."

"Goodbye."

When she hung up, Samantha thought about what she had just done. She didn't know why she has done it – yes she did. She had to know – she had to bring closure to this whole charade, if not for the Department then for herself.

As she dialed the lawyer's number, her mind was working forward. Roscoe had said that all transfers over $10,000 were reported so she would have to make two transfers again.

She heard a horn tone on the other end of the line. Oh, come on; be there, the young woman whispered. The tone sounded again and again. She waited almost five minutes, before beginning to give in. Then all of a sudden the horn stopped and a voice could be heard on the line.

"Hello!" she cried out.

"Hello!" came the reply.

"Mr. Offuya?"

"Speaking," a man's voice sounded.

"Mr. Offuya, this is Angelou Adams."

"Yes, Ms. Adams. I hear you."

"Mr. Offuya, I received your fax. I accept."

"Good, I'm glad. You must hurry though. They've called for elections. The Debt Reconciliation Committee will soon be dissolved."

"I'll wire it tomorrow. I'll make two transfers again."

"No, Ms. Adams, listen to me, you can't transfer any more money to me in Nigeria. This place is not safe. I can't send my articling student again to do a pick-up. It's too large. He might be tempted, or he might be intercepted and robbed or even killed. In addition, a transfer of that size would be flagged in the system several times and adverse interests who would never know of your affair would suddenly be all eyes and want a part. They might even try to stop me from representing you."

"Then how, Mr. Offuya?"

"You must bring the money to me in person."

"Mr. Offuya, I'm hiring you to represent me because I can't go to Nigeria."

"I'm not asking you to go to Nigeria Ms. Adams. That would be worse than a cash transfer. The moment you got off the plane, the bloodhounds would pick up your scent. They would surely try to rob you. They might even kidnap you and demand a ransom from your company. If they ever saw me with you, I'd be done."

"Then what are you asking?" she demanded.

"It's much easier to go from Baltimore to London than it is from Baltimore to Abuja. I know for a fact that a round trip could be done in twenty-four hours. It might take you a week to come here and go back. Also, I will be better able to hide your payment from the vicious factions, who live in Abuja. They might demand half of my fee. I have a bank account in London, where I personally can deposit the money."

Samantha had heard enough. She would have called it all off if he hadn't added.

"Ms. Adams, I must warn you. You should not try to bring that much cash into England in your bag. If it were discovered, the authorities would probably take it from you and notify your government. Much has changed in the world since your 9/11. England only allows travelers to bring in $9,999 in cash, which is not declared. After that they suspect, you are something to do with terrorism."

"How am I supposed to get to England and get there with $15,000 in cash?"

"Getting there is easy, simply book a flight and book a return for 24 hours later. I must meet you on a weekday, when the banks are open and when we can get through to a Solicitor to draw up a Power of Attorney. As for the $15,000, you can make two $7,500 transfers to yourself in London. When you arrive, go to Western Union, show your passport, give the secret words, and they will issue you the cash."

"Do you think they really will?"

"Of course they will, Ms. Adams. Other business people do it every day. Nobody carries cash anymore. I would have thought that a consultant would have known things like that."

"All of my consulting work takes place within the US. My clients take care of their own travel plans. How shall I meet you in London?"

"Yes, how shall I locate you in London? That is a good question. I take it you've never been to London?"

"No."

"Do you even have a passport?"

"Yes, I have a passport?"

"Let's see. There is a 99.9% chance that your plane will land in Heathrow, the main international airport south west of the city. There are two ways of getting into town from there. You can take the Heathrow Express or the Tube. I would

The Adams Sisters

advise the Express. Its last stop is Paddington Station. You can't get lost. There are also three of four dozen small English hotels within walking distance."

"What about American Hotels?"

"Not around Paddington."

"Ok then, I'll check into an English hotel around Paddington. That should be a no brainer."

"A what?"

"Nothing it's an expression. What next?"

"Both Hyde Park and Kensington Gardens are quite close by."

"You mean a walk?"

"Distances aren't large. If you don't like walking, there are plenty of cabs."

"Ok, I'll meet you in Kensington Gardens. After I've had a chance to look at a map, I'll decide whether I'll walk to the Gardens or not." She sucked in a deep breath and continued, "Ok, Mr. Offuya, I'm in the Gardens. What am I looking for?"

"Well, me of course, Ms. Adams."

"I know I'm looking for you Ibrim, but where will you be or how will I know it's you?"

"Enter the Gardens by the Marlborough Gate and turn to your right. You'll pass an old English House. Stay on the walking path. Almost immediately, you will come to four artificial ponds, which are called The Fountains. I'll be sitting in one of the benches that are spaced out along the edge of the four ponds. I hope it won't be raining, but it probably will be. I'll be wearing a black trench coat, and I'll have a white brolly across my knees or I'll be sitting under it."

"Excuse me, but what's a brolly?"

"Sorry, Ms. Adams, in American that's an umbrella."

"All right, we're almost there. Mr. Offuya, do you have a current picture of yourself?"

"I can have one taken within an hour."

"Good, would you do that, please and then fax me a copy? I know it won't copy or transmit exactly like you look, but that will help me make a positive ID."

"All right, Ms. Angelou, I believe we have everything covered. I'll fax you the photograph, and you will telephone me as soon as you have booked a flight. Try to book so that you will arrive at Heathrow early in the morning. Once I know when you're arriving, I'll make my travel arrangements."

"What if you can't get a flight?"

"There are several flights, between Nigeria and London, every day. It's our favorite destination. I may even retire there."

"I see. That's why you have a bank account there?"

"Exactly, any more questions?"

"What if I report you to the Nigerian Bar?"

"Your complaint won't go any further than the Bar. They will only say the fee is according to their schedule. You will miss getting your Release Certificate in time, and the Debt Reconciliation Committee will be dissolved, as soon as we have the elections in April."

"Ok, I have no more questions."

"Then I wish you God speed in making your plans."

"Good bye Mr. Offuya."

"Same to you Ms. Adams."

On Thursday, Samantha phoned her mother to tell her that she had to go out of town on business for the Department. At noon, she told the Office Manager that she wasn't feeling well and wouldn't be in the next day. It was 4:30 pm when she left the underground parkade, and there was no time to waste. The gold Lexus GT crossed over the Potomac River on the Roosevelt Memorial Bridge, followed the signage for Interstate 66 and was soon headed for the Dulles International Airport. The United Airlines plane would lift off at 6:10 p.m. and she would be in Heathrow Airport, at 6:20 a.m. Friday March 7th.

The plane was ninety percent filled. Samantha was traveling under her own name but had brought the Angelou passport just in case that crafty old lawyer should ask for it. After supper and a movie, the lights were dimmed, and most of the passengers nodded off.

As soon as she cleared Customs and Immigration at Heathrow, the young woman entered the travelers' area of the Terminal. It seemed small and cramped when compared to Dulles. The first thing she did was find a cash machine. To her surprise the machine dispensed English pounds. She was under the impression that she needed Euros and so looked for another cash machine. The next one too dispensed English pounds. She decided to go to the information desk.

A middle aged woman in a blue suit and white blouse asked, "Good morning Miss, do you need a map?"

Samantha had trouble understanding what she was being asked, because of the woman's accent. "Could you tell me where I can find a cash machine, which dispenses Euros? Those ones over there are all giving English pounds."

The Adams Sisters

"The Euro dispensers are in the Departures area, Miss. The machines in Arrivals only give Pound Sterling."

"I thought England was part of Europe and that, in Europe, the Euro was the currency."

"England is not part of the Monetary Union," The Courtesy Assistant informed her. "We still use pounds in England, not Euros."

Samantha thanked her and went back to one of the cash machines, where she withdrew 250 pounds, using one of her cards. She caught herself thinking how easy it would be if the whole world used the American dollar.

The Heathrow Express is a sleek, new above ground train with padded armchairs and overhead monitors, which doesn't make many stops on its way into the city. It cost four times as much as the Underground; however, for tourists and business travelers arriving from the sky, it's a welcomed alternative.

At 8 a.m. Friday morning she stepped out onto the platform in Paddington Station and followed the other passengers as they walked towards the exits. The first thing she saw was an American hamburger joint at the end of the platform, where several stores and restaurants were located. She stopped into a bookstore and bought a Visitors Guide & Map. It only took a few minutes to locate Paddington Station in the Guide.

The street names around the station were the same as those that Ibrim Offuya had given her. She followed the overhead arrows indicating the 'Praed St. Exit' and was soon out on the sidewalk in the early morning day. It was misting lightly. She spotted an American franchised coffee shop across the street and headed towards the location thinking to herself that this was just like the US, except for the funny money.

With coffee and Danish in hand, Samantha found a table and had breakfast. Afterwards, she dug into the tote bag, which was the only luggage she was carrying and found a list of Western Union locations that she had printed off the Internet back in Georgetown. It took a while, but she found one on Praed St. On the way out she asked the cashier,

"Do you know of any good hotels nearby?"

The young man came around the edge of the counter and motioned for her to follow him up close to the window. "There's one over there; there's one across the street there and there are dozens down the two side streets at both ends of this block, which are called London St. and Spring St." She thanked him and left.

Western Union was in the same block as the coffee shop, so she made her way there directly. A young black woman with a heavy Jamaican accent served her. She counted out four piles of 50 pound notes; let Samantha double count each pile for for the correct number of notes, then put them into a brown envelope along with several smaller notes, some change, and a receipt. Samantha put the envelope into a string shoulder bag that she was wearing inside her micro fiber, charcoal trench coat.

From Western Union, she proceeded to a large hotel located on the other side of the street. The desk clerk wasn't the least surprised that she didn't have any luggage. Once she had locked the room door behind her, she stripped off the black jewel-neck jacket and matching flared skirt that she had worn to work on Thursday, picked up the money and went straight into the shower.

After standing under the refreshing blast of water for ten minutes, the young woman dried herself. Then she put back on the same clothes she had been wearing and left the hotel room. It was 11 am when she arrived back on the sidewalk. The majority of the traffic was comprised of red double decker buses and traditional black Fairway cabs.

The thought of hailing a cab crossed her mind, but her body rejected it. The long trans-Atlantic flight had been enough sitting. The first thing she must become accustomed to was looking to the right instead of the left, when crossing the street.

In a matter of minutes, Samantha found Spring St. and then Sussex Gardens, which ran into Westbourne St. Soon she could see a high gate and open park beyond. Once through the gate, she turned right, as Ibrim Offuya had instructed and almost immediately was in front of the old English house he had mentioned. It was a two storey L shaped structure, built of grey brick with a high peaked roof. The windows were deeply recessed into the walls and made of pieces of cut glass fitted in a diagonal lead grid. A low iron gate blocked the path leading up to the door.

Off to her left, on the lower ground, she could see four fountains, which are located in an area known as the Italian Gardens. Several people were sitting on the benches on the far side of the ponds. As she approached them, she noticed an African man sitting off by himself with something white stretched across his knees. She walked up closer and caught his eyes following her. He was an older man, about the same age as her father. Before sitting down, she inquired,

The Adams Sisters

"Mr. Offuya, Mr. Ibrim Offuya?"

"Yes, it's me. Please sit down."

She sat on the outer edge of the bench, turned towards him and put out her hand. Instinctively he shook it and then said, "Please forgive my caution, but would you mind showing me your passport."

She slipped her hand inside her coat and produced the Angelou Adams passport. Once he had looked at it; he handed it back and continued, "Welcome to London Ms. Adams."

"I can't really believe that I'm sitting here talking to you."

"It's all real. How was your flight?"

"I dozed on and off for several hours, but I am tired."

"Ah yes, jet lag. It should be about your bed time now at home. But anyway, Angelou, we shouldn't sit here gabbing. I've reserved an appointment at a solicitor for any time between 1 and 5 p.m. Have you been to Western Union?" She patted her side. "Good, very good, what we should do is catch a cab and have the driver drop us near the solicitor's office. We could go for a bite, before seeing him."

"Sounds fine to me; I've only had a Danish today."

They were the first clients to arrive after lunch. A legal secretary showed them into a book lined library, where she had the documents laid out, which had been prepared in advance. Samantha had to show her passport again, sign an affidavit to the effect that she had the authority to represent Baltimore General Services and was duly authorized to give a Power of Attorney. The English solicitor, a middle aged man wearing a navy blue chalk stripped suit, would have preferred that she had a signed resolution from the Board of Directors bearing the company seal, but he let them go on that particular detail since the Power of Attorney was going to be executed outside England.

When they returned to the street, Ibrim cleared his throat loudly and asked, "Now then Angelou, do you have something for me?"

She pulled the brown envelope out of her coat and handed it to him. "There were $15,000 US dollars in the transfer when it started out. I'm not sure how many pounds are there now, but the receipt is included, and I haven't taken any of it out."

"I'm sure everything will be fine," he replied putting the envelope inside his trench coat. "What time is your plane?"

"I fly back at midnight tonight. I'm going to try to get some sleep, when I get back to the hotel."

"Well, I must be off to my bank. Let me hail you a cab."

"Where are we in relation to Paddington Station? I'd like to see something of this city before I rush back to the States."

"We're at the corner of Tottenham Court Road and Oxford Street a bit East of Oxford Circus. If you walk back West on Oxford and continue, when it changes into Bayswater Road, you will eventually pass right in front of Marlborough Gate, where you entered Kensington Gardens. From there, you should know your way."

She thanked him; they shook hands, and then he hailed a cab for himself. Samantha looked back over her shoulder and saw his cab pulling away from the curb. It had all seemed too simple to her. He hadn't even asked the name of her hotel. As she walked, everything turned over in her head. He's probably having me followed. I don't want him to find out that I'm not going back, until Sunday. I should run that old dodge routine we used in Manhattan. She looked for a store located on a corner. They were the shops, which had the best odds of having a side door opening onto another street.

She entered a large music store on Oxford Circus and then quickly took another exit through to the side street. There was a lane, directly across the street from her. She walked briskly to the opening between two buildings. At the other end she could see cars passing, so advanced. Arriving at the far end of the narrow passage, first she looked back over her shoulder to be sure she wasn't being followed and then she looked to her left, towards Oxford Street. Two cabs waited on the corner. She opened the door of the first vehicle in line and climbed in.

"Where to Miss?"

"I'd like to go to Paddington Station."

"Right you are."

As he was pulling away, she looked out through the back window. Once again, no one seemed to be following. When the cabbie let her out, she pretended to be entering the Station. After he had driven off, she doubled back and made straight for the hotel, where she fell asleep for five or six hours.

When Samantha awoke, she was hungry. Before leaving her parents' place on Thursday morning, the young woman had slipped several changes of underwear, a pair of soft soled leather shoes, a long sleeve acrylic sweater, a pair of white jeans and a boiled wool jacket into a shoulder bag. She got dressed in the casual clothes, flipped through the Visitor's Guide and went outside, where she got into another cab.

"Where to Miss?"

The Adams Sisters

"Take me to the West End, please."
"Any place particular in the West End?
"How about the Odeon?"
"The Odeon Pantheon or the Odeon West End?"
"West End will be fine."

The cinema was located on Leicester Square, which by night is one of the busiest spots in London. Street animators entertained the crowds with anything from an impromptu song to a political rant; tourists paid good money to have their faces ridiculed by cruel cartoonists and suburban youth lined up at several clubs to dance the night away. Samantha checked the billboard above a cinema. The Pianist by Polanski was starting at nine. She had two hours to have something to eat and explore the neighborhood.

By 9 am Saturday morning the mist had burned off. Samantha was eager to see some of the sights. Today she decided to be venturesome and try to go to the Houses of Parliament using the Underground. At Paddington station, she boarded a southbound train on the Circle line and was soon at Westminster Station. After Parliament, it was Big Ben. From there, she walked to the Westminster Pier and took a boat cruise along the Thames River as far as Greenwich. Some of the sights included: St. Paul's, The Tower of London, Tower Bridge and the Docklands. The return trip to the central city was on a bus having Paddington Station as its last stop.

Saturday evening, a young American bureaucrat ate late at a traditional pub, which served fish and chips, in addition to two dozen types of beer. Since she was alone, she took a high stool at the bar. The stools on both sides of her changed patrons twice, while she ate. Then, as she was ordering a second mug of sweet English lager, a tall casually dressed man sat down on the vacant stool to her right. He turned out to be from Australia. For an hour, she listened to stories about his life in the land-down-under.

Because she had to check out by 11 am Sunday morning, and since there was a light drizzle outside, Samantha decided to take a guided tour of the city in an animated double-decker bus. When it ended, she thought how lucky it had rained, as she may have spent the whole day wandering around on foot carrying a not so light shoulder bag, following a map and seeing little. In the late afternoon, the rain cleared up, and there was enough time to browse a few clothing stores, before she decided that she should start to make her way back out to Heathrow Airport. By then she was confident enough with the city and the Underground to take the Tube back to the airport, instead of the Heathrow Express.

****

The Adams Sisters

14 – Maybe

Late in March Sebastian received a small white card in the mail from Christina inviting him to attend her graduation, on Sunday May 25th. This was their first communication, since the day she had returned the house plans at the Club. He felt odd inside and leaned back in his leather executive's chair. His hands came up over his face, across the top of his head and then his fingers laced into each other, behind his neck.

Why did I get myself into this, he thought, closing his eyes? For a second, his mind flashed back to one of Penelope's paintings, which he hadn't bought. It was a girl in a white dress standing on the back of a yacht, throwing a round life preserver to a man who was struggling in the waves. The swells of foaming water were made of demons and devils, which lived under the water.

He opened his eyes, shook his head and reached for his Agenda. May 25th was open. He penciled in 'Christa's Graduation' then flipped back over the pages. Tomorrow the mechanical shovel was scheduled to go up to Welsh Valley, to remove the old foundation from the vacant lot so that construction could begin. He wanted to be there, at least long enough to shoot a few frames of film. Sebastian was planning to keep a complete a photographic record of the house from conception through to birth and moving in day. All his shots would be spliced together into a video.

The invitation said *rsvp* along the bottom and the return envelope was addressed to her. He flipped the card over and wrote.

*

Dear Christa,
  Congratulations!
  I can hardly wait to see you in your cap and gown.
Love,
Sebast

*

Sebastian went into the outer office, where an administrative assistant was busy preparing documents for an IPO. After sealing the envelope, he set it down on her desk.

"Would you make sure that gets in the mail today, please, Ms. Franklin?"

"Certainly, Sir," the thirtyish or so black woman replied.

"Thanks," he added politely, and then returned to his office. As he sat back down the telephone rang. He closed the Agenda, which still lay open at May 25th and answered the call.

"Sebastian speaking."

"Hi Sebastian, this is Aimee speaking."

"Aimee, I was just thinking about you."

"Sebastian, you probably say that to all the girls. How could you have been thinking of me, when we haven't seen each other in almost a month?"

"I kid you not, Aimee. Truth is my middle name."

"So Mr. Truth, how did I rate in your thinking?"

"Oh, you were being you."

"Where was I?"

"You were up in Welsh Valley with me, looking at the site."

"Have they started to work yet?"

"The heavy equipment arrives tomorrow to take out the remains of that old foundation. I'm going up for an hour or so in the morning to take a few pics."

"I've seen lots of framing and finishing of houses, but never a start."

"You haven't?"

"Nope."

"Wanna come?"

"Sure, I think I could fit that in, what time?"

The Adams Sisters

"I don't know yet exactly. The contractor is going to call me, when a flatbed truck and shovel are on their way. I'll call you as soon as I know and then I'll swing round and pick you up."

"Sounds fabulous!"

"Aimee, what were you calling about."

"Simply thought I'd touch bases," the illustrator replied.

"Glad you did. See you tomorrow."

"Bye," she purred into the phone.

At that moment, Sebastian had a second déjà vu. It was when he had gone to pick up Aimee the last time. She was coming down a set of stone stairs in a beige raincoat. A gust of wind caught the flap of her coat and flipped it open. Her long hair blew straight back over her shoulders. Sebastian remembered thinking how great she looked. Then he shook his head, smiled to himself and went back to work.

**

By mid-April, Samantha Adams had become a State Department Analyst I. She was assigned to Iraq and still reported to Roscoe Walters. To help her get her head into Bagdad, she was asked to submit a report on the toppling of Saddam Hussein's statue. Sometime later, Walters wanted to talk to her about the submission, so had emailed a meeting request, which she had accepted.

In the abstract of her research, she had summarized a number of observations of various aspects of the event.

1. *Notice the total lack of ordinary Iraqis in all the photos.*
2. *US troops appear to be in a loose, almost casual pattern about the statue, but if one looks closely, the soldiers have in fact set up a concentric control formation consisting of a tight inner ring and a second perimeter check-point part way up each street.*
3. *Notice the total lack of women, among the Iraqis militants who are toppling the statue.*
4. *The militants are all young males about the same age, who dress in a similar fashion.*
5. *Where did the flag come from? Are we to believe these young militants, who have been living in hostels or the streets for a long time, have managed to safeguard an Iraqis flag, which hasn't flown in the country for ten years.*
6. *Notice the similarity between this photo and the reproduction of a painting of American Patriots in New*

York, tearing down the statue of George III in 1776, while the Declaration of Independence was being read.

"This is a very astute hypothesis you put forward in this report Sam."

"I really haven't put forward a hypothesis Sir. It's only an analysis and several observations. I'm sure any military intelligence officer could refute it with little difficulty."

"We're not the military here Sam and because of that we must look at all possibilities and all angles."

"Do you mind if I ask you a few personal questions?"

"Not at all Sir."

"Have you ever been involved in any protests… maybe as a student?"

"No, I haven't. In addition, I've voted in every election, since I was old enough."

"How do you account for seeing, what might suggest a staged scene in these photos Samantha, when nobody else has? Can you say for certain that you haven't been influenced by the media, perhaps by Aljazeera?"

"Mr. Walters, we all thought that there were WMD's in Iraq, but none were found. Two courses in my Master's program were on the Analysis of Propaganda. The text books were full of examples of appearances not matching reality and reality not matching media reports."

"The guys around here will have to start doing their homework if they want to keep up to the new girl on the block."

"Have they read my report?"

"No, everything that everyone does here is confidential, except for me. I decide what will become known for general consumption, and it's always released at group briefings."

"I'm going to send your report along to my superiors."

"I hope it will be useful."

"That will be all. You may go now."

"Thank you, Mr. Walters."

She was at the door, when he spoke again, "Oh, by the way, did you know they've had their elections in Nigeria?"

"I saw it on the news."

"One of our staff at the American Consulate in Abuja sent us a newspaper clipping. Among other things, the article said t the Debt Reconciliation Committee has been dissolved by the new government."

She smiled at him and left.

The Adams Sisters

**

Tod Evans lay on his back in his room in the basement of the family house in Silver Spring. A form from the Veterinary College Employment Referral Department rested on the bed beside him. It had been in his possession for almost three weeks. Tomorrow was the last day of April and also the last day to return the employment referral form. The names of three potential employers were typed on the form. He had to rank them in order of preference 1, 2, 3. The indecision he felt was frustrating.

The first potential employer for after graduation was a commercial swine operation, in Delaware. The second opening was with a supplier of police horses, located near Blacksburg in south West Virginia. The third employment opportunity was a medium size dog and cat clinic on 19th Street NW at N Street NW in Washington, two blocks south of Dupont Circle.

Instinctively, the first choice went to Blacksburg. It would be great to work in a horse operation. He could use all the experience gained, during his practicum at the Cabot Club, to sell the selection committee at the interview. The pork operation in Delaware came in a close second. Industrial food operations paid very well, and the benefits were great. He probably wouldn't have even read the bio for the domestic pet practice had it not been for the location.

Christina Adams hadn't called him yet, and he really wasn't expecting she would. However, he was sure she would phone after her graduation ceremonies were over. If he took either one of the positions being offered in Delaware or Virginia, at best he would come back in DC on weekends. If he took the opening near Dupont Circle, he would be very strategically located, as far as he and she were concerned. She'd pass near there twice a day - once on the way to DC General and then again going back home in the evening. The pet clinic didn't pay anything near to what the position in Delaware was offering, but it was more than a bare living.

He stood up and flipped a coin. No, he thought that wasn't what he really wanted. He closed his eyes and pointed at a section of the page and then rejected that too. Finally, it had to be over. He marked the possible placements as 1, 2, and 3, picked up his car keys, went upstairs and headed for the University of Maryland campus at College Park.

**

On Thursday May, 22nd Christina Adams met Jewel Simpson early. They had breakfast in Georgetown village to discuss their Commencement weekend strategy. Wearing official Commencement regalia was mandatory. They could pick up caps and gowns from the 1st floor lobby of the Medical-Dental Building, between 9:30 a.m. and 12:00 p.m. that day. All graduates would assemble at 12:30 p.m. on the steps in front of the Wellington Hall Jesuit Residence, in the Southwest Quad. The group Grad Photos would be shot at 1:00 p.m. Pizza and beer would be provided by the Medical Students Association, after the shoot.

"So, Sebastian is really coming?" Jewel questioned her friend cautiously.

"Here look for yourself," Christina replied. "This is the invitation I sent him. There's what he wrote, '....*in your cap and gown*'."

"Good, I'll finally get to meet this mystery man."

"We could put him between us at the Commencement Reception on Sunday," Christina offered.

"It's a deal," Jewel affirmed shaking her best friend's hand.

Suddenly Christina exclaimed, "Look Jewel, it's already past 9:30 a.m. and we're still here gabbing. I want to see what I look like in the cap and gown, before I show up to have my picture taken in it."

"I do too, so let's get over to Medical-Dental right now. If we're the last, we won't have any choice."

They weren't the first, but neither were they the last. Both young women had a chance to choose between at least half a dozen combinations of the graduation regalia before they made their choice. Christina dropped Jewel at her apartment and then went straight home. At 12:30 p.m. the two soon to be graduating Medical students met up again on the steps at Wolfington Hall in cap and gown.

"What did you think when you saw yourself in front of the mirror?" Jewel asked.

"It makes me look fat," Christina complained.

"You're not fat," he friend assured her, "but I must admit that the gown hides all the perfect curves, I so painfully dieted to acquire."

Then Christina asked, "What did you really think of you as a graduate, Jewel?"

"It makes me look like one of those Salem witches. I wish I had more shoulders."

They both laughed and went to get in line according to height. The photographer showed them exactly where he

The Adams Sisters

wanted them to stand. At 1 p.m. sharp he put up his hand then exclaimed.

"Silence everybody we're going to do it, ready, aim, 3, 2 and 1 and shooting. Nobody move, we take five of these, ready, aim, 3, 2 and 1 and shooting."

When the snapping was over, a huge burst of conversation and laughter rose from the group. Second and third year students from the Med Student Association appeared pushing caterer's carts loaded with pizza and beer. One of them yelled at the top of his lungs.

"Chow time, chow time, come and get it."

The Graduating Class moved slowly down the steps. By the time they reached the stainless steel food carts, their picture taking stress had begun to subside.

"Watch your gowns folks." One of the student servers cautioned. "You don't want to smell like pizza and beer, when they hand you your diploma."

The photographer folded up his tripods and reflector screens and stowed them in his minivan. He looked over at the students milling about laughing and talking. Well, that's kick off done for another year; he thought to himself getting into the vehicle. There would be just enough time during the afternoon to develop these plates before 5 p.m., when he had to be back at the Gorman auditorium for the Magis/Master Teacher Ceremony and reception, where he would also be taking photographs.

The following day Christina, Charles, and Marsha met up with Jewel, Ben and Mr. and Mrs. Simpson at 5 p.m. in front of Healy Hall for the Warwick Evans Awards Ceremony and Reception. Both Christina and Jewel were to be recipients. As they walked into Gaston Hall to be seated, Roger Simpson looked at Charles and joked.

"I don't know which is the biggest event, marriage or graduation."

Charles winked and replied, "I haven't had the experience of the other yet, but I have a suspicion that it's not too far away, once this Commencement is by us."

"Maybe you'll be in Church sooner than you think," Roger Simpson commented. Charles looked at him with a puzzled expression wondering if his wife and daughter were hiding something from him. Roger laughed, "Only joking Charles, I mean Graduation Mass. It's tomorrow at 9:30 a.m. in Holy Trinity Church."

"Oh, right!" Charles sputtered. "I forgot all about the Mass."

At 10:45 a.m. on Sunday all graduates reported to the C Street NW entrance of the Daughters of the American Revolution Constitution Hall, with cap and gown in hand. When all were assembled, they proceed as a group to the D Street NW side of the Hall for robing and processional line-up. At 11:00 a.m. the graduating class proceeded down the right side aisle of Constitution Hall led by the Registrar.

Christina glanced sideways twice trying to catch a glimpse of her parents, Sebastian, and Samantha. There were too many people, and she had to keep moving. The graduates filled the front rows of the center section of the Hall. All remained standing, until the National Anthem was played.

The Dean presented the graduating class to the President of the University for conferring of degrees. As each graduate came on stage, they gave their identification card to the Dean and proceeded to regroup until their name was called. When it was their turn, each student walked to center stage, received their degree from the President and then continued across the stage to be hooded by a Faculty member.

Before Christina left the stage to return to her seat, she looked out across the attendance several times, until she located her family. When the last graduate arrived back at the reserved seats, the Oath of Hippocrates was administered. The Alma Mater was followed by a Benediction. During the recessional, the graduates followed the Registrar out of Constitution Hall, in double file. Once the procession began to break apart, Christina went quickly to Jewel's side. Her eyes were filling with tears.

"He didn't show up Jewel. Sebastian isn't here."

"He has to be," Jewel insisted.

"No, there was an empty seat between Samantha and my Dad. It was reserved for him."

"This can't be Christa. Why would he do a thing like that?"

"I can't go out there and face them Jewel," Christina sobbed. "I don't want to go to that Reception. It's too embarrassing."

"Here Christa, hold on to my hand. Squeeze tight, I'm here. We have to think our way out of this."

"There's no way out Jewel. Stupid Sebastian did it to me."

"I bet if you had of invited that Preppy, Yellow Cloud guy, he would have shown up."

Christina looked at her through the film of tears covering her eyes and agreed, "He probably would have."

The Adams Sisters

Jewel was grasping at straws. "You should phone him and ask him to meet you at the Reception." Christina wasn't thinking about what Jewel was saying, she only answered automatically.

"He lives too far away and I don't have my cell phone."

"I've got mine," her friend snickered wickedly and produced it from the folds of the gown.

"We weren't supposed to bring any personal possessions and especially not phones."

"This isn't a possession. It's part of my body." Both girls began to laugh from the tension.

"Jewel, I can't just phone Tod up like that."

"Oh, so now he's Tod is he. When did all this begin? You've been holding out on me Christa Adams."

"I was going to tell you."

"Sure you were."

"No, really I was. Things just needed to get right."

Jewel became very serious. "Christa, Sebastian didn't show up today. Does that mean that things have suddenly got right?"

Christina brushed the water away from the corner of her eye with the edge of the gown.

"Yes, it's all right now. I only hope it isn't too late."

"Well, give him a call and see if it's not too late. You need something to pick you up before we go to the Reception.

"What will I say to him?"

"I don't know, but you'll think of something. What's his number?"

"I don't know."

"Where does he live?"

"He lives in Silver Spring. His last name is Evans."

"There are probably two dozen Evans out that way."

"Try it anyway."

"Ok, I'm trying."

The telephone information assistant came back to her, "Yes, Miss I do have a Tod Evans. It's a double listing on the same number with John Evans."

Christina heard a woman's voice answer, "Hello."

"May I speak to Tod, please?"

"One moment, please. He's out in the back yard. I'll go call him."

Several minutes later she heard his voice saying, "Hello." A powerful shot of adrenaline rushed through her.

"Hi Tod, this is Christa speaking."

"Hi Christa. I've been waiting for you to call. Have you graduated yet?"

"We received our diplomas this afternoon and there's a reception later on."

"Congratulations!"

"Thanks."

"You wouldn't be calling to take me up on that rain check for a cup of coffee, would you?"

"You've already read my mind."

"That's great Christa. I can't believe you're really calling. I wish I were there."

"Do you really wish that Preppy?"

"Yes, I do."

"When do you want to have coffee?"

"Is this evening too soon?"

"Nope."

"Then I'll meet you at the coffee shop on Dupont Circle at 9 p.m."

"I'll be there. I have to go now. My parents are waiting to go to the reception."

"Have fun."

"See you later."

"Bye Christa."

"Bye."

Marsha couldn't believe what was happening. She had expected her youngest daughter to ask them to take her home because she wasn't feeling well. Instead, she was in the back seat laughing with Samantha, as Charles drove them to the International Trade Center, at 1300 Pennsylvania Ave. NW.

On Sunday evening at 8:30 p.m. Commencement was a thing of the past. Marsha was sitting in the living room knitting a cushion cover. She saw her daughter's running shoes coming down the carpeted steps from upstairs. The young woman was wearing chinos and a scoop neck T-shirt.

"Going somewhere Christa?"

"I thought I'd go out for a walk. Maybe I'll go as far as Dupont Circle and have a coffee."

"There's plenty of coffee here."

"I know, but I want to clear my head, breath in some fresh air."

"Well, come and have a chat with me before you go."

"Ok Mom," she said coming in and squatting on a white leather ottoman.

"What to talk about it?" her mother asked.

The Adams Sisters

"Talk about what?"

"Sebastian of course, your father was boiling. I told him not to say a word until I had a chance to have a chat with you. What's going on with you and Sebastian?"

"I don't know. You saw the rsvp card he returned to me."

"When was the last time you talked to him?"

"It's been a while."

"Did you see him when you went to Philadelphia to write the MLE?"

"No."

"You should have come to talk to me or Samantha. Does Jewel know what's going on?"

"No."

"Then it's time you started to talk to somebody about it. Bottling things up inside you will not solve anything. Did you and Sebastian have a fight?"

"It wasn't exactly a fight."

"What was it then?"

"Sebastian let it slip out that he had been seeing the illustrator who did the preliminary sketches for the house."

"That could have only been business, dear. How many women do you think your father has had to deal with in his professional life?"

"I know Mom, but it wasn't only business."

"Was he sleeping with her?"

"He said no."

"What was it then?"

"He told me that he was out having drinks with her, and she started talking about how much she would like to be the one living in the house that he's building. Before the night ended, they were half-jokingly and half seriously talking as if she was going to be the woman of the house. It was humiliating, and it hurt.

I told him he had some serious thinking to do about myself, himself and the illustrator. When he replied to my invitation to come to Commencement, I thought he had done his thinking and had his ducks lined up. I guess I was wrong."

"Nothing is ever easy between men and women Christa. We break up; we make up and then we break up again. Sometimes we're married for twenty-five years to the same man and then we go and renew our marriage to him with a second ceremony. But anyway, why don't you go for your walk and I'll keep on with my knitting."

"Thanks, Mom."

"Don't walk in any shadows, and stay under the street lights. This is a good part of town, but one never knows."

"I'll be careful."

Christina stood in front of the plate glass window of the coffee shop on the Dupont Circle. She found Tod's blond head of hair almost immediately. He already had a coffee and was reading something. She went in and bought a mocha café, before going over to his table.

When she sat down, he looked up and smiled the broadest most joyful smile she had ever seen. It was irresistible. Briefly, her fingers brushed the top of his hand.

"How was Commencement?" Tod enquired.

"Nerve wracking, but now I'm an MD, or at least I will be in 6 months, when my internship is completed."

"That's excellent! I'm so happy to stop studying too."

"Did you find a job?"

"Yea, I took one that I was offered through the school's Placement Service."

"Where is it?"

"Just a little bit south of the Circle, on the corner of 19th and N, at an Animal Clinic," he informed her.

"Doing what?" she exclaimed with surprise.

"Probably giving vitamin shots to cats and dogs," he joked.

"I thought for sure that you'd be going out into a rural district doing something with horses."

"That was a possibility."

"How did you end up taking an Animal Clinic?"

"I want to see, if there's anything in your *maybe*," he replied, avoiding her eyes. "Blacksburg Virginia is too far away for that."

Christina felt her stomach contract and then go all soft. She needed a deep breath but didn't want to take it. She had never felt this emotion before and wanted to keep it as long as she could. They talked well past the end of their cups of coffee. By the time she kissed him in the shadows, just before going into the Adams residence, they had inched past the day they spent together on Assateague Island, and were building something new between them.

****

15 - Beach Grass

The more Christina saw Tod, the more she wanted to see him, and it was the same from his side. They met for lunch; they met after work and then they started to meet going to work in the morning. If it wasn't possible for them to see each other, because of weather, schedules or outside demands; they talked on the cell phone while driving, walking, working, eating and just before falling to sleep. Christina would leave him at 9 or 10 p.m. on a week night and then as soon as she got in her room at home, she would click open the email to tell him one last thing she had forgot to say, during their time together. Often as not she would find that he had already sent her a text message while driving home.

It was the summer. There were so many things to do and places to be. They walked and talked, licked on ice cream and drank a lot of coffee. They played tennis, went horseback riding in Rock Creek Park, and sometimes attended a concert or a local club. If her mother asked where she had been or where she was going, she became evasive and said she was with Jewel or Jewel and Benjamin or some of the people from the Hospital. However; Marsha wasn't that easily fooled, and even suspected that her daughter was secretly seeing Sebastian.

On the weekends, the couple often mingled with the hundreds of thousand tourists visiting Washington, during the summer, as they toured the Smithsonian Castle, the Museum of American History, the Museum of Natural History, the National Gallery the Capitol Building. They even went for a walk around Arlington Cemetery.

One afternoon Tod surprised her when he told her that he had made an appointment for them to visit the Black Fashion Museum in the two thousand block of Vermont Avenue NW. The younger Adams had never seen the dresses that Elizabeth Keckley had designed for Mary Lincoln and didn't know that Ann Lowe had designed Jackie Kennedy's wedding gown.

In August Christina and Tod arranged for a weekend get-a-way together on the Jersey Cape. Also known as Cape May County, the Jersey Cape is a peninsula that stretches south from mainland New Jersey with the Atlantic Ocean on the east and Delaware Bay on the west. Along the Atlantic coast nature has created inlets, waterways, islands and beaches that give the Cape a unique character.

The 30 or so miles of continuous beaches along the Cape are dotted with mostly summer communities such as Sea Isle City, Avalon, Stone Harbor and the Wildwoods. These destinations have been popular since the 18th century. The town of Cape May, at the southern tip of the Peninsula, is home to over 600 Victorian homes, which have been restored.

Jennifer Evans was even more attentive to the change in her son, since graduating than Marsha was with her daughter. When she saw him in the passenger seat of the light blue BMW that was backing out of their driveway around supper time, on Friday August 22nd, she instinctively knew that he had finally got by Angie from Raleigh. As they drove off, she watched how he looked at the young black woman. He won't be getting out of it this time, by going off to study at the Virginia & Maryland School of Veterinarian Medicine, she thought to herself and smiled.

The couple had reserved two rooms in Cape May for the evening. From the Evans home, they drove to Annapolis then followed a series of secondary highways west across Maryland and Delaware to the Ferry Terminal, at Lewes. The daylight held during the hour long cruise across the mouth of Delaware Bay. Their boat was packed with cyclists, who were on the last lap of a coast ride back to New York City from Cape Hatteras in North Carolina, where they had flown with their bikes.

The Adams Sisters

Once the light blue BMW cleared the ferry ramp, they made their way quickly to the Cape May Inn. As soon as their bags were deposited in their rooms, the pair met up in the hall.

"Let's go walk on the beach for a while." she suggested.

"Sounds great," he replied, linking his hand with hers.

On the way to the Municipal Pier, they passed a bronze plaque, which explained the history of the town. Cape May was named after Captain Cornelius Jacobsen Mey, who was sent out by the Dutch West Indies Company to establish a trading facility in the region in 1620. English settlers later changed the name to Cape May.

On the beach, a mechanical rake drove along scooping off the top few inches of sand, before shaking it through screens to filter out litter and then projecting the sand back out onto the beach, in the direction from which it had come. Since the sky was still luminous, they could see the surf, of a receding tide, away off across the beach towards the Atlantic and decided to go and walk along the moist band of sand, just before the water, to avoid the litter rake. Once out of sight of the vehicles headlights, Tod stopped and drew her in close to him.

"What are you thinking about, Ms. Adams?"

She looked up and smiled, "How nice and warm your chest and legs feel against my skin."

"Are you cold?"

"No, I only like to feel your warmth."

He leaned down and pressed his lips gently on top of hers. She removed her arms from around his waist and locked them around his neck. When he straightened back up, she stood up on her toes and clung to him leaving her sandals behind on the sand.

"How's that for being close?" he asked.

"I can feel your skinny ribs and even the throb of your heart," she answered, before releasing her grip around his neck and sliding down his body, until her feet touched the sand again.

When they had walked far enough up the beach, to work out the stiffness of a day's work and the drive to the ferry, they went up to the seawall, found some stairs and came down into the world of the living on the other side. The smell of hot fat coming from a converted bus overpowered both, and they walked away from it each carrying a large paper cone of succulent deep fried clams. Once the clams were done, they stopped into an open air bar and bought two beers, which they drank at an outside picnic table.

The following day after breakfast, they headed for the Wildwoods and a second hotel, which they had reserved for Saturday night. There are three Wildwoods – North Wildwood, Wildwood by the Sea and Wildwood Crest. Their hotel was in Wildwood by the Sea.

In addition to its three miles of beach and famous boardwalk, Wildwood by the Sea has four amusement piers with hundreds of rides, movie theatres, shops, restaurants, and night clubs. In the morning, they browsed through the shops, had a light snack then headed to the beach. They stayed lying in the hot sand or jumped in the high waves, being pushed up by the incoming tide, until five o'clock. After an excellent meal of crab cakes, oysters, and shrimp salad, they went out onto the amusement piers. The couple rode the ferris-wheel, threw basketballs, shot 22 caliber rifles and ate cotton candy. Around 10 o'clock, they strolled into a night club and danced to a live band, until 1 a.m.

When they got back to their rooms, Tod asked to come in for a few minutes. She resisted.

"But why?" he asked.

"Because I want to wait until we're married," she explained.

"Are you asking me to marry you?" he joked while tickling her.

She burst out giggling and squirmed in his arms, "Are you accepting?"

He stopped tickling her and whispered, "Sure, I'm accepting."

She put her two hands on his chest, pushed herself away from his grip and seductively purred, "Then why don't you ask me outright."

"Ok, I'll ask you. Do you want to marry me, Christa?" She didn't make a sound, and he came back, "Ah, I see, it's all right for me to accept, but when it's your turn, you don't say a word."

She stopped struggling, "I am too, I'm accepting."

"Are you saying that you really want to marry me?"

She looked deeply into his eyes and said, "Yes, I really want to marry you."

"When?"

"As soon as possible," she blurted out and then covered her mouth with her hand.

"Why?"

"Because I'm in love with you, silly boy."

The Adams Sisters

He stopped smiling, lightly pressed his lips against hers and said, "I think I'm going to go to my room now."

"You don't have to go right away. Stay a little longer," she protested limply.

"No, I guess I'll go now," he said. "Everything is perfect the way it happened just now. I want to keep it like that."

He took three steps towards the door to his room and then turned back towards her, "You're not joking with me, are you?"

"No Preppy, I'm not joking," she declared, standing on her toes to kiss him. "I really want to be married to you."

"I'll see you in the morning Christa."

"Nite Tod." The door closed quietly behind him.

Next morning the young man was roused by a soft knocking.

"Preppy...Preppy....Hey Preppy, hoo-hah wake up. Come on Preppy, it's morning. Time to get up."

Eventually, he did wake up, pulled a blanket off the bed, which he twisted about himself like a caftan and opened the door. Christina stood in front of him in a white halter, white shorts, and a white headband.

"Tod, it's after eight. I thought you wanted to go surf fishing this morning."

"I did. I mean I am. Did you put a sedative in your perfume last night?"

"Don't be silly."

"All right, you go ahead on down to the dining room. I'll be there in less than ten minutes, no wait a maximum of ten minutes."

"Ok, see you downstairs."

"When he arrived in the dining room doorway, she made motions for him to go to the breakfast buffet. First he found fried eggs, scrambled eggs, poached eggs and boiled eggs. Then it was bacon, sausages, ham, meatballs, and liver paste. That was followed by waffles, toast, bagels, hot cereal, cold cereal, fruit cocktail, grapefruit, tea, coffee, milk and orange juice. He took a little of everything.

'So what are you going to do, while I'm surf fishing?" he asked her as he placed a tray on the table with one hand and pulled out a chair with the other.

"I have my book."

"What's it called?"

"Castle Umberto."

That's a weird name."

"It's Italian."

"What's it about."

"This guy, sort of a Duke brings his girlfriend home to meet his father and step mother. He ends up getting seduced by the step mother and the girlfriend by his father."

"Christa, I didn't know you read stuff like that."

"I hardly ever do," she replied defensively, "but this is a vacation. It's like candy. Everybody knows it's only fantasy. They're even very tasteful about it."

"As long as they're tasteful about it," he kidded, "I won't say anything more."

"Tod Evans."

"Yes, Madame?"

"Did I say anything about you going out fishing, on our getaway weekend?"

"But there're supposed to be Stripers out there and they're not fantasy."

"Says who?"

"Do you see that little guy over there beside the buffet table? "

"Do you mean the one wearing a black vest, who has a rattail moustache?"

"That's whom I'm referring to. He told me I should go up the beach around Wildwood Crest, cus it's better fishin around there."

"I didn't see you talking to him."

"You just weren't looking close enough."

"I never took my eyes off you for one second, while you were going through the buffet."

"We were using sign language."

"Tod."

"What?"

"Wipe the ketchup off your chin. People will be laughing at you."

He wiped his chin. "There's no ketchup on me."

Christina dabbed her finger in ketchup from her own plate; then touched him on the point of his chin, before saying. "Sure there is, look," and then she showed him her finger.

"Ok, I read it on a sign, when we were walking on the pier last night."

"Did you like our evening out last night?" she chirped, nibbling on a piece of bacon, which she was holding between her fingers.

The Adams Sisters

"It was fine," he replied squeezing another wrap made of toast and scrambled eggs into his mouth. "You really dance well."

"Wow, look who's talking. The Wave should have had you in a go-go cage, instead of behind the bar." He smiled back at her.

"It was the beer wasn't it," she joked.

"I only had a couple of beers during the whole evening," he replied defensively.

"Then you have no excuse. Do you remember what you said last night?"

"I remember."

"Wanna take it back?"

"Nope ... you?"

"Nope," she replied with a grin spread from ear to ear.

"Let's hurry up and finish breakfast," he said. "We'll take our bags with us and go up to Wildwood Crest."

"Sounds like a game plan to me, Preppy."

"I thought you weren't going to call me that anymore."

"Sorry, I mean Tod."

He moved his foot under the table and caressed her ankle with his toes.

When they arrived at the two mile strip of sand known as the Crest, Christina cruised along the beach road, until they were well past the parked cars. They found a huge driftwood log that was surrounded by beach grass. She settled down on a blanket, with her back against the log and watched him put his rod together, attached a three inch piece of silver painted lead, which was shaped like a double triangle, to the line and add a three barb hook, before set off for the surf.

Every fifteen minutes or so she looked up from Castle Umberto and watched him make long casts out into the boiling waves; then start to reel the line back in again. It was almost noon, when he came back up the beach carrying two striped bass, which he lay on top of several handfuls of grass, to keep them from touching the sand.

"We'll have to pick up a bag of ice cubes on the way back, so they don't get overheated," he cautioned.

"I don't get it," she exclaimed.

"Get what?" he asked casually.

"You didn't even have any bait and you came back with two fish."

"Stripers are a predator that strike on small fish caught in the surf. They thought my chunk of lead was a smelt, but it had three hooks in it."

He pulled out a long stem of beach grass and sat down beside her. She watched while he fashioned it into a small round coil. When it was finished, he said,

"Maybe you'll understand this."

"Understand what?"

"Give me your hand." She stretched out her right hand.

"No, the left hand," he insisted. She switched hands. He took hold of the third finger and slipped the coil of grass around it. "Do you understand that?" he asked, without looking at her.

"I understand," she replied softly. "It wasn't a midnight joke." Then she threw her arms around his neck and began kissing him until he had to plead for air.

"Why don't we have your fish for lunch?" she suggested. "There's a public grill over there on the beach and lots of driftwood."

"Yours is a better idea," he replied, recovering from her sudden display of emotion. "That way there won't be any ice melting all over your car. I'll get my knife from the trunk and go back down to the surf to clean them."

I'll clean the fireplace up a bit by rubbing the grate with a rock, while you're cleaning the fish," she added.

Jennifer Evans watched from behind the front room curtain, as her son removed his bag and fishing gear from the trunk of the BMW and set it down on the front lawn. She saw him, and his friend stand on the front lawn holding hands as they talked and then embrace for a long time, before the young woman finally got back into the car. Mrs. Evans knew she was going to be meeting this girl. The only question in her mind was when?

The next weekend was Labor Day, and while many Washtonians headed out of the city, the newly engaged couple went in town to window shop for a more permanent ring. Just for fun, their first stop was Pampillonia, which has been serving the distinguished tastes of a distinguished city, for five generations, from their Connecticut Avenue N.W. location. She tried on hidalgo – center rings and guard rings, diamond solitaires, two stone clusters, platinum round and gold round rings, before telling the clerk that she would have to think about it.

Once they were out on the sidewalk Tod exclaimed, "Wow, did you see the price of some of them."

The Adams Sisters

"I know," she replied. I couldn't believe that octagonal sapphire with diamond hearts on both sides was $49,000. That's more than my BMW." She looked at Tod. He was turning a lighter shade of pale. She poked him in the ribs with her elbow. "Don't worry Preppy, I'm not going to do that to you." Then she reminded him, "Remember, we agreed it was only going to be something a little less fragile than this band of beach grass."

"So do you have any ideas yet?" he asked feeling reassured, after hearing her say that.

"Yes, for the shape I prefer the marquis, and it's the blue sapphire I like the best."

"Yea, it's kind of cool."

At another jeweler, she settled on a 2 k., cut blue sapphire set in a platinum ring. The jeweler explained the phenomena of the gemstone to them. It was translucent with a small amount of internal iridescence and an adamantine luster. The band had to be adjusted for her finger. The jeweler told then to come back before 5 p.m., and it would be ready. Later, when they left the store for a second time that day, there was a small, square, white satin ring box in Tod's jacket pocket.

"Now I must find an appropriate place to give this to you," he joked as they walked hand in hand along the sidewalk.

"Why not over supper and I'm buying."

"Fair enough, since you're paying any preference?" he inquired.

"I'm burnt out from choosing all day long, Tod," she pouted affectionately. "You're in the driver's seat now."

"I feel like tapas tonight," he told her and playfully added, "any objections?"

"Oh yes, Spanish, great idea. We never have anything like that at home."

"I know a cozy little tapas bar in Morgan."

"Ok, let's go."

The waiter seated them, asked if they would like to begin with a drink; then motioned towards the hot bar, where *el cocinero* was waiting. They ordered *aceitunas, albondigas, chorizo, croquetas, gambas, patatas bravas, pimientos, and tortilla Espanola* and went back to their table. It wasn't long, before the waiter arrived with two good sized plates, a basket full of plain tortillas and a small jug of sangria. He lit the candle that was on the table, poured them each a glass from the jug and then disappeared.

As the soft notes of Spanish guitar music filled his ears, Tod lifted his glass and whispered, "To forever!"

Christina also lifted her glass against his and whispered in reply, "To forever."

When they had returned their glasses to the table, he reached into his pocket and removed the ring box.

"I'd like to put this on your finger before we start the tapas."

She extended her left hand, and he removed the remains of beach grass that were still wrapped around her finger, before slipping the platinum band over her knuckle. She brought her hand back, held it up close to her face and then extended it again so it was in the full glow coming from the candle.

"Thank you Preppy," she said lowly. "It's the most wonderful gift anyone has ever given me."

"Let's try some of this," he said, picking up his fork, as he entwined his feet in hers under the table.

While they ate, they began to talk about their immediate future.

"Have you told your family about me?" she asked.

"No, but my mother saw us arriving back from Jersey last Sunday and when I came in she ribbed me with, "looks like someone has the love bug.' I only smiled and bowed out politely. What about your parents?"

"They didn't even see you drop me off, the day we came back from Assateague. I don't know how I'm going to let them know. I don't want to blurt out, 'Hi Charles and Marsha, guess what? I'm engaged.'"

"They'll probably notice your ring and start asking questions."

She started to laugh, "I can just see the look on their faces." He twisted his mouth into a frown, and they laughed together.

"We better prepare ourselves in advance," she said seriously.

"I know, John and Jenny are going to want to know, when it all started and when we're planning to get married."

"We need to have the same story about when it all started," she agreed; "so, let's get synchronized. Let's not mention anything about DC Meets. I'm going to say that we met while we were working at the Wave.

He agreed, "There's no lie in that."

The Adams Sisters

I'll tell them that I liked you but that we were both too busy with school, so we've been emailing since then. How long ago was that now?"

He did a quick calculation, "Last Spring; that's about 15 months ago."

"Perfect, I'll tell them we've been building up to this for the past 15 months."

"All right, I'll say the same thing," he seconded her. "Now, what about, when do we want to get married?"

"I feel like saying as soon as possible," she replied, moving her toes up under the cuff of his pants.

"So do I."

"I can see Marsha's expression already. Excuse my Spanish, but she'll have a shit."

"You're excused."

"You know Preppy you're off the hook now that you've bought me this ring. It's Marsha and I and probably my sister Samantha, who will have to roll up our sleeves and make a wedding happen."

"I'll help, if you tell me what to do."

"That's not the boy's place," she reminded him. "So, if it's all right with you, I'll tell her that we would like to get married as soon as possible, but without causing her or Charles any inconvenience."

"No, we don't want to inconvenience anyone," he agreed putting out his hand.

She shook his hand and reconfirmed," Do we have our stories straight?"

"Yup!"

"I can't believe it," she exclaimed." We're sitting here discussing our own engagement and our marriage, and we're wondering what our parent's reaction will be. It's almost as if we're two kids who have done something wrong, and we know we're going to get caught."

"Families are an important part of getting married, because, in addition to our own, we're both going to be taking on another family," he said, reaching out to cup her hand between his two palms, until he could feel the sapphire on the engagement ring cutting into his skin.

"I know I'm going to be so shy with your clan," she replied, pulling her hand from between his closed palms. "I'm always shy around white people, when it's not a public place.

"Do you think I won't be feeling a bit odd too?"

"It's different, you're a boy."

"I won't say anything to John and Jennifer until you get Charles and Marsha up. Then I'll invite you over for supper to introduce you to my folks. I'll make sure none of my brothers or sisters are stopping by that evening, so you'll be able to feel more at ease."

"It sounds so funny when you call my parents, Charles, and Marsha."

"Want to know something that's going to sound even funnier?"

"What's that?" She asked, visibly showing excitement.

"One day I'm going to simply come out and say, 'Hey Dad what do you think of that.'"

"You wouldn't."

"Sure I will."

"My Dad is an extremely straight guy. I don't want you to say anything that might set him off. I don't think he would appreciate a white boy calling him Dad."

"I won't set him off. Tell you what, I'll call Marsha, Mom, first so he can get used to how it sounds."

"Yea, that's a better idea," she exclaimed, slapping her hands together. "Start with her. She's an old fuddy-duddy, but you can kid around with her easier than you can with Dad."

Marsha didn't notice the ring, until Wednesday morning at breakfast. When she did, she didn't know what to say and excused herself.

"I'll be right back in a minute Christa. I'm just going into the kitchen to see what your Dad is doing."

"Sure, Mom."

When she rounded the entrance to the kitchen, she put her finger up to her lips, so her husband wouldn't say anything and then whispered into his ear.

"She's wearing a ring on the third finger of her left hand, Charles."

Charles felt the third finger of his left hand; then looked seriously at her before saying, "That's her engagement ring finger."

"I know. That's why I'm whispering."

"Who?" he asked.

"Who else but Sebastian?" she replied.

'He's a dirty rotten stinker to have done that at her graduation and come up now with a ring."

"I told you then we had to let them work it out by themselves, and now it seems they have."

The Adams Sisters

"I'm still not ready to forgive him for what he did." Charles insisted. "Respect has to be earned, even by Sebastian."

"I agree, but how are we going to handle this? She'll think we're dead if we don't notice the ring."

"Ok, you go back and sit down." He suggested. "I'll come in a minute. Wait a little bit and then notice it. After you notice it, I'll say something too."

"Ok Dad, it's your call. I'm glad Mrs. Yamato doesn't come until 9 a.m."

Marsha went back to the breakfast table and sat down. Her husband wasn't long coming after her. She let him put milk and low calorie sweetener into his coffee and take a sip before she commented,

"That's a nice ring you're wearing Christa. Did you buy it recently?"

"No, it's a gift."

"From whom?"

"A boy I know."

"Which boy dear?" her mother asked trying to appear casual.

"His name is Tod."

Charles sucked in his breath too fast, coughed and sent a fine spray of coffee onto the table cloth in front of him.

"That's your engagement finger isn't it, Christa?" Marsha laughed lightly, trying to look composed.

"That's because it's an engagement ring, Mom."

This time, Charles, started choking and made for the kitchen again.

Mrs. Adams stood up quickly excusing herself, "I'll be right back. I must go see what's happening with your father."

"Sure mom."

She was no sooner in the kitchen, before he grabbed her by the arm. "What's happening Marsha? You said it was that snake Sebastian, but she's saying Tod. Who's Tod?"

"I don't know dear. I'm as shocked as you are."

"You're her mother."

"What's that supposed to mean?"

"Mothers are supposed to know these things. I rely on you."

"She's almost 27 Charles. I can't follow it all. Come on now, stop choking. We must go back in and get to the bottom of this."

She went in first with Charles following. "Excuse me both of you," he apologized. "A bread crumb went down the wrong way."

Marsha didn't waste any time, "Who's Tod, Christa?"

"He's a boy I met a while ago."

"Where?" she pressed politely.

"I met him when I was working at the Wave."

"I've never heard you mention his name before."

"We were only casual acquaintances, when we worked together, but I'm sure I mentioned his name a number of times."

Charles always had a soft spot, when either of the girls was being grilled by their mother. This was no exception. "I seem to remember her mentioning a Tod, Mother."

Marsha shot him a look of complete surprise; then turned her attention back to her daughter. "If you were only casual acquaintances at the Wave, how did you get to know him well enough for him to give you a ring?"

"We really got to know each other through email, after we stopped working at the Wave."

Charles rallied again. "I seem to remember now; he was a student, wasn't he Christa?"

"Yes, he was in 4th year of Veterinary Science at U Maryland in College Park while I was in the fourth year of Medicine. We both had too heavy study schedules to see much of each other, so we sent email messages back and forth almost every day, and besides that he lives in Silver Spring, which made meetings quite difficult."

Marsha continued, "Has he graduated yet?"

"Yes."

"Did he find a job after graduation?"

"Yes, he has a job in an Animal Clinic, just off Dupont Circle.

"Oh, I know that place," Charles interjected. "That's nice and close. It's been easier for the two of you to see each other since he's been working there?"

"We've been seeing each other all summer Daddy, sometimes twice a day."

"Were you with him two weekends ago?" her mother asked.

"Yes, but we had separate rooms. It was during the weekend that we got engaged. Is there something the matter Mom?"

The Adams Sisters

"No, no, there's nothing the matter. Your news is all very sudden, but I'm getting it. You're engaged to a young man named Tod."

"I must run now Mom and Dad or I'll be late for work."

Charles came to life. "Don't be late Christa; leave your dishes where they are. Mrs. Yakamoto will take care of them, when she arrives."

"Ok, Dad, I'll see you and Mom this evening. Maybe we can talk a little more about my news then."

"That's a very good idea," Marsha agreed. "We'll talk some more this evening."

After they heard the front door close, both the elder Adams sat staring at each other. Charles broke the tense silence. "Let's not make any snap judgments. We'll hear her out and then have a conference in the car somewhere, far from anybody accidentally overhearing us."

"You don't think that she's ....it's very sudden,." Christina's mother said cautiously.

"No, I don't think she's...... but it has taken me off guard."

"Yes, you're right."

"Of course I'm right. She's our daughter."

"Charles, may I ask you one little favor?"

"That depends on, what your one little favor is?" her husband replied.

"Sometimes in your insurance business you must find out things about people."

"Sure, lots of times. There are lots of people out there, who don't always tell the truth."

"Can you see what comes up on this Tod?"

"She didn't give us his last name."

"She said he finished in Veterinary Science at U Maryland in College Park this past spring and also that he worked at the Wave, when she was there."

"Ok, I can do you a favor, besides I wouldn't mind knowing something about him myself."

"Thanks dear, and call me when you have something."

Marsha was out working in the front flower beds, when Mrs. Yamato opened the front door around 11:30 a.m. and said,

"Mrs. Adams, it's the phone for you, Mr. Adams."

"I'll be right in." She took off her gloves, dusted off her gardening clothes and went into the hall, where the phone was located.

"Hello Charles."

"Ok, I've got some details for you."
"Go ahead."
"His name is Doctor Tod Evans and he turned 27 in June."
"Doctor!" she exclaimed.

"Yes, doctor, that's what they call Vets these days. He's got a couple of credit cards and no bad marks on his credit file. He owns a 7 year old Audi. The address on the license is at his parent's home.

His father's name is John, and the mother is a Jennifer. They live in their own home, in Silver Spring. He did work at the Wave the same time as she did and here's the corker. Are you ready?"

"Yes."

"He's a white boy."

"Oh, Charles."

"I know Marsh, but that's how it happens. They didn't grow up in the same world as you and I."

"I know, but there are so many nice black boys around. Couldn't she have found one her own color?"

"They're both just kids who've been cooped up in those brain factories for seven or eight years, Marsha."

"I know, but I thought it would be Sebastian."

"You did your best. I'll see you at supper Hon. I'm meeting a client for lunch"

"Okay bye and thanks Charles."

***

Samantha had only arrived back from lunch when her phone rang. It was Roscoe Walters. He wanted to see her in the briefing room. She picked up a pad of lined paper, two different color ball point pens and set off for the meeting. The door to the briefing room was open. Mr. Walters was seated at a long table with two men. She knocked softly on the door, before entering. Roscoe looked up and motioned for her to come in. Once she was seated, he introduced the two men sitting together across the table.

"Samantha, this is Agent Arnold Steinberg from the African Intelligence Division and on his left is Mr. Raconni, who's with the CIA. I'll let them tell you what this is all about."

Agent Steinberg began to speak, "Ms. Adams, about a year or so ago I had a call from your superior, Mr. Walters, concerning a letter he had come across, which was addressed to a Caravel Holdings in Baltimore. He asked me to come to see him. The envelope containing the letter bore a stamp from Nigeria. It was from a Dr. Lawrence Ossaga. He was making

The Adams Sisters

an inquiry about transferring $15,000,000 USD to Caravel's bank account. I filed a day report about our meeting. Mr. Raconni's research staff came across my notes and contacted me about a month ago. This morning we came to see Mr. Walters."

Samantha looked at her superior. His face was blank. She looked back at the two agents and began speaking, "I recall that letter Mr. Steinberg. It was the start of a file we ran for a while on a Nigerian Scam. They wanted us to send them $15,000. Mr. Walters said it wasn't a budgetary expense. He told me to send the file to archives, and he gave me a new assignment."

Agent Steinberg patted a file folder that was on the table in front of him. "We have a copy of the file here, Samantha."

"How may I help you gentlemen?" she asked cautiously.

Mr. Raconni began to speak, "Ms. Adams, I'll come directly to the point. I'm with the Money Laundering division of the CIA. We've found a bank account in Baltimore through, which $15,000,000 has passed in the last six months. You're the only signing authority on the account. Would you care to tell us what's been going on?"

Samantha felt a quick surge of panic grip her. Perspiration suddenly appeared under her arms, and her stomach pulled in tight. Walters still had the same blank look on his face. Without thinking she blurted out,

"There's nothing illegal. The Department isn't involved."

Raconni continued, "Would you care to start at the request from the lawyer Mr. Offuya and tell us what happened?"

Samantha collected her thoughts and began to speak,

"After Mr. Walters told me to send the file to archives, I felt somewhat cheated. It was my first real project here in Washington, and I wanted so much to win. I wanted to crack the Nigerian scam. I wanted closure.

I contacted the lawyer Offuya on my own, outside of work and told him Baltimore General Services would send him $15,000. He replied that I shouldn't send it to him; rather I should bring it to him. He said he would meet me in London England. I was advised to transfer money to me, via Western Union in two lots, less than $10,000 each. The government in England flags currency transactions over that amount.

Mr. Offuya told me how to get to Kensington Park in London, and that's where I met him. From there, we went to see a solicitor, who drew up a Power of Attorney between Baltimore General, myself and Mr. Offuya. When we left the solicitor's office, I gave him the money, which Western Union had converted into English pounds. He hurried off, because he wanted to deposit the money at a bank somewhere in London, where he had an account.

Near the end of March, I received a call from Doctor Ossaga. He asked me if I had received the money yet. I was completely shocked. I put him on hold and logged onto the company's bank account over the Internet. There it was fifteen million dollars. I took him off hold and told him it had arrived. He told me that he would fax me instructions on how the money was to be spent.

I received a list of items from him, which were quoted in dollar value plus shipping and insurance, rather than by quantity. For instance, I sent him one million dollars' worth of pickup trucks and one million dollars of economy cars. There were also backhoes, mini bulldozers, welding machines and an incredible variety of other things. I went to a dealership in Baltimore and bought a fleet of cars and a fleet of trucks. They handled getting them to the docks. It didn't take the Nigerians very long to burn through $12 million. Shipping and insurance are very expensive.

At that point, Doctor Ossaga told me that as per our arrangement I was to ship him one and a half million dollars' worth of artesian well drilling equipment, well liner, heavy gage electricity transmission wire, pumps and portable buildings, which could be used to house the pumps. His order was a separate shipment, sent to a different port and addressed to himself, not to a Nigerian company as had been the case with the construction equipment, vehicles, and other material."

Mr. Raconni interrupted her," Do you mean he used his own name?"

"Not Doctor or Lawrence, only L. Ossaga." she replied hurriedly.

"What did you do with the remaining $1.5 million?"

"I contacted the African American Health Organization and found out what they were short of in the way of medical equipment and supplies in Nigeria. I spent Baltimore General's share of the money to purchase a list of items the country needed, put them together with his pumps and items and shipped the whole thing to him."

"Do you really expect us to believe that you gave away one and a half million to somebody in Africa whom you have never seen?"

The Adams Sisters

"That's what I did Mr. Raconni. I have all the bills and receipts to show that's what I did. I also have copies of every invoice, bill of lading and insurance contract for the things I shipped to the others."

"Ms. Adams, this is a classical money laundering scheme. They sent you $15 million, which probably came from the drug trade, and you shipped them goods they can convert to cash and there is no paper trail. Didn't it ever occur to you to ask yourself where the money had come from?"

"Yes it did Sir."

"And?"

"I went to the bank in Baltimore, before I touched one cent and asked them for hard copy proof of the origin of the funds. They provided me with copies of two transfer documents from SWIFT. The money was transferred first from the account of the Nigerian Treasury to the account of the Nigerian Central Bank and then from the Nigerian Central Bank to the account of Baltimore General Services."

Mr. Raconni went silent. He gave her the same look that a wild animal gives a hunter, just after it has been shot. Mr. Steinberg came to life.

"Ms. Adams, where are the copies of all the documentation?"

"They're in my bedroom at home."

"When would it be convenient for you to get them for us?"

"I can get them right now if you want. It's only about 20 minutes' drive from here."

"Yes, we would appreciate it, if you would do that," Arnold Steinberg replied. "While you're gone, I'll show Mr. Raconni around the State Department." Both men rose and left Samantha and Mr. Walters alone."

"Am I going to lose my job, Mr. Walters?"

"As long as your documentation checks out, this is a private affair you've been telling us about. You used your money and your time to do this."

"But it started inside the Department and I didn't really close the file."

"Lots of people in the State Department have made social contacts with people off the job, whom they met through an assignment. Take me for instance. I was involved in the investigation of a very beautiful woman, whom we suspected of being a mole in the Interstate Department of Trade and Commerce. I was transferred to another assignment, and somebody else ended up confessing to being a mole. Later, I married the beautiful woman, and I still have my job."

"Thank you, Mr. Walters."

"Don't thank me Samantha. Thank your parents, your training, your instincts, and I hope your excellent capacity for keeping good records."

"I better go get them those papers."

"One last thing, before you go."

"Yes, Sir?"

"Is there any money left in the account?"

"About twenty-thousand."

"Did you take back the $15,000 you lent Baltimore General yet?"

"No."

"I suggest you write yourself a check for the balance that's in the account and then close it, after the check clears."

"Yes Mr. Walters, I mean Roscoe. I'll do that." She stood up and left.

****

16 - The Patio

Once Christina let Tod know that she had talked to Marsha and Charles; he didn't waste any time. John and Jennifer were put into the loop the very same evening. Mrs. Evans was already prepared since she had seen them together, after the Wildwood weekend and insisted that the couple come to a dinner for four, as soon as possible. It was the first Sunday in September, and Christina Adams had the hands free ear piece of her cell phone in place, as she sped northward along Georgia Street NW towards Silver Spring. She had told her fiancée that she would buzz him the moment she crossed into Maryland. As the BMW glided past the intersection with Alaska Avenue NW, her thumb pressed on the button, which brought the phonebook of her cell phone to the screen. His name and number were programmed to appear first. He answered in three rings.

"I'm almost there," she said anxiously. "Any last minute anything I should know."

"No, everything is cool. Mum's in the kitchen, and Dad is finishing washing his buggy. I'll meet you out front."

"Thanks. I'm really very nervous, even if it isn't showing."

"I believe you. I'm a bit unsure of myself too."

"You, why, they're your parents? This is your home ground."

"I'm not worried about tonight; it's the return engagement at your place next Sunday that has me hexed."

"Now Tod, don't start. They're both extremely nice people," she reminded him. "If you even hint that you're a Redskins fan, Dad will invite you to go to FedEx Field with him. He has two season tickets. My Mother sometimes goes and the rest of the time he invites anybody who's interested." Her attention was suddenly taken by the road again. "The sign says Colesville Road, next right. Where do I go from here, Tod?"

"Take Colesville and drive up three intersections, until you reach the Library. Noyes Dr. meets Colesville across from the Library. Turn left into Noyes Dr."

"I've got the Library. I'm turning left onto Noyes. Ok, I see you standing out front. I'm hanging up now." She pulled in the behind John Evan's SUV and switched off the ignition. Tod opened the car door for her, extended his hand and pulled her up out of the bucket seat. She straightened the soft pleats of her rainbow print chiffon dress and asked, "How do I look?"

"Just fabulous!"

"You're only saying that. I was so nervous I thought I was flying. I had to take a Gravol on the way here."

"Gravol doesn't relieve stress."

"I suppose it's all in my head, but that little pill calmed me down."

"Come on and meet my Dad. He's rolling up the hose in the back yard."

"Oh Tod," she began to fidget.

"Come on, he won't bite."

Mr. Evans was drying his hands on a rag as the young couple rounded the corner. Christina had imagined all sorts of ways he would look. It was fast, but she seized up the lean, six foot man wearing khakis and a pullover with one glance, saw his son in him and liked him instantly.

"Dad I'd like you to meet Christa, Christa Adams."

Now it was Christina's turn. She was sure she was blushing. "Good evening Mr. Evans. I'm very pleased to meet you. Her hand reached out towards him. He wiped his right hand on his pants one last time and shook her extended hand.

"Excuse my attire Christa; these are my car washing clothes."

Jennifer Evans saw them talking through the kitchen window. She also wiped off her hands, slipped out of her apron

The Adams Sisters

and came through the back door to greet them. She was wearing a printed silk shell with a full skirt. This time she was more at ease.

"You must be Christa," she said walking towards the threesome. "Tod hasn't stopped talking about you all week." She took the young woman's arm and hand with her both hands and squeezed lightly.

"He's told me a lot about you too," their guest replied.

"I think my husband would be more comfortable if we let him sneak off and change his clothes. Come in inside, we'll go into the living room."

They all followed her back inside and through to the front room. Christina noticed a crucifix carved from dark brown wood hanging on the kitchen wall and then that both the living room and dining room were on the front of the house. The living room was a much different style from the one she was accustomed to on R Street. Christina and Tod sat together on a cloth sofa, and his mother sat on the edge of the cushion of one of the upholstered arm chairs.

"Was there much traffic coming out from the city?" Mrs. Evans enquired?

"It was busy, until I got above Missouri. After that, it was a breeze. I hope these two men haven't had you locked up in the kitchen all day."

"The kitchen is no prison for me," the older woman laughed. "I do my most creative work there. Do you like to cook?"

"It's one of the many things I have on my to-do-list. Hopefully, now that school has stopped, I'll be able to get through to cooking more often."

"I have a glass of lemon aid on the go in the kitchen. I'm going to go and get it," Jennifer informed them as she stood up. "What would you two like to drink?"

"Do you have any ice tea?" her visitor inquired, and received an affirmative head nod.

"What about you Tod?"

"I'll have a Coke, please, Mom."

When his mother left, the young woman grabbed feverously for her fiancée's hand and said, "This is so neat Tod. You have your mother's hair and nose and your father's eyes and build."

"What about my mouth?"

"That's all mine," she joked, kissing him quickly.

Tod's father walked into the living room before his wife arrived back with the refreshments. "Where's Mum?"

"Getting us a drink."

"Oh, I better go tell her I want one too," he said and then disappeared again.

Christina noted that her father very seldom referred to his wife as Mum, when talking to his daughters. It was always – Marsh or your Mother. She didn't think he owned a pair of khakis, and she had never seen him wash his own car. The Evans both returned together and sat in the two unoccupied arm chairs.

"So Christa," John began, "Tod tells us that you're doing your internship at DC General."

"I have about 6 to 8 weeks left and then the real job starts. I think they're going to assign me to Pediatrics. At least that's what I overheard one of the doctors say."

"Oh, I'd love to do that," Jennifer said, "all those cuddly little babies."

"I don't think there's a lot of cuddling in Pediatrics," Christina assured her." It's divided into birth and aftercare. The new doctors get the birth, and the regular day doctors get most of the aftercare."

"Day doctors," Jennifer repeated.

"If a woman doesn't have a doctor or simply shows up in labor; she goes to the new doctors, who also usually get the evening or night shift. Invariably when it's their turn for a day shift, one of their assignees goes into labor at 2 a.m., and they get a call from the duty nurse to hustle on in."

Mrs. Evans looked at her son anxiously. "For you two's sake, I hope they don't put Christa into Pediatrics right away."

"Why, Mum?"

"That type of a schedule would be hard on newlyweds."

"If it's Pediatrics that she draws, we'll work it out," her son reassured her.

"John, why don't you come and help me bring everything in from the kitchen? Tod, you and Christa go find yourselves a place at the dining room table."

While they ate, they talked back and forth. First the parents would give her a tidbit on their son and then she would tell them something about herself or her family. When supper was over, Jennifer brought out the family photo albums. Tod's fiancée got to see a little of what he was like growing up and what the rest of the family looked like.

The Adams Sisters

After the albums, they all took a second cup of coffee from the tall sterling silver coffee pot that was on a tray on the buffet, beside the dining room table and went back to the living room. It was 9:30 p.m. when their son reminded them that his fiancée had to work in the morning. Mrs. Evans was visibly annoyed that the evening was coming to an end.

"Well, if it's like that, we'll have to let you two say your good nights, but I'm looking forward to seeing you again soon Christa, whenever you have a minute. Tod doesn't have to be here. We're all introduced now. Simply call and say you're dropping in for a cup of coffee."

"I will Mrs. Evans."

Call me Jennifer."

"Jennifer," then she turned to her fiancé.

"Come on Tod, walk me to my car." They both stood up. "Mr. Evans, I find your stories, about your son, so intriguing."

"Call me John too," he said standing up.

"I will and thank you both for a wonderful meal and such an exciting evening, bye-bye now."

"Drive carefully, on the way back down to Georgetown," Mrs. Evans called after them as they walked towards her car. "It's not dark yet, but it's almost and there are still a lot of people out on bikes in the night."

"I'll be careful. Thanks again."

"Bye."

***

Once Mr. Steinberg and Mr. Raconni had examined all the documents that Samantha brought in, the latter admitted that there was nothing in them for the CIA. She transferred the balance from the Baltimore General Services bank account into her personal account and then closed the business account and Post Office box. She also notified Fifth Dimension Internet offices that she wanted to close her account with them and have the automatic charge to her credit card stop. The company told her that they had already billed for the month of September and so would terminate the account on the first day of October. Finally, it was finished. She had real closure.

Samantha was as surprised as her parents at Christina's revelation. The news had acted as a kick start for her, and she was resolved to set up on her own and get back to a regular life as soon as possible. Who knows, maybe she and Ron Williams might get back together. She had seen him, on several occasions after the New Year's trip to Florida.

All the first weekend of September Samantha looked at rental accommodation. There were apartments in both Arlington and Alexandria, which were interesting, but they lost their attraction, when she looked at a condominium in the Waterfront area of Washington. At five p.m. on Sunday, the 7th of September there was only one place left on her list and then she would decide.

The gold Lexus moved slowly along Virginia Avenue in Foggy Bottom, heading west towards Georgetown. To the left was the Kennedy Center, Edward Durrell Stone's modern version of the Lincoln Memorial, which housed vast venues for the performing arts. Next came the East Block of the Italian-designed Watergate Complex, an address, which had been made famous by Richard Nixon's scandal. She turned right onto 25th Street, where it crossed H Street.

There was a double series of two storey town houses running from the corner with H Street, up the block to an eight level beige apartment building. The first group of town houses was made of red brick with mansard roofs and narrow upstairs dormers. The last unit in the string had a false facade over the mansard roof on the second storey, which was shaped like the end of a barn roof.

The next group of four, two storey townhouses were higher than the units south of them. They were fronted by a knee high brick retaining wall, at the sidewalk and individual sets of brick steps going up to the front door level. The first unit had a 'For Rent' sign hanging from a wrought iron frame.

Samantha parked the car and got out. Looking up 25th Street, she could see the beginning of a cluster of dozens of multi-shaped buildings, which were part of the campus of George Washington University. The property management agent, a tall brunette woman wearing a two piece navy pant suit and white blouse, opened the door, when she rang the bell.

"Thank you for calling. I wasn't sure, if you were still coming."

"Is it still for rent?"

"Yes," the woman said, closing the door behind them.

"I didn't realize the unit was this close to George Washington U until I arrived. How is it that this house is still for rent, when it's so close to the university and a new term is about to start?"

"Actually it was rented to a professor, who was to start at George Washington this term. He put down a deposit in

The Adams Sisters

August, and we were to receive the first and last month from him after Labor Day weekend. During the week, he called to say that he had accepted an offer at another university. He had to forfeit his deposit, and we were lucky to get this place back in the weekend paper."

"Have many people looked at it?"

"There were five yesterday and now you're the fourth today. They're all thinking about it. The unit is a tad pricey, if you're still a student."

Samantha let the agent show her through the house. It had been completely renovated inside. The floors were hardwood throughout. Door handles and hinges were made of aluminum. There was a gas fired, glass fireplace set three feet out from the wall in the living room. The kitchen had granite counter tops and a breakfast counter. A dinette was located between the kitchen and the living room. The stairs to the second level formed a semi-circle, as they went up. There were two bedrooms upstairs, which had skylights fitted into the buildings flat roof. The master bedroom had access to a large bathroom.

Samantha went all through it three times and then went out into the back yard. She definitely didn't have enough furniture, but she did have a start. The house was within walking distance to the State Department. It was a hop and a skip to her parent's residence in Georgetown. The condominium tower at Waterfront was nice and also convenient, but she would have to buy more furniture there too.

The young woman had lived in apartment towers in both Philadelphia and Manhattan, since leaving home. Coming back to R Street temporarily had made her realize how much she missed a house and instant access to the street. They were back in the living room looking at the fireplace, when she turned to the agent.

"I'll take it."

"You mean you're renting it?"

"Yes."

"I'll need a cheque and you'll have to sign a lease now."

"I have a check book in my purse and I'll sign the lease now."

"This is terrific," the property management woman exclaimed. "You won't regret it. This is a great location. There's almost instant access to the whole City, as well as

Georgetown. The Roosevelt Bridge is five minutes from here and then it's a straight line to Dulles Airport."

"Where do you want me to sign?"

"Let's go into the kitchen. It's easier to deal with paperwork on a counter top."

The following week Samantha had her furniture and household effects moved from a public storage depot into the house.

***

At 5 o'clock, on the second Sunday of September, Tod was just entering Georgetown, when he picked up his cell phone and called Christina's cell number. As they had agreed, he let it ring three times. Arriving on R Street NW, he remembered where the house was located from the afternoon when they had returned from Assateague Island. There was an unoccupied space on the curved, red brick driveway, so he parked there and then pressed redial on the cell phone, letting it ring three times again. Tod got out of the car and walked to the massive red front door.

His knock was answered by Charles, who was wearing a white shirt, bow tie and a pair of black trousers with a thin chalk stripe in them.

"Good evening Mr. Adams," the visitor greeted him politely.

"You must be Tod. We've been expecting you. Come right in." The young man heard the front door closing behind him. "Christa and her mother are still upstairs getting ready. Come on into the living room and sit down." Tod followed him and sat in an armchair. "What would you like to drink? I'm having a short Bourbon and soda on rocks."

"Any beer?" the young man asked.

"Sure, I'll be right back." When he returned, he put a tall glass of beer on a coaster on the end table beside his daughter's guest and then settled himself down on the white leather sofa. "Christa tells us you're a Doctor of Veterinary Science and that you're at the Dupont Circle Animal Clinic."

"Yes, to both, I finished in the spring and have been at the Clinic since graduating."

"How do you like it?"

"It's quite a learning curve. The staff performs all the same standard medical procedures on people's pets, as are performed on humans. This week we had an open heart surgery on a Labrador retriever. Today I prescribed medication for a cat that is suffering from high blood pressure."

The Adams Sisters

"Really, we've never had a dog or cat, so I haven't had to learn about how fast the pet world is evolving. However, from my work in insurance, I am aware that many people are starting to take out insurance policies on their pets."

"Some of the work we do is billed to insurance companies," the young Vet replied.

"Really. How would you like to earn a few extra bucks selling pet insurance for me at the Clinic?"

"I don't think it would be permitted, Mr. Adams."

"Of course not Tod, I'm only kidding."

At that moment, Christina and Marsha came down stairs and joined the men. Tod and Charles both stood up. Christina was wearing a grey flannel skirt and white silk blouse, which had no collar. Her mother wore a dress that was cut from an expensive piece of black and gold fabric. They started to apologize together, "Sorry, we're late. We couldn't get a hair dryer to work, and when it did, only low heat would come out of it."

"No problem Mother, your hair looks great. We've had a little man to man about Tod selling some insurance for me."

Christina looked at her fiancée who only shrugged his shoulders and smiled.

Marsha was more emphatic, "Forget about insurance, Charles; it's the weekend. Isn't somebody going to introduce us?"

"Excuse me," Christina said, clearing her throat. "Tod, this my father Charles, whom you've already met, and this is my mother Marsha. Mom and dad, this is my fiancé, Tod Evans." Both the Adams approached and shook his hand.

"I'm the bartender," Charles laughed. "What's everybody drinking?"

"Nothing for me Daddy," his daughter stammered nervously.

"I'll have a glass of red wine dear," his wife said, sitting down on the sofa. Christina took hold of Tod's hand and led him to the settee.

"So Tod," Marsha said, tell us all about yourself. We're dying to hear about you."

"Mother!" Christina snapped.

"It's ok, Christa. I don't mind," Tod said softly. "After all, this is our get to know each other evening. Once I've told your parents all about me, I'm not letting them off the hook. I want them to share a little of you with me." From there, he proceeded to unravel the story of his life in about twenty-five minutes.

"Good, that's great," Charles exclaimed clapping his hands, when their guest had finished. "You're a local boy who's played football; what an addition to the family. You know Tod I've had two season tickets to the Redskins for the past twenty years, and because my wife blessed me with two daughters, I never had a son upon whom I could bestow all my football wisdom."

"Dad, he's not your son yet," his daughter picked nervously. "I must become his wife first."

"Oh, that's only a formality Christa."

Marsha came to life, "Charles, are you insinuating that I am a formality?"

"Of course not Dear," he joked with her and winked at his daughter and her boyfriend. "You're my salvation. You know that."

Mrs. Adams relaxed. "Tod, Christa tells us you two want to get married as soon as possible and you only want a small wedding."

"That's right, Mrs. Adams, as soon as possible and only family and close friends."

"Do you have a license yet?" the middle aged woman pried.

"That's not a formality, son," his father-in-law to be joked. "Gotta have a license."

"We didn't get a license yet, Mom," her daughter informed her. "There's plenty of time for that."

"But it's going to be a Church wedding, isn't it Christa?" her mother continued.

Christina looked at Tod, and he replied for them both, "Yes, Mr. and Mrs. Adams, we want a Church wedding."

The parents looked at each other, smiled and relaxed. "You see Mother," Charles said, "now let's all take our glasses on into the dining room and plan a wedding while we eat."

"Yes, Christa, you show Tod into the dining room," Marsha said, "And Charles you come give me a hand with the platter and serving bowls."

"I can help with that, Mum." Her daughter offered.

"No, you take care of our guest. Your father and I can manage, can't we Charles."

"Certainly, you and Tod go on in and find yourselves a place. Your mother and I'll just be a minute."

The Adams Sisters

As soon as they were in the kitchen, Marsha bubbled over, "Oh Charles, I can't believe it. I get to plan a wedding. I'm so bored playing around in those damn flower beds. Planning a wedding is a real job, I've got to get my paper and pencil."

"What for," her husband asked?

"So I can take notes while we eat."

"Don't bother; your fingers will be all sticky. I'll turn on my dictating machine and give the tape to one of the girls at the office to transcribe for you."

"I don't want them to know all our private, family business around that office of yours. I'll get my pencil and paper."

After an entrée of artichokes marinated in lemon, they dined on a baked ham, Brussel sprouts smothered in blue cheese sauce, scalloped potatoes, and a side dish of cold slaw, which had raisins buried in it. Charles had been quiet while all the details of the ceremony and reception were discussed. They were back in the living room on coffee and black forest cake, when he suddenly came to life,

"Now there's one detail we haven't discussed, yet."

"What's that Daddy?"

"Your Mother's and my wedding present."

"No, Mom, make it a secret."

"There's no secret in wedding presents anymore, Dear," her mother assured her. "Every major store has a computerized, Wedding Gift Registry, these days. Both the couple and those giving gifts can even do the whole thing over the Internet. That's how I learned to use a computer. One of the clerks showed me the first couple of times, and now I can do it by myself. Your father and I have been discussing our wedding present to you both, all this week, before going to sleep."

Christina relented. "Ok, Dad, wedding present."

"After much discussion kids, we've decided to give you a two week trip to any place in the world that you want."

Tod looked at her." It's too much."

"It's not too much son," the elder Adams interrupted. "You've both been in school for seven or eight years, without a break and now you've started your careers, without even the traditional trip to Europe. You don't have to decide where you want to go now. Let us know when you've talked it over, and we'll have a travel agent handle all the details for us."

"You see, I told you they were nice people," Tod's wife to be said, cradling his hand in hers.

"But that's a lot of money Christa," Tod objected again.

"No, it's not," Marsha assured him. "Do you two have and sort of daydreams about where you would like to go for a honeymoon?"

"Go ahead Tod, tell them."

"We had talked a little about going for a visit to Spain someday," he admitted.

"Well, talk a little more and see if you'd like to honeymoon in Spain," Charles urged them.

"Tod, do you feel like going for a little walk?" Christa urged. "We could go over to Montrose Park. A walk would help your supper go down."

Christina put on a coat sweater and on the way by his car; he picked up a wind breaker. Once they were inside the park, he stopped and put his arms around her waist. Their lips met without either even thinking about it.

When they arrived back at the Adams residence, almost an hour later, Marsha did notice that her daughter's hair was mussed, but she didn't have time to think about it, because the couple told them that they had decided that they would accept a week in Spain, for a wedding present, because they wanted to see Spanish horses.

***

Once Samantha had all her things unpacked at the new rented townhouse, she began to see that she would need quite a few pieces to fill in the bare spaces around the house. However, first she decided to replace some of what she had brought with her from Manhattan, if it was worn or just looked cheap. The week after she moved in, she began to look for new bedding, during her lunch hours. On Wednesday at noon, she was browsing in a linen store in downtown Washington, when her cell phone rang inside her purse.

"Hello!"

"Hello, is this Ms. Angelou Adams?"

Samantha was full of panic. She hadn't noticed the distinctive ring pattern on the cell phone and had answered without thinking. Dam, she thought. Why didn't I have that Fifth Dimension account canceled sooner?

"Yes, Angelou Adams speaking."

"Good afternoon Ms. Adams, this is Doctor Lawrence Ossaga speaking."

"Yes, good afternoon Lawrence. You're coming through very clear today."

"That's because I'm in the United States."

"Well, fancy that."

The Adams Sisters

"Pardon?"

"Nothing Lawrence, where are you?"

"I'm in Washington."

"How long have you been in Washington?"

"Two weeks. I haven't had a chance to see Baltimore yet, but I'm told it's very nice."

"How long will you be staying in Washington?"

"For now, it looks like a year."

"A year," she exclaimed.

"Yes a year."

"What are you doing in Washington?"

"I've been given a one year contract to perform Commercial Attaché functions at the Nigerian Embassy."

"You have."

"Yes."

"That's incredible."

"Angelou, I'd like to come to Baltimore to see you."

"What for Lawrence?"

"Well, I would like to meet you in person and I'd like to ask you something."

"What would you like to ask me?"

"I was going to wait, until I saw you."

"I ... I would really like to know what you want to ask me," she pressed.

"Very well, the embassy is having a reception next Thursday night. I don't know anybody in this city yet. On the map, Baltimore doesn't seem to be very far from Washington. I was going to ask you, if you would like to accompany me to the reception next Thursday evening."

Samantha felt herself relaxing, "Well, that's very thoughtful of you Larry; I'm going to call you Larry. That's what everybody calls people named Lawrence, in America."

"I don't mind."

"Washington is full of women Larry. The magazines say there are ten women for every man in the city."

"I didn't know that," he replied awkwardly.

"With that many women there, I'm sure you wouldn't have any trouble finding someone to be your escort at the reception. Talk to some of the staff in the embassy. They'll have lots of contacts."

"Maybe they will, but they wouldn't be like you."

"I'm not special Larry. I'm just another business woman."

"That's not so, Ms. Adams."

"Why do you say that?"

"Ms. Adams, it was me who went to the docks to pick up the equipment for the wells that my people needed. It's me and only me who knows what you did."

"What did I do Larry?"

"You gave Baltimore General's share of the 15 million dollars to my people in the form of medicine and medical equipment. I would like to say thank you on behalf of all the people who will never know how much you helped them. That's why I would like you to be my guest at the reception."

"I don't know Larry. I'm just a little nobody in America."

"Please, Angelou?"

She was silent for almost a minute.

"Are you still there?" he inquired.

"All right, Dr. Ossaga, I'll accept your invitation. Do I need a pass or anything?"

"No card, your name will be on the guest list. Simply identify yourself at the door."

"Fine, I'll see you next week. My lunch is almost finished. I must get back to work."

"Bye then."

"Bye."

The following Thursday Samantha parked her metallic gold Lexus outside the Nigerian embassy and went to join the other guests, who were going through the front door. Once inside, the door man checked off her name on the list, and she went on into the reception. A waiter was circulating with a tray of drinks. She accepted one from him and then asked.

"Do you know what Doctor Lawrence Ossaga looks like?"

"Yes Ms."

"Can you point him out to me?" she continued.

"That's him over there in the gold and black tribal robe."

"Thank you."

Samantha sipped on her beverage and watched him. He looked a bit like Sebastian. He was talking to two older men. She finished her drink and then freshened it and began to walk towards the three men.

"Dr. Ossaga," she said.

The tall African in traditional regalia turned. He recognized her instantly. "Ms. Adams, you have come."

"Yes, I have."

He extended his hand, and she shook it. The other men were showing considerable curiosity. She noticed it and smiled at them. Lawrence began to speak.

The Adams Sisters

"Ms. Adams may I introduce you to a colleague and one of our guests in Washington this week. This is Colonel Ochim Jocommo, who arrived from Nigeria this afternoon, and this is Dr. Ojibwa, our ambassador to the United States."

She nodded her head and said, "My pleasure gentlemen."

"The pleasure is ours, Ms. Adams," they both replied together. "Tell us Lawrence, how do you come to know such an attractive woman in Washington?"

Dr. Ossaga laughed, "Ah, you two, it's a very long story, and I'm sure Ms. Adams doesn't want to go into all that."

She shook her head no.

"Would you please excuse us? We have a little catching up to do."

"By all means," ambassador Ojibwa said, "I must circulate among our guests anyway."

Ossaga and his guest walked to the back of the reception room and then out onto a torch lit patio. Other guests had already sought out the cooler outside air.

"I'm so glad you came."

"I'm glad I came too."

"You look different in person, so beautiful."

"You're quite a bit different than I imagined too."

"How different?"

"Much more handsome," she replied, flattering him ever so lightly.

"Thank you, you're too generous."

They talked for several more minutes and then he said, "Perhaps it's too cool out here for you?"

"No, no, I'm fine. There are a few things I want to tell you. Lots has changed in the past six months."

"Changed how?"

"To start, I'm no longer associated with Baltimore General Services."

"What happened?"

"The other shareholders didn't appreciate what I did with the company's share of your contract. There was a Special Meeting of Shareholders and Directors. They exercised a Shareholder's Covenant and bought me out."

"That's terrible."

"No, not really, I had other interests that I wanted to spend more time on."

"Like what?"

"Consulting."

"Is that as good as what you were doing?"

"I'm starting to like it more and more. As a matter of fact, I'm currently working on a contract for the American Government."

"Really."

"Yes, it's with the State Department here in Washington."

"Are you commuting from Baltimore?"

"I was until two weeks ago. Now I've rented a place here and moved my things."

"How wonderful."

"Yes, Washington is great a great city and it's also where I grew up."

"How did you get to Baltimore?"

"I had an unhappy engagement, which didn't end in marriage and I needed a change. The Baltimore opportunity was there for the taking, and I took it."

"But if you're no longer with Baltimore General Services and you're living in Washington, how was I able to telephone you."

"That was my private line at work. When I left, I had all my calls on it forwarded to my cell phone."

"Can you do that?"

"It's very common in America. That old number in Baltimore is to be canceled for good at the end of September."

"If I need to speak to you again, after the end of September, how will I contact you?"

"I'll give you my cell number," she said, digging in her purse for a pen and pad. "You should give me your number too. I may want an escort for lunch someday."

"I hope you will want one and soon."

Samantha smiled at him as she passed him her number.

"There's one more thing."

"What is that?"

"Not all of the shareholders were happy merely expulsing me from the company; some also wanted to take all my assets."

"I must admit; it's the same in Nigeria," he told her. "I've heard of shareholders losing their life for a lot less than what you did."

"That's why I'm using my other name."

He looked surprised. "What other name?"

"My full name is Samantha Angelou Adams," she explained. "While I was in Baltimore I shortened it to Angelou Adams, because I wanted to make myself as invisible as possible for my ex-fiancé. For the reasons you have just

The Adams Sisters

alluded to, I've been using Samantha Adams, since moving to Washington."

"Then should I call you Samantha Adams?" he asked hesitantly.

"If you want to find me in the phone book, you'll have to look under Samantha. Also, my family and all the people whom I've met here, during the past six months, know me as Samantha or Sam."

"Then I'll keep your secret and nobody will ever know what Angelou Adams did."

"If you can keep that secret Larry; then maybe you and I will get to know each other outside a fax machine."

He raised his near empty glass of wine and clinked it against hers saying, "To Samantha!"

"I'll drink to that Larry. Now why don't we go back inside and find a refill for you?"

He put out his elbow saying, "May I have the honor, Ms. Samantha Adams?"

"Certainly Doctor," she replied, linking her hand in the crook of his arm, as they walked back inside.

****

17 - Finca Sierra

Marsha Adams devoured half a dozen large print, illustrated books and three videos on wedding planning, all within the same week. By the third weekend in September she was ready to sit down and start to discuss the ceremony, the reception and the wedding as a whole. Since the frost would be on the pumpkin, she and her daughter decided that autumn would be the nuptial theme, and given the perchance of rain or strong winds at that time of the year; they decided both the ceremony and reception would be held inside.

The wedding would take place at Holy Trinity Church, where the family had attended Sunday service, since Christina was a young girl. The bride to be had vetoed a reception at Cabot. It was too far a drive from the Church, and there were negative memories associated with it for her. She also said no to the Georgetown Inn, making it understood that she wanted a reception, which had an aroma of autumn, was surrounded by trees, and built with stone and wood. The final choice was an Inn on MacArthur Boulevard, in Potomac MD, along the old C&O Canal.

The Inn had a large reception room downstairs with a fireplace and a wide spiral staircase to the dining area upstairs. Once Saturday, October 25th was confirmed by both the

The Adams Sisters

Church and the Inn, invitations went out. In keeping with the couple's wishes to have a small intimate wedding, each side received 15 invitations to send to their choice of aunts, uncles, friends or professional associates. In motif, on the front of the cards, there were dried wild flowers and herbs wrapped in the colors of autumn. A week before the ceremony the couple rented a one bedroom apartment on Ordway Street. NW, in Cleveland Park, which is straight up Connecticut Avenue from downtown and on the east side of the Zoo, in Rock Creek Park. The unit would come vacant on November 1st.

Christina wore a long, white satin gown with a loose hood and no part of the dress trailing behind her on the isle. At 3 p.m. the piano started playing and the choir broke out into "I Will Always Love You", she felt her father's hand take her firmly by the arm and begin to move her forward. As she walked up the aisle, the young woman was aware of the people in the pews but couldn't see them. She couldn't even feel the floor underneath her feet, when the Processional finished.

Samantha came forward and read a passage from the Bible, which her sister and brother-in-law to be had chosen. Then following a short recitation on the meaning of marriage, the exchange of vows began. Christina heard the young man in the tux beside her say "I do!" and then it was her turn.

"Do you Christina Adams take Tod Evans as your lawful husband, to have and to hold, from this day forward, for better or for worse, for richer and for poorer, in sickness and in health, to love and cherish, until death do you part?"

"I do."

She turned to face her husband, and he slipped a platinum band over the knuckle of the third finger of her left hand. Without waiting to be told, he leaned over and brushed his lips over hers. An audible sign was heard coming from those sitting in the pews.

Christina's bouquet was made of dried wildflowers and autumn herbs. As she drew back her arm to toss it into the waiting wedding party, the sun caught her in the eyes, and she couldn't see to aim in the direction, where Samantha stood. A few seconds later Tod's younger sister Gwyn started jumping up and down holding the bouquet in her hand. A volley of cheers and clapping was heard. Once the pictures were taken, and the bride and groom had entered the lead car, everyone went to their vehicles. The wedding procession drove to M Street and then out along MacArthur Boulevard.

It wasn't a long drive and soon the wedding guests were inside the Inn, where the décor was autumn and a bright fire was burning in the field stone fireplace. Branches of colorful leaves hung down from the rough hued beams. On one of the long tables from which apple cider or wine were being served, a bushel basket of russet apples lay on its side with the fruit spilling out onto the white tablecloth. On another table, there were pumpkins and on a third bunches of wild grapes that were still attached to the vine.

Before the wedding party went up the wide spiral staircase, the bride and groom worked their way around the reception introducing each other to members of their family or old family friends. Christina was curious about the tall black man, who had accompanied her sister. Skillfully she steered herself and her new husband towards them. As soon as they were within touching distance, the sisters flung their arms around each other laughing hysterically.

"Oh, Christa it was so perfect," Samantha cried with visible tears.

Tod waited until they had calmed, before saying, "Samantha; we so appreciated your reading that passage from the Bible."

"I would have volunteered, if you hadn't asked me," his new sister-in-law declared.

"Samantha, aren't you going to introduce us?" the bride asked.

"Oh, excuse me, Larry I'd like you to meet my sister Christa and her husband Tod. Everybody, this is Dr. Larry Ossaga."

"Do you work in Washington, Dr. Ossaga?" the bride asked politely.

"Yes, as a matter of fact I do Christa. I'm a Commercial Attaché at the Nigerian Embassy."

Christina looked at her sister and raised her eyebrows. Next it was Jewel and her husband Benjamin Denton.

"Oh, Christa I'm so happy for you!" her friend exclaimed, hugging her closely.

"Jewel, if you hadn't been carrying your cell phone that day, this might not be happening."

"I'll never tell."

"Neither will I," Christina gushed, taking Tod by the arm. "Thank you so much for being my maid of honor."

"That's what friends, for the eight years, do for each other," Jewel giggled.

The Adams Sisters

"Those were my exact words to you, when you thanked me for escorting you to the Chuppah in July," Christina reminded her.

Jewel squeezed Ben's arm and smiled at Christina mischievously saying, "I see my parents over there. Banjo and I are going to go talk with them."

"Don't forget you and Ben are seated at our table. Tell your parents that their seats are reserved at my parent's table. Tod's parents will also be seated there."

After half an hour had passed, the Host mounted two or three steps of the staircase and held a small silver triangle above his head. While circling a silver bar inside it, to gain the guests attention, he called out, "Good afternoon ladies and gentlemen, welcome to the Inn. We are ready to serve you now, so if you please, follow me upstairs."

The centerpieces on the nuptial tables were low copper buckets filled with gourds, pine cones and clusters of acorns. Silk, autumn colored leaves, were scattered here and there on the table cloths. Each guest's name was neatly printed on a small white setting-card. There were platters of Brie, Gouda and Roquefort cheeses, as well as a selection of biscuits, crackers and pumpkin bread in baskets at every second place, to get the guests started while dinner was being served.

The wedding meal began with Chesapeake Bay crab chowder or an autumn salad. Following that, food carts went back and forth between the tables; while the waiters served dinner plates with slices of roast beef, servings of sea bass, grilled chicken or vegetarian pasta, along with roasted root vegetables, asparagus, mashed potatoes, pan fried potatoes, stewed mushrooms and gravy. As well as serving the meal, they also filled or refilled glasses with water, cider and white or red wine.

Every five minutes, someone, would start clinking silverware against a glass, and when the others joined in, Tod and Christina would give them a kiss. While they ate, a number of people from both families stood up and made short speeches on the merits of the bride or groom and in general, the wonders of married life. When the end of the main meal was cleared away, the wedding cake was wheeled in, and the newlyweds held the warmed knife together, while it sliced down through the frosting and into the fluffy interior.

After coffee and a slice of wedding cake, Tod stood up and thanked everyone for coming and for their many gifts. He explained that he and his new wife would be leaving shortly, as they had to change and drive out to Dulles Airport, where they were catching a plane to Spain for their honeymoon. Before sitting down, he invited them all to stay – have second or third helpings and get to know each other.

Hardly had the groom regained his chair, when Charles rose and announced that everyone was invited back to the Adams house following the reception and that parking along R Street was permitted. As an added incentive, he told them that he had engaged a singer and three musicians. They would attempt to play all requested songs and tunes, and provide dance music for as long as anyone stayed.

***

At 10.00 a.m. on Monday September 26, an American Airlines Boeing jet left the Atlantic Ocean behind and began to fly in over Portugal. Half an hour later the pilot announced that they had begun their descent down from thirty thousand feet that they would be at the docking gate at 11 a.m. Madrid time and that the temperature on the ground was twenty-five degrees Celsius. Following this announcement, the Cabin Attendant passed out Visitors Immigration Cards for them to fill out as all passengers not carrying an EU passport would be asked for the card and their passport by the Spanish Authorities. The first Spanish word that they saw was Aeropuerto on the Terminal building, as the plane landed at Barajas airport. They were both excited and jokingly greeted each other in Spanish, as their mental preparation for a week on the ground in another language began.

Once they were through immigration, the couple looked for the nearest cash machine. As soon as they inserted their plastic cards a language menu choice appeared on the screen. They each withdrew three hundred Euros. From there, they went to find the car rental company through which reservations had been made.

Tod and Christina had mapped out their route in advance. From the airport, they would head west to Zaragoza then south to Barcelona. Then they would travel west along the Mediterranean as far as Valencia, where they would turn inland towards Albacente, before returning to spend the balance of their honeymoon in the Spanish capital city of Madrid. As they pulled out of the rental car lot, Tod bugled,

"Ok, Mrs. Evans, have you fastened your seat belt?"

"Si Capitan!"

"Are you ready to navigate us out of here and onto Zaragoza?"

The Adams Sisters

"I think so, Honey. I've got two maps, a Spanish/English dictionary, a guide book and a magnifying glass. We're looking for any sign that says E90 or direction arrows pointing to Guadalajara."

"How do you spell that, Senora?"

"G U A D A L A J A R A."

The first main artery was Avenida de la Hispanidad.

"I'm glad they drive on the same side of the road, as we do in America," Tod remarked.

"I never thought of that," she admitted. "Look the sign says Eisenhower. They're just as American as we are."

"Check the map to see where Eisenhower goes."

"Oh, you should take Eisenhower," she exclaimed.

"Which way?"

"East."

"What's east in Spanish?"

"Este."

"Thanks, I should have remembered and west is oeste."

"Right you are Preppy. We'll really be Sergio and Sonia by the time we get back to DC if we keep it up like this."

The full name for Eisenhower was Glorieta de Eisenhower, and as they traveled east, it became N II and then E90. After they had driven 25 km the first sign for Guadalajara appeared. Both of them relaxed and began to enjoy the drive. They were in Zaragoza by 4 p.m...

Zaragoza is the political and cultural center of the autonomous community or province of Aragon. It was founded in 14 BC by Augustus, as a retirement colony for Roman veterans. After they had left the Autovia or turnpike, Christina guided him along a series of streets, until they were in the area of the Plaza del Pilar. There were a number of Hotels and Hostals in the small side streets around the Plaza.

The guide book explained that a Hotel was much the same as in the US and that a Hostal was less expensive, usually didn't include breakfast and that rooms came either with a bathroom or with the use of a bathroom in the corridor. They decided to stick with a hotel so picked one that looked as if it might suit their tastes, entered and walked towards the registration desk, where they intended to use their Spanish. Each of them took a turn ordering a room, but had to keep asking each other how to say some word or another. Finally, the clerk asked them if they spoke English. Both their faces lit up with smiles as they exclaimed together,

"Si, si!"

Then the Spaniard asked, "A room?"

"Si, con bano," Tod said.

"All the rooms come with a bath, Sir," the Spaniard replied and Christina laughed along with her husband.

The clerk told them what the price was in Euros for the night. They simply said they would take it and then they filled out the registration card.

Once their room door closed behind them, they dropped their bags, burst out laughing and hugged each other.

"Well, I guess we can now say that we've officially landed," Tod remarked.

"Oh, we're landed all right," she agreed, "and it wasn't that bad."

"I can't believe that Autovia," he continued. "It's better than the interstate highways in the States."

"It's not V Tod. You have to say B."

"B what?"

"It's pronounced Autobia and not Autovia."

"Oh yes, I remember now, a V is a B in Spanish."

"We didn't see many horses this afternoon," she lamented. "I was expecting to see Mustangs and Andalusians everywhere, beside the road. Instead, all I saw were huge black silhouettes of bulls on hills and those windmill things."

"Aren't those wind turbines unreal, there must be thousands of them," Tod replied as he pulled back the curtain and looked at the courtyard behind the hotel. "They look like something out of the War of the Worlds."

"I wonder if we're going to start making electricity with those things at home," she pondered.

"There are already quite a few in California," he confirmed, "but I think they should try to harness the tides, before we start playing around with something as fickle as the wind. Tides go up and down twice a day, rain or shine. If they could be harnessed, electricity would become as cheap as the air."

"Air is free, Tod."

"That's what I mean."

"Let's get showered and go back outside to see some of this city, before I'm tempted to see how soft that bed is," she suggested.

"Ok, first we'll find a place to have supper and then we'll see what's happening this evening."

"Maybe the desk clerk can suggest something."

"You try to talk to him later, but for now come on in and have a shower with me," he urged.

The Adams Sisters 241

Christina laughed and began to slip out of her soiled travelling clothes. "That's right, we're Mr. and Mrs. That means we can take a shower together."

"We can do more than take a shower together," he taunted.

"I know; it's still our wedding night and we haven't consummated our marriage yet," she replied jokingly, with a wide smile on her face.

"There'll be plenty of time for consummating," he assured her.

"I wouldn't be so sure of that," she said looking at his nakedness. "Time may have just run out for you, Mr. Preppy Evans."

He approached her casually, "Are you challenging me, Mrs. Evans?"

She grinned and arched her back so that her chest was thrown forward. "It's half past challenging time, big boy," she purred as they wrapped their arms around each other.

"I don't have any ahhhhhh," he stammered.

"You don't need any ahhhhh, we're married," she replied taking a step towards the bed, with him in her arms. "Besides, this is my safe time."

"Is this called Giant Steps and Baby Steps?" he asked.

She smiled up at him and walked him another step towards the bed. "Yea, I'm the giant and you're the baby."

"I guess I'll have to give in then, if it's like that," he said as he faked losing his balance and fell backwards onto the bed, with her on top of him.

"Are you ready for your medicine, big boy?" she cajoled, as she leaned forward and kissed him.

Half an hour later she rolled away from him and giggled, "I hope I don't become addicted to that."

"And if you do?"

"I might not want to go to work anymore."

"So, I'll work for the both of us."

"But it would be you who I'd be addicted to, so you'd have to stay home too."

"Then we'd have a problem," he agreed and asked,. "Do you want to try to make it through to the shower now?" She nodded her head to say yes. "Come on," he said kneeling up on the bed, taking hold of one of her hands.

Once they were dressed, they went downstairs. There was a new attendant at the desk. He told them exactly what they needed to know, as well as the fact that siesta was just finishing in the town, and many people would soon come into the center of the city to walk and talk, until at least 11 o'clock. Following the desk clerk's directions, the couple found themselves in Plaza de Santa Marta. It was brimming over with *tapas bars* and small shops selling chocolate-dipped and candied fruits.

"Let's do tapas," she suggested, stepping ahead of him and spinning about on one foot. "I so much liked that one we ate in Morgan when you gave me my ring. If we still have room after tapas, I think I'd like one or two chocolate covered, candied strawberries, like those in that window."

"Fine by me, but let's look at the menus posted outside each restaurant's doors. Some of them seem to specialize in one dish and others in another."

"You chose the place and once I've eaten, I'll tell you whether you've made a good choice or not."

After a light meal and several cups of wine, they joined in with the Zargozans strolling through the streets. At one point, they came across an archeological dig, which was lit up and occupied a whole city block. Following Christina's guide book, they made it back through the maze of streets, which changed their names every block or so, and into the vast square known as Plaza del Pilar, which contains an aluminum obelisk, at least four stories high and which is surrounded by a fusion of other architectural shapes. Not far from there they found a massive Baroque structure, which is the Basilica that was protected by the Virgin through two bombings, during the Spanish Civil War. At the end of their walk, they resolved to go for a tour through the Museo Camon Aznar, which houses a permanent exhibit of Goya, after breakfast in the morning and then to strike out for Barcelona.

On Monday morning at 11 a.m. the newlyweds gassed up their vehicle and started to find their way through a series of traffic circles, which led them on a zigzag route, back out to the major highways. Near the outskirts of the city, they started to see signs, which indicated both Madrid and Barcelona. All of a sudden, a large green overhead arrow loomed in front of them, and Christina reacted fast.

"There Tod, it says Barcelona E90, take that direction." Tod was already in the outside lane of the traffic circle and veered off in the direction, which the arrow indicated. Soon the overpasses and clover leafs disappeared, and they were on their way to Barcelona.

The Adams Sisters

"See if you can find out what the E and N mean in front of the numbers on these highways."

She searched the symbol key on the map and replied. "E means European and N means National."

"These European routes are like major interstate throughways in the US," Tod commented. "We cover a lot of distance very quickly, but if we stay on them, we won't end up seeing very much of Spain."

"I know," his wife agreed, "but counting today, we have only 6 full days left. All the horse ranches I looked up are in the south of Spain, between Madrid and the Mediterranean. They're not on major highways so it may take us extra time to find them. Also, we should really arrive back in Madrid early Friday because there is a lot to see there too, and it will be the weekend. If we use these turnpikes, when they're available; we won't run short of time at the end."

"Ok, we'll use them, when we're traveling between cities."

Before long, they were driving through a very old mountain chain known as the Sierra de Alcubierre. Eons of wind and rain had worn away the jagged peaks, until they were nothing, but buttes and grass covered rolling hills. In places the ribbon of asphalt, on which they drove, spanned deep gorges, which were a quarter of a mile wide at the top. Double spans of trestles rose up, almost a quarter of a mile from the canyons' floors to support the highway.

At the half way marker to Barcelona, the honeymooners decided to break for lunch at one of the huge, futuristic service centers, which were built on the median of the Autovia. The southbound parking lot was half filled with trucks, campers, and cars. The couple walked through a clear Plexiglas tube over the traffic racing past underneath them, on the Autovia, to reach the dining and amenities facility.

There was something for every taste in the Center. If travelers were hungry, they had a choice. There were fast food, self-serve, a sit down enclosed dining room and a bar. There was a kiosk selling CD's and sun glasses and also a small store selling local produce such as wine, cheese; honey and vacuum packed smoked legs of lamb. An arcade filled with electronic games beckoned to the kids. In an open space, several coin operated vibrator beds offered relief to stiff drivers. Baby change rooms, stocked with free paper diapers were a reprieve to both infants and mothers.

As they continued driving south, after leaving the rest stop, the greenery turned brown and then in some areas the countryside looked as if it was only fine sand. The closer they approached Barcelona, the more the traffic increased and the number of lanes on the highway first doubled and then tripled.

"This is worse than LA.," Tod commented.

"I always thought Spain was people riding around on donkeys. How did they get so Americanized?"

"I don't think America has any monopoly on the growth of these mazes," her husband assured her. "This is what comes with the automobile and increased mobility."

The twelve lane highway they were driving on began to split into a Y. To the left the signs indicated Centro or Downtown and to the right Puerto or Port. "Keep following all the signs that say Centro," Christina advised him.

Before long both sides of the highway were crowded with massive construction sites, cranes and partially completed concrete superstructures. From a distance, several seemed as high as the Empire State Building. Many supported the names of well-known international and multi-national corporations.

"Stay over on the left," Christina advised. "That's the way to Gran Via. It's one of the principal streets in Centro."

Barcelona is the gateway, not only to Catalunya, but also to the Mediterranean. It's an urban carnival squeezed in between the mesmerizing blue waters of the Mediterranean and the green Tibidabo hills. The surrealism of Dali, Picasso and Mio has spilled over into the architecture of the city's buildings, whether they are of Moorish or modern inspiration.

Christina navigated them through to an area of the city known as the Plaza de Catalunya, which has fountains and statues. The Plaza was surrounded by a huge modern shopping center called the Triangle and older multi-story apartment buildings that were built of sandstone.

"This is insane," Tod exclaimed, "they double park everywhere."

"Watch out Tod, that car is turning."

"He didn't even give a signal."

"Tell that to the rental company," she warned.

Once the car was parked, they returned to the square. Christina took pictures of the fountain, the statues, and Tod. She even asked a pedestrian to snap them together.

"Oh, look," she exclaimed. "They call their subway the Metro, just like we do in DC."

His mind was elsewhere. "I really like their money."

"Pardon?"

"These ten, twenty and fifty cent pieces are like our dollar."

The Adams Sisters

"I hadn't really thought about it," she had to admit.

"Do you feel like going into that Triangle complex and spending a few Euros?" he asked.

"Maybe later, but for now, let's walk. The guide book says a stroll down Las Rambles is worthwhile. Look it starts over there, see the street sign."

The walk down Las Rambles, a wide sidewalk boulevard with one way streets on either side, proved to have been the right choice. The 12 block Boulevard kept changing every hundred feet. At first there were flower sellers and vendors with cages full of colorful birds. Then the sidewalk gave way to a maze of outside cafés, restaurants, bars and an amazing assortment of artists displaying oil paintings, ceramic jewelry, and pottery or painting portraits. It all ended at the harbor, and a statue of Christopher Columbus standing on the top of a high column with his arm outstretched out towards the Mediterranean.

The couple found a Hostal for the night and rode an open cage elevator up eight floors with their bags, to a room, which had a bath. That evening they went into a large upstairs restaurant overlooking a busy intersection. Their meal started with a basket of warm bread, a cold bottle of white wine and an oval tray covered with twelve different kinds of thinly sliced, cured meats. After the entrée, they ordered a main course of vegetables and grilled lamb, sliced from a spit above an open charcoal fire, in the middle of the room.

Early Wednesday afternoon found them in Valencia - the heart of Costa Blanca, which is a 466 kilometer ribbon of Mediterranean shoreline that alternates between soft dunes and jagged promontories. They spent what remained of the day on the sand, out front of the Casino, where they were staying that night. In between bouts of splashing in the warm sea, they ate huge, juicy oranges, which came from a fruit stand in front of one of the dozens orange groves; they had passed earlier, while driving.

"I can't believe how my Spanish is coming back to me," Christina remarked as she passed a wholly peeled orange to her husband.

"I know," he replied, "I bought and paid for these oranges, without missing a word. I'm sure they thought we were from another part of Spain."

"Let's hope we have as much luck tomorrow. These are touristy places we've been around so far. I don't know what Albacete is going to be like."

"So, what's on the agenda?"

"If we arrive in town early enough, we should be able to catch the weekly horse sale, which is held from 9 a.m. until noon."

"That won't be a problem. Albacete is half way between here and Madrid and Madrid is only about 350 clicks."

"I also have addresses and maps for three breeder's ranches outside the city. Two of them have a bed and breakfast arrangement for people visiting the farm."

"I can hardly wait to smell horse manure again," he joked.

She burst out laughing, "Me too!"

"If we win big on the slots tonight, we'll enquire about buying a horse tomorrow."

"Wouldn't that be unreal," Christina exclaimed. "I'd so much love to bring a Spanish horse back to the States."

"Come on; let's go in the water again, I'm getting all sticky from these oranges."

The purebred Spanish horse or Andalusian, descends from the earliest known saddle horses. One of the few natural breeds of the world; they come from the same ancestral stock as the Numidian, Libyan or Berber horses, which came from the wild horse of Central Asia. The Spanish horse is better than any other horse, because of its agility, its resilience and the distension of its rhythmic movements.

A foal born from an approved breeding stallion and mare must be inspected by the Spanish Military before it is five months old. Information held in the Spanish State Stud Book for the purebred Spanish horse is so comprehensive that all details, of all registered horses and their progeny are listed, from the late 1800's on. This includes blood type information, breeder's brands and cross references to ancestors, progeny, and their progeny's progeny.

The next day the Evans arrived in the interior town of Albacete, a little before 9 a.m. The first person they asked gave very explicit directions to the horse sale. The event was only starting, when they took a place in the wooden bleachers, which surrounded the indoor, earth floor ring. First came the mares; then the colts and lastly the stallions. There were warm bloods, show jumpers, colored sport, and dressage horses.

When the sale was over, the couple had lunch and then began to try to find their way to one of the breeding farms called, Finca Sierra or Mountain Ranch, for which Christina had an address. On the edge of town, a gas station attendant

The Adams Sisters

told them that the ranch was about twenty-five kilometers north. He said to follow the signs.

The owner's wife was remarkably young and very attractive. After signing them in and showing them to their rooms, in halting English with a British accent she urged, "If you hurry, you will be able to find the orientation tour. My husband José gives it once a day. Take these cassette players and ear plugs. His explanations are only in Spanish."

Christina and Tod hurried back outside to join a group, which had gathered about the old well, in the center of the courtyard. At exactly 2 p.m., a handsome young Spaniard introduced himself as José and invited the group to follow him for a tour of the stables. When he stopped in front of one of the stall doors over the top of which reached the head and mane of a well groomed jet black stallion, their guide began to speak in Spanish. The young American couple switched on their cassette players.

"The purebred herd at Finca Sierra originated in the 1980's with the purchase of several mares. First there was Guadalajara, born in 1965, under the Parladé brand and then came Osborne and Urquijo, who were younger. They were bred initially to Hermoso VIII and Remache, who had Yeguada Militar bloodlines. Later all three were bred with Brioso IV and Novata V, who were both born in 1970, under the Buendía brand and were 100% true bloodlines. This is the stallion Jebel II, who is a direct descendant from the first herd."

When José had finished, he moved to another open stall door and continued with the same sort of explanations. This was repeated for fourteen other horses. When they reached the far end of the stables, a wide door opened back out into the bright afternoon sun.

"I hope you have enjoyed the tour. Please feel free to browse through the stables and paddocks on your own. Don't forget to visit our modest gift shop at the ranch house, before leaving. You'll find a large collection of, one-of-a-kind items, all related to horses."

That night before falling to sleep, the Evans couple quietly discussed all that they had seen and heard, during the day.

"Visiting this place alone was worth a trip to Spain," Tod whispered in her ear.

"I know, I'd like to bring a horse back with me," his wife admitted.

"When we get back home, I'm going to do a little write up on this location and send it into an equestrian magazine that I subscribe to."

"I'll give you some photos to include with your article," she offered.

"Can you imagine setting up a horse operation like this in the States?"

"Yes, and I'll bet that you're the type of person who could do it."

"Do you really believe that?"

"I do!" she replied, unbuttoning his pajamas jacket.

He stroked her silky hair, ran his hand gently over her back and drew her in close against him. She began to feel excited and her mouth found his. When they were fatigued, they drifted off into a deep sleep, loosely holding each other in their arms.

The next morning, after a delicious breakfast, which began with a glass of thick pulpy *naranja or orange juice*, and was followed by double servings of *huevos rancheros or ranch style eggs* and *café con liche*, the newlyweds left Finca Sierra and followed the rural, paved highway back to Albacete. On the outskirts of the town, they picked up the National III, which would take them north to Madrid.

Near noon, the rental vehicle arrived in the south east corner of the Comunidad de Madrid and began to make its way through a series of ring roads, which encircles the ancient Spanish capital city, much like the Capitol Beltway does in DC.. Vehicles filled all lanes and traffic slowed to 30 km per hour. Heat waves shimmered up off the black asphalt.

"Is everything okay navigator?" he asked.

"I'm fine," she assured him coming out of her Finca Sierra daydream. "Follow all the signs for El Centro. We'll try Hostal Citadel first. It's in El Centro, and the Metro Station Sol is nearby."

"Good, as soon as we find a place, I want to return this buggy to the airport, and then come back to the Hotel on the Metro."

"Are you sure we shouldn't keep the car, until we take off."

"We can get around easier on foot, in the part of Madrid that we're planning to see. It's such a hassle getting through the traffic and finding parking. While you were in the bath this morning, I checked over the map. It's a 13 minute Metro ride from El Centro to the airport. If we plan on taking the Metro to catch our plane, we won't have to leave the downtown four

The Adams Sisters

hours before the flight to avoid traffic jams and allow time to return the car."

"Okay then we'll take it back today," she agreed.

"How much is a room per night at the Hostal Citadel?" he inquired.

"About seventy Euros, but if we don't like the look of it, there's an American chain not far away, which is three hundred and fifty Euros a night."

"I'd rather bring back some nice gifts for everybody with the money we'd save, as long as the Hostal is safe and clean."

"I'd also like a little Spanish character," she emphasized then continued, "I'll come to the airport with you. Once the car is returned, we can roam around Madrid until we're tired and then hop the Metro back to the Sol station."

"Sounds like a game plan to me."

The Hostal Citadel turned out to be very suitable. There were quite a number of young Americans in the lobby. Some wore backpacks and others pulled suitcases, which glided along on hidden wheels. The room was pleasant, light-filled and had a full-bath. It also included a hairdryer, telephone, TV, air conditioning, heating, a valuables safe and free wireless (WIFI) internet access. To top all this off, there was a small wrought iron balcony.

After leaving their luggage at the Hostal, it took an hour and fifty – five minutes to drive out to Barajas, where the Aeropuerto was located. When the paperwork was completed, they left the automobile concessionaire and entered the Main Terminal, where they followed the Metro signs. The train cars from the airport to the Nuevos Ministerios Station were huge and even more modern than those in Washington. Once they transferred to the Blue Line, it was just like any other subway. They got off at the Banco de Espana Station and began walking in the general direction of their Hostal.

By now both Tod and Christina were acclimatized and ready to take on the restless energy, which seemed to pulsate everywhere. They knew siesta had started, because the church bells were chiming, and some of the stores were closing; however, the majority of the crowds on the street paid little attention. The hot, dry air and the buzz of the Madrilenos cast a spell over them, and they entered into the colorful, tide of people, which moved along the sidewalks. After some time, they spotted signs for the Sol Metro station and passed on to Plaza Mayor, which is the hub of Centro. It was there that Christina started to buy souvenirs and gifts.

Early Saturday morning the couple headed towards the Huertas, one of Madrid's five main neighborhoods, to explore the city's three great museums. Christina was overwhelmed by the collection of women's fashion dating from the 18th century to the present, which covered a whole level in the Queen Sofia Museum. Lunch was a pitcher of sangria and a platter brimming with chocolate delights, individually chosen from a buffet of one hundred and fifty items, made entirely or partially of chocolate.

That evening Christina and Tod went to see a Spanish play at 7:30 p.m., which was about a young couple settling in after their honeymoon. The new wife had to get used to a husband, who now seemed to never dress in anything, but a singlet undershirt and who was unshaven more often than he was shaved. He, on the other hand, had never seen her in hair rollers, and now the ironing board was a permanent fixture in their kitchen. Around 10:30 p.m., they wandered into a Café for supper and were just in time to catch a flamenco dancer's performance.

On Sunday morning, they checked out at ten, temporarily stored their bags in the room beside the Front Desk and then went out to roam around El Rastro or the Flea Market. It was an incredible experience that took them through a labyrinth of side streets, lanes, and arches. Christina almost bought an antique chair from an overzealous street merchant. She couldn't seem to say no. As much as their senses were overwhelmed by the sights, sounds and smell coming from every direction, around noon they cut short their visit to the people's market, had a quick tapas and coffee, and then headed for the Plaza de Toros, where there was an early bullfight.

Bullfights have changed considerably since Hemmingway's days. There really isn't much of a fight anymore. Today the picadors ride horses, which are encased in light-weight, armor. After each bull is stung by the horsemen, the matador dutifully frees him from his existence. They watched for an hour and then as pre-arranged, went back to the Hostal to collect their bags and took the Metro out to Barajas.

Late Sunday evening, Air traffic control directed a new Boeing out of the main jet stream and began leading it up The Dulles Airport Access Expressway into its final approach, to an available runway. When the Tod and Christina Evans cleared US customs, they immediately collected their baggage from a

The Adams Sisters

long revolving conveyor belt. The airport was crowded with people arriving for Monday morning appointments in the Capitol. The couple quickly piled everything onto a push cart, went outside and loaded it all into a cab.

That night they slept together in Christina's room at the Adams house. They would stay there, until their apartment in Cleveland Park would be set up enough to live in. Neither of them had any furniture, but there had been many wedding gifts.

On Monday morning November 3, Tod walked to work for the first time in his life. When Christina arrived at the General Hospital, she went to her pigeon hole and retrieved her routing slip. It indicated the name of the doctor she was to report to in Pediatrics. Since no one, but Human Resources, knew she had been on her honeymoon, it was a quiet reintegration into the hospital for her.

****

18 - Gilbert's Corner

Charles Adams had followed the Washington Redskins for years. Almost since the beginning, he had purchased season tickets. So many important things had happened on those bleachers. A score of insurance deals were closed while the teams moved back and forth out on the playing field. Marsha had told him that she was expecting Christina as they hugged each other, after an overtime touchdown. He had brought Christina to FedEx Park to help her get over a crush that went sour in high school. It was there too that Samantha had told him she had been jilted in Manhattan and had applied for a job back in Washington.

Now it was happening again. At his daughter's insistence, he had invited this tall, athletic Nigerian, Larry Ossaga, to a cold, late-season Saturday game at FedEx Park, which is located due east of the south-east corner of DC, in Prince George County Maryland. The man knew nothing about football. Every time Charles turned towards the African to explain the play, the man started asking him questions about his daughter Samantha.

Charles had once been bewitched by Marsha, and he detected all the signs of bewitchment in Larry. How had Samantha ever become involved with this man? The father in him had been so sure she was through with the ups and downs

The Adams Sisters

of love and was going to content herself with being a career woman, now that she was back in Washington. When he and Larry parted in the parking lot after the game, Charles knew instinctively that he would be seeing more of this man.

The month of November had been a frenzied rush of looking for, buying and scheduling the delivery of the furnishings Tod and Christina needed for the apartment in Cleveland Park. It had been a stressful time for them. Christina didn't like a lot of what they were buying. On a number of occasions, she caught herself, just before snapping at Tod about her displeasure, with an item or a furnishing. In December, the hospital put her on four weeks of the 11p.m. to 7 a.m. shift. This seemed to increase the below the surface irritation, which they both sensed between them. It wasn't until between Christmas and New Year's that they really had a chance to get back in touch with each other.

The couple ate Christmas Day breakfast with his parents and dinner with Marsha, Charles, and Samantha. After that, they both had two days off. It was their first chance to go exploring around Cleveland Park. On Boxing Day afternoon, they went to see a movie at the Uptown theatre, which boasts DC's largest movie screen. When the show was over, they walked across Connecticut Ave. NW and had supper at a quaint French restaurant. Since they didn't have to drive home, the meal ended up being several courses of wine, washed down with a little food.

When the pair arrived back at the apartment, their coming together began, as soon as the door closed behind them as they danced to the soft chords of a Spanish guitar. It finished with love making on the new living room rug, and then falling to sleep. Tod woke at 2 am feeling cold. He carried his wife into the bedroom, and she didn't wake up.

When Christina woke in the morning, all the stress of the past two months was gone. They cuddled and talked in bed until 9:30 am, then got up, and heated up left over pizza from the refrigerator.

"Christa, I know you don't like some of the things we bought, just so we'd be able to furnish this apartment."

"I never said anything."

"You didn't have to. It was in your eyes and your mood."

She smiled at him. "Preppy, you have an over active imagination. What you saw in my eyes and my mood was my frustration at not being able to see you enough. For the last two months, as soon as we finished supper it was rush, rush,

rush, to go out looking for something or other we needed. This December night shift has been the worst thing I've had to do in my entire life. Here I am a newly married woman and some nights I was sitting in the staff room having a coffee at 3am. I'd start thinking of you sleeping here without me and tears would come to my eyes."

"You mean you don't really mind that chair over there?" he asked, pointing to a large fanning wicker patio chair, without a seat cushion.

She clinked her water glass against his and replied, "It gives the place a breezy, islands atmosphere. Besides, we'll probably replace most of this over the next few years. These are startup things."

During January, Christina pulled three consecutive weeks of 3 to 11 pm shifts and one 11 to 7am..

*

Doctor Ojibwa stood in the window watching an embassy car pull away. It had been a good visit, up to about fifteen minutes before Jocommo left. The Colonel had waited until then to tell him that the government had decided not to renew Dr. Ossaga's contract in Washington, when it expired. The old ambassador hadn't even blinked or even asked why. Perhaps it was his nonchalant attitude, even disinterested reaction that had prompted the military man to give him the reason for the recall, as they were shaking hands at the door.

On a cold Sunday afternoon in mid-January, Samantha was curled up in the corner of her sofa reading. A fire burned in the thick glass fireplace stove, which stood on its own on the living room floor. She felt good. The State Department had settled down; Christina's wedding had passed without a hitch and she had spent Christmas with her parents. Today she started into a novel, which was her Christmas present to herself. Already three chapters had been devoured. Around three pm, the phone in the hall toned. She thought of letting it ring through to the answering machine and then decided that she wouldn't.

"Hello!"

"Hello Samantha!"

"Larry, I thought you were working all day?"

"It's 3 pm and enough is enough."

"Good for you – all work and no play."

"I haven't heard that one."

The Adams Sisters 255

"Never mind! Would you like to come over? I did a super grocery order yesterday and can offer you the choice of five or six main dishes."

"Over, yes I'd like that, but as for supper, I'm not sure yet."

"Well, let's start with over and then we'll work on supper. Who knows, I may I'll even invite you to stay the night."

"Stay the night?"

"On the sofa Larry, on the sofa."

"Yes, right, on the sofa," he confirmed with an embarrassed tone.

"Ok, I'll be waiting for you and drive carefully. We've had an inch or so of snow this afternoon. You must start braking well before you want to stop."

"I'll be careful. See you in about half an hour."

When he arrived, she let him in, gave him a big smack on his surprised lips and then hung his long over-coat in the entrance closet. They started off by discussing the novel she had been reading and half a dozen other topics, before he became silent. She sensed his agitation.

"What's bugging you today Larry?

"Huh?"

"You've got something on your chest."

"Only my shirt and sweater."

"Funny," she grinned, "let's try this again. Is there something you want to talk to me about?"

"How did you guess?"

"Call it women's intuition."

"It all started a bit before I called you."

"Let's back track. What all started?"

"I was talking to Dr. Ojibwa at the embassy and he told me."

"Told you what, Larry?" she asked with excitement, thinking he was going to get a promotion.

He hesitated and then replied," Dr. Ojibwa told me that when my current contract is up in April. I'm being recalled."

"Recalled?" she squeaked.

"Yes!"

"To Nigeria?" she exclaimed.

"Yes!"

"But you've only just begun."

"That's what I told the Ambassador."

"What did he say?"

Larry continued, "He said something has come up."

"What something has come up?"

"He wasn't supposed to tell me."

"But he did. What is it?"

"The authorities in Nigeria have discovered that a million and a half dollars' worth of medical supplies entered Nigeria somehow, which were traced directly to me."

"Oh Lawrence, I'm so sorry. It was me who sent you those medical supplies. Now they've come back to haunt us."

"I could have refused to accept them."

"But you didn't."

"No!"

She began to fret, "What are you going to do?"

"I can't go back to Nigeria. Fist it will be the medical supplies and then, it will be the artesian well equipment. They'll finish by finding everything that you shipped to all of them and it will be confiscated."

"Oh Larry, I was so stupid to do that."

"It's over and done with Samantha. We can't change the past."

"Do you have any money?"

"All my pay from the embassy position has been deposited into an account in Nigeria. I've only transferred spending money here."

"What are you going to do?"

"I'm going try to find a way to stay in America."

"There are thousands of people who simply stay in the US every day," she informed him.

"I mean stay legally."

"You'll have to have a job."

"I know."

"I can't picture you being a waiter."

"Neither can I. My thinking was more along the lines of professor."

"Professor of what?"

"Economics, I do have a Ph.D.," he explained.

"But that's from England and you don't have any teaching experience."

"Then I'll be an assistant professor."

"It's the same for assistant professor. Most schools require that you were a TA running seminars or labs while being a grad student. "

"Then what do you suggest?"

"The husband of one of my girlfriends completed a Ph.D. in Geography, at the University of Arkansas. He started off

The Adams Sisters

marking term papers and exams in the school, at the end of this street."

"Which school are you talking about?"

"George Washington University."

"Then I'll start off marking term papers and exams at George Washington University too and after that I'll be an assistant professor."

"Please stay for supper Larry?"

"Do you think that's a good idea, considering I'm being recalled and could spend the rest of my life in a Nigerian prison?"

"All the more reason."

He looked at her with very soft eyes and smiled before answering, "Then I'll stay."

From that moment, until when he left at 9:30 pm, they talked of nothing but George Washington University and visas. After supper Samantha called her old girl friend and husband, who was now an assistant professor in the Geography department. The four of them had a speaker phone conference call.

Larry took notes as fast as he could. When they hung up, he had everything he needed to know about putting in the motion an application to be a marker at GWU's Economics Department. As he was leaving, he put his hands on Samantha's hips and gave her a soft kiss, before saying good night.

By the time April rolled around, Lawrence Ossaga had made ample preparations for staying in the US. A visit to immigration revealed that he was entitled to apply for an automatic, four month visitor's visa, when his diplomatic functions ended. It was the host country courtesy, which allowed departing embassy staff time to put their US affairs in order, before returning to their own country. Early in April he had an interview with the Economics Department at GWU. The afternoon session with the committee went so smooth that he even phoned Samantha to tell her that he was sure they were going hire him.

On the last Friday in April, Lawrence has an exit interview with the ambassador, Dr. Ojibwa.

"You know Lawrence; I'm going to be sad to see you go. You have excellent skills and a winning personality. I was sure we would make a diplomat out of you."

"You might still, Doctor," his assistant replied, as always showing loyalty for the President and government, and with no hint of the terror he was feeling about what might happen to him back in Nigeria.

"Then you really don't know anything about a million and a half dollars' worth of medical supplies, which someone has linked to your name?"

"It's a mystery to me. I'm sure someone has made an error and it will all be straightened out, when I return; however, I'm grateful to you for letting me see what was behind the recall."

"I may not have done it for another, but your work has been first class and you applied such diligence to even the smallest matters. I felt impelled to treat you as a fellow professional. I suppose you'll be leaving immediately."

"Actually, I'm going to stay in Washington for a few weeks. I've been seeing an American woman."

"That Ms. Adams you introduced to us?"

'Yes, her!"

"Do you think she will go back to Nigeria with you?"

"I'm not sure yet. I want to take a few weeks to discuss the situation with her. There are a number of issues and perhaps we can find solutions, which are mutually acceptable."

"One must always work through a number of issues with a woman, whether she is Nigerian or American."

They both smiled, shook hands and then Lawrence excused himself. After he left, the ambassador filed a copy of the exit interview by email to his superior in Abuja. He added a PS to the effect that Dr. Ossaga would be staying on in Washington for a few weeks, while he worked things out with an American woman, who he has been seeing.

*

A number of people, whom Tod had met, while working at the Wave, took their dogs and cats to the Pet Clinic. Soon they became his regulars. Quite often, they invited him to parties or gatherings, when they picked up their pets. At first he declined, but then Christina received almost two months of afternoon and evening shifts. As the days passed, he found that he didn't like sitting in the apartment alone. It wasn't long before he started to run with a Dupont Circle crowd, several evenings a week, while his wife was at work.

Usually, he was home and most times in bed, before she arrived around midnight. She did, however, smell the alcohol on him, when she got into bed and at first simply thought he'd had a few beers while watching TV. When it continued, she mentioned the drinking. Tod told her that some of his old

The Adams Sisters

buddies from Silver Spring had been looking him up and that he met up with them, after work on a number of occasions.

"But you shouldn't be drinking and driving Tod. Just think if you got hit with a DUI. You wouldn't be able to drive, and the authorities might suspend your Veterinary license. What would you do then?"

"I won't be getting hit with a DUI and my license won't be getting suspended," he assured her and then his tongue slipped. "If you were home in the evenings, I'd never be meeting the guys for anything."

"How's that supposed to make me feel?" she snapped back. "Do you think I enjoy my schedule at the hospital? It's their system, and I must run in it until they decide I've passed Go. We haven't had decent cuddle time, since New Year's Day."

"I've been doing my best, Christa."

"I'm not saying it's you. I just feel so stressed all the time, and I know, if we were making out more regularly, I wouldn't be. The other night I came home really wanting you, but you smelled like beer and I couldn't get you to wake up."

"Let's stop. I've been inconsiderate, and I'm finished going out after work."

For a time, Tod did change. Several times a week, they made love, before she left for the hospital. What she didn't know was that, on a number of occasions, he went out, after she left for work, to have a night cap with some of the Dupont Circle crowd. In his mind and in the mind of the veterinarian who owned the clinic, this after work socializing was strictly business. Some quite chic Washtonians were starting to bring their pets into the clinic and ask for him.

In April, the uneasiness between Tod and his wife returned. She was sure she smelled mouth-wash masking alcohol, more than once. It was not a good month for them. During another argument, he explained to her that his going out for a few drinks was only business and that the people he was seeing were giving him excellent referrals.

"My Dad sold insurance for years, and there was lots of evening work, but he didn't seem to always be drinking."

"It's not that I want to drink."

"Then why do you?"

"They're an established crowd and they meet in bars around Dupont Circle for supper and a few drinks after work. Today I had a top fashion model come in, to have the nails clipped on her pink poodle. Before she left, she gave me a hundred dollar tip."

"A hundred dollars, she must want to sleep with you."

"Please Christa, don't talk nonsense. It's strictly business. There's no bed; there's no hint of bed and there never will be any bed except with you."

"What did you do with the hundred dollars?"

"I bought you a bunch of tulips and two tickets to the current production at the Kennedy Center. They're in the bedroom on your night table."

She felt embarrassed and looked at the floor. "Excuse me for what I just said Tod. I wasn't even thinking. It simply popped out."

"You're forgiven Honey, now come on, let's have supper. I'm famished."

Near the end of April, she arrived at the apartment one evening as usual, a little before midnight. She slipped out of her clothes and slid into bed, as quietly as possible. After a moment, she noticed that she couldn't hear her husband's breathing. She put her arm out, but he wasn't there. Then she sat up in bed and turned on the light. The covers on his side hadn't been disturbed. She got up, put on a terry towel robe and went to sit in the living room. The sliding glass panel on the French door was open about six inches as she had left it earlier in the day. Every time she heard a car pull into the curved driveway, in front of the apartment building, she got up and watched from behind the curtain, but it was never him.

Finally around 3 am she heard a lot of laughing and talking as a car pulled into the entrance drive down below. Once again she went to look. She saw Tod climbing out of the space behind the seats of a sports car. Even from there she recognized the girls. They were the two waitresses from the Wave, who had been squeezed in beside him, the first time she had seen him driving away from work. They're not business; she said to herself and then thought that it was time she had a serious talk with her husband.

Christina waited until she heard the door close behind him and then she flicked on the light. Tod stood in front of her like a rabbit staring into oncoming headlights.

"Good evening Mr. Evans," she blurted out sarcastically. "It's so nice of you to come home this evening, or should I say this morning."

"Christa, what are you doing up?"

"Waiting for you, what else, Dear?"

The Adams Sisters 261

"I can explain."

"I think we're past your explanations Tod. I saw who drove you home. Been out doing a threesome? I thought the party dude from Silver Spring hung up his running shoes and was going to be a husband."

"I haven't seen either of them since I stopped working at the Wave."

"You're supposed to be a married man and a professional."

"I am a married man and a professional. It was my boss, the owner of the Pet Clinic who took me to the party, where I met them."

"Blame it on the boss," she sneered, "how convenient!"

"It's the truth. I didn't touch either of them, not even a good night kiss. They only gave me a ride home. They said I looked as if I'd had too much to drink."

"The blind leading the blind. Where's your car?"

"I left it down near Dupont Circle."

"Well, I'm tired Tod, and I want to go to sleep, but first we have something to decide."

"What's that, Hon?"

"Who's going to sleep on the sofa tonight?"

"Sofa?"

"Yes, you or me?"

"I'll sleep on the sofa," he replied sheepishly.

"Fine, but we're not finished with this."

"Ok Christa, I'll sleep on the sofa. Go on back to bed and get some sleep."

The following morning he got up and went to work without going into the bedroom. When he came home at 5:30 pm there was a piece of paper taped to the molding around the entrance to the kitchen. The writing was neat and legible.
"Dear husband,

I've gone to stay with my parents, until we decide how we're going to handle this."
Your wife."

He went into the bedroom. All her clothes were gone from the closet. Her dresser drawers were empty. There wasn't a cosmetic to be seen anywhere in the bathroom.

Two weeks went by, and Christina had no news of Tod. At length, she decided to drop by the Pet Clinic on P Street to see him. When she arrived, the receptionist said he no longer worked there. The confused young woman remembered the owner's name and requested to speak to him. After a ten minute wait, a tall man wearing a white jacket approached her. He had graying hair and appeared to be in his late forties.

"Good afternoon, I'm Doctor Harris. I understand you're inquiring about Doctor Tod Evans?"

"Yes!"

"How may I help you?"

"I was wondering if you could tell me why he is no longer working here and where he has gone?"

"I'm afraid that's confidential information. I couldn't release it without his express permission."

"I'm Tod's wife, Doctor Christa Evans." The veterinarian looked at her oddly. "Tod and I had a misunderstanding and communications have broken down between us. I'd be grateful for anything you could tell me."

"I don't know where he's gone to Mrs. Evans. On Monday this week he came to me at the end of the day and said that something very wrong had happened in his private life and that he had to stop working here at the clinic. He's a talented young man and has a knack for attracting high end clients. I told him that I would hold his place open, as long as possible."

Christina thanked the veterinarian for the information and left. From there, she drove to Cleveland Park and went into their apartment. In a matter of minutes, she discovered that everything personal he owned was gone. Now it seemed almost like a hotel suite.

Immediately she pulled out her cell phone and pressed on the code for his number. All she received was a recorded message from the carrier stating that the customer she was calling was not available and that his voice mail box was full. Quickly she called Mrs. Evans.

"Hello Jennifer, this is Christa, Tod wouldn't happen to be over there, would he?"

"No, I haven't seen Tod for several weeks now. I called him last week, but his voice mail was full. Is there anything the matter?"

"No, it's all right Mrs. Evans. I simply thought he may have gone over to visit you. He's probably off with some of his buddies. When I catch up with him, I'll tell him to give you a call."

"I'd appreciate that. His father's birthday is coming up."

"I'll give him the message, bye now."

*

The Adams Sisters

Near the end of May Dr. Lawrence Ossaga received a confidential letter from the committee, which had interviewed him for the position at George Washington University.

**

"Dear Dr. Ossaga,

We were very pleased with the interview that was held last month for the Economics Department's, Senior Marker position. You have excellent credentials, and we are sure that you are the caliber of person, who would flourish in the university environment. Unfortunately, at this time we are unable to offer you a position for the autumn term.

Our decision is based solely on objective criteria. For further information, please consult the academic applicant interview score sheet, which is attached.

Should you rectify the deficiencies indicated on the score sheet, before August 15th, please contact us immediately. While we cannot guarantee you a position at that time, you will still qualify for a September start, should a vacancy exist."
Yours Truly,
Sheryl Henderson
Employment Committee Chairperson

Immediately he flipped over to the interview score sheet, which was paper clipped to the letter and quickly ran his eye down over the twenty odd check marks. He had scored very well. At the bottom of the list was a question with Yes and No boxes. Is the applicant legally permitted to work in the United States? The No box had been checked.

The following week the young African made an appointment with immigration and now on the last Thursday of the month, he was sitting in front of an Immigration Review Officer's desk, feeling quite nervous.

"You see, Dr. Ossaga, if you had applied for a professorial position and it was only the legal working requirement that was blocking you, we could issue you a two year Professional Visa. However, this is more of an academic assistant position and as such does not qualify.

I realize that you are caught between a rock and a hard place because, without teaching experience, the university won't hire you as a professor. The Senior Marker position would give you excellent experience. You could use that experience to apply for something later, more along the lines of assistant professor. For that, we could issue a visa."

After Lawrence left the official's office, he felt uneasy somewhere inside. He had now used up one month of the diplomatic staffs' four month Visitor Visa. In 90 days, he would have to report in to the Ministry in Abuja or go into exile, probably in the UK. He knew he could stay there for years, as he had already long ago researched the whole question, when devising a backup plan in case anything had gone wrong, when he was sitting on the Debt Reconciliation Committee.

"You know Larry," Samantha said to him apologetically, "it's entirely my fault you're in this predicament."

"We've been through this Sam," he replied patiently, "anything could have happened with that project at any point along the way, even while I was still back in Nigeria. The day I accepted the fact that the only way I was going to get the equipment for the artesian wells my father's former villages needed, was the day I put myself in fate's hands."

"Maybe you could get hired as a professor someplace else – say a small private university?"

"That's what I was thinking, but it would have to be within driving distance of DC. I'm not going to apply to something in Fargo, North Dakota."

"You'd freeze to death there."

"And I wouldn't be able to see you."

"But you hardly know me."

"But I've started to know you."

She looked away, wondering if she really wanted this. Then she made her decision. "If you want Larry, I'll help you look. We can check the Internet, academic magazines, placement agencies or even call the colleges."

"You're really up for that?"

"Yes!"

"Then I accept your offer," he said, taking hold of both her hands and squeezing them lightly.

"When do you want to start?" she asked.

"I'll start tomorrow to rough out a plan and then on the weekend we can focus in on the details, once you are finished with your chores."

"My chores," she laughed. "You know I have chores?"

"Everybody has chores Sam. I don't want to abuse your generosity."

"That's considerate of you. Would you like to know something else?"

"Something else what?"

"That's the first time you've ever called me Sam."

The Adams Sisters

He grinned back at her, then lowered his eyes and offered, "If you let me, I'll relieve you of the chore of preparing supper this evening."

"What did you have in mind?"

"How about the Tayac?" he suggested.

"On 22nd Street?"

"Yes!"

"It's expensive," she warned.

"I've eaten there and I'm inviting."

"Ok, if you're inviting," she replied squeezing his arm.

"I'm inviting," he repeated.

*

Tod Evans reached down and turned on his cell phone, before moving out of the driveway onto the John Mosby Highway in Loudoun County, Virginia. He turned east towards Gilbert's Corner, which is about fifty miles west of DC. His aging Audi passed over the stone bridge, which spanned the Little River and was soon at the intersection of Virginia state highways No. 50 and No. 15. A direction arrow pointed north, up No. 15 towards Leesburg. Crossing through the intersection, the John Mosby became highway No. 50. He followed it south-east, until it joined Interstate 66 heading in the direction of Washington.

Since leaving Cleveland Park, he only opened his cell phone long enough to make any necessary calls and then it was immediately turned off again. He never checked the voice mail box, which had long since filled to the brim. Right or wrong, it was the solution he had opted for. He had succeeded in stopping all calls from the Dupont Circle crowd and he knew that, in a couple of months, they would forget all about him. Today he was expecting a call from a veterinary supply house, which had promised to let him know if they could locate items not available, at another supplier. He was expecting them to call soon.

Christina was on Wisconsin Street, driving towards Foggy Bottom. She had promised to give her Sis three hours on Saturday morning, during which time they would map out a strategy to find a professor position for Samantha's new boyfriend, Larry. She picked up her cell phone to call Samantha. Without noticing it, she pressed the wrong stored number in the phonebook. After three rings, it answered.

"Hello!"

She was stunned. It was her husband. She didn't know what to say.

"Tod, what are you doing there?"

"Christa, is that you?"

"Yes it's me. Why are you at Samantha's? Is this some kind meeting that the two of you arranged?"

"I'm not at Samantha's. I'm driving east on Interstate 66, a little west of Arlington."

Quickly she looked at the face plate of her phone and saw that she hadn't dialed her sister's number. "Oh, my God, it's you. Where have you been for the last month? I must have called your number ten dozen times, but the computerized voice always said you were unavailable and that your mail box was full."

"I've been here all along."

"Why didn't you call me? I've been so worried."

"I had to think things out. I had to get my head straight. I had to break off with the Dupont Circle crowd."

"What have you been doing?"

"I'm working."

"Where?"

"In Virginia, a bit east of Dulles Airport."

"Tod, we have to talk."

"I know. What are you doing today?"

"I'm on my way to Sam's place to help her with some research for a couple of hours."

"I'm going to be busy, until noon picking up supplies and medicines," he told her, and then continued, "let's have lunch. I'll call you when I have rounded up everything on my list."

"Promise?"

"Yes, promise Christa. I'll call to you later."

Tod arrived at the diner before his wife, went inside, put two salads, two wraps and two sodas on a tray. After paying, he went back outside and walked towards a picnic table, which was under a wide shade tree. He saw her pull into the parking lot and waved so that she would see him.

When Christina arrived at the table, her place was set. He was smiling up at her with a shy little boy look on his face. She couldn't resist and smiled back.

"Get everything settled at your Sis's place?" he asked.

"I hope so; we were looking for a professor job, for her new boyfriend."

"New boyfriend?"

"Larry."

"The Nigerian?"

"That's him."

The Adams Sisters

"What have you been doing with yourself?" he prodded.

"Delivering babies," she moaned. "It never stops. I've delivered at least a baby a day and sometimes two, since the first of last November."

"I never realized there were that many births."

"So, what about us Tod?" she asked becoming serious. "What's happening with us? What about our apartment?"

"The rent's being paid. I gave the landlord 3 postdated cheques the day I moved out my gear."

"Tod."

"Yes."

"Are we separated?"

"We're not separated."

"What are we then?"

"We're going through a process of realignment."

"Realignment!"

"That's right."

"Realignment to what?"

"To a lifestyle that's more compatible with you and me."

"Ok, I won't press you for any more details now, but I'm glad we're not separated. I told Mom and Dad we were going through a disagreement."

"That's exactly what I told my parents too."

"What are you doing, way out there, on the other side of the airport?"

"A locum."

"For who?"

"An old Vet named William Yodeler, who had a heart attack and decided he would like to see some of the world, before it was too late. He and his wife are in the Greek Islands at the moment. They'll be gone for a year."

"That's a lot of responsibility for someone who's recently graduated."

"I can handle it."

"So where is it exactly?"

"It's out in the countryside east of Fairfax, about five miles past Gilbert's Corner. The road out front of the house is called the John Mosby Highway."

"Is it a farm?"

"There are about fifty acres, a stone house, and two small barns. One of the outbuildings is made of wood and the other stone. The man has a horse practice. The surrounding countryside is full of horse farms."

All of a sudden she cupped his two hands in hers and said, "It was stupid of me to move out on you like that Tod. I was acting like a spoiled child."

"You did what you had to do at the time Christa and now we're getting by it."

"How far are we by it?" she asked smiling.

He started to laugh, "We're getting there."

"Tell me how to get to your new place. I might come out for a visit."

"It's really simple. Take Interstate 66 west to the highway 50 exit, and then continue along it, until you come to Gilbert's Corner. There's nothing there, but a flashing four way stop. Go through the intersection. There's a stone bridge over a river, and old mill, some antique places and then you're back out in the fields again."

"You'll come upon a one storey sandstone house with two dormers in a silver tin roof, located out near the highway, on the right hand side. There're a chimney and a closed in back porch on the end that you'll be approaching from. There are also trees, bushes and a nice lawn around the property. Across from the sandstone house, on the other side of the highway, there's a low white wooden house with a veranda. If you see a red brick building on the left, called Mount Zion Church, you've gone too far."

"Ok, I've got it. We've been out that way before with my Dad for Sunday afternoon drives, when I was young."

"I can't stay too long Christa. I have some sick horses that are waiting for the medicine that's in my car."

"All right, I'll let you go, but call me and leave a message, if I'm not available. My mail box is always empty."

"I'll leave a message," he assured her.

"Can we kiss before we leave?"

"I don't have any objections," he replied, opening his arms towards her.

*

Samantha sat in her kitchen early on last Sunday morning in June with a warm breeze blowing through the partially open back door. She decided to grind more beans and have a second coffee. When it was prepared, her musings returned. She felt anxious, frustrated and something that she couldn't quite label.

Contrary to what she had supposed, there hadn't been that many openings in the smaller colleges and private schools, for Economics professors. She and Larry had contacted every position that was advertised and then had started doing cold calls to schools, which hadn't advertised. It seemed that Economics was another discipline that was in oversupply. Some of the institutions told them that they had waiting lists of recent graduates, who would even do substitute work.

For the first time, she began to focus in on the dilemma. Larry's visa was up in eight weeks, and he had already told her that he wouldn't stay in the US illegally. There was no possibility that he would return to Nigeria under the present administration. Some of his old friends had emailed him that the police had been around asking them general questions about his habits and acquaintances.

He told her that he would go to England, where he had the right to work, because Nigeria was part of the British Commonwealth. From there he would apply to immigrate to the US, through the front door. She was able to relate somewhat to England since her short jaunt there to deliver the money the lawyer Offuya.

Samantha set her cup down and looked up at a hanging, potted ivy that the breeze had caught hold of. It was going round and round. It gave her the impression of a whirlpool. Suddenly she found a label for what had been bothering her. It was the same feeling she had in Manhattan, after the restaurant meeting with her fake fiancée and his new woman. It was a feeling of losing.

Why had she let this happen? Why had she let this big, handsome African, who was so unaccustomed to American ways, get through her defense shield? If she had encouraged Ronnie Williams only a tiny bit, she wouldn't be in this predicament now.

Samantha knew she needed to get out of the house. She rose, went over and shut the back door; then moved the two security bolts back into their imbedded slots. Once upstairs, the young woman turned on the water in the tub and tossed a scooper of crystals in under the faucet. When the soap bubbles were almost six inches above the edge of the tub, she let the silk robe slip off her sleek body and fall into a crumble on the bath mat, before stepping into the tub and sliding down under the foam.

When Samantha re-emerged an hour later sitting behind the wheel of her Lexus, she was wearing a pink hooded-polo top, designer jeans, clog running shoes, and no bra. While, in the tub, she had decided to go and walk around with the tourists on the Mall; however, when she arrived downtown, she turned the car in the direction of Capital Square, which is located a little south of L'Enfant Plaza on G Street, between 7th and 9th. The Nigerian Embassy owned a small unit in a complex that Lawrence Ossaga was renting. Even before she parked, she saw him standing out on the balcony. He was dressed in a traditional tribal robe and was wearing a pill box cap.

He called out from above, as she walked across the front lawn. "Samantha, why didn't you phone to warn me?"

"Are you expecting some of your African buddies over?" she jested.

"No, why?"

"I thought today was some special occasion, from the way you're dressed."

"You mean this," he asked, holding up an arm, to better display the robe."

"Yup!"

"I was feeling vulnerable, after a week of employment rejections and went for my security blanket."

"Bit of an identity crisis?" she joked.

"You might say that. Are we going stand out here and discuss the world situation or would you like to come up?"

"I feel like being outside in the sun today. Would you like to go for a walk?"

"Wait there, I'll be down in a few minutes."

Five minutes later he came out the door in a blue muscle shirt, black shorts and sandals. Samantha marveled at his bare muscular shoulders, as they started down the street. In Banneker Park Larry bought them both ice cream cones from a peddle cart vendor. They licked on the cones, as they walked past the Maine Avenue Fish Market, under the Francis Case Memorial Bridge, along the edge of the Washington Channel and over onto the island section of West Potomac Park.

"No, if I talk to them, it might get back to Nigeria and that would raise suspicions. For all intents and purposes, I'm supposed to be tying up the loose ends here, and they are expecting me in Abuja the first week of September."

"What loose ends were you supposed to have?"

"You!"

She looked at him, burst out laughing and then bounced the palm of her hand off his huge right bicep. "I didn't know you cared like that."

"I didn't either, until the last few weeks," he replied

The Adams Sisters

"I know what you mean. I didn't know either," she added.

He looked puzzled. "You mean you could tell that I?"

She interrupted him, "No, I mean me." They both started to laugh and linked their hands together.

They stopped to look down into the Potomac River, not far from the inlet to the Tidal Basin, which had originally been built for flushing out the nearby Washington Channel with fresh river water. Two large catfish were nibbling at a slice of bread that was floating on the surface, wedged between two twigs.

"I wish I hadn't got you involved in all this," he said, without looking at her.

She replied while continuing to watch the fish, "You know there is a possible way out of your not being legally able to work in the US."

"There is?"

"Yup!" she assured him.

"Do you know somebody in high places?"

"Nope!"

"Then what?" he asked eagerly.

"If we were married, you'd be eligible for the Senior Marker job."

He stood up straight, turning towards her, but she didn't look at him. "You'd do that for me, Sam?" he stammered awkwardly.

"For us Larry."

"This isn't a joke, is it, something you're saying to make me feel better?"

"No, I'm not joking."

"What do I have to do?"

"You should know the answer to that," she replied seriously. "You're a man."

"I must ask you, right?"

"Right you are."

"And after I ask you?"

"Usually a man buys the woman an engagement ring."

"Do you know I'm a Moslem?"

"I only said that it was a possible way out of your and our predicament," she reminded him.

"What comes after the engagement ring?"

"We get married and I start to call myself Mrs. Samantha Ossaga."

He took hold of her hand, and she turned her gaze from the water and into his eyes. "Do I get to kiss the bride?"

"Just a little one, I don't like showing affection in public."

He leaned over and kissed her softly on the lips while whispering, "Will you marry me, Samantha."

"Yes, I'll marry you, Larry," she replied, smiling up at him.

"Come on," he said taking her by the hand and starting to walk towards the Jefferson Memorial.

"Where are we going?"

"I want to find some bushes, where I can kiss you properly."

She started to giggle and followed him.

*

While Samantha and Larry were looking for a secluded spot along the Potomac, Christina was cruising along the John Mosby Highway in Virginia, looking for the house Tod had described. She passed through Middleburg and then Aldie. The countryside alternated between wooded stretches, large open fields and corn.

In one field, she saw a deer standing close to a huge roll of hay that was twice the size of it. Suddenly a large red brick church appeared ahead on the left side of the road. She knew that she had gone too far and turned into its driveway. Closed green shutters covered the windows. A large plaque caught her attention. Leaving the car idling, she got out and went to read it.

The Mount Zion Baptist church was founded in 1851. On July 6, 1864 Mosby Rangers routed one hundred and fifty Union cavalrymen nearby. One Ranger and almost one hundred of the cavalrymen fell in action. Many of them were buried in the cemetery, just west of the church.

She re-entered her car and turned back the way she had come. This time she found the house and drove into its driveway. Tod's car was parked beside the white wooden barn. She got out, went up to the back door and knocked loudly, but no one came. Perhaps he's in one of the buildings she thought, going back down the steps.

There was a red cross, similar to the ones painted on field ambulances, attached to the outside wall of the small sandstone building. The overhead sliding door was open. As she entered, she heard Tod's voice somewhere inside. When her eyes had adjusted from the bright June sun, she went in the direction of his voice.

Tod was kneeling down in the hay at the hind end of a mare that was lying on the stall floor. His hands were gripping a filmy membrane sac, which he was drawing out from the inside of the horse.

The Adams Sisters

"Come on girl, push. That's my girl; you can do it. It's almost half way out. That's my girl. What a beautiful baby you're going to have!"

Christina didn't dare move for fear she would frighten the horse. She listened to how he talked to the mare. It was that same strong, confident voice he had when they were making love.

When the foal was finally out, and the membrane peeled away, she walked in quietly and knelt down beside him. Tod's hands didn't stop moving, and he didn't stop talking to the new mother. He took a soft sponge from a pail of warm water and began to wash off the new born. When one side of the foal was clean, he turned the young animal over and then motioned the sponge towards Christina.

She took the sponge from him and began to wipe off the tiny, quivering body the same way she had seen him do it. He stood up and went to examine the mare's mouth. The tone and flow of his words didn't change, but now the words were directed at Christina. He told her not to talk and that once the foal washed off, they would put it against the mother's side and leave them to get acquainted.

Suddenly the mare lifted her head, whirled around and looked the young woman in the eye. Christina froze. A minute later she felt Tod take the sponge from her hand and lift her to her feet before he placed the young animal at its mother's side. They left the stall together and shut the bottom door softly. He took her by the hand again and led her back outside.

Christina put her hand up to shade her eyes from the bright mid-afternoon sun and exclaimed, "That was impressive Tod, and you were impressive."

"She's the third pregnancy I've had since taking over. Quite a few of the neighboring farms bring their mares here to foal. The last one wasn't as easy as today."

"Your arms and face are all splattered with blood and mucus," she told him.

"I need to take a shower. Are you coming in?"

"Sure!"

"Any trouble finding the place?"

"I went past it once, but circled back. This is really a beautiful setting. It's hard to believe we're so close to Washington."

"You're right," he said, opening the door to the back porch. "It's a landscape painter's delight."

"Oh, it's so cool in here," she commented, walking into the kitchen.

"The house has the stone walls," he explained. "They're at least a foot thick and really block the heat. I'm going to go and wash up now. I'll show you around the house after."

She waited until she heard the shower running and then went into the bathroom to wash the smell of the newborn off her hands. A thin film of vapor had formed on the clear glass door of the shower stall, but she could see his silhouette. It aroused a mild desire in her. She wondered what he would say if she opened the door.

"Having fun in there," Christina called out?

"Are you in the bathroom?"

"Yes, I need to wash my hands. Get ready, the water temperature might change for a minute."

"Ok, go ahead."

When she was finished, she told him that she would wait for him in the living room and left him to finish showering. However, before settling onto the sofa, she took a quick look through the house, which included the upstairs. There was a master bedroom and a child's bedroom, as well as a small bathroom equipped with a wash basin and toilet, under the eaves on the second floor.

Christina was flipping through a magazine, when Tod came into the living room, towel drying his hair and wearing only a pair of athletic shorts. He sat on the edge of an armchair across from her.

"Is there any particular motivation in this visit?" he inquired.

"Only curiosity, but I must say, this suits you much better than a Dupont Circle clinic."

"I knew that from the beginning, but I might have lost you, by comeing to a place like this straight from graduation. If you remember, we were setting up cell phone meetings morning, noon and evening around that time."

"And you don't think you've lost me?"

"I said it was realignment."

"I won't comment on that, but would you care to enlarge upon what you mean?"

"I'm forming a plan."

"What type of a plan?"

"It's small now, but there's lots of potential."

"Good things have small beginnings," she said encouraging him to continue.

The Adams Sisters

"I'm going to buy an Andalusian breeding stallion and bring it to the States. I've already contacted the Finca Sierra ranch in Spain, where we stayed during our honeymoon. The stallion will stay here until Dr. Yodeler comes back. It should be able to start breeding with mares on surrounding farms, as soon as it arrives. I've already had several expressions of interest."

She was amazed, "That's quite a realignment, Andalusians are very expensive."

"I know. I've talked to my Dad. He'll co-sign with me on a loan"

She was eager. "That's something I could really align myself with, Mr. Evans."

"I'm starting to get hungry," Tod told her as he stood up to finish drying his hair. "I've been in that stable, since eight o'clock this morning. It was a long delivery. Care for a snack, Christa?"

"I had lunch and I told Marsha that I'd be back for supper, so I think I'll pass; but why don't you sit back in that chair and let me fix you a surprise."

He looked at her grinning. "Give me a shout, if you can't find anything."

"I'll be fine," she replied. "You just relax. I know how tensed up I am, after delivering a baby. Usually, I start with a coffee. Would you care for a cup?"

"Yes please," he answered, leaning back in the arm chair.

*

Samantha felt like a high school girl, when Larry pulled her into a clump of cherry trees, surrounded by bushes, not far from the Jefferson Memorial. Once she was sure they couldn't be seen by anybody walking by, she covered his faces with kisses and drew him in tight against her. He did likewise but was careful, remembering her remark about not liking to show emotion in public. In the end he was glad that he had kept control of himself because she suddenly pulled away from him saying,

"We shouldn't forget our walk. Have you ever visited the Memorial?"

"No, I've been too busy."

"Come then," she urged pulling him back out onto the open grass. "I'll give you a guided tour."

The Jefferson Memorial, which was completed in 1943, is a miniature open-air Pantheon that looks out across the Tidal Basin towards the cherry trees on the far shore. Rudolph

Evan's bronze statue of the third president, Thomas Jefferson, stands amid ionic columns and four panels upon which have been etched stirring excerpts from Jefferson's speeches and writings.

After the tour, they walked back down the multiple layers of terraced steps towards the sidewalk that followed the water and Samantha said,

"We have a lot to discuss and plan, in a very short period of time."

"I know, I can't even put all the pieces together in my mind, but I know where to start," he replied taking hold of her hand again. "I must get you a ring. Let's go shopping now."

"Do you want me to help you pick it out?"

"Yes, I insist."

"That might be bad luck," she replied remembering that it was she who had picked out her first engagement ring.

"Not in my country it isn't."

"Would you like to come over to Mum and Dad's for supper with me, tonight?"

"Sure, we will be able to show them your new ring."

She laughed, "It might require sizing for me."

"Then we'll size it too."

Samantha flipped open her cell phone and called her mother to say she was bringing a guest to supper with her. When her mother pressed her, Samantha told her that it was Larry Ossaga, who had come to Christina's wedding with her.

*

When Christina returned from the kitchen, she was carrying a cup of coffee in one hand and a platter of Buffalo wings in the other, which she set on the coffee table in front of the sofa.

"Come and get it Rover," she hollered.

"I see you found my stash of frozen deli-food," he joked, pulling himself up out of the deep padded chair to come and sit beside her.

"I sampled one. It passed."

"Have another."

"No, I don't want to spoil my supper."

"What time are they eating?"

"Marsha said that she would be serving at six. I had her wake me up at noon, so I could drive out here this afternoon. I'm going to try to sleep for a few hours, after supper, before going into work."

The Adams Sisters

He took one bite then said, "Thank you for getting this ready. I didn't know how hungry I was, before tasting them"

As he ate, they talked. Periodically he would lean back, roll his head from side to side and then revolve each shoulder in its socket. When the chicken wings were all gone, she asked, "I can't help notice the contortions that you're going through with your neck and shoulders. Have you got a pinched nerve?"

"I seem to have strained a muscle on both shoulders, during that delivery. I must have been kneeling down with my arms stretched out in front of me, for three or four hours."

"I could give you a shoulder massage if you like?" she volunteered.

"That would be considerate of you."

"Turn sideways then," she said, getting up and kneeling on the couch. He did as she said and she started to rub and chop at his thick shoulder muscles for five minutes. Finally, she had to stop. "Whew, now it's my shoulders that are getting strained."

He swiveled around to face her, "Care for a little shoulder massage yourself?"

"Well, now that you're asking," she replied turning her back towards him.

For the next ten minutes, his strong hands moved back and forth, across her back, over her shoulders and along the length of her arms. Finally, she leaned into his chest murmuring, "I'm fine now."

He whispered into her ear, "Could I offer you a tour of the upstairs, Mrs. Evans?"

"I don't think I have enough energy to climb the stairs," she whispered back.

"How would it be, if I carried you?"

"That would be fine," she said, slipping an arm around his neck.

"I must leave no later than five o'clock," she reminded him, as he began to lift her up off the sofa. "There's a lot of traffic on Sunday afternoon."

"No later than five," he confirmed.

She looped her other arm around his neck and the couple started up the stairs.

****

19 - July 27th

Samantha parked the gold Lexus in one of the spots on the curved driveway of the big red brick house on R Street NW and then she and Lawrence Ossaga got out of the automobile. She led him off to the side of the house to a gated, flag stone path, which went around to the back yard. They surprised Charles and Marsha Adams sitting outside on the cedar deck, which came out several feet from the house in front of the dining room sliding glass door. Her parents were having a martini while they waited for their daughters to arrive for Sunday evening dinner. Since Mrs. Yamato didn't come on the weekends, the elderly Adams couple had enjoyed doing all the preparations themselves, and they were now talking about it.

"Oh, Samantha," Marsha exclaimed as her eldest daughter came round the corner of the house. "You surprised me. I didn't know who it was."

"Hi Mom! This is my friend Larry, who you met at Christa's wedding."

"Pleased to see you again, Mrs. Adams," the tall African said, taking hold of her outstretched hand.

"You don't have to Mrs. Adams me, Dr. Ossaga. Call me Marsha, even my daughters do, well sometimes."

"Ok, Marsha and I am simply Larry, not Dr. Ossaga."

Samantha moved on, "You've met my Dad Charles."

The Adams Sisters

"Yes we have," Charles said standing up. "If it hadn't been so late in the season, I may have been able to teach him more about football."

"There's always next year, Sir."

"Right you are, can I offer you two a martini? The shaker is still half full. I'll grab two more glasses."

"Yes, sit down," Marsha said motioning her arm towards two wooden deck chairs, which were so well made they could easily pass for inside furniture. "We'll finish our drinks with you, before going in.

Lawrence was quite taken up with the Adams back yard. "You have half a tennis court and one basketball hoop?"

"That's correct," the elder Adams replied passing him a cut crystal glass.

"Did you have sons, in addition to your two daughters?"

"No sons, you'll have to get the particulars on that out of Mother, but I didn't let that stop me. Both girls can dunk a mean hoop, but tennis is their specialty. Do you play tennis, son?"

"No, that's not one of my accomplishments, but I'm making attempts at golf since coming to America."

"Good, I'll invite you out to play with me at Cabot someday. Golf's even better than football."

"Samantha has introduced you as Doctor, Larry," Marsha said. "Are you a specialist?"

"That's correct, a Doctor in Economics, not medicine."

"Where did you study that?"

"I went to a university in England."

"And you were born in Nigeria, not England?"

"Yes, I was born west of Lagos, which is the country's main commercial city. My father was a hereditary tribal chief for nine hundred thousand people, who live in five villages."

"How many people live in Nigeria?" Marsha pressed him.

"The official count is about 130 million, but it could be close to 150 million."

"That's half the population of the United States."

"I know and they're squeezed into a country about the size of Texas."

"Why didn't you take over the Chief from your father?"

'My father said it was time for his people to evolve and that he would be the last hereditary chief. He sent me away to study and then transferred the power to an elected Mayor and 20 councilors. It's working very well."

Marsha turned her attention to her husband, who had been listening intently. "Charles, why don't we take our glasses and what's left in that martini shaker and move into the living room?"

"Good idea, dear, everybody follow me."

They had hardly sat down on the white leather furniture, when the front door opened and Christina walked in.

"Hope I'm not late? There was traffic." Christina explained before the question could be asked.

"No, you haven't held up anything," her father replied. "We're still talking."

Christina took a seat across from them and nodded to Larry, who returned her acknowledgement. She couldn't help being amazed at how the white leather sofa accentuated his blackness. She wondered if the Adams had ever been that black.

"What's for supper, Mom?" the younger daughter asked.

"African food, but I'm not sure I can pronounce everything."

"Did you prepare it?"

"After Sam called to say she was bringing Larry, your father and I and went to the African deli in town. We picked out a few things from West Africa, to which I added a little Afro-American of my own."

"What kind of Afro-American?" Christina pried.

"You know dear, African-American baked rack of lamb."

"What's from the deli?" her daughter continued.

"You tell her Charles, I can't remember how to pronounce those foods."

"Along with the rack of lamb your mother and I are serving okra soup, kenkey, gari, fufu and moi-moi." Then he laughed and looked at Larry, "but you'll have to ask our guest what we're really eating."

"Let me think a minute," Samantha's friend said. "Ah yes, okra soup is thick and it contains okra, tomatoes, corn, and bacon. Kenkey balls are made of mixed portions of fermented cooked maize meal and raw maize. Usually, they're boiled. Gari is that green paste, which is served with sushi. Some people like to put it on the Kenkey balls. Fufu is like your mashed potatoes, only it's made with yams and moi-moi are little cakes made from black peas. I like to eat them with salsa sauce."

"Sounds like a win-win to me," Christina laughed and smiled back at him.

The Adams Sisters

"How did you know what you were ordering at the deli, Mother?" Samantha asked.

"There were American labels on the dishes, beside the African ones."

"What did they call Gari, Mom?"

"Ginger sauce," Mrs. Adams replied authoritatively.

"I'll get the address for that place from you, before I leave," her eldest daughter said.

"Has everybody finished their martini?" Marsha asked. "Yes!" she replied to her own question, after reading their nods to the affirmative. "Then let's move to the table. We can continue this conversation there."

When everyone was seated, Charles began his usual blessing. "Dearly beloved Creator, we are gathered here to partake of the gifts and blessings you have bestowed on us. We thank you for your bounty and ask that you don't forget the hungry of this world. Amen."

"Here Samantha, serve yourself and Larry some of these Kenkey balls," Mrs. Adams urged, passing a platter to her daughter. Samantha reached out with her left hand to take a dish from her mother.

"My, but that's a nice ring you're wearing," the older woman commented. "Is it new?"

"Yes, it's new. Larry bought it for me this afternoon."

"Larry bought it. Show me your hand; I want to have a closer look."

"Samantha, is this what I think it is?"

"It's what you think it is Mum."

She turned towards her husband declaring, "Charles, do you see what's happening here?"

"What's happening, Mother? Isn't the lamb cooked enough?"

"It's not the lamb, it's your daughter. She's got engaged."

"Engaged, let me see. Oh, oh, what a beautiful ring, when did all this happen?"

"This afternoon Dad."

"Ho, ho," he exclaimed getting up from the head of the table to come and hug his first born from behind. "This calls for a celebration. Larry...... here Larry let me shake your hand. Congratulations! There isn't a luckier man than you on the planet at this minute. Let me assure you of that.

Mother, grab that cheap bottle of wine off the table, before anybody has a drop. I'll be right back. I'm going to get a vintage label from my private stock, which has been waiting a year for an occasion like this."

Christina also rose from where she was sitting at the other end of the table and came to see the single diamond that was on Samantha's left hand."

"Oh Sis, it's beautiful," she exclaimed. "May I try it on?"

Her sister slipped off the ring and passed it to her. Christina was flooded with memories of her own engagement and marriage. As she began to take the ring off, her mother cried out, "Now me Christa. I want to try the ring too." Her younger daughter brought it around to the other side of the table and put the small band of gold onto her mother's palm. Then she remembered Larry and went back to where he was seated. Before he could say a word, she threw her arms around his neck and kissed him on the cheek.

Charles was back from his wine storage holding an open wine bottle in his hands. "It's a Barola from Italy, 1985 and it's chilled too. Hold up your glasses everyone; we've got a toast to make." He went around the table filling each glass in mid-air and then went back to the head of the table, where he held his glass out in front of himself declaring,

"To love, to engagements, to marriage, to babies and to family! May Samantha and Lawrence have a great life!"

They all stood up, touched their glasses together and said, "To Larry & Samantha!"

Everyone had only just started to eat when Christina said, "I have an announcement to make too."

"What is it?" her sister asked, glad to find something to turn the attention away from herself.

"I'm moving back to our apartment this week?"

"So you and Tod have made up?" Samantha questioned.

"We're aligned again."

"What are you aligned on?" Her mother asked suspiciously.

"Tod's buying an Andalusia stallion and I get to ride it, when it's not being used for breeding."

Charles coughed loudly looking his wife straight in the eye. "I knew that Evans kid had his head screwed on the right way."

For the rest of the meal, their conversation drifted here and there but Marsha didn't hear much of what anybody was saying. She was wondering if Samantha's children would be as black as their father and if Christina's children would have their father's blond hair.

*

The Adams Sisters

It was eleven thirty in the evening on the last day of the Fourth of July long weekend. Samantha had seen her fiancée three times over the holiday and had squeezed in at least twelve hours of required reading on Libya and Iran, which were the new buzz words at the Watch. Now she lay in the dark, on top of the covers in her bedroom.

The air conditioner was laboring not far from her, trying to cut out a square, where she could sleep, in Washington's midsummer, urban oven. Yet it wasn't the heat or the noise of the machine that was keeping her awake. She had been rushing around in a cloud of excitement for the past four days and now she couldn't get herself down and she had to be in the office in eight hours.

Suddenly a cell phone on the bedside table hummed. In the dark she located the green light, which glowed on the instrument's face plate and reached out for it. Her thumb pressed the answer button.

"Hello!"

"Samantha."

"Larry."

"I couldn't sleep."

"Neither could I."

"What were you thinking about?" the young woman asked eagerly.

"I was remembering all the new people, who you introduced me to this weekend. I'm simply amazed at how much fuss they made about your engagement ring."

"Girls are like that. You should see how we carry on, when it's a new baby."

"It's already a week."

"I know.

"We'll have to set a date to get married," he reminded her.

"We can't get married without a license Mr. Lawrence Ossaga."

"A license?"

"Yes, a license."

"But what for?"

"Because that's the law."

"Then it isn't only in the movies. That's really how it happens in America."

"That's really how it happens all over the world, boy. They probably even have marriage licenses in Nigeria."

"So that means we must go to City Hall and get a license."

"There is no City Hall in Washington and before we apply for a license, we'll have to get a blood test."

"A blood test, what for?"

"Because it's the law," she repeated.

"I can't believe that this huge city doesn't have a City Hall?"

"No City Hall," she reiterated.

"But there's a Mayor, I've seen him on TV."

"Yes there's a Mayor, but there's no City Hall. If you think that international diplomacy and the US federal government are complicated, wait until you enter into the municipal life of the nation's Capital."

"Tell me all about it," he laughed.

"Well, it's like this, the D in DC stands for District and districts don't have City Halls.

"You're kidding me."

"I kid you not. Washington is like a colony. We have no state representatives and we don't have any representatives in Congress."

"Well, why doesn't somebody do something about it?"

"They have been trying to do something about it for 200 years, but it's still not fixed."

"What have they done?"

"When I was a young girl, the popular rage was Home Rule, but that eventually ended when the powers, who thought they could be, couldn't fund their budget. During the eighties, it was statehood. There was even a Statehood Party and some of the Ward councilors ran on statehood."

"What happened to statehood?"

"The President said he didn't like it and Congress beat the proposal 2 to 1."

"These councilors then, where do they sit?"

"On the DC Council," she informed him.

"And where is the DC Council?"

"At the DC Government."

"Why doesn't the DC Government send somebody to Congress to represent you?"

"They do. DC residents elect a delegate to the House of Representatives and two shadow senators, but they can't vote and they don't get paid."

"Alright Samantha, let's get back to the Marriage License. Tomorrow I should go to the Council at the DC Government and see about it, right."

The Adams Sisters

"Wrong, marriage licenses are issued by the Superior Court of DC."

"You wouldn't happen to know where the Superior Court is located, would you?"

"It's on Indiana Ave. NW, in the low numbers, probably between one and one thousand. However, let's start by both getting a blood test from an accredited laboratory and when we have the results, we'll go to the Superior Court together."

"So now we're through to getting a blood test," he exclaimed.

"Did you want to get married in a church, Larry?"

"How about a mosque," he replied?

"That's convenient."

"Why?"

"The churches are probably all booked up for the rest of the summer."

"The mosques probably are too. I liked the church wedding your sister had. Since we don't have too much time though, maybe we should get married at City Hall for now and then we can get married in a church or a mosque later."

"Get married twice."

"Sure, it happens in American movies all the time."

"I'll take your word for it," she laughed. "After we get a license, we'll request a Civil Wedding at the Superior Court. I've heard it takes about ten days."

"Ten days, in Vegas we could start getting married sixty seconds after we have a license."

"That's Vegas and this is DC."

"I think I'm ready to sleep now Samantha. My mind is more settled. I feel good."

"Ok, but don't forget, blood test tomorrow."

"I won't forget."

"Nite Larry."

"Nite!"

Samantha still didn't feel like sleeping and decided to call Christina to see how her move back to hers and Tod's apartment had gone.

"Hi Sis, are you still up or have you gone to bed."

"I only now arrived from work Samantha."

"How was work?"

"At the beginning of my shift, we lost a beautiful little girl, who had been in the incubator for a week; but then we all bounced back, when a healthy little boy was born a few hours later. He had such fine blond hair on the top of his head and his mother is black."

"I wonder if he'll keep the blond hair, as he grows up."

"They rarely do."

"Are you're all moved in at the apartment now?" Samantha asked.

"Yes, it took me three loads. That BMW doesn't hold much."

"Mom still doesn't know that you're living there alone, right?"

"No, and that's the way it's going to stay forever. It's just like your Manhattan engagement ring. They are never to know about either."

"Agreed, we'll never snitch on each other. How's Tod?"

"I didn't see him this weekend, but I was there last Sunday, before coming to the supper where you announced your engagement. His outlook and attitude have changed."

"Obviously, or you wouldn't have moved back to the apartment, especially to be all alone."

"Then you knew my moving back in wasn't only because of the fact that he's buying a horse, which I get to ride?"

"Horses are bribes between a father and a daughter Sis, not between a husband and wife."

"How are things with your future husband?" Christina prompted her.

"I was on the phone with him, before I called you. We're planning a civil marriage, as quickly as we can arrange it. We're both going to try to get a blood test tomorrow."

"That is quick. What's the matter," she joked, "are they planning to deport him."

"No, he has a possible job offer at George Washington U, if he can get legal work status, before August 15th. "His temporary visa expires at the end of August."

"I didn't realize it was like that. Do you love him?"

"Yes, it's not like you and Tod. It's hard to love like the first time again and I've been holding back, because of Manhattan and because of the fact that his future was so uncertain; but I do love him and I'm sure that it will be a bigger love in a year from now."

"Does he love you?"

"Yes, he's staying in the US because of me. Guess what he said about ten minutes ago?"

"I can't imagine."

The Adams Sisters

"He said that we'll get a civil marriage now, because it needs to be quick; but in a year or so, when we have time to plan it; we'll get remarried in a church or a mosque."

"That is sweet."

"Anyway Sis, you must be tired from work. I only wanted to say boo. I'll call you in a few days."

"Bye Sam."

First Christina went to the refrigerator and poured a glass of juice. Then she walked into the bedroom and turned the air conditioner back to low. Now she was sitting on the sofa looking at two small silver objects on the coffee table in front of her. One was the remote for the TV and the other was her cell phone. She leaned forward, stretching out her arm, picked up the cell phone, flipped it open and pressed on a programmed key.

"Hello!"

"Tod?"

"Hi Christa, I'm glad you called. I've been keeping my phone on all the time, since last Sunday."

"Instead of keeping your phone open, why didn't you call me?"

"I wanted to give you time."

"Guess what I did in the time you gave me?"

"Tell me."

"I moved back into our apartment. In fact, I'm sitting on our sofa at this very instant."

"Oh, wow, you should have let me know. I would have surprised you, after work tonight."

"You can surprise me some other night or if you come into town for supplies, during the day, when I'm here, drop by and climb into the sac for a few hours with me."

"We're going to have to watch it. That's how couples end up making babies."

"I'm taking lots of precautions. We'll have babies; but on our time."

"How about last Sunday?"

"I wasn't expecting that to happen, but I checked my calendar and it was a low risk day."

"So now we're a two house family," he joked and continued. "What have you been doing besides moving?"

"I was on the phone to Samantha, before I called you. She and Larry have got engaged and they're getting married, as soon as possible."

"Is she pregnant?"

"No, he was recalled to Nigeria, but wanted to stay here with her and now he needs legal status, so that he might get a job at George Washington U."

"When's the wedding?"

"They're not going to have a wedding as such, for the moment. It's going to be a civil ceremony and probably this month."

"That is fast. Are we going?"

"She hasn't said anything yet. Tod, would you laugh, if I ask you something serious."

"Try me."

"Promise?"

"Ask me," he prompted.

"What would you think about renewing our vows by getting remarried along with Sam and Larry?"

"Can people do that?" he inquired. "I mean is it legal? Washington isn't Vegas."

"I think so."

"What do you think about the idea yourself?"

"I asked you first," she objected.

"It would be different."

"That's not an answer," she complained.

"Can you let me think on it?"

"How long?" she fretted.

'Over night."

"Fair enough, call me in the morning. I should be awake by 9 am and Tod."

"Yes."

"Just so you know, even if you don't want to get married to me again, I've still moved back into our apartment."

"That's good to know," he told her, feeling more confident. "I'll call you a bit after nine in the morning."

"Thanks."

The following morning her phone buzzed at 9:05 am.

"Christa, it's me. I can't talk long. A pick-up truck and trailer are coming into the yard. They have a sick cow on board. Have you talked to Samantha about this double marriage idea?"

"No."

"Talk to them. If they have no objections, then I'm in."

"Oh, Tod I love you."

"I knew you did and I love you too. That's why I'm willing to get married to you again. I have to go Christa; they're walking towards the door."

The Adams Sisters

"I'll call you after I've talked to Sam. Bye!"
*

The H. Carl Moultrie Courthouse is a massive 7-storey, 654,000 square foot structure, which occupies a full city block on Washington's Judiciary Square. From the outside, one is struck by the building's windows, which are narrow vertical openings, spanning all five floors. Once inside, one is equally surprised to discover soft hidden panel lighting, cool lime-green walls and silver beams and columns supported by brightly tiled floors, inlayed with geometrical shapes.

On Tuesday July 27th, nine people waited on the modular furniture in the waiting area of the Family Court, which was partially enclosed by thick glass panels upon which were etched futuristic designs, similar to those on the tiled floor. At 3:55 pm, a tall, sleek woman, dressed in a lace fringed wrap around black dress, left her LCD computer screen, at the Court Clerk's counter and walked to the waiting area.

"Good afternoon everybody," she greeted. "I wonder if I could have you all proceed to the Marriage Celebration Room now? There's a plaque on the double doors, just down that hall."

They had hardly seated themselves again, in the Marriage Celebration Room, when a tall mahogany door near the far end of the chamber opened and a petite brunette woman, in a bright orange dress and matching orange shoes, strode in and greeted them.

"Good afternoon folks," she exclaimed, using her index finger to loosening a pink, silk scarf, which was wrapped about her throat. "My name is Anita Jones-Livingston and I'm an Associate Judge for the Superior Court of the District of Columbia. I have been asked to perform the ceremony this afternoon as the regular person has been called away unexpectedly. Are we all ready?" She read their nod to the affirmative. "Could I have Samantha Adams and Lawrence Ossaga step forward, please?"

The couple separated themselves from the others, and moved through the low swing gates in the middle of the solid railing, which divided the room. Samantha was wearing a black skirt suit, which had a pin dot jacquard jacket and silk georgette bias-cut full skirt, as well as black high-heel halter slings and a string of white pearls. The associate judge took the couple by the elbows and steered them into position on the floor. Then she went to the register table, picked up a leather bound procedures book and returned to them. Before she began to read, she smiled and said,

"You are a beautiful looking bride and groom."

And then began the time worn questions, which would bind them as one. The ceremony didn't take long. Suddenly Samantha was hearing the marriage official say,

"Lawrence, you may kiss your bride now and then I'd like both of you to come over to the desk with me to sign the Register. Also, may I have a witness for the bride and groom accompany us, and also sign the Register?"

Roscoe Walters pushed back the swing gate and followed the wedding party to witness for Samantha. Once the bride and groom had signed, in the appropriate places, their witness picked up the pen and attested to what he had seen. Associate Judge Anita Jones-Livingston signed the bottom of the document and thanked the three of them.

The Judge waited until Samantha, Larry and Roscoe had returned to where they had been and then she began to speak again,

"Would the next couple please step forward?"

Christina stood up and was followed by Tod. This afternoon she was dressed in a moon blue woven matte jersey dress and jacket, with a matching handbag and keyhole sling-back pumps. The couple stood at the same spot where Sam and Larry had only moments ago taken their vows. When all were settled, the Magistrate began the second ceremony,

"Do you Christina Evans take Tod Evans to be your lawfully wedded husband, to love and cherish in sickness and in health? "

"I do."

After a few short questions and sentences, the woman of law turned and asked the witness for the bride and groom to come forward. A tall Navy man in full dress gently pushed open the gate before him and followed his brother and sister-in-law to the Register desk.

When their vows were bound in law, the Associate Judge wished both couples all the best in their future lives together and told them that they could have their Marriage License certified at the Court Clerk's counter down the hall. She then turned and walked towards the door by which she had entered, less than half an hour ago.

Marsha felt disappointed and let her husband know in a low whisper, "Is that all?"

"They're married, dear," he whispered back.

The Adams Sisters

"But there was no music or flowers," she continued.

Once again her husband leaned over close to her ear and said, "They told you, you're going to get all that, when they get married in a church. Would you rather have them live in sin, until then?"

"No."

"Then cheer up and go and congratulate your daughter and new son-in-law." While she was doing that, Charles stepped through the swing gate and addressed the wedding party.

"I hope all of you came by taxi as we requested?" Some nodded their heads and others said yes. "Good," Charles continued. "As soon as these young people have their Licenses certified, I'd like you to follow me outside to a waiting limousine, which will take us all to the Lincoln Club for the wedding meal."

While the wedding party were taking pictures on the Courthouse steps, a sleek black limousine pulled away from the curb, where it had been waiting and stopped near them. The chauffer got out, walked to the other side of the vehicle and opened the double doors in anticipation of the approaching group. Once they were all in and seated, he carefully shut the doors behind them.

Inside the limousine, there were flowers everywhere. At the back of the compartment, a large bottle of champagne was chilling in a silver bucket full of ice. A rack of long stem glasses hung down from the ceiling. As the chauffer pulled away from the Courthouse steps, strains of a popular love song filled the back compartment.

"Alright everybody," Charles exclaimed as he removed the bottle of bubbly from the ice. "It's party time. Get yourselves a glass."

The limousine made its way across town, from the Capitol Hill area to Connecticut Avenue, about a block north of the White House. Inside the cool air conditioned vehicle, the wedding party talked and laughed as they sipped fizzy champagne and watched five o'clock Washtonians and tourists moving on the streets through the tinted, one way windows.

The Lincoln Club is an elegant, relaxing restaurant, which transports its patrons through time, to the social clubs of India, during the British Raj era. The elegant interior of pale pastels, wooden ceiling fans, and a profusion of plants make one quickly forget the city outside. Since the private club like dining room and outdoor patio beyond, didn't open until 6 pm, the wedding party settled themselves into deeply cushioned cane arm chairs and settees, which surrounded a large, low round glass topped cane table and ordered martinis. Samantha slipped off her shoes and buried her toes in the rich Indian carpet, which covered the floor. Soon the drinks arrived.

Lawrence Ossaga's white suit and straw fedora seemed so appropriated to this environment. As he scanned the wedding party he noted his former superior sitting across from him, held up his glass and called over, "Cheers, Doctor Ojibwa. I'm so glad you came.

"So am I Lawrence, I love weddings."

"Did you get introduced to everybody in the limo?"

"Briefly, but I'm still not sure who everybody is."

"Let me run through the names again for you. These good people are my wife's parents, Charles, and Marsha Adams. This is my wife's sister, Christa, and her husband Tod. Our witness over there is Mr. Roscoe Walters. He's my wife's Director at work. I'm afraid I'll have to ask my sister-in-law Christa, who their witness is."

Immediately Christina leaned forward. "This is my brother-in-law and my husband's brother, Morgan, who went through the Annapolis Naval Academy."

"I'm very pleased to meet you all," Dr. Ojibwa exclaimed, holding his glass into the air.

"And now Doctor it's your turn," Larry said. "Everybody, my I present to you Dr. Victor Ojibwa, Nigeria's Ambassador to the United States and my former Director at the embassy."

"Call me Victor," the old man pleaded.

It wasn't long before a young man, wearing black pants, a vest, and a bow tie came to tell them that the dining room was now open and would they please accompany him. They followed him through a maze of set tables and out onto the patio, which was furnished almost the same as inside, except that the floor was made of varnished teak planks that were not covered with carpets.

The young man seated the wedding party in the red velvet lined chairs, which surrounded a large round wooden table, under a blue canopy. The table was covered with a white table cloth and elaborately set with sterling silver, folded white napkins, crystal glasses, flowers, and candles. A woman in a traditional sari, with her hair in one braid extending down the middle of her back as far as her waist, came to introduce herself,

The Adams Sisters

"Welcome everybody, my name is Jasbir and I am your hostess for the evening. Please don't hesitate to call on me for any help you may need with ordering or whatever."

She waved her hand and the same young man, who had shown them to their seats, appeared carrying a stack of menus and expertly placed one in front of each guest. When he had finished, their host waved her hand again and a younger women began to push a small square wheeled cart towards the table.

On the cart rested a bucket of frost covered ice cubes and two cut glass pitchers of water, which themselves contained ice cubes. Effortlessly she removed the tall glass from in front of each of them, put a scoop of ice cubes into the bottom of the glass and then filled it to the brim with cold water.

Their hostess said, "I'll leave you now for a few minutes to give you time to read the menu. Mr. Adams has already ordered wine in advance for the table. We'll bring you chilled carafes of Pinot Gris in a moment."

The menu was immense. It was divided into eight sections – Appetizers, Vegetarian, Goon, House, Northwest Frontier, Paris, Mongolia and Dessert.

"How did you choose this place Dad?" Christina asked her father.

"You'll have to talk to the boss on that one," her father replied, smiling at his wife of thirty-five years.

"I'm not the boss Charles," his wife objected joking. "We decided together. First there was Larry, who is from Nigeria and Samantha, who is with the State Department. Then we were told that ambassador Ojibwa and Mr. Walters would be attending. With all these international connections, we decided that our theme for the reception would be international. I personally visited a dozen restaurants, before settling on the Lincoln. Charles agreed it was a good choice as he had been here several times for lunch."

"You couldn't have made a better choice," Victor complimented her. "I simply adore Indian food."

"As do I," interjected Roscoe Walters.

For the next fifteen minutes, they examined the various sections of the menu, stopping here and there to suggest to one or other that they should order this or that. At the same time a new waiter arrived, carrying a tray on which there were five tall crystal carafes. After placing four of them in the center of the table, within reaching distance of all; he poured the contents of the fifth, which was larger than the others into the smaller glass, which was beside each person's water glass.

Several other tables on the patio had filled, when Samantha leaned forward, half whispering, "Roscoe!"

"What?"

"Look who has just come in."

Walters did a half turn, without it seeming that he had moved at all. However, he had a full five seconds to look at the couple coming through from the dining room.

"It's Senator Hugh Russell of the Foreign Affairs Committee and Senator Elizabeth Brown."

"I didn't think those two were that close," his understudy commented.

One never knows," her superior replied. "There are strange things done, beneath the Washington sun, by those who morn for more."

"I'll second that," Samantha replied.

Has everyone about decided?" Charles asked, and then waved towards their host.

"Are we ready, Mr. Adams?" Jasbir inquired.

"As ready as we will ever be," he replied.

"I believe there are two brides and two grooms?"

"There are."

"We'll start with their orders first," Jasbir said while motioning to the woman who had served the water. "Jasmin, would you begin with this young lady," she said, indicating Christina, "and I'll take the other bride's order."

The waitresses made their way around the table in a counter clockwise direction, helping each one of the guests decide if they really wanted, what they were ordering. Samantha and Larry started with an appetizer of marinated sautéed jumbo shrimp cooked in mango chutney while Christa and Tod each ordered Tandoori Scallops.

Roscoe liked it hot and spicy, so chose a Goan dish called Lamb Vindaloo. Goa is a state along India's western coastline, which was originally colonized by the Portuguese.

Morgan thought he'd stay with something more familiar and decided on Lobster Malabar. Marsha followed his lead and stuck to her choice of lamb chops cooked with ginger and green herbs. Dr. Ojibwa, who was more experienced, ventured forth ordering a traditional Parsi chicken curry with potatoes in an onion and tomato based sauce with herbs and spices.

The two bridal couples' appetizers were served first and then Charles, Marsha Morgan and Roscoe received their Club

The Adams Sisters

Calamari. Surprisingly, Victor started with an Empire Salad. For the next hour plates, dishes, bowls and baskets of poppadum bread appeared and disappeared, as if they were riding on a magic carpet. When a carafe of Pinot was emptied, Charles held it up and it was replaced by another, At times, four conversations were going at the same moment.

"Mr. Walters, if you're Samantha's superior, you must also be with the State Department."

"I am ambassador."

"Which section are you with?"

"I handle mostly administration and research. Currently, our project areas are Iran, Syria, and Lebanon. However, I do recall hearing your name mentioned around the Department on at least one occasion. It was rather a humorous story," Roscoe replied.

"I'd love to hear it, if you can remember what it was," the Nigerian ambassador assured him.

"It was more than a year ago now, at a White House reception. A junior Secret Service agent had been assigned to note all people, who talked with the President. During the evening, an African in traditional dress penetrated the ring of official well-wishers, who always surround the President at such functions. He turned out to be a Colonel Jocommo from your country, who had a meeting with the President the following day.

The Secret Service said that it couldn't be the Colonel as he was in uniform standing elsewhere with another soldier. When we looked into the matter, the person who had spoken with the President was Jocommo and we suspected that you had engineered the meeting. You smiled and waved at our Mr. Steinberg as you left the reception with your country man, who was wearing traditional robes. "

The ambassador laughed jovially, "I recall that evening distinctly, Roscoe and you are correct. It was my maneuverings that got Jocommo through to the President."

Victor Ojibwa turned his attention towards Larry, who had been listening. "Lawrence, now that you have officially resigned and have informed Abuja that you will be staying in the US, I don't think there would be any harm in my telling you that it was Colonel Jocommo, who informed me that your were to be recalled, after your name came up in that medical supplies investigation."

"Medical supplies investigation?" Roscoe repeated, casually catching Samantha's eyes."

"Yes, before Lawrence came to work for me here in Washington, he sat on the Debt Reconciliation Committee in Nigeria. Recently, approximately a million and a half US dollars of medical supplies surfaced and some people were saying that Lawrence had fraudulently used Committee money, to import supplies and medicine for his tribe."

Roscoe turned to Larry saying, "I don't wish to insult the bridegroom, but you simply don't look like the type of person, who would be capable of something like that."

Samantha looped her arm in under her new husband's and laughed, "Believe me Mr. Walters. Larry's just not capable of anything like that."

"Exactly what I thought too, Samantha," Victor added. "That's why I let him know about the nasty rumors being stirred up against him back home."

When the main course had all been cleared away, their hostess wheeled up a cart, which supported a three level, white frosted cake. A long sterling silver knife lay on either side. Both the wedding couples rose and together the four of them cut pieces from the cake. A restaurant photographer added several pictures of this to the others he had been snapping during the evening. Other patrons on the patio thought a double birthday celebration was taking place under the blue canopy.

It was approaching 9 pm, when the wedding party rose and began to make their way back through the restaurant. Charles had called the chauffer on his cell as they were leaving the patio. The limousine was ready, when they came out the front door of the restaurant. Since Roscoe, Victor and Morgan elected to take cabs, only the two couples, and the sisters' parents re-entered the long black vehicle.

They seemed hardly to have pulled away from the restaurant, when the limousine turned off K Street NW and stopped under the overhanging roof at the entrance to the Colonial Hotel.

"Why are we stopping here?" Samantha asked.

"To let you and Larry off," her mother replied. "Your father and I booked you a suite here for the evening."

"But Mother, I've heard the rooms at the Colonial are as high as $3,500 a night and besides that, all my things are at my place. Our bags are there too. We have everything packed and we planned to take a cab to Regan Airport in the morning."

"We didn't pay $3,500 Samantha and your bags are up stairs dear. Christina lent me your key. Put the clothes you're

The Adams Sisters

wearing in the empty piece of luggage and leave it at the Front Desk, when you check out. Your father will pick it up some time tomorrow."

"Sis!" Samantha exclaimed, looking at Christina.

"I had no choice in the matter, Sis. You know what Marsha's like, when she makes up her mind."

The chauffer was standing with an open door and Samantha gave in saying, "Thank you very much Mom and Dad. Come on Larry; let's go see our wedding night hide away. Bye everybody!"

The Colonial Hotel is built in the style of an Italian Renaissance Palace. It's decorated with Louis XVI chandeliers and furnished with European antiques. The address has been a Washington oasis for traveling royalty, presidents, and prime ministers for almost one hundred years. A valet accompanied them to the Front Desk, where Larry said,

"Mr. and Mrs. Lawrence and Samantha Ossaga, we have a reservation."

The Desk Clerk looked down her list and replied, "Yes, Dr. Ossaga, we have you and Mrs. Ossaga booked for one night in the honeymoon suite. Jose, would you accompany these people to Suite 888."

"Certainly Ms. Peters!" The valet replied. "No baggage Doctor?"

"It has been put in the room earlier during the day."

"Would you and your wife be so kind as to follow me?"

"Certainly," the African replied, putting out his elbow for his new wife to take hold of.

Jose led them along a white marble floor, which was covered with Persian carpets from the middle through to the wall that was made of a continuous series of French doors, with heavy gold drapes gathered on either side. Glass top coffee tables and padded straight back, oak arm chairs were arranged in clusters along the full length of the carpet. A number of these were occupied by well-dressed people, who were chatting together quietly. Drink glasses or coffee cups lay on the low tables in front of them.

The eighth floor was made up of several main corridors running in the direction of the building's wings. Each of these intersected with a number of smaller corridors along their length. These led off to alcoves or suites. Jose turned into one of them and stopped in front of a large, white-maple door bearing three brass eights. He inserted a plastic card in the slot and the door swung back. After placing the card in groom's palm, the Valet hung a Do Not Disturb sign on the door's outer handle and stepped back.

"There you are Doctor. I hope everything is to your entire satisfaction and that you have a memorable stay at the Colonial. If you require anything what so ever, simply press the red button on the bed side table. The Concierge will immediately call you."

Larry put a twenty dollar bill into the valet's hand and the man disappeared. "Are you ready, Mrs. Ossaga?"

"Ready for what?"

Without saying anything else he bent down, swooped up Samantha and carried her into the suite.

"Wow, Larry, you don't look that strong!"

"Looks can be deceiving," he replied, going back to close and secure the door.

The suite contained a sitting room, a bedroom, and a huge bathroom, half of which was taken up by a heart shaped, whirl pool tub. The sitting room was elegantly furnished with antiques, a Persian rug and sofas similar to those they had seen near the elevators on the main floor. An uncorked bottle of champagne was chilling in a bucket of ice, on the low glass topped coffee table.

The bedroom was more than simply green – the walls were covered in richly textured, green cloth wall paper. A heavy embroidered green quilt covered the bed, the skirts around the bedside tables were a fluffy green. The upholstery on the headboard, as well as the heavy velvet curtains, were each their own shade of green. Attached to the ceiling above the bed was a huge mirror, encased in an elaborately configured green plaster frame.

The couple found their luggage stowed neatly in the double closet and laid out on the bed were a white silk night gown for her and a pair of light grey silk pajamas for him.

Samantha laughed when she saw them, "That's my Mother."

"What would you say to me taking that bucket of champagne and the glasses into the bath and getting the whirlpool tub going?" Larry asked.

"I'd say that you have been reading my mind. Go on in and get it going. I'll slip on a nightie and come to join you." He was already in motion when she called after him, "Be sure to use lots of bubble crystals."

The Adams Sisters

Five minutes later she appeared in the doorway of the bathroom, framed in white silk. He was buried in a mountain of bubbles holding up two glasses of champagne.

"Come and get it," he laughed.

She slinked across the distance between them, and slid into the rushing water with her husband.

The following morning Samantha and Larry packed their wedding clothes in the spare bag that Charles and Marsha had left. She dressed casually in a tropical punch double scoop-neck sweater, white Irish linen pants with a yoke and flared legs, a mauve silk scarf for a sash and white patent leather flower slides on her feet. He slipped into a pair of summer weight plaid hounds-tooth trousers, a wave print silk shirt and a pair of soft-leather, light-blue sandal-loafers, without heals. When they were dressed, he called the Hotel Butler to take their bags to the main lobby.

Arriving on the main floor, the newlyweds went into the dining room, where breakfast was being served. They both ordered fresh fruit, waffles, and eggs Benedictine, which were served in white English bone china, with had a large splash of blue in it. While they ate breakfast, the couple quietly discussed the previous night.

"Larry, where did you learn to do all those wonderful things, you did to me last night?"

He looked at her shyly and then defended himself, "You're no stranger to the pursuit of pleasure yourself."

She smiled cattily and then purred, "I warned you, I was engaged once. Maybe if my ex-fiancé and I had waited, until our wedding night, we might have made it to the altar."

"That would have been my loss," he said, but to answer your question, "The women in our tribe shower the Chief's son with attention, hoping that he will remember them, when he becomes the Chief. I had a lot of admirers, before I went away to England."

"It's a lucky thing for me your father never told them his plans didn't include you succeeding him," she purred again, reaching out her foot to caress his leg.

Larry started to laugh, "I thought I was in a movie last night, every time I looked up, it was us in the mirror above the bed."

"We are staring in a movie dear Larry. It's called the Honeymoon movie, and we're about to move on to the next scene."

After breakfast they signed out, picked up their bags and caught a cab for Regan National Airport, which is less than a ten minute drive from the hotel, in south Arlington, on the site of the old Abingdon Plantation. Over the years, the Capital's metropolitan airport has been through as many changes as the seasons.

The current terminal is composed of two long side by side structural steel buildings draped with glass. The roof is made of a continuous series of semi-circle domes, which span both structures. The steel ribs and metal skin of the ceiling above the long wide interior halls give one the impression of being in a cathedral. After the Ossaga's checked in and gave up their luggage to security; they had a short wait in a departure loading area, before boarding the plane that would take them to Santa Fe, New Mexico.

Santa Fe, which is the nation's oldest capital city, is nestled in the foothills of the Rocky Mountains. It was founded by Spanish explorers in 1607 and has been claimed by the Pueblo Peoples, the Spanish Crown, Mexico and the Confederacy. Mexico ceded it to the US in 1846. Today it is internationally known for its cultural sophistication, Opera and home to the third largest art market in the US.

At the Santa Fe Airport, the new husband and wife rented a vehicle and then headed into town to find a hotel, which would be their home base for the next few days. Larry was immediately struck by the architecture of the terminal building and the residential suburbs, during the drive into the city.

"These houses look as if they are made of red clay and yet they're so new," he said to Samantha, who was driving. "I almost feel as if I'm someplace in Africa."

She laughed when he said that he almost felt as if he was in Africa and replied, "I've heard that there are lots of old clay buildings in New Mexico, but these new homes we're seeing are probably made of cement or a wooden shell colored with a thick layer of clay colored stucco."

The city was clogged with August tourists. When they arrived in the historic Plaza district, she suggested they look for accommodation first and then sight see after. "What do you feel like Larry, a hotel, a motel or a bed and breakfast?"

"I think that a bed and breakfast would suit me fine, after the opulent luxury we soaked in last night," her husband replied.

"I couldn't agree more. See what the guide book has for B&B's and navigate me to one."

The Adams Sisters

The first place they visited was called Casa del Cielo. It was located on a historic hill in downtown Santa Fe and was only a four block walk from the Plaza, the museums, the restaurants and the shops. When the Ossaga's arrived, another couple was checking out of the Navajo Room. As soon as the newlyweds saw how it was decorated with regional textiles, antiques, and artwork; they said they would take it. There was even a view of the sun set over the mountains, during the early evening.

The heart of historic Santa Fe is a jig saw of low buildings made of stone, wood, and clay. Huge tree trunks and wooden beams support wide sloping roofs or portals that reach out from the buildings to cover equally wide sidewalks, which are sometimes paved with decorated clay tiles. Every available inch of wall space along the sidewalks, under the portals is occupied by Native Americans, who are selling jewelry, silverware, loose gem stones, decorative modern and traditional clothing, as well as brightly painted clay pots and earthenware objects. The street vendors spread their wares on colorful rugs, which have Pueblo designs woven into them. Samantha wanted to buy everything she saw.

Early Friday morning the honeymooners left the Capital and headed north along El Camino Real Byway, the old Spanish Royal Highway of the Interior Land. Before lunch, the couple toured a winery near Dixon, in the Embudo Valley. In the early afternoon they arrived at Taos and decided that was as far as they would go. After renting a unit at an upscale motel, Samantha drove a few miles outside the village for a visit to the Taos Pueblo.

The pueblo has been inhabited continuously, for fifteen hundred years, by the Taos Pueblo Tribe. The dwellings, which are made of clay plastered over wood and straw frames, resemble clusters of terraced apartments, stacked up on top of each other. During a guided tour they were shown outdoor cooking ovens, the church and the cemetery and the pueblo.

Their guide, a Taos girl, who was studying software engineering at University of New Mexico in Albuquerque, during the winter, told them that her grandmother lived in an apartment in the pueblo and that she would inherit it. The girl also informed them that in spite of the fact that most Americans didn't have much use for the former President Nixon, the Taos are grateful to him, because he restored their Blue Lake to them, which had been taken away, by the US government during the 18th century Indian Wars.

That evening the Ossaga's drank a bottle of the vintage, they had purchased at the winery, earlier in the day and then went for a swim in the motel's pool. It was near 9 pm when they left for a stroll down through the village looking for a place to have supper and found that there were more stores selling Native American crafts than there were restaurants.

The following day Samantha took state highway 64 and headed West across country towards Farmington NM. A little before the town, she turned south towards the Chaco Canyon Historical Park, which is one of America's most significant and fascinating cultural and historic areas. Between AD 850 and 1250, it was a major center of the ancient Anasazi, who were the ancestors of the present day Pueblo, Hopi, and Navajo. The Chaco site, which is world renowned for its monumental public and ceremonial buildings, engineering feats, astronomy, artistic achievements, and distinctive architecture; was designated a World Heritage site in 1987.

After leaving the moonscape, prehistoric stone structures on the Chaco Canyon floor, the Ossaga's headed north, towards Durango, in the south west corner of Colorado. It was near sunset when they reached their destination. The town was bustling, as the Fortune 500 Executives Harley Davison Club had stopped in Durango for the night and both sides of the main street were lined with motor cycles. Honky-tonk piano music poured out the open double doors of several saloons.

Samantha and Larry decided not to even try the motels, most of which displayed NO Vacancy signs. Instead, they walked into the largest saloon and asked if there was a room available. Luckily there was and they were able to refresh themselves downstairs amid the swirl of can-can girls and waiters wearing suspenders and pork-pie hats, before climbing up the wide oak staircase to a wonderful sleep in a bed that boasted a down filled mattress.

In the morning, the adventurers set off early for nearby Mesa Verde to see the cliff dwellings that the Anasazi had left behind. The ruins proved to be awe inspiring. First they visited Cliff Palace, which is a stone village build high up in the side of a cliff, on a ledge that was carved out of the sandstone, when the ocean covered this area. It amazed Larry how these lost ancients had built dwellings and public buildings here in the 8 century A.D., which had perfectly plumb corners and perfectly square windows and doors. From the Cliff Palace the couple went to visit a second site called, Balcony House.

The Adams Sisters

Samantha was watching Larry, who had climbed down into an open chamber in the rock, when her cell phone's chime signaled. She unsnapped the device from her belt and answered the call.

"Hi, it's me Christa."

"Hi Sis!"

"How's the honeymoon?"

"We couldn't have made a better choice."

"What have you been doing?"

"We're simply roaming around, without a set plan. In Santa Fe, we went to the Opera.

We've also visited a real pueblo and toured a winery."

"Where are you now?"

"We're in Colorado going through a cliff dwelling site called Balcony House. Larry has climbed down into a chamber in the rock that's called a kiva. A prehistoric native people called the Anasazi built all these cliff dwellings and they would go down into the kivas to worship God, who they believed was a woman. I'm sending you a picture of Larry with my phone. You'll have it in a second."

"Oh, yes," Christina agreed a few seconds later. "I've definitely got to go see that place. Anyways Samantha, I went by Larry's apartment yesterday to check his mail, like you asked. There's an envelope here with a George Washington University logo."

"Just a sec."

"Larry, it's Christa. She has an envelope from the school for you."

"Tell her to open it," he yelled.

"Christa, he says to open the envelope."

"Ok, I have the letter out and it says,

*

Dear Dr. Lawrence Ossaga

We have reviewed the additional information submitted in your file for the Senior Marker Position and are happy to say that all is now in order and we are pleased to offer you a position. Please contact me as soon as possible to make an appointment to come in and sign a contract for the term beginning September 6th.

Regards,
Sheryl Henderson
Executive Director"

*

Samantha wanted to yell 'Larry you got it' to the top of her lungs, but restrained herself as there were too many other tourists. "I haven't got a pen Christa, Text me Sheryl Henderson telephone number please. How's things with you?"

"Not bad, when we hang up I'm leaving to spend the afternoon and night with Tod out in the Virginia countryside. He stayed here at the apartment over night, after the Lincoln Club and then came back again on Friday."

"Then the world's your oyster?"

"Well, not quite."

"What do you mean not quite?"

"I missed my monthly."

"Have you been to see a Doctor? What am I talking about? You are a Doctor."

"I've used an HCG test strip yesterday."

"And?"

"There were distinct and consistent color bands on the control and test regions."

"Which means?"

"That's positive, but I'm going to have a blood test this week."

"When do you think it happened?"

"I'm quite sure it was that Sunday afternoon, before the supper at Mom's, where you showed us your ring."

"That's quite a while ago. Wouldn't it have shown up in the blood test you had to get for the marriage license?"

"They were looking for syphilis, not a glycoprotein hormone."

"Are you happy?"

"Yes, very happy and I'm going to show Tod how happy I am this afternoon."

"Then I'm happy for you too, for both of you. I'm going to go now Christa. Larry has climbed back up out of the worshiping well. I want to tell him the good news, both parts of your good news. We're heading back to Santa Fe this afternoon and flying from there to DC tomorrow afternoon. Let's meet for lunch on Wednesday. I have a bottle of New Mexico vintage for you and I'm dying to hear more about this baby you're expecting."

"It's a deal," her younger sister replied.

"Bye Christa."

"Bye Sis!"

The End

Made in the USA
Charleston, SC
08 March 2015